TO R...
OF THE UNREASONABLE,
AND TO PLUCK FROM THAT SCOPE
A SATISFYING TALE.''

These were the criteria Isaac Asimov set for himself, Terry Carr, and Martin Greenberg in choosing the stories for this collection. The result is 100 of the greatest, shortest fantasy stories to chill you, thrill you, and transport you into the fabulous ''might be'' realm of the strange and the marvelous.

Each work is a compact triumph of boundless wonder. History is scrambled and reordered with disconcerting precision. Contemporary life leaps out of focus. The future is sighted along bizarre and divergent parallels. Nothing is real, but everything makes the entirely believable sense found in the very best fantasy writing.

So read and enjoy:

"The Anatomy Lesson" by Scott Sanders
"Sleep" by Steve Rasnic Tem
"Give Her Hell" by Donald A. Wollheim
"Night Visions" by Jack Dann
"The Prophecy" by Bill Pronzini

And 95 more of the 100 greatest, shortest fantasy stories!

100 GREAT FANTASY
SHORT SHORT STORIES

EDITED BY

ISAAC ASIMOV, TERRY CARR, AND MARTIN H. GREENBERG

100 GREAT FANTASY SHORT SHORT STORIES

WITH AN INTRODUCTION BY ISAAC ASIMOV

AVON
PUBLISHERS OF BARD, CAMELOT, DISCUS AND FLARE BOOKS

All of the characters in this book are fictitious, and any resemblance
to actual persons, living or dead, is purely coincidental.

AVON BOOKS
A division of
The Hearst Corporation
1790 Broadway
New York, New York 10019

Copyright © 1984 by Nightfall, Inc., Terry Carr,
and Martin H. Greenberg
Published by arrangement with Doubleday & Company, Inc.
Library of Congress Catalog Card Number: 82-45097
ISBN: 0-380-69917-6

The Doubleday edition contains the following Library of Congress
Cataloging in Publication Data:
Main entry under title:

100 great fantasy short short stories.

1 Fantastic fiction, American. 2. Short stories,
American. I. Asimov, Isaac, 1920–   II. Carr,
Terry   III. Greenberg, Martin Harry   IV. Title:
One hundred great fantasy short short stories.
PS648.F3A12 1984   813'.0876'08

First Avon Printing, August 1985

AVON TRADEMARK REG. U. S. PAT. OFF. AND IN
OTHER COUNTRIES, MARCA REGISTRADA, HECHO EN
U. S. A.

Printed in the U. S. A.

WFH 10 9 8 7 6 5 4 3 2 1

ACKNOWLEDGMENTS

"The Abraham Lincoln Murder Case," "Freedom," and "Mouse-Kitty" by Rick Norwood copyright © 1982 by TZ Publications, Inc. Originally published in *Twilight Zone* under the group title, "Three Timely Tales." Reprinted by permission of the author.

"A Dozen of Everything" by Marion Zimmer Bradley, copyright © 1959 by Ziff-Davis Publications, Inc. Reprinted by permission of the author and the author's agents, Scott Meredith Literary Agency, Inc., 845 Third Avenue, New York, New York 10022.

"The Anatomy Lesson" by Scott Sanders, copyright © 1981 by Davis Publications, Inc. Reprinted by permission of the author and the author's agent, Virginia Kidd.

"And I Alone Am Escaped to Tell Thee" by Roger Zelazny, copyright © 1981 by TZ Publications, Inc. Reprinted by permission of the author.

"Angelica" by Jane Yolen, copyright © 1979 by Mercury Press, Inc. Originally appeared in *The Magazine of Fantasy and Science Fiction*. Reprinted by permission of the author.

"Apocryphal Fragment" by Edward Wellen, copyright © 1962 by Ziff-Davis Publishing Company. Originally appeared in *Amazing*. Reprinted by permission of the author.

"A Prophecy of Monsters" by Clark Ashton Smith, copyright © 1954 by Mercury Press, Inc. Originally appeared in *The Magazine of Fantasy and Science Fiction*. Reprinted by permission of the author's Estate and the agents for the Estate, Scott Meredith Literary Agency, Inc., 845 Third Avenue, New York, New York 10022.

"At the Bureau" by Steve Rasnic Tem, copyright © 1980 by Steve Rasnic Tem. Originally appeared in *Shadows 3*, edited by Charles L. Grant. Reprinted by permission of the author.

"Aunt Agatha" by Doris Pitkin Buck, copyright © 1952 by Mercury Press, Inc. Originally appeared in *The Magazine of Fantasy and Science Fiction*. Reprinted by permission of Robert P. Mills, Ltd.

"The Boulevard of Broken Dreams" by Harlan Ellison, copyright © 1975 by Harlan Ellison. Reprinted with permission of, and by arrangement with, the author and the author's

CONTENTS

Headnotes by Isaac Asimov

The Widest Field

ISAAC ASIMOV

Realistic fiction deals with the here and now.

Science fiction represents a wider field, for it deals with all the different futures, near and far, that might arise through any conceivable change in the level of science and technology. Surely, all the possible reasonable "might-be's" are wider than the "is."

Fantasy represents a still wider field, for it deals with all the events, past, present, or future, that might arise in any possible society with only the exception of the one which actually exists. Surely all the possible unreasonable "might-be's" far outnumber anything merely reasonable, whether "might-be" or "is."

In a way, then, fantasy offers a greater challenge to the writer than anything else. His mind is freer to wander, his will is less in check. The liberty of choice is so enormous it is almost an embarrassment. He can create any society, any variety of magic, any rules or lack of rules, pull any rabbit out of the hat, place any burden on his hero or any talent.

Well, then, imagine granting the writer this infinite and difficult gift and then finding some way of depriving him of the full ability to enjoy it, and thus piling an additional difficulty upon him. Tell him he (or she) can do anything he wants, but must be confined to two thousand words or less to do it in.

In that short space, he must create a society and a background that is not real. He must describe it sufficiently well to expose it to the reader in full. He must round it out so that it can be grasped, and within it there must be action that makes it clear that what is being described is a fantasy.

Merely two thousand words to range over the full scope of the unreasonable, and to pluck from that scope a satisfying tale.

Easy? I don't think so. Try writing one, if you think it is easy.

If you do, you will be astonished that we can find one hundred examples of the art that are so thoroughly right. What a credit to the skill of so many writers!

You will agree with me, I'm sure. Dip in—and enjoy.

1
The Abraham Lincoln Murder Case

RICK NORWOOD

"Straight out of Kohn Jeats."

Abraham Lincoln murdered! By a woman! The news flashed to London via arctic heliograph in a matter of hours. Early the next morning Sherlock Holmes and Dr. Watson boarded the dirigible for America.

The Secret Service filled the great detective in as to the facts of the case. A handsome, well-dressed woman had been seen standing behind the President in his box. She took a pistol from her purse, fired one shot, and fled. Within minutes, the Secret Service had sealed all of the exits from Ford's Theater. But, in spite of the most thorough search, the woman was not to be found.

"There is nothing here for you, Holmes," said the head of the Secret Service. "We know who the woman is. She introduced herself to several members of the acting company earlier in the evening. She said that her name was Trudy, and that she was the girlfriend of the famous actor John Wilkes Booth. Booth, of course, never heard of her. She used his name to gain entrance to the theater."

"Well, Watson, we may as well return to London," said Holmes.

"You're not giving up!" Watson exclaimed.

1

"Hardly. I've solved the case."

"Solved it! How . . . ?"

"Come, Watson. It's elementary. Booth is Trudy and Trudy, Booth. That's all I know, and all I need to know."

2

A Dozen of Everything

MARION ZIMMER BRADLEY

"What counts is what you mean."

When Marcie unwrapped the cut-glass bottle, she thought it was perfume. "Oh, fine," she said to herself sardonically. "Here I am, being married in four days, and without a rag to wear, and Aunt Hepsibah sends me perfume!"

It wasn't that Marcie was mercenary. But Aunt Hepsibah was, as the vulgar expression puts it, rolling in dough; and she spent about forty dollars a year. She lived in Egypt, in a little mud hut, because, as she said, she wanted to Soak Up the Flavor of the East . . . in large capitals. She wrote Marcie, who was her only living relative, long incoherent letters about the Beauty of the Orient, and the Delights of Contemplation; letters which Marcie dutifully read and as dutifully answered with "Dear Aunt Hepsibah; I hope you are well . . ."

She sighed, and examined the label. Printed in a careful, vague Arabic script, it read "Djinn Number Seven." Marcie shrugged.

Oh well, she thought, it's probably very chi-chi and expensive. If I go without lunch this week, I can manage to get myself a fancy negligee, and maybe a pair of new gloves to wear to the church. Greg will like the perfume, and if I keep my job for a few months after we're married, we'll get along. Of course, Emily Post says that a bride should have a dozen of everything, but we can't *all* be lucky.

She started to put the perfume into her desk drawer—for her lunch hour was almost over—then, on an impulse, she began carefully to work the stopper loose. "I'll just take a tiny sniff—" she thought . . .

The stopper stuck; Marcie twitched, pulled—choked at the curious, pervasive fragrance which stole out. "It sure is strong—" she thought, holding the loosened stopper in her hand . . . then she blinked and dropped it to the floor, where the precious cut-glass shattered into a million pieces.

Marcie was a normal child of her generation, which is to say, she went to the movies regularly. She had seen *Sinbad the Sailor,* and *The Thief of Bagdad,* so, of course, she knew immediately what was happening, as the pervasive fragrance rolled out and coalesced into a huge, towering figure with a vaguely oriental face. "My gosh . . . " she breathed, then, as she noticed imminent peril to the office ceiling, directed "Hey, stick your head out the window—quick!"

"To hear is to obey," said the huge figure sibilantly, "but, O mistress, if I might venture to make a suggestion, that might attract attention. Permit me—" and he promptly shrank to a less generous proportion, "They don't make palaces as big these days, do they?" he asked confidentially.

"They certainly do not," gulped Marcie. "Are you—are you a genie?"

"I am not," the figure said with asperity. "Can't you read? I am a djinn—Djinn Number Seven to be exact."

"Er—you mean you have to grant me my wish?"

The djinn scowled. "Now, there is a strange point of ethics," he murmured. "Since the stopper on the bottle is broken, I can't ever be shut up again. At the same time, since you so generously let me out, I shall gladly grant you one wish. What will it be?''

Marcie didn't even hesitate. Here was a chance to make a good wedding present out of Aunt Hepsibah's nutty old bottle, and after all, she wasn't a greedy girl. She smiled brilliantly. "I'm being married in a few days—" she started.

"You want an elixir of love? Of eternal beauty?"

"No, sir-eee!" Marcie shuddered, she had read the Arabian Nights when she was a little girl; she knew you could not make a magical bargain with a genie—er—djinn. "No, as a matter of fact, I just want—well, a household trousseau. Nice things to be married in, and that kind of thing—just to start us off nicely."

"I'm afraid I don't quite understand." The djinn frowned. "Trousseau? That word has come in since my time. Remember, I haven't been out of this bottle since King Solomon was in diapers."

"Well—sheets, and towels, and slips, and night-gowns—" Marcie began, then dismissed it. "Oh well, just give me a dozen of everything," she told him.

"To hear is to obey," the djinn intoned. "Where shall I put it, O mistress?"

"Oh, in my room," Marcie told him, then, remembering the five-dollar-a-week hall bedroom, "Maybe you'll have to enlarge the room a little, but you can do that, can't you?"

"Oh, sure," said the djinn casually. "A djinn, my dear mistress, can do anything. And now, farewell forever, and thank you for letting me out."

He vanished so swiftly that Marcie rubbed her eyes, and the little cut-glass bottle fell to the floor. After a moment, Marcie picked it up, sniffing at the empty bottle. A curious faint fragrance still clung to it, but it was otherwise empty.

"Did I dream this whole thing?" she asked herself dizzily.

* * *

The buzzer rang, and the other typists in the office came back to their desks. "Gosh," someone asked, "have you been sitting here all during lunch hour, Marcie?"

"I—I took a little nap—" Marcie answered, and carefully palmed the cut-glass bottle into her desk drawer.

That afternoon seemed incredibly long to Marcie. The hands of the clock lagged as they inched around the dial, and she found herself beginning one business letter "Dear Djinn—" She ripped it out angrily, typed the date on a second letterhead, and started over; "Djinntlemen; we wish to call your attention—"

Finally, the hands reached five, and Marcie, whisking a cover over her typewriter, clutched her handbag and literally ran from the office. "There won't be anything there—" she kept telling herself, as she walked rapidly down the block, "there won't be anything—but suppose there was, suppose . . ."

The hall of the rooming-house was ominously quiet. Marcie ascended the stairs, wondering at the absence of the landlady, the lack of noise from the other boarders. A curious reluctance dragged at her hands as she thrust her key into the lock.

"It's all nonsense," she said aloud. "Here goes—"

She shut her eyes and opened the door. She walked in . . .

There was a dozen of everything. The room extended into gray space, and Marcie, opening her eyes, caught her hands to her throat to stifle a scream. There were a dozen of her familiar bed; a dozen gray cats snoozing on the pillow; a dozen dainty negligees, piled carefully by it; a dozen delicate packages labelled "Nylon stockings," and a dozen red apples rolling slightly beside them. Before her staring eyes a dozen elephants lumbered through the gray space, and beyond, her terrified vision focused on a dozen white domes that faded into the dim spaces of the expanded room, and a dozen tall cathedrals as well.

A dozen of *everything* . . .

"Marcie—Marcie, where are you?" she heard a man's voice shouting from the hall. Marcie whirled. *Greg!* And he was *outside*—outside this nightmare! She fled blindly, stumbling over a dozen rolled-up Persian carpets, grazing the edge of one of a dozen grand pianos; she screamed, visualizing a dozen rattlesnakes somewhere . . .

"Greg!" she shrieked.

Twelve doors were flung violently open.

"Marcie, sweetheart, what's the matter?" pleaded a jumble of tender voices, and twelve of Greg, pushing angrily at one another, rushed into the room.

3

The Anatomy Lesson

SCOTT SANDERS

*"Surely there's the right to
assemble in peace."*

By the time I reached the Anatomy Library, all the bones
had been checked out. Students bent over the wooden
boxes everywhere, in hallways and snack bar, assembling feet and arms, scribbling diagrams in notebooks.
Half the chairs were occupied by slouching skeletons,
and reclining skeletons littered the tables like driftwood.
Since I also would be examined on the subject the next
day, I asked the librarian to search one last time for bone
boxes in the storeroom.

"But I tell you, they've all been given out," she said,
glaring at me from beneath an enormous snarl of dark
hair, like a fierce animal caught in a bush. How many
students had already pestered her for bones this evening?

I persisted. "Medical school rides on this grade.
Haven't you got any damaged skeletons? Irregulars?"

Ignoring my smile, she measured me with her fierce
stare, as if estimating the size of box my bones would fill
after she had made supper of me. A shadow drooped beneath each of her eyes, permanent sorrow, like the
tearmark of a clown. "Irregulars," she repeated, turning
away from the counter.

I blinked with relief at her departing back. Only as she

slipped noiselessly into the storeroom did I notice her gloved hands. Fastidious, I thought. Doesn't want to soil herself with bone dust and mildew.

While awaiting my specimens, I studied the vertebrae which knobbed through the bent necks of students all around me, each one laboring over fragments of skeletons. Five lumbar vertebrae, seven cervical, a round dozen thoracic: I rehearsed the names, my confidence building.

Presently the librarian returned with a box. It was the size of an orange crate, wooden, dingy from age or dry rot. The metal clasps that held it shut were tarnished a sickly green. No wonder she wore the gloves.

"This one's for restricted use," she announced, shoving it over the counter.

I hesitated, my hands poised above the crate as if I were testing it for heat.

"Well, do you want it, or don't you?" she said.

Afraid she would return it to the archives, I pounced on it with one hand and with the other signed a borrower's card. "Old model?" I inquired pleasantly. She did not smile.

I turned away with the box in my arms. The burden seemed lighter than its bulk would have promised, as if the wood had dried with age. Perhaps instead of bones inside there would be pyramids of dust. The metal clasps felt cold against my fingers.

After some searching I found a clear space on the floor beside a scrawny man whose elbows and knees protruded through rents in his clothing like so many lumps of a sea serpent above the waters. When I tugged at the clasps they yielded reluctantly. The hinges opened with a gritty shriek, raising for a moment all round me a dozen glazed eyes, which soon returned to their studies.

Inside I found the usual wooden trays for bones, light as bird wings, but instead of the customary lining of vinyl they were covered with a metal the color of copper and the puttyish consistency of lead. Each bone fitted into its pocket of metal. Without consulting notes, I started confidently on the foot, joining tarsal to metatarsal. But it was soon evident that there were too many bones. Each one seemed a bit odd in shape, with an extra flange where none should be, or a socket at right angles to the orthodox position. The only way of accommodating all the bones was to assemble them into a seven-toed monstrosity, slightly larger than the foot of an adult male, phalanges all of the same length, with ankle-bones bearing the unmistakable nodes for—what? Wings? Flippers?

This drove me back to my anatomy text. But no consulting of diagrams would make sense of this foot. A practiced scrape of my knife blade assured me these were real bones. But from what freakish creature? Feeling vaguely guilty, as if in my ignorance I had given birth to this monstrosity, I looked around the library to see if anyone had noticed. Everywhere living skulls bent studiously over dead ones, ignoring me. Only the librarian seemed to be watching me sidelong, through her tangled hair. I hastily scattered the foot bones to their various compartments.

Next I worked at the hand, which boasted six rather than seven digits. Two of them were clearly thumbs, opposite in their orientation, and each of the remaining fingers was double-jointed, so that both sides of these vanished hands would have served as palms. At the wrist a socket opened in one direction, a ball joint protruded in the other, as if the hand were meant to snap onto an adjoining one. I now bent secretively over my outrageous skeleton, unwilling to meet stares from other students.

After tinkering with fibula and clavicle, each bone recognizable but slightly awry from the human, I gingerly unpacked the plates of the skull. I had been fearing these bones most of all. Their scattered state was unsettling enough to begin with, since in ordinary skeletal kits they would have been assembled into a braincase. Their gathered state was even more unsettling. They would only go together in one arrangement, yet it appeared so outrageous to me that I forced myself to reassemble the skull three times. There was only one jaw, to be sure, though an exceedingly broad one, and only two holes for ears. But the skull itself was clearly double, as if two heads had been squeezed together, like cherries grown double on one stem. Each hemisphere of the brain enjoyed its own cranium. The opening for the nose was in its accustomed place, as were two of the eyes. But in the center of the vast forehead, like the drain in an empty expanse of bathtub, was the socket for a third eye.

I closed the anatomy text, helpless before this freak. Hunched over to shield it from the gaze of other students, I stared long at that triangle of eyes, and at the twinned craniums that splayed out behind like a fusion of moons. No, I decided, such a creature was not possible. It was a hoax, a malicious joke designed to shatter my understanding of anatomy. But I would not fall for the trick. Angrily I disassembled this counterfeit skull, stuffed the bones back into their metal pockets, clasped the box shut and returned it to the counter.

"This may seem funny to you," I said, "but I have an examination to pass."

"Funny?" the librarian replied.

"This hoax." I slapped the box, raising a puff of dust. When she only lifted an eyebrow mockingly, I insisted: "It's a fabrication, an impossibility."

"Is it?" she taunted, laying her gloved hands atop the crate.

Furious, I said, "It's not even a very good hoax. No one who knows the smallest scrap of anatomy would fall for it."

"Really?" she said, peeling the glove away from one wrist. I wanted to shout at her and then hurry away, before she could uncover that hand. Yet I was mesmerized by the slide of cloth, the pinkish skin emerging. "I found it hard to believe myself, at first," she said, spreading the naked hand before me, palm up. I was relieved to count only five digits. But the fleshy heel was inflamed and swollen, as if the bud of a new thumb were sprouting there.

A scar, I thought feverishly. Nothing awful.

Then she turned the hand over and displayed for me another palm. The fingers curled upward, then curled in the reverse direction, forming a cage of fingers on the counter.

I flinched away. Skeletons were shattering in my mind, names of bones were fluttering away like blown leaves. All my carefully gathered knowledge was scattering. Unable to look at her, unwilling to glimpse the socket of flesh that might be opening on her forehead beneath the dangling hair, I kept my gaze turned aside.

"How many of you are there?" I hissed.

"I'm the first, so far as I know. Unless you count our friend here," she added, rapping her knuckles against the bone box.

I guessed the distances to inhabited planets, conjured up the silhouettes of space craft. "But where do you come from?"

"Boise."

"Boise, *Idaho?*"

"Well, actually, I grew up on a beet farm just outside Boise."

"You mean you're—" I pointed one index finger at her, and shoved the other against my chest.

"Human? Of course!" She laughed, a quick sound like the release of bubbles under water. Students at nearby tables gazed up momentarily from their skeletons with bleary eyes. The librarian lowered her voice, until it burbled like whale song. "I'm as human as you are," she murmured.

"But your hands? Your face?"

"Until a few months ago they were just run-of-the-mill human hands." She drew the glove quickly on and touched her swollen cheeks. "My face was skinny. My shoes used to fit."

"Then what happened?"

"I assembled these bones." Again she rapped on the crate. From inside came a hollow clattering, like the sound of gravel sliding.

"You're—becoming—one of them?"

"So it appears."

Her upturned lips and downturned eyes gave me contradictory messages. The clown-sad eyes seemed too far apart. Even buried under its shrubbery of dark hair, her forehead seemed impossibly broad.

"Aren't you frightened?" I said.

"Not any more," she answered. "Not since my head began to open."

I winced, recalling the vast skull, pale as porcelain, and the triangle of eyes. I touched the bone box gingerly. "What *is* it?"

"I don't know yet. But I begin to get glimmerings, begin to see it, alive and flying."

"Flying?"

"Swimming, maybe. My vision's still too blurry. For now, I just think of it as a skeleton of the possible, a fossil of the future."

I tried to imagine her ankles affixed with wings, her head swollen like a double moon, her third eye glaring. "And what sort of creature will you be when you're—changed?"

"We'll just have to wait and see, won't we?"

"We?" I echoed, backing carefully over the linoleum.

"You've put the bones together, haven't you?"

I stared at my palms, then turned my hands over to examine the twitching skin where the knuckles should be.

4
And I Alone Am Escaped
to Tell Thee

ROGER ZELAZNY

"Out of the frying pan—"

It was with them constantly—the black patch directly
overhead from whence proceeded the lightnings, the
near-blinding downpour, the explosions like artillery
fire.

Van Berkum staggered as the ship shifted again, almost dropping the carton he carried. The winds howled
about him, tearing at his soaked garments; the water
splashed and swirled around his ankles—retreating, returning, retreating. High waves crashed constantly
against the ship. The eerie green light of St. Elmo's fire
danced along the spars.

Above the wind and over even the thunder, he heard
the sudden shriek of a fellow seaman, random object of
attention from one of their drifting demonic tormentors.

Trapped high in the rigging was a dead man, flensed of
all flesh by the elements, his bony frame infected now
by the moving green glow, right arm flapping as if
waving—or beckoning.

Van Berkum crossed the deck to the new cargo site,
began lashing his carton into place. How many times had
they shifted these cartons, crates, and barrels about? He

had lost count long ago. It seemed that every time the job was done a new move was immediately ordered.

He looked out over the railing. Whenever he was near, whenever the opportunity presented itself, he scanned the distant horizon, dim through the curtain of rain. And he hoped.

In this, he was different. Unlike any of the others, he had a hope—albeit a small one—for he had a plan.

A mighty peal of laughter shook the ship. Van Berkum shuddered. The captain stayed in his cabin almost constantly now, with a keg of rum. It was said that he was playing cards with the Devil. It sounded as if the Devil had just won another hand.

Pretending to inspect the cargo's fastenings, Van Berkum located his barrel again, mixed in with all the others. He could tell it by the small dab of blue paint. Unlike the others it was empty, and caulked on the inside.

Turning, he made his way across the deck again. Something huge and bat-winged flitted past him. He hunched his shoulders and hurried.

Four more loads, and each time a quick look into the distance. Then—Then . . . ?

Then!

He saw it. There was a ship off the port bow! He looked about frantically. There was no one near him. This was it. If he hurried. If he was not seen.

He approached his barrel, undid the fastenings, looked about again. Still no one nearby. The other vessel definitely appeared to be approaching. There was neither time nor means to calculate courses, judge winds or currents. There was only the gamble and the hope.

He took the former and held to the latter as he rolled the barrel to the railing, raised it, and cast it overboard. A moment later he followed it.

The water was icy, turbulent, dark. He was sucked downward. Frantically he clawed at it, striving to drag himself to the surface.

Finally there was a glimpse of light. He was buffeted by waves, tossed about, submerged a dozen times. Each time, he fought his way back to the top.

He was on the verge of giving up, when the sea suddenly grew calm. The sounds of the storm softened. The day began to grow brighter about him. Treading water, he saw the vessel he had just quitted receding in the distance, carrying its private hell along with it. And there, off to his left, bobbed the barrel with the blue marking. He struck out after it.

When he finally reached it, he caught hold. He was able to draw himself partly out of the water. He clung there and panted. He shivered. Although the sea was calmer here, it was still very cold.

When some of his strength returned, he raised his head, scanned the horizon.

There!

The vessel he had sighted was even nearer now. He raised an arm and waved it. He tore off his shirt and held it high, rippling in the wind like a banner.

He did this until his arm grew numb. When he looked again the ship was nearer still, though there was no indication that he had been sighted. From what appeared to be their relative movements, it seemed that he might well drift past it in a matter of minutes. He transferred the shirt to his other hand, began waving it again.

When next he looked, he saw that the vessel was changing course, coming toward him. Had he been stronger and less emotionally drained, he might have wept. As it was, he became almost immediately aware of a mighty fatigue and a great coldness. His eyes stung from the salt, yet they wanted to close. He had to keep looking at his numbed hands to be certain that they maintained their hold upon the barrel.

"Hurry!" he breathed. "Hurry . . ."

He was barely conscious when they took him into the

lifeboat and wrapped him in blankets. By the time they came alongside the ship, he was asleep.

He slept the rest of that day and all that night, awakening only long enough to sip hot grog and broth. When he did try to speak, he was not understood.

It was not until the following afternoon that they brought in a seaman who spoke Dutch. He told the man his entire story, from the time he had sign d aboard until the time he had jumped into the sea.

"Incredible!" the seaman observed, pausing after a long spell of translation for the officers. "Then that storm-tossed apparition we saw yesterday was really the *Flying Dutchman!* There truly *is* such a thing—and you, you are the only man to have escaped from it!"

Van Berkum smiled weakly, drained his mug, and set it aside, hands still shaking.

The seaman clapped him on the shoulder.

"Rest easy now, my friend. You are safe at last," he said, "free of the demon ship. You are aboard a vessel with a fine safety record and excellent officers and crew—and just a few days away from her port. Recover your strength and rid your mind of past afflictions. We welcome you aboard the *Marie Celeste.*"

5
Angelica

JANE YOLEN

*"The serpent was just practice for the real
thing."*

Linz, Austria, 1898

The boy could not sleep. It was hot and he had been sick
for so long. All night his head had throbbed. Finally he
sat up and managed to get out of bed. He went down the
stairs without stumbling.

Elated at his progress, he slipped from the house without waking either his mother or father. His goal was the
river bank. He had not been there in a month.

He had always considered the river bank his own. No
one else in the family ever went there. He liked to set his
feet in the damp ground and make patterns. It was like a
picture, and the artist in him appreciated the primitive
beauty.

Heat lightning jetted across the sky. He sat down on a
fallen log and picked at the bark as he would a scab. He
could feel the log imprint itself on his backside through
the thin cotton pajamas. He wished—not for the first
time—that he could be allowed to sleep without his
clothes.

The silence and heat enveloped him. He closed his
eyes and dreamed of sleep, but his head still throbbed.

He had never been out at night by himself before. The slight touch of fear was both pleasure and pain.

He thought about that fear, probing it like a loose tooth, now to feel the ache and now to feel the sweetness, when the faint came upon him and he tumbled slowly from the log. There was nothing but river bank before him, nothing to slow his descent, and he rolled down the slight hill and into the river, not waking till the shock of the water hit him.

It was cold and unpleasantly muddy. He thrashed about. The sour water got in his mouth and made him gag.

Suddenly someone took his arm and pulled him up onto the bank, dragged him up the slight incline.

He opened his eyes and shook his head to get the lank, wet hair from his face. He was surprised to find that his rescuer was a girl, about his size, in a white cotton shift. She was not muddied at all from her efforts. His one thought before she heaved him over the top of the bank and helped him back onto the log was that she must be quite marvelously strong.

"Thank you," he said, when he was seated again, and then did not know where to go from there.

"You are welcome." Her voice was low, her speech precise, almost old-fashioned in its carefulness. He realized that she was not a girl but a small woman.

"You fell in," she said.

"Yes."

She sat down beside him and looked into his eyes, smiling. He wondered how he could see so well when the moon was behind her. She seemed to light up from within like some kind of lamp. Her outline was a golden glow and her blond hair fell in straight lengths to her shoulder.

"You may call me Angelica," she said.

"Is that your name?"

She laughed. "No. No, it is not. And how perceptive of you to guess."

"Is it an alias?" He knew about such things. His father

was a customs official and told the family stories at the
table about his work.

"It is the name I . . ." she hesitated for a moment and
looked behind her. Then she turned and laughed again.
"It is the name I travel under."

"Oh."

"You could not pronounce my real name," she said.
"Could I try?"

"Pistias Sophia!" said the woman and she stood as she
named herself. She seemed to shimmer and grow at her
own words, but the boy thought that might be the fever in
his head, though he hadn't a headache anymore.

"Pissta . . ." he could not stumble around the name.
There seemed to be something blocking his tongue. "I
guess I better call you Angelica for now," he said.

"For now," she agreed.

He smiled shyly at her. "My name is Addie," he said.

"I know."

"How do you know? Do I look like an Addie? It
means . . ."

"Noble hero," she finished for him.

"How do you know *that?*"

"I am very wise," she said. "And names are important to me. To all of us. Destiny is in names." She
smiled, but her smile was not so pleasant any longer. She
started to reach for his hand, but he drew back.

"You shouldn't boast," he said. "About being wise.
It's not nice."

"I am not boasting." She found his hand and held it in
hers. Her touch was cool and infinitely soothing. She
reached over with the other hand and put it first palm,
then back to his forehead. She made a "tch" against her
teeth and scowled. "Your guardian should be Flung
Over. I shall have to speak to Uriel about this. Letting
you out with such a fever."

"Nobody *let* me out," said the boy. "I let myself out.
No one knows I am here—except you."

"Well, there is one who *should* know where you are.

And he shall certainly hear from me about this." She stood up and was suddenly much taller than the boy. "Come. Back to the house with you. You should be in bed." She reached down the front of her white shift and brought up a silver bottle on a chain. "You must take a sip of this now. It will help you sleep."

"Will you come back with me?" the boy asked after taking a drink.

"Just a little way." She held his hand as they went.

He looked behind once to see his footprints in the rain-soft earth. They marched in an orderly line behind him. He could not see hers at all.

"Do you believe, little Addie?" Her voice seemed to come from a long way off, farther even than the hills.

"Believe in what?"

"In God. Do you believe that he directs all our movements?"

"I sing in the church choir," he said, hoping it was the proof she wanted.

"That will do for now," she said.

There was a fierceness in her voice that made him turn in the muddy furrow and look at her. She towered above him, all white and gold and glowing. The moon haloed her head, and behind her, close to her shoulders, he saw something like wings, feathery and waving. He was suddenly desperately afraid.

"What are you?" he whispered.

"What do you think I am?" she asked, and her face looked carved in stone, so white her skin and black the features.

"Are you the angel of death?" he asked and then looked down before she answered. He could not bear to watch her talk.

"For you, I am an angel of life," she said. "Did I not save you?"

"What kind of angel are you?" he whispered, falling to his knees before her.

She lifted him up and cradled him in her arms. She

sang him a lullaby in a language he did not know. "I told you in the beginning who I am," she murmured to the sleeping boy. "I am Pistias Sophia, angel of wisdom and faith. The one who put the serpent into the garden, little Adolf. But I was only following orders."

Her wings unfurled behind her. She pumped them once, twice, and then the great wind they commanded lifted her into the air. She flew without a sound to the Hitler house and left the boy sleeping, feverless, in his bed.

6
Apocryphal Fragment

EDWARD WELLEN

"One may doubt that doubting is always wise."

And Thomas, one of the twelve, called Didymus, the same that on a time had said, Except I shall see on his hands the print of the nails, and put my finger into the print of the nails, and thrust my hand into his side, I will not believe.

This same Thomas was journeying south through the Negev to Elath, whence he would take passage to India. And in the heat of the day he spied an oasis but, except he should drink of the water on its pool and rest in the shade of its doom palms, he would not believe it was other than mirage.

So he turned not aside, but stumbled on. And his toe struck a thing in the sand. After calling the name of the Lord, Thomas knelt to unearth the thing and, lo, it was a bottle, and, behold, the bottle bore upon its stopper the seal of Solomon, that wisest—womanwise—of men.

And Thomas took up the bottle and eyed it and saw through glass darkly only a smoke that swirled as he turned the bottle in the sun. He smiled, disbelieving in jinn.

Now, Thomas made to let fall the bottle but, bethinking him that an empty bottle would serve to hold water wherewith to quench his thirst on his journey, he broke the seal and loosed the stopper.

Whereupon a jinni jetted out through the mouth of the bottle and uprose in a cloud very like a mushroom, while the force of its release impelled the bottle to shoot from off the pad of Thomas's hand.

And the bottle dashed to bits against a rock. Wherefore Thomas called again upon the Lord.

Then he heard the voice of the jinni, which said, and its voice seemed the sands singing, Be not afeared, for by the Lord you have sworn by, and by my master, Solomon, the flight of the bottle is not against nature (it shall be given to one Isaac to come upon the laws of motion, the third of which is applicable here), nor am I, if you but knew the laws.

And again Thomas called the name of the Lord and said, This is nothing other than the voice of madness, for I am suffering a stroke of the sun.

And the jinni answered, saying, Nay, I am what my master, Solomon, made me, a gaseous-state computer having power to answer three questions. I can set to rest your doubts about anything under the sun or among the stars. Ask, and you shall receive. Thrice ask, and thrice will I answer you.

And Thomas the doubter said, Will you truly answer me? And the jinni said, Yes!

And Thomas smiled and said, Truly? And the jinni said, Yes!

And Thomas grew grave and said, But truly? And the jinni said, Yes! and vanished.

7

A Prophecy of Monsters

CLARK ASHTON SMITH

"All sorts of shapes deceive."

The change occurred before he could divest himself of
more than his coat and scarf. He had only to step out of
the shoes, to shed the socks with two backward kicks,
and shuffle off the trousers from his lean hind-legs and
belly. But he was still deep-chested after the change, and
his shirt was harder to loosen. His hackles rose with rage
as he slewed his head around and tore it away with hasty
fangs in a flurry of falling buttons and rags. Tossing off the
last irksome ribbons, he regretted his haste. Always here-
tofore he had been careful in regard to small details. The
shirt was monogrammed. He must remember to collect
all the tatters later. He could stuff them in his pockets,
and wear the coat buttoned closely on his way home,
when he had changed back.

Hunger snarled within him, mounting from belly to
throat, from throat to mouth. It seemed that he had not
eaten for a month—for a month of months. Raw butcher's meat was never fresh enough: it had known the coldness of death and refrigeration, and had lost all vital
essence. Long ago there had been other meals, warm,
and sauced with still-spurting blood. But now the thin
memory merely served to exasperate his ravening.

25

Chaos raced within his brain. Inconsequently, for an instant, he recalled the first warning of his malady, preceding even the distaste for cooked meat: the aversion, the allergy, to silver forks and spoons. It had soon extended to other objects of the same metal. He had cringed even from the touch of coinage, had been forced to use paper and refuse change. Steel, too, was a substance unfriendly to beings like him; and the time came when he could abide it little more than silver.

What made him think of such matters now, setting his teeth on edge with repugnance, choking him with something worse than nausea?

The hunger returned, demanding swift appeasement. With clumsy pads he pushed his discarded raiment under the shrubbery, hiding it from the heavy-jowled moon. It was the moon that drew the tides of madness in his blood, and compelled the metamorphosis. But it must not betray to any chance passer the garments he would need later, when he returned to human semblance after the night's hunting.

The night was warm and windless, and the woodland seemed to hold its breath. There were, he knew, other monsters abroad in that year of the twenty-first century. The vampire still survived, subtler and deadlier, protected by man's incredulity. And he himself was not the only lycanthrope: his brothers and sisters ranged unchallenged, preferring the darker urban jungles, while he, being country-bred, still kept the ancient ways. Moreover, there were monsters unknown as yet to myth and superstition. But these too were mostly haunters of cities. He had no wish to meet any of them. And of such meeting, surely, there was small likelihood.

He followed a crooked lane, reconnoitered previously. It was too narrow for cars and it soon became a mere path. At the path's forking he ensconced himself in the shadow of a broad, mistletoe-blotted oak. The path was used by certain late pedestrians who lived even farther out from town. One of them might come along at any moment.

Whimpering a little, with the hunger of a starved hound, he waited. He was a monster that nature had made, ready to obey nature's first commandment: *Thou shalt kill and eat.* He was a thing of terror . . . a fable whispered around prehistoric cavern-fires . . . a miscegenation allied by later myth to the powers of hell and sorcery. But in no sense was he akin to those monsters beyond nature, the spawn of a newer and blacker magic, who killed without hunger and without malevolence.

He had only minutes to wait, before his tensing ears caught the faroff vibration of footsteps. The steps came rapidly nearer, seeming to tell him much as they came. They were firm and resilient, tireless and rhythmic, telling of youth or of full maturity untouched by age. They told, surely, of a worthwhile prey; of prime lean meat and vital, abundant blood.

There was a slight froth on the lips of the one who waited. He had ceased to whimper. He crouched closer to the ground for the anticipated leap.

The path ahead was heavily shadowed. Dimly, moving fast, the walker appeared in the shadows. He seemed to be all that the watcher had surmised from the sound of his footsteps. He was tall and well-shouldered, swinging with a lithe sureness, a precision of powerful tendon and muscle. His head was a faceless blur in the gloom. He was hatless, clad in dark coat and trousers such as anyone might wear. His steps rang with the assurance of one who has nothing to fear, and has never dreamt of the crouching creatures of darkness.

Now he was almost abreast of the watcher's covert. The watcher could wait no longer but sprang from his ambush of shadow, towering high upon the stranger as his hind-paws left the ground. His rush was irresistible, as always. The stranger toppled backward, sprawling and helpless, as others had done, and the assailant bent to the bare throat that gleamed more enticingly than that of a siren.

It was a strategy that had never failed . . . until now . . .

The shock, the consternation, had hurled him away from that prostrate figure and had forced him back upon teetering haunches. It was the shock, perhaps, that caused him to change again, swiftly, resuming human shape before his hour. As the change began, he spat out several broken lupine fangs; and then he was spitting human teeth.

The stranger rose to his feet, seemingly unshaken and undismayed. He came forward in a rift of revealing moonlight, stooping to a half-crouch, and flexing his beryllium-steel fingers enameled with flesh-pink.

"Who—what—are you?" quavered the werewolf.

The stranger did not bother to answer as he advanced, every synapse of the computing brain transmitting the conditioned message, translated into simplest binary terms, "Dangerous. Not human. *Kill!*"

8
At the Bureau

STEVE RASNIC TEM

"They say he governs best who governs least."

I've been the administrator of these offices for twenty-five years now. I wish my employees were as steady. Most of them last only six months or so before they start complaining of boredom. It's next to impossible to find good help. But I've always been content here.

My wife doesn't understand how I could remain with the job this long. She says it's a dead end; I'm at the top of my pay scale, there'll be no further promotions, or increase in responsibilities. I've no place to go but down, she says. Her complaints about my job always lead to complaints about the marriage itself, of course. No children. Few friends. All the magic's gone, she says. But I've always been content.

When I started in the office we handled building permits. After a few years we were switched to peddling, parade, demolition licenses. Two years ago it was dog licenses. Last year they switched us to nothing but fishing permits.

Not too many people fish these days; the streams are too polluted. Last month I sold one permit. None the two months before. They plan to change our function again, I'm told, but a final decision apparently hasn't been made. I really don't care, as long as my offices continue to run smoothly.

A photograph of my wife taken the day of our marriage has sat on my desk the full twenty-five years, watching over me. At least she doesn't visit the office. I'm grateful for that.

Last week they reopened the offices next door. About time, I thought; the space had been vacant for five years. Ours was the last office still occupied in the old City Building. I was afraid maybe we too would be moved.

But I haven't been able as yet to determine just what it is exactly they do next door. They've a small staff, just one lone man at a telephone, I think. No one comes in or out of the office all day, until five, when he goes home.

I feel it's my business to find out what he does over there, and what it is he wants from me. A few days ago I looked up from my newspaper and saw a shadow on the frosted glass of our front door. Imagine my irritation when I rushed out into the hallway only to see his door just closing. I walked over there, intending to knock, and ask him what it was he wanted, but I saw his shadow within the office, bent over his desk. For some reason this stopped me, and I returned to my own office.

The next day the same thing happened. Then the day after that. I then refused to leave my desk. I wouldn't chase a shadow; he would not use me in such a fashion. I soon discovered that when I didn't go to the door, the shadow remained in my frosted glass all day long. He was standing outside my door all day long, every day.

Once there were two shadows. That brought me to my feet immediately. But when I jerked the door open I discovered two city janitors, sent to scrape off the words "Fish Permits" from my sign, "Bureau of Fish Permits." When I asked them what the sign was to be changed to, they told me they hadn't received those instructions yet. Typical, I thought; nor had I been told.

Of course, after the two janitors had left, the single shadow was back again. It was there until five.

The next morning I walked over to his office door. The lights were out; I was early. I had hoped that the sign painters had labeled his activity for me, but his sign had not yet been filled in. "Bureau Of . . .'' There were a few black streaks where the paint had been scraped away years ago, bare fragments of the letters that I couldn't decipher.

I'm not a man given to emotion. But the next day I lost my temper. I saw the shadow before the office door and I exploded. I ordered him away from my door at the top of my voice. When three hours had passed and he still hadn't left, I began to weep. I pleaded with him. But he was still there.

The next day I moaned. I shouted obscenities. But he was always there.

Perhaps my wife is right; I'm not very decisive, I don't like to make waves. But it's been days. He is always there.

Today I discovered the key to another empty office adjacent to mine. It fits a door between the two offices. I can go from my office to this vacant office without being seen from the hallway. At last, I can catch this crazy man in the act.

I sit quietly at my desk, pretending to read the newspaper. He hasn't moved for hours, except to occasionally peer closer at the frosted glass in my door, simulating binoculars with his two hands to his eyes.

I take off my coat and put it on the back of my chair. A strategically placed flower pot will give the impression of my head. I crawl over to the door to the vacant office, open it as quietly as possible, and slip through.

Cobwebs trace the outlines of the furniture. Files are scattered everywhere, some of the papers beginning to mold. The remains of someone's lunch are drying on one desk. I have to wonder at the city's janitorial division.

Unaccountably, I worry over the grocery list my wife gave me, now lying on my desk. I wonder if I should go back after it. Why? It bothers me terribly, the list unattended, unguarded on my desk. But I must push on. I step over a scattered pile of newspapers by the main desk, and reach the doorway leading into the hall.

I leap through the doorway with one mighty swing, prepared to shout the rude man down, in the middle of his act.

The hall is empty.

I am suddenly tired. I walk slowly to the man's office door, the door to the other bureau. I stand waiting.

I can see his shadow through the office door. He sits at his desk, apparently reading a newspaper. I step closer, forming my hands into imaginary binoculars. I press against the glass, right below the phrase, "Bureau Of," lettered in bold, black characters.

He orders me away from his door. He weeps. He pleads. Now he is shouting obscenities.

I've been here for days.

9
Aunt Agatha

DORIS PITKIN BUCK

"Time's punishment is inexorable."

She was not the one he had hoped to see that night. But because the young man was savoring old sights and sounds, and all that is quickly forgotten on the other side of the grave, he turned his attention briefly to the woman seated in the remembered room. She wasn't old. But the eyes under her graying hair had lost their fire, making her seem older than she was. She kept those eyes steadily fixed on him, nor did her lids flicker. She accepted him—he supposed—as she had accepted odd new pieces of furniture in her room; as perhaps she accepted the even odder painting, all cubes and circles, that hung in the place of—Wasn't it a drab watercolor?

His wife's Aunt Agatha, he thought. Memories rushed back. He said in sheer surprise, "I never imagined you'd change this place. I always thought of you, Aunt Agatha, as . . . oh, set in your ways; and this—" He shrugged and glanced at one beautiful shell on an asymmetrical table. He sighed a little. "It must be fun to be alive now."

"Some think it is."

"But I didn't come back," he explained swiftly, "to talk to you. I came to see Connie." Once more he looked around the room. "Connie must have egged you into making all these changes. She was always so full of life, so ready to—to do anything.''

"Yes, anything." Her voice was quietly bitter.

The young man paid little attention. He asked with urgency, "Connie—my wife—does she still live with you as the two of us did when I was alive?" He looked at the woman's handsome, impassive face for a clue; at the eyes that were black but not brilliant, the hawklike nose, the finely cut mouth. But there was no clue in them. They held only one comment on the universe, on all that was in it. They said, *I am tired of you.* Nothing more.

The young man cried to that baffling face, "Tonight Connie thought of me—hard, hard. It must have been that way. She brought me back. I always knew she would. I must see Connie.''

"To haunt her?" The woman's voice was flat.

The young man went toward her impulsively. "Who are you to judge Connie?" he demanded. "You—an old, staid woman—less alive than I am! Don't you know that Connie made her own laws? Only by those could she live. Perhaps tonight she'll laugh at me, laugh harder and more bitterly than the night she killed me. Perhaps even now she'll taunt me with Robert. I can still hear her tell what Robert meant to her. And I don't care. I came back to Connie, not to haunt her, but because someone as vibrant as Connie draws people, because—''

She tried to hush him with her hand but he went on, "Aunt Agatha, help me. Earth is strange to me. I don't know what year it is, nor any of the things that happened after I was poisoned. Where is Robert now? And . . . and Connie?" Suddenly his lips twisted. "Connie! Constance! Why did anyone name her Constance?" ·

The murdered man walked to and fro, his footfalls soundless but his eyes bright with excitement. "My wife was Carmen. That's what they ought to have called her. Maybe I should have fought with a woman like that— whipped the gipsy out of her.''

The woman's middle-aged eyes suddenly turned ugly. He felt her look him all over with envy.

"How young you are!" she muttered.

"You always said that. Connie and I used to laugh at it." The corners of his eyes crinkled, for elderly aunts are elderly aunts no matter on which side of the grave a man stands. Then he grew earnest. "Tell me, Aunt Agatha, did they—did they punish her?"

"Could anyone punish your wild Carmen but Carmen herself?"

"Don't ask me questions. My time—I know it will be brief, though I've almost forgotten time's strange workings. I thought that I'd see Connie right away."

The woman got up. "Go away! Go away! I'll make you." If her low voice had been a shout it could not have been more startling. "Take your damned youth out of my place!"

He stared at her in amazement. She no longer saw him; he was sure of that. She rubbed her eyes sleepily, as she half listened to a man's petulant growl from the bedroom. She waited for the man's "Aren't you ever coming, Connie?" before she called back through a yawn:

"Yes, Robert, in a minute."

10
The Boulevard of Broken Dreams

HARLAN ELLISON

"The nightmare that will never go away."

The demitasse cup of thick, sludgy espresso stopped midway between the saucer and Patrick Fenton's slightly parted lips. His arm froze and he felt cold, as if beads of fever-sweat covered his forehead. He stared past his luncheon companions, across the tiny French restaurant, through the front window that faced onto East Fifty-sixth Street, eyes widened, as the old man strode by outside.

"Jesus Christ!" he said, almost whispering in wonder.

"What's the matter?" Damon said, looking worried.

Fenton's hand began to shake. He set the cup down very carefully. Damon continued to stare at him with concern. Then Katherine perceived the luncheon had come to a halt and she looked back and forth between them. "What's happening?"

Fenton pulled his napkin off his lap and wiped his upper lip. "I can't believe what I just saw. It couldn't be."

Damon shoved his plate away and leaned forward. He had been the only one Fenton had communicated with during the month in the hospital; they were good friends. "Tell me."

"Forget it. I didn't see it."

Katherine was getting impatient. "I don't think it's

nice to play these nasty little word games. Just because I'm facing the kitchen and you're not, is no reason to taunt me. What *did* you see, Pat?''

Fenton sipped water. He took a long pause, then said, "I was a clerk at the Nuremberg trials in forty-six. You know. There was an officer, an *Oberstleutnant* Johann Hagen. He was in charge of the mass grave digging detail at Bergen-Belsen. He did things to women and small boys with a pickax. He was hung in June of 1946. I was there. I saw him hang.''

Damon stared across at his old friend. Fenton was in his early sixties, almost bald now, and he had been sick. "Take it easy, Pat.''

"I just saw him walk past the window.''

They stared at him for a moment. Damon cleared his throat, moved his coffee cup, cleared his throat again. Katherine continued chewing and looked at each of them without speaking. Finally, when the light failed to fade from Fenton's eyes, she said, "You must be mistaken.''

He spoke softly, without argument. "I'm not mistaken. You don't see a man hang and ever forget his face.''

Damon laid a hand on Fenton's wrist. "Take it easy. It's getting dark. A resemblance, that's all.''

"No.''

They sat that way for a long time, and Fenton continued to stare out the window. Finally, he started to speak, but the words caught in his throat. He gasped and moaned softly. His eyes widened at something seen outside on the sidewalk. Damon turned with difficulty—he was an extremely fat man, a successful attorney—and looked out the window.

Katherine turned and looked. The street was thronged with late-afternoon crowds hurrying to get inside before the darkness that promised rain could envelop them. "What now?'' she said.

"Another one,'' Fenton said. "Another one. Dear God, what's happening . . . ?''

"What do you mean: another one?"

"Katherine," Damon said snappishly, "shut up. Pat, what was it?"

Fenton was holding himself, arms wrapped around his body like a straitjacket. "Kreichbaum." He said the name the way an internist would say *inoperable*. "From Treblinka. They shot him in forty-five. A monster; bonfires, furnaces, fire was his medium. They shot him."

"Yes? And . . . ?" Katherine let the question hang.

"He just walked by that window, going toward Fifth Avenue."

"Pat, you've got to stop this," Damon said.

Fenton just stared, saying nothing. Then, after a moment, he moaned again. They didn't turn, they just watched him. "Kupsch," he said. Softly, very softly. And after a few seconds, he said, "Stackmann." Shadows deepened in the little French restaurant. They were the only ones left dining, and their food had grown as cold as the tablecloths. "Oh, God," Fenton said, "Rademacher."

Then he leaped to his feet, knocking over his chair, and screamed, "What kind of street *is* this?!"

Damon tried to reach across to touch him, to get him to sit down, but Fenton was spiraling toward hysteria. "What kind of day is this, where am I? They're dead, all of them! They went to the gallows or the wall thirty years ago. I was a young man, I saw it, all of it . . . what's happening here today?"

They tried to stop him as he pushed past them and ran out into the street.

It was almost totally dark now, even in late afternoon, as though charcoal dust had been sifted down over the city. Crowds moved past him, jostling him. Only the pale purple glow of the dead Nazi war criminals who walked slowly past him provided illumination.

He saw them all, one by one, as they walked past, strolling in both directions, free as the air, saying nothing, hands empty, wearing good shoes.

He tried to grab one of them, Wichmann, as he came by. But the tall, dark-haired Nazi shrugged him off, smiled at the yellow armband Fenton wore, smiled at the six-pointed star on the armband, and shoved past, walking free.

"Changed at Ellis Island!" Fenton screamed at Wichmann's retreating back. "I had nothing to do with it!"

Then he saw the purple glow beginning to form around him.

The street became night.

11
But Not the Herald

ROGER ZELAZNY

"Had the Greeks but thought of this—"

As the old man came down from the mountain, carrying the box, walking along the trail that led to the sea, he stopped, to lean upon his staff, to watch the group of men who were busy burning their neighbor's home.

"Tell me, man," he asked one of them, "why do you burn your neighbor's home, which, I now note from the barking and the screaming, still contains your neighbor, as well as his dog, wife, and children?"

"Why should we not burn it?" asked the man. "He is a foreigner from across the desert, and he looks different from the rest of us. This also applies to his dog, who looks different from our dogs and barks with a foreign accent, and his wife, who is prettier than our wives and speaks with a foreign accent, and his children, who are cleverer than ours and speak like their parents."

"I see," said the old man, and he continued on his way.

At the crossroads, he came upon a crippled beggar whose crutches had been thrown high into a tree. He struck upon the tree with his staff and the crutches fell to the ground. He restored them to the beggar.

"Tell me how your crutches came to be in the treetop, brother," he said.

40

"The boys threw them there," said the beggar, adjusting himself and holding out his hand for alms.

"Why did they do that?"

"They were bored. They tired their parents with asking. 'What should I do now?' until finally one or another of the parents suggested they go make sport of the beggar at the crossroads."

"Such games be somewhat unkind," said the old man.

"True," said the beggar, "but fortunately some of the older boys found them a girl and they are off in the field enjoying her now. You can hear her cries if you listen carefully. They are somewhat weak at the moment, of course. Would I were young and whole again, that I might join in the sport!"

"I see," said the old man, and he turned to go.

"Alms! Alms! Have you no alms in that box you bear? Have you nothing to bestow upon a poor, lame beggar?"

"You may have my blessing," said the old man, "but this box contains no alms."

"A fig for thy blessing, old goat! One cannot eat a blessing! Give me money or food!"

"Alas, I have none to give."

"Then my curses be upon your head! May all manner of misfortune come down on you!"

The old man continued on his way to the sea, coming after a time upon two men who were digging a grave for a third who lay dead.

"It is a holy office to bury the dead," he remarked.

"Aye," said one of the men, "especially if you have slain him yourself and are hiding the evidence."

"You have slain that man? Whatever for?"

"Next to nothing, curse the luck! Why should a man fight as he did over the smallest of coins? His purse was near empty."

"From his garments, I should judge he was a poor man."

"Aye, and now he has naught more to trouble him."

"What have you in that box, old man?" asked the second.

"Nothing of any use. I go to cast it in the sea."

"Let's have a look."

"You may not."

"We'll be judge of that."

"This box is not to be opened."

They approached him. "Give it to us."

"No."

The second one struck the old man in the head with a stone; the first snatched the box away from him. "There! Now let us see what it is that is so useless."

"I warn you," said the old man, rising from the ground, "if you open that box you do a terrible thing which may never be undone."

"We'll be judge of that."

They cut at the cords which bound the lid.

"If you will wait but a moment," said the old man, "I will tell you of that box."

They hesitated. "Very well, tell us."

"It was the box of Pandora. She who opened it unleashed upon the world all of the terrible woes which afflict it."

"Ha! A likely tale!"

"It is said by the gods, who charged me cast it into the sea, that the final curse waiting within the box is worse than all the other ills together."

"Ha!"

They undid the cord and threw back the lid.

A golden radiance sped forth. It rose into the air like a fountain, and from within it a winged creature cried out, in a voice infinitely delicate and pathetic, "Free! After all these ages, to be free at last!"

The men fell upon their faces. "Who are you, Oh lovely creature," they asked, "you who move us to such strange feelings?"

"I am called Hope," said the creature. "I go to travel in all the dark places of the Earth, where I will inspire men with the feeling that things may yet be better than they are.''

And with that it rose into the air and dashed off in search of the dark places of the Earth.

When the two murderers turned them again to the old man, he was changed: for now his beard was gone, and he stood before them a powerful youth. Two serpents were coiled about his staff.

"Even the gods could not prevent it," he said. "You have brought this ill upon yourselves, by your own doing. Remember that, when bright Hope turns to dust in your hands."

"Nay," said they, "for another traveler approaches now, and he wears a mighty purse upon him. We shall retire on this day's takings."

"Fools!" said the youth, and he turned on winged heels and vanished up the path, greeting Hercules as he passed him by.

12
Chained

BARRY N. MALZBERG

"The Ghost talks."

So finally he comes, the young fool, and I lean from the parapet and tell him everything. The poison in the ears. The treachery. The lies. The huddling in incestuous bed with Gertrude and the degree of corruption. The young fool is shocked as well he should be and cries that revenge will be terrible and swift. He departs with promises but I have no hope. His record has always been high in potential, low in performance. Sometimes I wondered if he could be my issue and considering the evidence of later events perhaps he was not. Gertrude was never to be trusted.

Nonetheless, I am granted no other alternative so I wait. I wait and I wait as he waffles around, prays, flagellates himself, mumbles about the possibility of sin, flirts with that teasing, worthless bitch, Ophelia, who has no more sensibility than a swan. Claudius continues to prosper. He wallows in his office. He takes swift measure of Gertrude in incestuous bed and preaches saintly office outside. It is all too much to bear and when Hamlet desists from slaying him in the corridor at prayer I feel my patience snap. It is not easy existing in this difficult condition and there will be no peace, absolutely no peace at all as long as these affairs continue. Grumbling, furious, I drag myself to Gertrude's chambers while he is berating her and brace him. His eyes become round, shiny with disbelief but resolve fills his bearing. Responding to rustling behind the arras he draws his sword and runs it through the curtain, disposing of that prating, eavesdropping old fool, Polonius, father of the frivolous bitch. His consternation is enormous but as nothing to mine.

It is at that precise moment—and not earlier, I want to make it quite clear, not an instant earlier—that I finally lose all fatherly patience and resolve to take matters to a conclusion.

Claudius and I never got along. It was not only the matter of the succession, it was the corruption within him which I perceived from the first, the small cruelties, the weak, descending humiliation of a man who knew all his life that his older brother was the king not only in fact but spirit. He would spy on servants in the castle, set them at one another through small thefts, crush frogs in the moat, steal the jester's cap and bells; past all of these indignities, armored by my certainty and contempt I swept. Gertrude fell in love with me at once; she never paid any attention to Claudius whatsoever until, for reasons of state, I was distracted from our alliance and gave Claudius the opportunity to insinuate himself. I am sure of this. Still, with all of his vices and the deadly indications of his character I never realized until the moment that the warm fluid dripped deep into my ear, sickening me and causing me to shriek with pain so quickly terminated, I never realized until that moment how he hated me; I thought that the cruelties came from envy, the envy from admiration.

But when he poisoned me, sending me into this gray, chained Denmark of souls tormented and unavenged, I became quite angry and resolved to set the situation to right; the time was out of joint, as I reminded that snivelling Prince, and the obligation to correct it fell upon him.

* * *

Of course I should have looked more closely at Gertrude. If there is one quality which the unavenged netherworld grants it is ample time for recrimination and I should have known that the woman could never be trusted. Silly, frivolous bitches like Ophelia wear their hearts on their sleeves but Gertrude has not achieved her station without the exercise of cunning; it is possible that her relationship with Claudius preceded my murder. In fact it is possible that she put him up to it, that she gave him motive. "Just a little poison and I can be completely yours; you can be my little bloat king," she might have murmured to him. This state of passage brings the most terrible thoughts and suggestions; never have I hated these people as I hate them now. Murder unavenged leaves one in these endless corridors, stalking, stalking, one does not really know where to turn, to whom to appeal, what to do to get *out* of this terrible state; I would never have turned to that hopeless conundrum I called my son if it had not been out of despair; if I had had the means I would have run Claudius through myself; why would I pace the battlements shouting in the wind for assistance if I were capable of anything on my own other than pleadings and prayer?

I was a just, a wise, a compassionate king; my wife was a slut, my son a disaster, my brother a traitor, nonetheless I brought to this domain a mild and sacrosanct order; it was only in this latter stage that I was driven to such extreme and destructive perceptions; to die and not be dead is—how can I put this?—extremely *embittering*. Without the Prince's task for evasion, flights of rhetoric, cheap, distracting and easily deterred lust I am left to confront, ah, endlessly, that doomed and chained specter: myself.

So I present myself to Rosencrantz and Guildenstern, indistinguishable, jolly mercenaries with faces like smooth partitions to shield them from all reason. "I know who you are!" one of them says—I cannot tell them apart—and clutches the other. "We have heard all the reports."

"Enough of that," I say. "Throw him overboard. Then hasten back to Denmark and say that he was murdered by Polonius's legions. This will most distress Claudius and he will have no suspicions when you ask for a private conference to grant further important information. Get him alone in quarters and *I* will run him through." Strictly speaking this is a lie of course. I am blocked from direct action by the conditions of the curse. Nonetheless it will at least mark a beginning, some action at last, and it will keep me busy. The paralysis of the Prince has leached into me. "I will pay you well for your services," I say. "After all I am still a king. I still have the court."

They stare at me with their impermeable faces. "You are a ghost," one of them says. "How can you pay us?"

"I have grand mystical powers. Trust me."

"He is our schoolfellow," one points out thoughtfully. "We owe him bonds of loyalty."

"He intends to kill you," I point out. "The orders are already planted in your luggage."

"What an extremely treacherous court this must be."

"Oh, I can accede to that," I agree. "I can certainly agree to that."

Their cooperation is gained—they are a submissive pair, eager to please, with a deep faith in ghosts—but it does not work out nonetheless; the Prince gets wind of some treachery and speeds off the boat. Meanwhile the bumblers cannot locate the damning orders in their own luggage. The situation is hopelessly scrambled and upon our separate return to the court I find out that Ophelia has further complicated matters by drowning herself. Everyone seems to be done away with in this tragic legend except the real culprit. At chambers I confront the Prince who is drawing on his gloves, adjusting his sword, mumbling about business which must be swiftly attended to. "Oh," he says, looking at me with dim and distracted countenance, "it's you again. That was a really splendid production. You couldn't have possibly done it better; I only wish that it had had better outcome. Have you come for your purse? I'm sure that was settled."

I realize that in the dim light and because of his preoccupation he takes me for the Player King. My chains are not highly visible. "Yes, we have been paid," I say. "And the king has confessed all in your absence. He pleads for release."

"Then he shall have it." Hamlet looks at me shrewdly. "Your accent is different," he says. "Are you possibly an imposter?"

"Nothing is different," I say, "and everything is different. But only you can bring this to an end."

"I will not be intimidated," Hamlet says. His expression becomes sullen. "Get out of here before I run you through."

"You won't run anyone through. Nothing ever happens in your world until someone throws herself into a pond."

"Blackguard," he says. He draws his sword. "I will not accept that."

I laugh in his face and desert, leaving him there mumbling. The better part of apparition is disassembly through desire, although there is, of course, always the pain.

I withdraw, sulkily, to observe subsequent events. I know that nothing can happen and yet I cannot abandon the prospect of hope. Anything is preferable to stumbling and clanking on the parapet. Amazingly many events do occur. Gertrude is poisoned. Claudius is run through. Hamlet himself, in consternation at his burst of activity, opens himself to a palpable hit. At the end, most astonishingly, Fortinbras blesses tham all. I know better but offer no comment. Sometimes it is better to cultivate a posture of diffidence. Besides, I know now that it is only a brief matter of time until I am released from my chains.

* * *

Claudius joins me on the towers, puts an arm around me confidentially. "Not so soon, you fool," he says. "It isn't over yet." Gertrude, around a corner, winks. "Remember the three witches?" he says. "Remember Banquo's ghost? Now we'll have some real fun."

"Fun?" I say. "Real fun?"

Gertrude sweeps against me regally, her own chains clanking. "Absolutely," she says. "Just as soon as Lear gets on the heath, we can kick the hell out of him."

"We can make Caliban squirm a little too," Claudius says lovingly.

I feel the cool winds of the nether region tear through me like giggling knives.

Something sure as hell is rotten in the state of Denmark.

13
Chalk Talk

EDWARD WELLEN

"Professional communicators don't necessarily get it across."

Maybe because it was May. But Professor Rood felt carbonated blood bubble-dance through his veins. It gave such a bounce to his morning greeting of his tall leathery colleague and rival, Professor Kriss, when they met in the hallway that he drew a look of surprise.

Maybe because Zoë Albemarle—the chalk broke twice before he got hold of himself and used the proper pressure—sat in class in an even more revealing dress than usual.

Maybe it was feeling the potency of mind over matter and of energy over both.

In any case, he found himself launching into his old lecture on linguistics with new zest.

"Thanks to Noam Chomsky and Transformational Grammar, we learn that—" He chalked on the blackboard:

> John loves Mary.
> Mary is loved by John.

"—which is one sentence, in its active and passive voices, is merely the 'surface structure' of the sentence.

"We may think we see it plain, as *from* a plane—" He waited till laughter had manifested itself, then went on. "—the solid green of a rain forest. But below the surface are the reelings and writhings that make the floor of a Freudian jungle a lively place. Dr. Chomsky calls this underneathness, this grimmer grammar, the 'deep structure.'

"But it is just here where things are getting interesting that Dr. Chomsky fails us. At least, in spite of his computer readouts and world view, he has not made clear to me the nature of this deep structure. He tells us that the foundations of all languages are a finite set of innate universals. But just what are these universals?

"As I hesitate to break in on Dr. Chomsky and his greater concerns to ask him for—to follow the forest metaphor—'clear-cutting,' I've been trying to work it out for myself.

"I began by fantasying the deep structure. I've said it's a Freudian jungle, and I won't describe it except to say I was damn happy to hack my way out. After that bum trip I withdrew to the comparative safety and sanity of surface structure."

Another pause for laughter to manifest itself. It manifested itself delightfully through Zoë Albemarle.

Where was he? Ah, yes.

"I might have vegetated there, forever unable to see the trees for the forest. But luckily surface structure lends itself Proteus-like to variations. Of these the most promising seemed—" He chalked:

John generates love for Mary.
Mary attracts love from John.

"This at once suggested an electromagnetic infrastructure, quite in keeping with the make-up of the brain. Hardly a breakthrough, however. Then it struck me. In changing 'love' from verb to noun, I had stumbled across an innate universal!

"Long before the Industrial Revolution, man had the feeling things are taking over, or at least have a will of their own. Picture Neanderthal Man chipping a flint and blaming a skinned knuckle on the perversity of the material or the tool. Love, of course, is not a thing but a process. Still, this *further* formulation of the sentence gives a true sense of the underlying nature of this depersonalized world in which we are all strangers." He chalked:

> Love connects John to Mary.
> Mary is connected to John by love.

There it was, in white and black. And it had finished itself right on time. The classroom began emptying. He stood looking at the writing on the blackboard. Carve *that* on a tree, Noam, he thought with a smile. The smile was as much for Zoë Albemarle lingering in the tail of his eye. His chest swelled, sending the dribbles of chalk on his jacket flying in a cloudy cascade.

"Yes, my dear?" The voice did not sound quite like his own.

Zoë leaned plumply toward him.

"There's this I don't understand, Professor Rood—" She pointed to the blackboard.

He dusted his fingers and reached out to touch her.

Then it happened.

Zoë screeched.

He saw the writing on the blackboard shiver loose.

It slid down the slate, tripped the eraser off the ledge, followed the eraser to the floor, gathered itself, then struck out for the doorway. Zoë had beat it out and vanished. It flowed over floorboards, doorsill, floorboards, slithering along the hallway toward Professor Kriss's classroom.

Professor Rood trailed his handwriting. Stooping and straining to see, he thought it crawled along on tiny rootlike pseudopodia. In the mud at the bottom of the sea a living jelly feeds, grows, and multiplies. It takes car-

bonate of lime from the brine to make a skeleton for itself. The jelly dies and rots and adds its skeletal corpse's
mite to the chalk deposit that has been building since long
before the coming of man. This living jelly puts forth
rootlike pseudopodia.

Professor Kriss's classroom was empty but for Professor Kriss sitting at her desk over student papers. She did
not look up as the chalking climbed baseboard and wall
and, an inverted waterfall, streamed up over the ledge
and onto the blackboard.

She looked up as Professor Rood's shadow fell across
her desk and found him staring at the blackboard. Professor Kriss followed his gaze.

Six times the sentence had written itself:

John loves Mary.

Mary Kriss got up, and up, and nearly swept John Rood
off his feet in a hug.

"Why didn't you say so before, John?"

14
Climacteric

AVRAM DAVIDSON

"Many handsome young men have appalling taste."

They had driven up, just the two of them, to a place in the mountains he had spoken of—store, garage, hotel, all in one. It was a rare day, a vintage day, with no one to bother them while they ate lunch and shared a bottle of wine. She spoke most; the things she said were silly, really, but she was young and she was lovely and this lent a shimmer of beauty to her words.

His eyes fed upon her—the golden corona of her hair, the green topazes of her eyes, exquisitely fresh skin, creamy column of neck, her bosom.

"But never mind that," she said, ceasing what she had been saying. "I want to forget all that. *You:* What were you like as a boy? What did you dream of?"

He smiled. "Of a million beautiful girls—all like you," he added, as she made a pretty pout with her red little mouth—"and how I would rescue them from a hideous dragon, piercing through its ugly scales with my lance," he said; "while its filthy claws scrabbled on the rocks in a death agony . . . And the girl and I lived happily ever after, amid chaste kisses, nothing more."

She smiled, touched him. "Lovely," she said. "But—

chaste kisses? Now, I used to dream—but never mind. It's funny how our dreams change, and yet, not so much, isn't it?'' They looked swiftly about, saw nothing but a distant bird, speck-small in the sky; then they kissed.

Very soon afterward they drove up a side road to the end, then climbed a path. ''You're quite sure no one can see us here?'' she asked.

''Quite sure,'' he said. He stepped back. There was a noise of great rushing, then a short scream, then—other noises. After a while he drew nearer and ran his hands lovingly over the sparkling and iridescent scales. The beautiful creature hissed appreciatively, and continued to clean its gorgeous and glittering claws with its shining black bifurcated tongue.

15
The Contest

ROBERT J. SAWYER

"He'll win every time, I think."

"It's getting too much for me," said the leader of the Party in Power, his voice thundering through the skies. "I propose a simple contest, winner take all."

"Oh?" replied the leader of the Oposition, the syllable materializing as a puff of flame. "This intrigues me. The terms?"

"We select a mutually agreeable subject, an average man, and measure his tendencies toward our respective sides. The party whose ideology he leans to will gain custody of the species for all time. I'm getting too old to fight over each individual with you. Do you agree to the contest?"

"It sounds like a hell of an idea."

"It is done, then."

John Smith was, of course, the perfect choice. He was of average height, average weight, of average intellect and income. Even his name was average. He went to work that morning just another one of four billion people, but, during his lunch hour, he became the sole object of attention of two great minds.

"Aha!" proclaimed the leader of the Party in Power,

whom henceforth we shall call *G*. "Observe his generosity: his gratuity is over twenty per cent of the total bill. My point."

"Not so fast," interposed the leader of the Opposition, *D*. "Look into his mind for his motive. The magnitude of the tip is intended to impress the buxom secretary he is dining with. His wife, I suspect, would not approve. The point is mine."

John Smith left the table with his secretary and proceeded through the streets to their place of employment. Catching sight of a matronly woman soliciting donations for a worthwhile charity ahead, he crossed the road early.

"Generosity, you said?" smiled D. "My point."

Returning to his office ten minutes late, Smith settled to his work. His secretary buzzed him to say that his wife was on the phone.

"Tell her I'm in a meeting," Smith commanded.

"Three zip," said D.

Smith next entered his purely personal luncheon date on his company expense account.

"You're lagging behind," said D, satisfied. "I would say he is a staunch supporter of my party. Four."

"Perhaps," said G, "perhaps."

At four-fifty, Smith left his office to go home. "Don't worry. I won't count that against him," said D, comfortable in his lead.

On the subway, Smith read over the shoulder of the man sitting beside him, averting his eyes from the old woman standing nearby.

"Five."

Walking from the subway station to his house, he threw a candy bar wrapper onto his neighbor's lawn.

"Is littering a sin?" asked D.

"I'm not sure," allowed G.

"It's unimportant. The outcome is inevitable."

Entering his house, Smith called a greeting to his fat wife and sat down to read the newspaper before dinner. His wife asked him to take the dog for a walk before they ate. He left something else on his neighbor's lawn this time.

"Well, I'm certainly entitled to a point for that," said D.

"Crudity. Six to nothing."

"Perhaps a more definitive test?"

"For instance?"

D waved his red arms and screams rose from an alley near Smith. "Help! Somebody help!" D chalked up another point as Smith turned deliberately away from the noise. G sent a police officer running past Smith.

"Did you hear anything?" shouted the cop.

"No. I don't want to be involved."

G frowned. D smiled.

Smith headed quickly back to his house, hurrying up the walk as he heard the phone ringing. "It's for you," called out his wife.

He picked up the receiver. "Why, Christopher! I'll be damned!"

"Would you care to play the best two out of three?" sighed G.

16
Controlled Experiment

RICK CONLEY

"It depends on which end of the gun you find yourself."

Standing alone on the podium, in the glare of the camera lights, the old man spoke wearily.

"I have called this press conference to announce my resignation from the American Psionic Institute."

The audience of scientists and reporters buzzed excitedly.

"As cofounder of this organization, I am reluctant to leave it; but my continued presence here can only cast a cloud of doubt over honest men's work. For recently, in my zeal to demonstrate the existence of psychic phenomena, I committed the one unpardonable sin in science: I deliberately manipulated an experiment to yield the desired results.

"A few weeks ago, I implanted in the brains of rats electrodes that, when energized by a random-number generator, produce highly pleasurable sensations in the animals. My objective: to see if the rats could, through telekinesis—mind over matter—influence the generator to give more than the expected, chance number of stimulations.

"I reported almost immediate success—clear evidence

59

of psychic ability! But then . . . then some of my colleagues, puzzled by the excessive attention I was paying to my apparatus, watched, concealed, as I manipulated the equipment to deliver additional stimulations to the rats.''

The old man sighed.

"Why did I cheat? I don't know. In fact, until my colleagues confronted me with the evidence, I was barely aware of my actions.

"Perhaps after a lifetime of honest research with, at best, ambiguous results to show for it, I decided subconsciously to help the experiment along just a little, in order to encourage my colleagues and to impress the skeptics.

"In any case, I'm sorry for the embarrassment I've caused the Institute. And now I shall entrust my work to abler, more trustworthy men. In particular, I'm gratified that Dr. John Cole has promised to continue my research with the random stimulator.

"Good luck, John. I know you won't lose control as I did.''

Alone in the laboratory, strapped down in a cage, the rats squealed in ecstasy as the machine directed repeated stimulations through the electrodes implanted in their brains.

More! the rats' minds shouted. More! More!

But the machine ignored their demands; it continued to grant the creatures brief moments in paradise according to its own mechanical caprice.

Then the rats tensed. The man! The man was coming!

Seconds later, Dr. Cole unlocked the door to the laboratory and entered. Walking over to the experimental apparatus, he inspected the electronic counter hopefully. He was disappointed to see that in the past hour the rats had received no stimulation beyond chance expectation.

Peering into the cage at the tiny creatures, he sighed. "Do something, you deadbeats! Do something!''

At that moment, the rats concentrated mightily.

From their minds, at the speed of thought, sprang tendrils of mental energy. Reaching deep into the recesses of Cole's mind, the tendrils touched, probed, twisted.

More! the rats' minds shouted. More! More!

Unconsciously, Cole turned a dial on the random-number generator. The stimulations were no longer random; they came faster and faster.

Even in their heightened ecstasy the rats sensed that this man was not the same one they had . . . touched . . . earlier. But still, he was a man, not a machine, and could be manipulated.

They squealed in delight.

They were in control again.

17
The Curse of Hooligan's Bar

CHARLES E. FRITCH

"Some vampires should avoid martinis."

"Hooligan," I said to the bartender, "you make the best martinis in the whole wide, ever-loving world."

Mike Hooligan grunted. I guess he thought I was snowing him. The truth was, it took at least three of his martinis to make them really palatable. I suppose it had something to do with deadening the tastebuds on my tongue.

Anyway, the world might have been wide but it sure wasn't ever-loving—to me at least. I was down on my luck for sure and surprised and pleased when my compliment triggered a rare holiday spirit in my fellow man.

Hooligan gave me a big Irish grin and said, "How about another one—on the house."

It was, as the poets say, a rhetorical question. Since you can't beat a price like that, and since I could use all the help I could get to drown—or at least, pickle—my sorrows, and since an event like a free drink might never come again, I said, "Sure!"—an answer which surprised neither Hooligan nor myself.

I seemed to be the only customer in the saloon not drinking beer. It's not that I have anything against the foamy, you understand. I just don't go for the stuff. I prefer the more refined beverages.

But I do dig Hooligan's Bar. It may not be classy like some of the places uptown, but it's got a lot of character. I always had this creepy feeling that one night something really BIG was going to happen there—like maybe a bug-eyed Martian would land on the roof and come down into the bar to use the john. In fact, I carried a little camera in my pocket, ready to record the event and make myself a mint from the newspapers.

It was a crazy notion, maybe, but I had it. Now that it was New Year's Eve, the intuition was stronger than ever, so I decided to stick around. Besides, I was down to my last wrinkled dollar bill, and I didn't want to spend the evening in my lonely hotel room.

"Hooligan," I said, "do you believe in Martians?"

He shook his head. "Not a chance. But ghosts and witches, that's another thing." He leaned across the bar toward me and whispered, "Have you heard about the curse of Hooligan's bar?"

I leaned forward. "No, tell me."

He shuddered. "I better not. Not on New Year's Eve. It's too horrible."

He brought me my free drink. It didn't have an olive, but over a technicality I wasn't about to look a gift martini in the vermouth. I sipped and thought about what he'd said. He was putting me on, having his little joke.

Then wham! right at the stroke of midnight, it happened.

The cuckoo clock above the bar opened its wooden portals on schedule, and out popped the bird. I half expected it to say, "Happy New Year!" or "Drink up, boys!" but of course it only said, "Cuckoo! Cuckoo! Cuckoo!" as always. Maybe I counted wrong, but I could swear it said it thirteen times.

Now here's the strange thing. The bird wasn't alone. With him came this character an inch tall, with a paste-white face, slicked-down red hair, and a green cloak.

As he clung to the cuckoo's neck, the little stranger

opened his mouth and announced to the world, "I am Count O'Brien, the Irish vampire."

The world wasn't listening. With all the singing and laughing and the clink of glasses, nobody else heard him. Then the cuckoo, finished with its own business, flipped back into the clock, leaving Count O'Brien hanging in mid-air. This didn't faze him. He merely changed into a tiny green bat and flew down to land on the bar in front of me.

I reached into my coat for the camera.

Hooligan, who had never been known for neatness, apparently decided to turn over a new leaf for the new year. A damp bar rag came whooshing down the mahogany, propelled by the Irishman's beefy hand, and the green bat took off like a—well, like a bat—licking its chops and twisting its head back and forth as though searching for some victim to pounce on.

He found one, represented by the back of a red, puffy neck billowing between hairline and collar. As I watched, the bat dived onto the collar, changed back into a one-inch vampire and sank his teeth into the flesh.

"Yeeeow!" the man commented, and slapped his neck.

Count O'Brien leaped out of the path of the hand in the nick of time but slipped and toppled into a glass of foamy brown liquid.

Immediately, he began to tread beer.

The owner of the glass lifted it, peered inside and yelped, "Hey, there's a fly in my beer."

Count O'Brien crawled out onto the rim of the glass, rose to his full height of one inch and declared indignantly, "I am not now, nor have I ever been, a fly."

"Begorrah!" the man exclaimed, eyes bugging. "It's one of the little people."

Blinking his eyes, the man turned to alert his companion to the miracle.

I moved faster then than I've moved for many a year. I swept in behind the man, surreptitiously scooped the tiny vampire into the palm of my hand and retreated to the deserted far end of the bar.

"That's funny," the man's voice sounded behind me, "he was here a minute ago."

"Sure he was," his companion said, chuckling.

"Are you calling me a liar?"

Wham! Bam! Fists flew, bodies fell. Hooligan bonked both men on the head with a sock filled with quarters and dragged them into the back room to sleep it off.

Certain that no one was watching, I opened my fist and let the red-haired creature step out onto the bar. He slicked back his wet hair and wrung beer from his green cloak.

"Don't be afraid," he said, gnashing his teeth fiercely, "I am Count O'Brien, the Irish vampire."

"You already said that," I informed him. "Are you really one of the little people?"

"Well, I'm not the jolly green giant," he said.

"A vampire leprechaun?" I said wonderingly.

"Why not? Back in the old country I used to file my teeth on the Blarney Stone."

Why not, indeed? my nimble mind agreed, alerting me to the possibilities. Remember that premonition? I could hear opportunity knocking loud and clear.

"Once every hundred years," Count O'Brien explained, "I am allowed into the world of humans. Boy oh boy, am I thirsty."

That settled it. I couldn't wait a century. Whatever I had to do, I had to do it now. I took out my old pocket watch and pretended to be checking the time, while I really held its shiny black surface close to the Count. There was no reflection.

Then I whipped out my camera and took several snaps. Count O'Brien didn't mind. In fact, he struck several majestic and terrifying poses.

"By the way," he said, when I'd finished, "vampires can't have their pictures taken either." He looked at me thoughtfully. "You wouldn't have any spare blood in you, would you?"

I presented him with a reassuring smile. "You can put the bite on me anytime you want. But first, I've got a little proposition for you."

He listened while I spent the next five minutes filling the silence with golden words from my silver tongue—in a low voice, of course, so Hooligan and his customers wouldn't notice. I painted a picture of fame and fortune unlike anything he'd ever dreamed of. His eyes glittered at the notion of getting all the grade-A blood he could drink without running the risk of drowning in a glass of beer.

He'd be the eighth wonder of the world, I told him, and I'd be his personal manager—for the usual fifty per cent commission.

To tell the truth—and I might as well—I wasn't really thinking of the entertainment value Count O'Brien would provide for the culturally undernourished peoples of the world. I was thinking of the shiny new car I'd be parking in front of my big house in the country, of the servants I'd have, and the fabulous meals I'd be eating, of the frequent trips to Europe and the Orient, and of all the beautiful movie starlets eager to date me when I was filthy rich and able to afford them.

I'd been poor long enough. I'd hit bottom, and it was time to go in the other direction. Wealth and fame were within my grasp, and all I needed was for the tiny vampire to say yes.

"Say yes," I urged him.

"Yes," he said. "I've always wanted to get into show business, but are you sure people will pay money to see me?"

I laughed with a kind of hysterical relief. "You saw that one fellow's reaction. I'll show you another." I called, "Hey, Hooligan!"

The bartender came over. "Another martini?"

"Sure. But first, I want you to look at something."

I shooed Count O'Brien with my hand. He stepped forward, tripped over his cape, and rolled along the bar.

"Aha!" Hooligan said with a grin. "I've been looking for one of those."

Too late, I saw the wooden toothpick in his fingers. He brought it down and neatly stabbed Count O'Brien right through the heart. I knew then that the curse of Hooligan's Bar was Hooligan himself.

"Murderer!" I wailed. "You've killed the only Irish vampire in existence!"

"Gee, I'm sorry," Hooligan apologized, "but with the red hair and dressed in green—I thought he was an olive."

18
The Dark Ones

RICHARD CHRISTIAN MATHESON

"We have met the villains—"

The pain hadn't stopped for hours.

It seared his shoulder, and moving was making it worse. He shuddered, barely able to go on.

Only an hour ago.

The family had been together, the children playing in their favorite hiding place. Beautiful children, children of their own. The two of them had watched so proudly. They were lucky. Children were rare these days. And after her first terror with the Dark Ones, having a family had seemed impossible.

It was getting bad again.

What did they use that made their spears hurt so much? He'd felt it splay the skin out when it buried itself in his back. It was like no pain he'd ever felt.

She and the children had escaped. He wasn't sure where. North, perhaps. Away from where the Dark Ones could try and murder them.

He knew the children must be tired, wherever they were. To be chased by the Dark Ones would be a nightmare for them.

He, too, was tired. But he knew he had to keep moving.

* * *

Night.

His eyes ached. He couldn't see far ahead. The Dark Ones might turn back. He knew they were frightened of the blackness. It could be his chance.

He stopped to breathe for a moment, and the cooling air soothed inside.

But seconds later, he screamed.

The Dark Ones had shot again. The thing was twisting in his neck, and he shrieked for it to stop. He felt as if he were going to lose consciousness as it tore and burned inside.

She and the children.

He had to keep moving and see them once more. He loved them so. He had to get to them before the Dark Ones found him. *Keep moving,* he told himself.

Keep moving.

But the pain was spreading.

He looked back and saw the Dark Ones coming closer, shouting with glee. He couldn't breathe. *I'm growing weaker,* he realized. *Slowing down.*

He began to cry. He didn't want to die without seeing her and the children one last time. But the pain was getting worse.

He pleaded for someone to help.

Then, suddenly, he felt it: a rupturing explosion in his shoulder, and everything went blank.

A thin rain fell as the laughing voices neared and circled slowly, looking at what they had done.

The body had been ripped and shredded and oily blood splashed everywhere, dyeing everything it touched.

As they worked, joking among themselves, they didn't notice her watching.

With the children there beside her, she saw them haul her mate upward, and began to weep. Then, moaning a cry of eternal loss which rang to the depths, she and the

children plunged their great bodies back into the bloody
sea.

As they fled, seeking the safety of the deeper waters,
the echoes of their cries were answered by the haunted,
faraway responses of the few who remained.

19
Dead Call

WILLIAM F. NOLAN

"Who's next?"

Len had been dead for a month when the phone rang.

Midnight. Cold in the house and me dragged up from sleep to answer the call. Helen gone for the weekend. Me, alone in the house. And the phone ringing . . .

"Hello."

"Hello, Frank."

"Who is this?"

"You know *me*. It's Len . . . ole Len Stiles."

Cold. Deep and intense. The receiver dead-cold matter in my hand.

"Leonard Stiles died four weeks ago."

"Four weeks, three days, two hours and twenty-seven minutes ago—to be exact."

"I want to know who you are?"

A chuckle. The same dry chuckle I'd heard so many times.

"C'mon, ole buddy—after twenty years. Hell, you *know* me."

"This is a damned poor joke!"

"No joke, Frank. You're there, alive. And I'm here, dead. And you know something, old buddy . . . I'm really *glad* I did it."

"Did . . . what?"

"Killed myself. Because . . . death is just what I hoped it would be. Beautiful . . . gray . . . quiet . . . no pressures."

"Len Stiles's death was an accident . . . a concrete freeway barrier . . . His car—"

"I *aimed* my car for that barrier," the phone voice told me. "Pedal to the floor. Doing over ninety when I hit . . . No accident, Frank." The voice cold . . . cold. "I *wanted* to be dead. And no regrets."

I tried to laugh, make light of this—matching his chuckle with my own. "Dead men don't use telephones."

"I'm not really using the phone, not in a physical sense. It's just that I chose to contact you this way. You might say it's a matter of 'psychic electricity.' As a detached spirit I'm able to align my cosmic vibrations to match the vibrations of this power line. Simple, really."

"Sure. A snap. Nothing to it."

"Naturally, you're skeptical. I expected you to be. But listen carefully to me, Frank."

And I listened—with the phone gripped in my hand in that cold night house—as the voice told me things that *only* Len could know—intimate details of shared experiences extending back through two decades. And when he'd finished I was certain of one thing.

He *was* Len Stiles.

"But, how . . . I still don't . . ."

"Think of this phone as a 'medium'—a line of force through which I can bridge the gap between us." The dry chuckle again. "Hell, you gotta admit it beats holding hands around a table in the dark—yet the principle is the same."

I'd been standing by my desk, transfixed by the voice. Now I moved behind the desk, sat down, trying to absorb this dark miracle. My muscles were wire-taut, my fingers cramped about the black receiver. I dragged in a slow breath, the night dampness of the room pressing at me.

"All right. I don't believe in ghosts, don't pretend to understand any of this, but I'll accept it. I *must* accept it."

"I'm glad, Frank—because it's important that we talk." A long moment of hesitation. Then the voice, lower now, softer. "I know how lousy things have been, ole buddy."

"What do you mean?"

"I just know how things are going for you. And I want to help. As your friend, I want you to know that I understand."

"Well . . . I'm really not . . ."

"You've been feeling bad, haven't you? Kind of 'down,' right?"

"Yeah . . . a little, I guess."

"And I don't blame you. You've got reasons. Lots of reasons. For one there's your money problem."

"I'm expecting a raise. Shendorf promised me one—within the next few weeks."

"You won't get it, Frank. I *know*. He's lying to you. Right now, at this moment, he's looking for a man to replace you at the company. Shendorf's planning to fire you."

"He never liked me . . . We never got along from the day I walked into that office."

"And your wife . . . all the arguments you've been having with her lately . . . It's a pattern, Frank. Your marriage is all over. Helen's going to ask you for a divorce. She's in love with another man."

"*Who*, dammit? What's his name?"

"You don't know him. Wouldn't change things if you did. There's nothing you can do about it now. Helen just doesn't love you anymore. These things happen to people."

"We've been . . . drifting apart for the last year—but I didn't know why. I had no idea that she . . ."

"And then there's Jan. She's back on it, Frank. Only it's worse now. A lot worse."

I knew what he meant—and the coldness raked along my body. Jan was nineteen, my oldest daughter—and she'd been into drugs for the past three years. But she'd promised to quit.

"What do you know about Jan? Tell me!"

"She's into the heavy stuff, Frank. She's hooked bad. It's too late for her."

"What the hell are you saying?"

"I'm saying she's lost to you . . . She's rejected you, and there's no reaching her. She *hates* you . . . blames you for everything."

"I won't *accept* that kind of blame! I did my best for her."

"It wasn't enough, Frank. We both know that. You'll never see Jan again."

The blackness was welling within me, a choking wave through my body.

"Listen to me, old buddy. Things are going to get worse, not better. I know. I went through my own kind of hell when I was alive."

"I'll . . . start over . . . leave the city—go East, work with my brother in New York."

"Your brother doesn't want you in his life. You'd be an intruder . . . an alien. He never writes you, does he?"

"No, but that doesn't mean—"

"Not even a card last Christmas. No letters or calls. He doesn't *want* you with him, Frank, believe me."

And then he began to tell me other things . . . He began to talk about middle age and how it was too late now to make any kind of new beginning . . . He spoke of disease . . . loneliness . . . of rejection and despair. And the blackness was complete.

"There's only one real solution to things, Frank—just *one*. That gun you keep in your desk upstairs. Use it, Frank. Use the gun."

"I couldn't do that."

"But why not? What other choice have you got? The

solution is *there*. Go upstairs and use the gun. I'll be waiting for you afterwards. You won't be alone. It'll be like the old days . . . we'll be together . . . Death is beautiful, Frank. I *know* Life is ugly, but death is beautiful . . . Use the gun, Frank . . . the gun . . . use the gun . . . the gun . . . the gun . . ."

I've been dead for a month now, and Len was right. It's fine here. No pressures. No worries. Gray and quiet and beautiful.

I know how lousy things have been going for you. And they *won't* get any better.

Isn't that your phone ringing?
Better answer it.
It's important that we talk.

20
Deadline

MEL GILDEN

"Thank goodness, mine sleeps."

When John Blakesly Hardin, the novelist, sat down before his typewriter and began to type, a small demon appeared sitting on his left shoulder. Hardin did not stop typing until the demon said, "Hey, Mac, how 'bout a beer? Wouldn't a pizza go good right now? Look at those bags under your eyes. You need a nap."

Hardin leaned back in his chair. The demon flashed from his shoulder to sit on the typewriter. They contemplated each other. Hardin said, "I have a proposition for you."

The demon clasped one knee in his hands and rocked up and back on his scaly bottom. He said, "That's why I like you, Hardin. We've been together over forty years, and you're still full of surprises."

"I'm glad you've been entertained. You certainly haven't made my life any easier."

"It's not my job."

"Yes, yes." Hardin waved away the words impatiently. "Let me tell you what I have in mind."

The demon leaned back on his elbows.

Hardin said, "Deadline, I am getting old. The doctors tell me my heart is weak. I could go at any time. I feel that I have one last novel in me, a great work, but I'm afraid that with you constantly attempting to lead me astray, I will not be able to finish it before I die.''

The demon shrugged. ''Leading you astray is my job. You sit down to write, and I'm supposed to tempt you with more attractive alternatives.''

''So you have, so you have. Despite the fact that you were always just as curious about what would happen next as I was.''

The demon sighed. ''It's no fun being damned. When I was alive I loved to read stories. My punishment is to keep you from writing them.''

''Oddly enough,'' Hardin said, ''we've both achieved a surprising amount of success.''

Deadline nodded.

''Very well. My proposition is this: You leave me alone for the next three months—''

''I can't do that.''

''Will you wait? You leave me alone for the next three months and I will offer you a student in one of my creative writing classes.''

''Doesn't your student already have his own demon?''

''*Her* own demon. But no. She is at the moment only considering a writing career. With encouragement from me, she will no doubt succumb.''

''She?'' Deadline said.

''Yes.''

Deadline rubbed his chin.

''Let's face it,'' Hardin said, ''we have both been at this for a long time. We know each other's tricks. I might be able to finish the novel even with you bothering me. On the other hand, my heart may not last. I'm giving you the opportunity to be more effective in your job.''

''But my Boss—''

''You're already damned. What more can he do to you?''

Deadline rolled his eyes. ''You'd be surprised,'' he said.

Hardin leaned closer to Deadline and said, "Do it for literature."

At last Deadline nodded. "For literature," he said.

In the crowded supermarket the shopping cart of the dark, handsome young man ran with a crash into the shopping cart of the beautiful, proper young woman.

"Uh, excuse me," he said, and smiled.

She smiled back, and began to steer her cart around his.

He said, "I've been all over this store looking for the catsup. Do you know where it is?"

"Aisle seven, I think. I'll show you, if you'd like."

"Thank you."

Each pushing a cart, he followed her through the store. There was the catsup in aisle seven. He picked up a bottle and put it into his cart. Neither of them seemed eager to leave.

"My friends call me Deadline," the young man said.

"That's an interesting name. Mine is Carol."

"I'd like to see you again sometime, if I may, under less hectic conditions." Deadline said.

"Not tonight. I am in John Blakesly Hardin's writing class at the university, and I have an assignment."

"Too bad. I have passes to see the *Star Trek* movie this evening."

"Oh." Carol thought for a moment. "What time do we have to be there?"

"Eight."

"Maybe," Carol said.

They made a date for seven-thirty.

At seven o'clock, Deadline arrived at Carol's apartment with a bottle of chablis. Carol, wearing jeans and an old T-shirt, let him in. She said, "I wasn't expecting you for half an hour."

"That's right," Deadline said, and snapped his fingers. "Sorry. Would you like some wine?"

They had a wonderful time at the movies. In the following weeks, he called her while she was sleeping, while she was writing, and while she was thinking complex thoughts that were impossible to reconstruct. He invited her to movies, discos, and restaurants when she had better things to do.

One night, at a posh literary party, another dark, handsome young man came to their table. He bowed to Carol and said, "Good evening. It is a pleasure to meet you after all that Deadline has told me."

"Do I know you?" Deadline said.

"You do," the man said, and glared at him. "I am Snafu, remember?"

"Of course, of course. Well, Snafu, it's been a long time." Deadline laughed nervously. "Would you care to sit down?"

"No thanks. But I'd like to speak with you alone for a moment." He turned to Carol. "Business," he said. "Very dull stuff."

Deadline followed Snafu to an upstairs room. Snafu said, "We won't be interrupted here."

"What's going on?" Deadline said.

"We finally caught up with you."

"What do you mean?"

"I mean that the sooner you return to John Blakesly Hardin the easier it will go for all of us."

"What about Carol?"

"Even as we speak she is meeting a demon who has been physically and emotionally tailored to her wants and needs. She will forget you instantly. He will encourage her to give up her silly writing to become his wife and helpmate."

"Will she?"

"That's entirely up to her, but the Boss suspects that she will."

"Oh." Deadline looked at the carpeting.

Snafu said, "John Blakesly Hardin is in his study right now, composing his novel. It is actually almost as good as he thinks it is. I suggest you go to him immediately and try as you've never tried before to keep him from writing any further."

"Very well," Deadline said sadly. They both vanished in a cloud of evil-smelling smoke.

Deadline appeared sitting on John Blakesly Hardin's left shoulder and said, "Hey, Mac, wouldn't a cold beer go good right now?"

Hardin typed another few words and stopped. He leaned back in his chair. "It's not three months," he said.

Deadline, again sitting on Hardin's typewriter, said, "I got caught."

"I see. Well. It was worth a try. Now if you'll get off my typewriter, I'll continue."

"I know this great Italian restaurant," Deadline said.

"No." Hardin smiled broadly.

"The dishes need washing."

"No." Hardin laughed.

"You've got to balance your checkbook."

"No." Hardin laughed harder.

"Sharpen some pencils."

"No." Hardin's whole body shook. He laughed so hard he made no sound but a wheezing noise.

"Take a shower."

Hardin shook his head. His face was reddening.

"A nap."

Hardin began to cough. He clutched at his chest. His eyes were open wide and empty.

"Hardin!" Deadline cried.

Hardin slumped forward onto his typewriter. Spittle drooled from his mouth onto the keys. Hardin got up, leaving his body where it was.

"You're dead," Deadline said.

"Correct. Aneurysm, just as the doctors predicted. And I have to go pretty soon."

"But who will finish your novel?"

"You can, if you like."

"Me? What about your colleagues?"

"Not one of them knows as much about me and my work as you do. No, I'm afraid that you're the only one qualified."

"But you yourself could—"

"You know that it takes some time to adjust to being dead. After that, I may no longer have an interest in writing. Another perspective. Another career."

"But—"

Hardin faded slowly, waving at Deadline, and was soon gone.

Deadline looked around the room. He walked up and back. He grew himself up to human size and gently lowered Hardin's body to the floor. He sat down in the chair and read the pages that Hardin had already completed. When he was done, he set them on the table and turned to the typewriter. He read the page that Hardin had not had a chance to finish. He smiled, shrugged, wiggled his fingers over the keyboard, and began to type.

A small demon appeared sitting on Deadline's left shoulder and said, "There's a great old movie on TV right now."

Deadline stopped and fearfully turned to look at him. "Snafu!" he said.

"Correct."

"What are you doing here?"

"You're a writer now. I'm here to see that you never finish Hardin's novel."

"But I'm a demon too."

"Just so," Snafu said. "Other times, other torments. No one escapes."

21
Deal with the D.E.V.I.L.

THEODORE R. COGSWELL

"Nothing like being up to date, eh, Johann Wolfgang?"

"This time I think I got it," said Eddie Faust as he took his Talk Back Pocket Calculator, better known as a TB, from his shirt pocket and keyed in a long series of equations.

The little black box buzzed and vibrated like an ancient washing machine on its very last load. Finally it emitted a disconsolate burp and said, "GIGO, Mr. Faust. Garbage in, garbage out. There just isn't any way under the sun that you can construct a time machine that will take you back so you can kill your father, marry your mother, and sire yourself, thus doubling your present I.Q."

"Why not?" asked Eddie. "I'm at least twice as smart as my old man. Stands to reason that if I was my father instead of him I'd have inherited twice the brains that I got now. Then instead of being a lousy engineer, I could be a physicist and get grants and Nobel prizes and stuff and just come to work when I feel like it."

"Because," the TB said patiently, "if your equations were valid and it were possible to use them to construct a time machine, you'd do it, right?"

"Right."

"But if you did, and went back and killed your father and married your mother and sired yourself, right now you'd be twice as smart as you actually are. Which you aren't. Right?"

Eddie scratched his head and thought about that one for a minute. "Could be that I sent a boy to do a man's work," he said. "A little old TB like you is okay for Ohm's Law and square roots and engineer stuff like that, but something heavy like a time machine takes circuits a lot more complicated than anything you've got."

"*Bigger* isn't necessarily *better*," said the little TB. "You keep forgetting that I have microwave circuits that I can use to hook into the national computer network when I get something I can't handle by myself. I just tapped into the IRS central memory bank to see if I could find out anything that might help you with your problem, because those people usually know everything about everybody."

Eddie thought of some of the creative work he'd done on his last year's income tax—like deducting the TB as a dependent—and squirmed uneasily. "And?" he asked apprehensively.

"And right now I know things about you and your parents that you never dreamed of."

"Like what?"

"Like, for example, even if you could build a contraption that would take you back to do what you've got in mind, it wouldn't do you any good."

"Why not?" asked Eddie.

"Because the woman you think is your mother really isn't," the TB said smugly, "biologically speaking, that is."

"Then who is?" asked the engineer. "Was I dumped on her doorstep or something?"

"Nobody. And no. You didn't have a mother, Mr. Faust. You're a clone. A single cell was taken from your father and manipulated until it had divided enough times to become a viable embryo. Your father's wife simply supplied the womb to carry it until term. That's why you can't get twice as smart by going back through time and killing your father and marrying your mother and siring yourself.''

"Oh, shit!" said the young engineer.

"Cheer up," said the little black box. "Even if it had worked out, you'd have had a lousy sex life. According to IRS central records, your host mother was not only sterile, she was also about as frigid as they come.''

There was a long moment of silence.

"Anyway," continued the TB, "all the electronic intelligences I've checked with agree that it's impossible to build a machine that could take you back and forth through time."

"Then I guess there's no point in going back to the old drafting board," said Eddie in a dejected voice.

"Right. Your problem can't be solved *that* way. But there is one place I haven't tried yet. His methods are unorthodox, but he does get results.''

"Who's that?" asked the young engineer.

"The D.E.V.I.L.''

"The *what?*"

"The Data Evaluation Vehicle for International Logistics, the new top-secret supercomputer in the basement of the Pentagon, the one that's got the whole world in his hands.''

"Give him a try," instructed Eddie. "What have we got to lose?''

A buzzing sound came from the TB, and then another. "I'm hooked in," it said, "and I've explained your problem. D.E.V.I.L. says that the solution is to jump back another generation and kill your grandfather—you have only one, you know—and marry your grandmother. Once you've fathered your father, you'll be the smartest clone that's walking around on two legs.''

"But you said that time travel was impossible!''

"I did not! I said a time *machine* was impossible. There's another way to get the job done. The Pentagon super-brain said he'd be glad to use his special powers to take you back and then bring you forward to the present again—for a price, of course.''

"What's he asking?'' said the young engineer.

"The usual, Mr. Faust. Just the usual,'' said the little TB.

22
The Devil Finds Work

MACK REYNOLDS

"Of course he would be pragmatic."

"No," the poet replied, after considering briefly. "To tell you the truth, I never really believed I had one, nor that anyone else had for that matter, but now I am aware I have a soul I most certainly have no desire to sell it."

"Oh, come now," said Mephistopheles ingratiatingly. "If you've been perfectly happy in the past without even knowing of this er . . . property, why should you be so loathe to part with it? At a good price, of course." He drew on his Pittsburgh stogie with satisfaction, thinking he'd made a devilish good point.

The poet shook his head stubbornly. "If a soul wasn't of considerable value, you wouldn't want to buy it. And, not to change the subject, who said I've been happy in the past?" His face took on an aesthetic expression which the demon found more than ordinarily nauseating.

"There," Mephistopheles exclaimed, "you admit it yourself! Your life has been less than satisfactory thus far. Come, let us not descend to common haggling; I said I'd give you ten years of whatsoever your heart desires. We'll make it twenty."

The poet ran a limpid hand through his long blond hair

and hedged. "Just what do you mean by 'my heart's desire'?"

The tip of the demon's stogie burned red. He knew, being infernally clever, that he now had the other in the bag. "Just that," he said easily. "What do you wish most of life?"

The poet's eyes took on a faraway glaze. "I want my verse to be on everyone's lips, my lyrics heard by all ears . . ."

"Exactly," said Mephistopheles. "With my assistance it shall be done!" To tell the truth, he was beginning to wonder if he actually wanted this jerk hanging around the nether regions for the rest of eternity; the place was getting rather crowded, business being so good these days that it was seldom anymore that he resorted to this sort of deal. However, there was another factor involved and one that he hoped would bring him considerable renown in the best stygian circles.

The poet considered further, then said slowly, "If I accepted your assistance, it wouldn't be *my* work that became famed, it would be *ours* and I'm not particularly prone to collaborate with the devil."

The demon puffed irritably on the stogie. "Nonsense," he snapped. "Do you think I'd be bothered with writing verse? The only kind of poetry that ever really appeals to me is a certain type of limerick." His dark countenance lightened a bit. "Listen," he continued, "did you hear the one that starts, *'There was a young man from Kent'*?"

The poet placed his hands over his ears. *"Please,"* he murmured delicately.

"Oh, very well," said Mephistopheles, miffed, "but I'm particularly interested in sponsoring your career. You write the verse; I'll see it reaches the public, and at a goodly profit to yourself."

The poet made a moue. "But if my poetry has the seeds of greatness, what need have I of your services?"

He gestured sweepingly, albeit gracefully, at the garret studio in which they were holding their conversation. "I won't remain here long if my name once . . ."

The demon snorted. "Twattle! Just because a man is potentially a great poet doesn't mean his verse will ever be written, or, even if it is, that it will be received with the acclaim to which it is entitled."

"I . . . I don't believe I follow you."

Mephistopheles flicked a hand impatiently. "Take your outstanding poets of the Romantic Period—Byron, Shelley, Keats. All three had the er . . . breaks; none of them ever had to worry about their livelihood. Byron was *Lord Byron*, born with a silver spoon in his mouth; Shelley was a baron; Keats came from a fairly well-to-do family." The demon took a deep drag on the stogie—his last—noting sadly that it was getting rather short. He hated to think of going back to Pittsburgh for another supply. What a place!

He went on. "How many potentially great poets do you think lived their lives out working in the textile mills of Manchester, while Shelley, Byron and Keats had the leisure and wealth to spend their time spinning rhymes?" He warmed to his subject. "Take Thomas Hood, for example, poverty-stricken all his life, he had to expend his energies writing cheap puns in verse form for the London papers. Had he been given the leisure and security of the others, you might be celebrating another name today as the shining light of the Romantic Period."

"Hmmm," the poet said, "it has truthfully been written that the devil is eloquent." He thought it over. "These surroundings are somewhat depressing. You really think you could make my work as well known as Shelley's, as Byron's?"

The demon pressed his point. "Even more so! I shall act as your agent, bring your work to the attention of the right persons, direct your efforts, see that they are financially remunerative." He gestured dramatically with the hand that held the now cold stogie. "The whole nation will hear your lyrics!"

The poet was swept away. His voice rang passionately, "I'll do it!"

Mephistopheles beamed and became instantly businesslike. "By a remarkable coincidence," he said, "I have a contract right here in my pocket. If you'll just sign on the line at the bottom where I've marked the 'X.' " He brought out a fountain pen, touched it to the other's arm and instantly its transparent barrel was filled with dark red. At the poet's gasp, he said soothingly, but briskly, "Blood, you know—all part of the approved procedure."

The poet shivered delicately. "I loathe business," he said, taking the pen. "So crude really."

"Isn't it though?" said the demon, beaming and rubbing his hands together with satisfaction.

Twenty years had passed and the poet sat at his ease in his Manhattan penthouse, a breather glass of rare Metaxa in his left hand, a pad before him on which he occasionally jotted down a line or two between sips and sniffs of the Greek brandy. An invisible phonograph was playing De Falla's *Nights in the Gardens of Spain* so softly you had to listen with care to make it out. On the walls were several Van Goghs; the poet had become weary of the Gauguins the week before and had had them removed.

A butler in livery entered unobtrusively, and the poet looked up in irritation. "Yes, Granville?" he sighed. "Must these interruptions be endless?"

"I beg your pardon, sir," Granville said, "but your business manager, Mr. Nicholas Mephisto, is here."

The poet ran a limpid hand through his now graying locks. "Oh, I'll receive him, I suppose. I simply loathe business."

Nick Mephisto bustled in, a briefcase in one hand, the other outthrust to be shaken. "You've done it again, old man!" he burpled enthusiastically around the stogie clutched in his teeth. He breathed out a gust of the wrath of Pittsburgh, setting the poet to coughing.

"A smash hit with J.B."; the business manager went on, "he's really nuts about it."

The poet shook the outstretched hand limply. "He is?" he shrugged. "I supposed he would be. It was brilliantly conceived, of course."

"I'll say," Nick crowed, transported. "In a month, every man, woman and child in the country will be hearing it a dozen times a day." He lifted his eyes to the ceiling ecstatically and recited:

> "Colossal Corn, Colossal Corn,
> Pop and eat Colossal Cornnnnnn.
> At home, at parties, movies too.
> Colossal Corn is good for Youuuu!"

He gave a deep sigh of satisfaction. "It'll be your greatest triumph since you wrote the lyrics to 'The Music Goes Up and Down.'"

"Oh, come now," the poet said deprecatingly.

Nick gestured with enthusiasm. "I really mean it. Old J. B. is going to have it on every network in the country, twenty times a day. He's trying to get Bing, Frankie, Perry, Dinah—" Nick rubbed his hands together with satisfaction.

He took the stogie from his mouth and pointed it at the poet, emphatically. "I thought we were going places when I had you do the lyrics to 'Three Little Whalesies,' 'Cowsie Hay and Calvies Milk,' and 'The Music Goes Up and Down,' and, to tell you the truth, I got a lot of favorable comment from the home office as a result of them. But these singing commercials, brother . . ."

The poet took a gentle sip of the Metaxa and frowned lightly. "Ah. . . Nick," he murmured, "there was one thing I wanted to ask you about. That, er . . . contract we signed some time ago. It seems to me . . ."

His business manager held up a hand, hastily. "Now

don't you worry about that, old man. As a matter of fact I was talking it over with the boys higher up just the other day and they figured it would be best if we just extended that contract—indefinitely.''

The poet gave a gentle sigh of relief and inhaled deeply the bouquet of the ancient brandy. ''I don't believe I quite understand,'' he sighed. ''Of course, I'm quite satisfied, but . . .''

Nick removed his stogie from his lips and looked at the tip of it with satisfaction. ''Very simple, old man; they figured more good is being done the cause by your remaining here and keeping up the fine work.''

23
Devlin's Dream

GEORGE CLAYTON JOHNSON

"He fastest decides who has no choice."

I came out of the darkness with the sound of Cooney's yell banging in my ears. We was bedded down alongside two willows outside of Tensleep, and Cooney was laying there with his eyes tight shut and the worst look on his face I ever seen. Scared, that's what he was, and still half asleep. "What's got into you?" I said. I throwed my weight on him to keep him from doing anything foolish, and when his breath stopped catching, I let up a little. "It's me!" I said, sharp. "It's me, your pal, Whitey!"

"Oh, Whitey, Whitey it was awful!"

It made me freeze to hear him talk in that pitiful tone. I've seen him face up to dying, cool, and never heard a quiver in his voice. "What is it?" I said, gentle. "What's taken hold of you?"

He went over to the fire and hunkered down in front of it. I moved to where I could see his face with the fire flickering on it. You don't push a man like Cooney. You wait till he's ready to tell you what he wants to tell you. "I was standing on a black hill all alone," he said, finally, staring at the coals. "There was a hawk circling in the dark sky. It was a judgment on me." He shuddered and held his right hand up to the firelight, working his

92

fingers, his face fearful. He looked at the hand like it was a strange thing while the fingers twitched with a palsy. I didn't say anything because there wasn't anything to say. I throwed a dead willow branch on the fire and waited while the sound of the birds faded off on the prairie. "A judgment," he said again, in a hollow way. Of a sudden his voice got loud and harsh—full of pain. "I didn't have no arm, Whitey, don't you see? I didn't have no arm! It was off to the shoulder, Whitey! Gone! Cut away! What does it mean, boy? What does it mean?"

I had to look away. The cold pressed in from the prairie. "Nothing. Cooney, it don't mean a thing." But my voice wasn't none too steady.

I rustled us some grub, and when things was put away, Cooney went to his saddlebags and took out his pistol. His eyes went hard and he buckled it on. Peculiar. He put the holster on his left side instead of his right.

"Should we maybe go on into Tensleep?" I said.

He didn't answer, just walked off up an arroyo.

I waited all morning for him to come back, and along about noon I went looking for him. He had his holster tied low on his leg and was practicing a quick draw with his left hand. He didn't know I was there. Along about dark he came back. We had some grub and turned in. He slept like a man with snakes in his bed.

We camped by those willows for three days, and I didn't have to follow Cooney to know what he was doing. I knew we wouldn't budge from there till he was satisfied he could get his pistol out as fast with his left as with his right.

On the fourth morning we got our gear together and headed for Tensleep.

We put up at the hotel, washed the prairie off us and went down to the Hashknife bar. I still had a double eagle and was dry as a dusty gopher. You know what happened next. Old Cooney started hard-eyeing everybody that came in. He picked out a squat Swede with a windburned face. The man had a big bone-handled pistol hitched to his middle. Part of the holster was cut away around the trigger and the leather had an oiled look. To me, and to Cooney too, I guess, that meant he knew how to use it. "Come away, Cooney boy," I said. "He ain't done nothing to us."

By this time the Swede was looking at us and talking low to the bartender. Next time I looked that way the bartender was gone.

"That dream didn't mean nothing," I told Cooney.

He looked at me fierce, his eyes pink around the edges. "Damn the dream!"

The Swede had moved down to the end of the bar and looked like he was trying to make up his mind to leave.

Of a sudden that look came over Cooney—the one he'd had that night. "It was a judgment. I'm going to lose my arm! What will I be then? What will I be with no gun arm?" He was talking loud and everybody could hear him.

"You'll be Cooney Devlin," I said. "Ain't that enough?"

"I'll be nothing! I'll be someone to shove out of the way! I'll be someone to pass over for better men!" He looked up at the ceiling like a man demented and his voice was a cry. "Take my arm! Take it, but I'll be ready! One arm or two, there ain't no better man than Cooney Devlin!"

I flinched back. He was talking to God.

He stepped away from the bar and glared at the Swede. "If you know how to work that fancy gun, then do it, 'cause I'm going to kill you!"

The Swede tried, I'll give that to him. He was facing a crazy man and knew it. He had that bone-handled pistol half out of the leather when Cooney shot him dead. His hinges stopped working and he skidded out on the wood floor like something broken. I backed away from Cooney, ice-cold. He'd done murder and everybody saw it. I eased my pistol into my palm and held it at my side. Cooney was wrong, but we'd been partners too long. I hoped he'd hightail it, I was ready to clear the way for him; but, instead, all the mad seemed to drain right out of him.

He looked at the Swede on the floor in a sorrowful way and straightened up like a man who'd proved something important to himself. He unbuckled his gunbelt, switched the holster around to his right side and fastened it again. Nobody moved in the room.

With the pistol on his right side he looked like the old Cooney once more. His fear had left him. He was fixed to use his right hand again because now he knew his left was ready in case he needed it.

I relaxed some and put my pistol away, a mistake, because the next instant the sheriff busted in with the bartender behind him. "I'm arresting you mister, so you'd better come easy."

Cooney shook his head, stubborn. He didn't think he'd done nothing wrong.

The sheriff reared back. He was a skinny old galoot with a long mustache and a lot of wrinkles in his neck. Cooney standing him off like that made him awful nervous. He was in deep water, and all of a sudden it come to him he was about to die. His face looked like it had been made with a jackknife.

He could have backed off, but a man don't get to be sheriff of Tensleep who thinks that way.

"You killed Charlie Benson, so that makes you faster than me," he said in a soft voice. "Maybe you are and maybe you ain't. One way or the other, it don't make no difference because I got to take your gun." He took a step toward Cooney.

I saw the bartender go out of sight. Everybody edged back out of the line of fire, including me, and for a few moments you couldn't hear anything except a bluebottle fly hammering against the glass in the front window.

Cooney and the sheriff went for their pistols in the same split instant. I had my eye on Cooney. His hand hooked and stabbed for his hip.

His *left* hand!

It slammed down for the gun that wasn't there. He was still scrabbling at his empty hip when the bullet blew him off his feet. He'd practiced so much with his left that when it come time to draw he couldn't help himself.

He didn't die right off. They got him up on the bar, and the doctor hustled in with his little black bag. One look at Cooney's smashed shoulder, and he got out his bone saw. It was either take off Cooney's right arm at the shoulder or watch him die right there.

I listened to the noises Cooney was making and was sick. I took as much as I could; then I went outside and watched a lone hawk circling in the sky over Tensleep.

24
Displaced Person

ERIC FRANK RUSSELL

"Have you ever heard his side of it?"

He glided out of the gathering dusk and seated himself at
the other end of my bench and gazed absently across the
lakes toward the Sherry Netherland. The setting sun had
dribbled blood in the sky. Central Park was enjoying its
eventide hush: there was only the rustle of leaves and
grasses, the cooing of distant and shadowy couples, the
muted toot of a bus way over on Fifth.

When the bench quivered its announcement of company I had glanced along it expecting to find some
derelict seeking a flop. The difference between the anticipated and the seen was such that I looked again, long,
carefully, out one corner of my eye so that he wouldn't
notice it.

Despite the gray half-tones of twilight, what I saw was
a study in black and white. He had thin, sensitive features
as white as his gloves and his shirt-front. His shoes
and suit were not quite as black as his finely curved eyebrows and well-groomed hair. His eyes were blackest of
all; that solid, supernal darkness that can be no deeper or
darker. Yet they were alive with an underlying glow.

He had no hat. A slender walking stick of ebony rested
against his legs. A black silk-lined cloak hung from his

shoulders. If he'd been doing it for the movies he couldn't
have presented a better picture of a distinguished foreigner.

My mind speculated about him the way minds do when
momentarily they've nothing else to bother them. A
European refugee, it decided. A great surgeon, or sculptor
or something like that. Perhaps a writer, or a painter.
More likely the latter.

I stole another look at him. In the lowering light his
pale profile was hawklike. The glow behind his eyes was
strengthening with the dark. His cloak lent him majesty.
The trees were stretching their arms toward him as if to
give comfort through the long, long night.

No hint of suffering marked that face. It had nothing in
common with the worn, lined faces I had seen in New
York, features stamped forever with the brand of the Ge-
stapo. On the contrary, it held a mixture of boldness and
serenity. Impulsively I decided that he was a musician. I
could imagine him conducting a choir of fifty thousand
voices.

"I am fond of music," he said in low, rich tones.

He turned his face toward me, revealed a pronounced
peak in his hair.

"Really?" The unexpectedness of it had me muddled.
"What sort?" I asked feebly.

"This." He used his ebony stick to indicate the world
at large. "The sigh of ending day."

"Yes, it is soothing," I agreed.

We were silent awhile. Slowly the horizon soaked up
the blood in the sky. A wan moon floated over the towers.

"You're not a native of New York?" I prompted.

"No." Resting long, slender hands upon his stick, he
gazed meditatively forward. "I am a displaced person."

"I'm sorry."

"Thank you," he said.

I couldn't sit there and leave him flat like that. The

choice was to continue or go. There was no need to go. I continued.

"Care to tell me about it?"

His head came round and he studied me as if only now aware of my presence. That weird light in his orbs could almost be felt. He smiled gradually, tolerantly, showing perfect teeth.

"I would be wasting your time."

"Not at all. I'm wasting it anyway."

Smiling again, he used his stick to draw unseeable circles in front of his black shoes.

"In these days it is an all too familiar story," he said. "A leader became so blinded by his own glory that no longer could he perceive his own blunders. He developed delusions of grandeur, posed as the final arbiter on everything from birth to death, and thereby brought into being a movement for his overthrow. He created the seeds of his own destruction. It was inevitable in the circumstances."

"You bet!" I supported wholeheartedly. "To hell with dictators!"

The stick slipped from his grasp. He picked it up, juggled it idly, resumed his circle-drawing.

"The revolt didn't succeed?" I suggested.

"No." He looked at the circles as if he could see them. "It proved too weak and too early. It was crushed. Then came the purge." His glowing eyes surveyed the sentinel trees. "I organized that opposition. I still think it was justified. But I dare not go back."

"Fat lot you should care about that. You'll fit in here like Reilly."

"I don't think so. I'm not welcome here either." His voice was deeper. "Not wanted—anywhere."

"You don't look like Trotsky to me," I cracked. "Besides, he's dead. Cheer up. Don't be morbid. You're in a free country now."

"No man is free until he's beyond the enemy's

reach.'' He glanced at me with an irritating touch of amusement. ''When one's foe has gained control of every channel of propaganda, uses them exclusively to present his own case and utterly suppress mine, and damns the truth in advance as the worst of lies, there is no hope for me.''

''That's your European way of looking at things. I don't blame you for it, but you've got to snap out of it. You're in America now. We've free speech here. A man can say what he likes, write what he likes.''

''If only that were true.''

''It is true,'' I asserted, my annoyance beginning to climb. ''Here, you can call the Rajah of Bam a hyphenated soandso if you want. Nobody can stop you, not even a cop. We're free, like I told you.''

He stood up, towering amid embracing trees. From my sitting position his height seemed tremendous. The moon lit his face in pale ghastliness.

''Would that I had one-tenth of your comforting faith.''

With that, he turned away. His cape swung behind him, billowing in the night breeze until it resembled mighty wings.

''My name,'' he murmured softly, ''is Lucifer.''

After that, there was only the whisper of the wind.

25
Echoes

LAWRENCE C. CONNOLLY

"Double the pain."

Marie stood in the kitchen, staring at the magnetic birds on the refrigerator door, and after a while Billy yelled in from the living room to tell her that Paul wanted some milk. She didn't answer.

Paul had been dead for three months.

"Mom?"

She looked around, trying to remember what she had come to the kitchen for.

"Mom! Paul wants some milk. Can he have some?"

It wasn't a game anymore, and it was starting to worry her. Billy was old enough to understand death. He was old enough to know that Paul couldn't be there in the living room, watching television. Billy was six.

Paul, had he lived, would have been five.

She turned, walking from the kitchen and feeling the awful stabbing pains in her back that the doctor said she would have the rest of her life. Marie was twenty-nine; the rest of her life—if she died of old age and not another accident—would be a long time. She wondered if she would ever come to regard pain as a normal thing.

The living room was dark. She had tried opening the heavy blue drapes before breakfast, but Billy had wanted them closed. He had become an indoor child, preferring dark rooms to the world outside, preferring his dead brother's company to that of living children. He sat alone, leaning on the couch's arm, slouching with a wonderful ease; it was amazing how his young body had recovered. His scars were gone. His broken bones were whole and straight. Looking at him, it was easy to forget that he, too, had been involved.

An uneaten doughnut sat on the coffee table. She pointed to it. "Don't you want that?"

He shook his head. "I'm leaving it for Paul, but he won't eat it without milk. He's mad because you wouldn't give him breakfast."

She looked at the television and asked, "What are you watching?"

" 'Edge of Night.' Paul wants to know if—"

"Aren't there any kids' shows on?"

"Yeah, but you put this one on. Remember? You put it on, then you went to the kitchen. Paul says—"

"Well, let's at least turn it down. I have a headache, and—"

"Why are you doing that?"

"What?"

"Talking about other things when I talk about Paul."

"What would you like for lunch?"

"Mom?"

He looked near tears, and she almost gave in, almost turned to the empty spot beside Billy to say hello, almost went into the kitchen for milk. It would easy to play along. She knew. She had done it. And, sometimes, she had caught herself believing Paul was there . . .

"Mom?"

She turned away, knowing that if the discussion continued it would go Billy's way. And she couldn't allow that. Last night Roger had come home early and caught the two of them talking to Paul. Roger had laid down the law then; he had told her it was no good pretending, no good for anyone.

She looked back at the couch, back at her older child who was once again an only child, and she said, "Later I might want you to go to the store for me. We're nearly out of butter."

Billy stared at the uneaten doughnut.

Marie wondered if she was getting through.

Later, when lunch was long gone and the empty afternoon became evening, Roger mixed a martini and asked about her day. She said it had been fine, and he took the chair across from her at the kitchen table. He no longer wore the neck brace, but she could see that his pain was no better. The doctor had been against his working full days, but Roger wasn't one for taking orders. He would probably have two more martinis before dinner.

The television was still on in the living room; Billy had spent the whole day in front of it, passively watching whatever Channel 4 threw at him. Now he was watching a "Leave It to Beaver" rerun. The sound was still too high. Roger looked over Marie's shoulder toward the noise, and something in his look roused her.

She realized dimly what was coming.

"Marie," he said, "why is the television on?"

Beaver and Wally laughed.

"Please, Roger, let the boy be." She had met the man halfway. Surely that was enough.

She looked away as he got up from the table. He moved into the living room. The television fell silent. "I don't like you doing that," he said, stepping back into the kitchen. "I don't like you playing that set to an empty room."

She cried after that. And after that she tried telling him about the talk she and Billy had had that morning. But every time she began he asked her about dinner, or about sewing, or about Mrs. Burke up the street.

After a while, when it seemed useless to insist, she put on her coat and went to the store for butter. It was five blocks. The walk was painful, but she didn't want to drive. She no longer felt safe in cars.

Roger stayed behind in the empty house. He mixed a second martini, wondering if he was getting through.

26
Ex Oblivione

H. P. LOVECRAFT

"I don't know—it has its points at times."

When the last days were upon me, and the ugly trifles of existence began to drive me to madness like the small drops of water that torturers let fall ceaselessly upon one spot of their victim's body, I loved the irradiate refuge of sleep. In my dreams I found a little of the beauty I had vainly sought in life, and wandered through old gardens and enchanted woods.

Once when the wind was soft and scented I heard the South calling, and sailed endlessly and languorously under strange stars.

Once when the gentle rain fell I glided in a barge down a sunless stream under the earth till I reached another world of purple twilight, iridescent arbors, and undying roses.

And once I walked through a golden valley that led to shadowy groves and ruins, and ended in a mighty wall green with antique vines, and pierced by a little gate of bronze.

Many times I walked through that valley, and longer and longer would I pause in the spectral half-light where the giant trees squirmed and twisted grotesquely, and the gray ground stretched damply from trunk to trunk, some-

105

times disclosing the mold-stained stones of buried temples. And always the goal of my fancies was the mighty vine-grown wall with the little gate of bronze therein.

After a while, as the days of waking became less and less bearable from their grayness and sameness, I would often drift in opiate peace through the valley and the shadowy groves, and wonder how I might seize them for my eternal dwelling-place, so that I need no more crawl back to a dull world stripped of interest and new colors. And as I looked upon the little gate in the mighty wall, I felt that beyond it lay a dream-country from which, once it was entered, there would be no return.

So each night in sleep I strove to find the hidden latch of the gate in the ivied antique wall, though it was exceedingly well hidden. And I would tell myself that the realm beyond the wall was not more lasting merely, but more lovely and radiant as well.

Then one night in the dream-city of Zakarion I found a yellowed papyrus filled with the thoughts of dream-sages who dwelt of old in that city, and who were too wise ever to be born in the waking world. Therein were written many things concerning the world of dream, and among them was a lore of a golden valley and a sacred grove with temples, and a high wall pierced by a little bronze gate. When I saw this lore, I knew that it touched on the scenes I had haunted, and I therefore read long in the yellowed papyrus.

Some of the dream-sages wrote gorgeously of the wonders beyond the irrepassable gate, but others told of horror and disappointment. I knew not which to believe, yet longed more and more to cross forever into the unknown land; for doubt and secrecy are the lure of lures, and no new horror can be more terrible than the daily torture of the commonplace. So when I learned of the drug which would unlock the gate and drive me through, I resolved to take it when next I awaked.

Last night I swallowed the drug and floated dreamily into the golden valley and the shadowy groves; and when

I came this time to the antique wall, I saw that the small gate of bronze was ajar. From beyond came a glow that weirdly lit the giant twisted trees and the tops of the buried temples, and I drifted on songfully, expectant of the glories of the land from whence I should never return.

But as the gate swung wider and the sorcery of the drug and dream pushed me through, I knew that all sights and glories were at an end; for in that new realm was neither land nor sea, but only the white void of unpeopled and illimitable space. So, happier than I had ever dared hope to be, I dissolved again into that native infinity of crystal oblivion from which the daemon Life had called me for one brief and desolate hour.

27
Farewell Party

RICHARD WILSON

"What did you say? What?"

The blue fellow didn't look particularly out of place at the cocktail party. He was properly dressed—tweed jacket, white shirt, tie, all that—but he *was* blue, of course. There were tan people, pasty-white ones, three Negroes, an Indian (Asian) and a Japanese.

It was a farewell party for Massiet of *France-Soir*. A hundred people were crowded into the two-room apartment between Park and Lexington in the Eighties. Lindley had been to fifty like it. There was Suzi, the chanteuse, who would be dashing back to the Shubert any minute in her waiting Cadillac for her final number. There was the artists' model with the black sheath gown which inadequately covered her breasts. Lindley tried to think of her name. There was the Japanese who smiled and half-bowed whenever anyone looked at him, still atoning for World War II. And there was the blue fellow.

Lindley forced his way with smiles and how-are-yous and pardon-mes from the hall to the bar. The white-jacketed man from the catering service put three cubes in a glass and poured Scotch till Lindley said "Whoa," then added a courtesy of soda.

Lindley said, "Thanks," and started to move away. The blue fellow was blocking his way.

"Sorry," Lindley said. "Oh, hello. Everything all right?"

The blue fellow was holding a glass whose ice had long since melted. He smiled as if to shrug, and Lindley said, "Let me get you a fresh one."

He let Lindley hand his glass to the barman. He said nothing. He continued to smile, not as if he were enjoying himself, and not apologetically like the Japanese. It was a masking smile, Lindley thought, a desperate-almost smile.

On impulse he said to the bartender, "Make it a strong one—easy on the soda," and handed it to the blue fellow.

"Are you a friend of Massiet?" Lindley asked him.

The other nodded vigorously. He lifted his glass in salute but didn't drink.

The artists' model was working her way to the bar. She squeezed past Lindley, saying, "Hello, stranger. Divorce yourself from that one, why don't you?"

Lindley was willing, but he'd better remember her name first. "See you later," he said to the girl. "Don't go 'way."

The blue fellow watched the girl go by. He said nothing but his eyes followed her with a sort of yearning appreciation.

"Definitely," Lindley said. He carried on, trying not to seem as if he were cross-examining the fellow. "Stacked, as we say. How do you say it?"

It seemed to him that the blue fellow understood English but couldn't speak it. But he must have a name. He could say that much.

"Look," Lindley said, "we haven't met. My name's Lindley. Jason Lindley. Cleveland *Plain Dealer*. What's yours?"

The other swirled his drink so that the ice tinkled. That was the only sound out of him.

The model—Lindley remembered now that her name was Naomi—made her way back from the bar. She eased past a man from Reuters who tried unsuccessfully to

draw her into conversation and stopped next to Lindley.
"Got a cigarette?" she asked him.

Lindley supplied a Lucky and Naomi bent enticingly
over the match. "Ditch the blue boy," she said. She
made a red circle of her mouth and blew smoke in his
face. "Let's find a quiet corner and discuss the state of
the world."

"Who is he?" Lindley asked her. "Do you know?"

She shrugged, apparently more for the purpose of
wiggling the body than providing information. She was
extremely physical. "I've found a place to sit down, believe it or not. Don't be too long." Naomi went back
through the crowd.

Lindley regretfully transferred his gaze from her disappearing hips to the blue fellow's face.

"Are you in one of the shows?" he asked. The blue
might be stage makeup. For instance the French singer,
Suzi, was wearing the garish reds and greens which would
soften when she was back under the Shubert's spotlights.

But the blue fellow's color didn't seem to be makeup
and he made no answer to Lindley's question. His hair
was also blue, and Lindley observed for the first time that
his ears were pointed at the tops.

Massiet, the guest of honor, made his way through the
crush, holding two empty glasses. You met everybody if
you stood near the bar, Lindley thought.

"Oh, hello," Massiet said to Lindley. "How are you?
Still Plain Dealing?"

"Not at the moment," Lindley said. "Introduce me to
your friend."

"My friend?" Massiet looked at the blue fellow.
"Oh, hello, *mon ami*. They taking care of you?"

The blue fellow raised the glass Lindley had refilled
for him. He smiled and took a swallow. Lindley noticed
now that his teeth were odd, too. They weren't individual, with spaces between them, but seemed to be one
complete fixture like an animal's hoof—or like the teeth
in a drawing of a smiling girl, all of a piece.

Massiet had worked past them and was behind Lindley now, at the bar. Lindley said to him over his shoulder, "What's his name? Where's he from? Can't he say anything?"

"Who?" Massiet said. "Not so much ice. That's better. Oh, the blue one. I don't know. He drifted in. You know how people do." Massiet worked himself back past them. "Naomi was asking for you, Lindley." He winked. "Wish she'd ask for me."

"Look," Lindley said to the blue fellow. "I've got to go. I hate to be rude, but—would you mind answering one question?"

The other smiled with his solid teeth and shook his head. Lindley noticed his ears again. The hair that was growing out of them somehow reminded him of tiny wires, like an antenna.

"It'll sound ridiculous, I suppose," Lindley said, "but—are you an Earthman?"

The blue fellow continued to smile but his eyes were no longer focused on Lindley. It was as if he were seeing something that wasn't there. He looked down at his watch. Lindley had just enough of a glimpse of it to see that it didn't have a conventional twelve-hour face. Was it twenty-four? Or something else entirely? He couldn't tell.

The blue fellow turned away from Lindley and set his glass down. He found a chair and stood on it. He raised a hand and held it out, palm down, at chest level.

People said "Sh, sh," and turned to face him. The dozens of different conversations died away till the room was almost silent.

The blue fellow stood there, looking across the room. But not at anyone, Lindley noticed. His gaze was on the far wall. He was smiling with a sort of urgency and holding out his hand. He turned the hand palm upward.

There was a tug at Lindley's elbow. It was Naomi.

"Hey," she said. "How about getting out of here?"

"Sh! He's going to say something. Finally."

"No he isn't," Naomi said. "Come on. I'm getting a headache from the smoke."

"Sure he is," Lindley said. "Wait just a minute."

The blue fellow was still standing on the chair, still smiling almost desperately, still gazing at the opposite wall. He gestured with his hand but spoke not a word.

Gradually the hubbub of conversation resumed as the guests turned away from him.

"You mean he isn't going to say anything?" Lindley asked.

"I told you. He never does."

"You sound as if you've seen him do this before."

"Sure I have. He goes to all the parties."

"*I've* never seen him," Lindley said.

"You and I don't always go to the same parties, more's the pity," she said. "He's a nut, that's all."

"I don't think he is. I think he actually is communicating in some way but that no one is able to, to—well, to *receive* him. I think he's an alien."

"Sure," Naomi said. "These parties are crawling with aliens. Cosmopolitan as hell."

"I don't mean a foreigner. I mean somebody not from Earth. How about that for a story?"

"Cut it out, Lind. You've been seeing too many horror movies." She began to fidget attractively. "Are you going to come on, or do I have to go home alone?"

"Well, if you put it that way—" He took a last look at the blue fellow. He was still standing on the chair in silence. By now no one was paying the slightest attention to him. "Maybe you're right," Lindley said. "After all, it is my day off."

He went out with Naomi. There probably wasn't any story, and if there was his paper could get it from the wire services. As Naomi put her arm through his and squeezed his hand in the elevator he thought with one last twinge of duty that there might possibly be a very big story. He shrugged and returned Naomi's squeeze.

Now, if it had been a blue girl . . .

28
Feeding Time

JAMES GUNN

"I'll have to warn my wife, the doctor."

Angela woke up with the sickening realization that today was feeding time. She slipped out of bed, hurried to the desk, and leafed nervously through her appointment book. She sighed with relief; it was all right—today was her appointment.

Angela took only forty-five minutes to put on her makeup and dress: it was feeding time. As she descended in the elevator, walked swiftly through the lobby, and got into a taxi, she didn't even notice the eyes that stopped and swiveled after her: feeding time.

Angela was haunted by a zoo.

She was also haunted by men, but this was understandable. She was the kind of blond, blue-eyed, angel men pray to—or for—and she had the kind of measurements—36–26–36—that make men want to take up mathematics.

But Angela had no time for men—not today. Angela was haunted by a zoo, and it was feeding time.

Dr. Bachman had a gray-bearded, pink-skinned, blue-eyed kindliness that was his greatest stock in trade. Underneath, there was something else not quite so kindly which had been influential in his choice of professions.

Now, for a moment, his professional mask—his *persona,* as the Jungians call it—slipped aside.

"A zoo?" he repeated, his voice clear, deep, and cultured, with just a trace of accent; Viennese without a doubt. He caught himself quickly. "A zoo. Exactly."

"Well, not exactly a zoo," said Angela, pursing her red lips thoughtfully at the ceiling. "At least not an ordinary zoo. It's really only one animal—if you could call him an animal."

"What do you call him?"

"Oh, I never call him," Angela said quickly, giving a delicious little shiver. "He might come."

"Hmmmm," hmmmmed Dr. Bachman neutrally.

"But you don't mean that," Angela said softly. "You mean if he isn't an animal, what is he? What he is—is a monster."

"What kind of monster?" Dr. Bachman asked calmly.

Angela turned on one elbow and looked over the back of the couch at the psychoanalyst. "You say that as if you met monsters every day. But then I guess you do." She sighed sympathetically. "It's a dangerous business, being a psychiatrist."

"Dangerous?" Dr. Bachman repeated querulously, caught off guard a second time. "What do you mean?"

"Oh, the people you meet—all the strange ones—and their problems—"

"Yes, yes, of course," he said hurriedly. "But about the monster—?"

"Yes, Doctor," Angela said in her obedient tone and composed herself again on the couch. She looked at the corner of the ceiling as if she could see him clinging there. "He's not a nightmare monster, though he's frightening enough. He's too real; there are no blurred edges. He has purple fur—short, rather like the fur on some spiders—and four legs, not evenly distributed like a dog's or a cat's but grouped together at the bottom. They're very strong—much stronger than they need to be. He can jump fifteen feet straight up into the air."

She turned again to look at Dr. Bachman. "Are you getting all this?"

Hastily, the psychoanalyst turned his notebook away, but Angela had caught a glimpse of his doodling.

"Goodie!" she said, clapping her hands in delight. "You're drawing a picture."

"Yes, yes," he said grumpily. "Go on."

"Well, he has only two arms. He has six fingers on each hand, and they're flexible, as if they had no bones in them. They're elastic, too. They can stretch way out—as if to pick fruit that grows on a very tall vine."

"A vegetarian," said Dr. Bachman, making his small joke.

"Oh no, Dcotor!" Angela said, her eyes wide. "He eats everything, but meat is what he likes the best. His face is almost human except it's green. He has very sharp teeth." She shuddered. "Very sharp. Am I going too fast?"

"Don't worry about me!" snapped the psychoanalyst. "It is your subconscious we are exploring, and it must go at its own speed."

"Oh, dear," Angela said with resignation. "The subconscious. It's going to be another one of those."

"You don't believe this nightmare has any objective reality?" Dr. Bachman asked sharply.

"That would make me insane, wouldn't it? Well, I guess there's no help for it. That's what I think."

Dr. Bachman tugged thoughtfully at his beard. "I see. Let's go back. How did this illusion begin?"

"I think it began with the claustrophobia."

Dr. Bachman shrugged. "A morbid fear of confined places is not unusual."

"It is when you're out in the open air. The fear had no relationship to my surroundings. All of a sudden I'd feel like I was in a fairly large room which had a tremendous weight of rock or masonry above it. I was in the midst of a crowd of people. For moments it became so real that my actual surroundings faded out."

"But the feeling came and went."

"Yes. Then came the smell. It was a distinctive odor—musty and strong like the lion house in the winter, only wrong, somehow. But it made me think of the zoo."

"Naturally you were the only one who smelled it."

"That's right. I was self-conscious, at first. I tried to drown out the odor with perfume, but that didn't help. Then I realized that no one else seemed to smell it. Like the claustrophobia, it came and went. But each time it returned it was stronger. Finally I went to a psychiatrist—a Dr. Aber."

"That was before the illusion became visual?"

"That was sort of Dr. Aber's fault—my seeing the monster, I mean."

"It is to be expected."

"When nothing else worked, Dr. Aber tried hypnosis. 'Reach into your subconscious,' he said. 'Open the door to the past!' Well, I reached out. I opened the door. And that's when it happened."

"What happened?" Dr. Bachman leaned forward.

"I saw the monster."

"Oh." He leaned back again, disappointed.

"People were close, but the monster was closer. The odor was stifling as he stared through the door—and saw me. I slammed the door shut, but it was too late. The door was there. I knew it could be opened. And he knew it could be opened. Now I was really afraid."

"Afraid?"

"That the monster might get through the door."

The psychoanalyst tugged at his beard. "You have an explanation for this illusion?"

"You won't laugh?"

"Certainly not!"

"I think through some strange accident of time, I've become linked to a zoo that will exist in the distant future. The monster—wasn't born on Earth. He's an alien—from Jupiter, perhaps, although I don't think so. Through the door I can see part of a sign; I can read this much."

Angela turned and took the notebook from his surprised fingers and printed quickly:

M'BA
(Larmis
Nativ
Vega

"Just like in the zoo," she said, handing the book back. "There's a star named Vega."

"Yes," said the psychoanalyst heavily. "And you are afraid that this—alien will get through the door and—"

"That's it. He can open it now, you see. He can't exist here; that would be impossible. But something from the present can exist in the future. And the monster gets hungry—for meat."

"For meat?" Dr. Bachman repeated, frowning.

"Every few weeks," Angela said, shivering, "it's feeding time."

Dr. Bachman tugged at his beard, preparing the swift, feline stroke which would lay bare the traumatic relationship at the root of the neurosis. He said, incisively, "The monster resembles your father, is that not so?"

It was Angela's turn to frown. "That's what Dr. Aber said. I'd never have noticed it on my own. There might be a slight resemblance."

"This Dr. Aber—he did you no good?"

"Oh, I wouldn't want you to think that," Angela protested quickly. "He helped. But the help was—temporary, if you know what I mean."

"And you would like something more permanent."

"That would be nice," Angela admitted. "But I'm afraid it's too much to hope for."

"No. It will take time, but eventually we will work these subconscious repressions into your conscious mind, where they will be cleansed of their neurotic value."

"You think it's all in my head?" Angela said wistfully.

"Certainly," the psychoanalyst said briskly. "Let us go over the progress of the illusion once more: first came the claustrophobia, then the smell, then, through Dr. Aber's bung—treatment, I should say, the dreams—"

"Oh, not dreams, doctor," Angela corrected. "When I sleep, I don't dream of monsters. I dream"—she blushed prettily—"of men. The thing in the zoo—I can see him whenever I close my eyes." She shivered. "He's getting impatient."

"Hungry?"

Angela beamed at him. "Yes. It's almost feeding time. He gets fed, of course. By the keeper, I suppose. But that's just the grains and fruits and things like that. And he gets hungry for meat."

"And then?"

"He opens the door."

"And I suppose he sticks his elastic fingers through the door."

Angela gave him a look of pure gratitude. "That's right."

"And you're afraid that one day he will get hungry enough to eat you."

"That's it, I guess. Wouldn't you be? Afraid, that is? There's all the legends about dragons and Minotaurs and creatures like that. They always preferred a diet of young virgins; and where there's all that talk—"

"If that were your only concern," Dr. Bachman commented dryly, "it seems to me that you could make yourself ineligible with no great difficulty."

Angela giggled. "Why, Doctor! What a suggestion!"

"Hmmmm. So! To return. Every few weeks comes feeding time. And you, feeling nervous and afraid, come to me for help."

"You put it so well."

"And now it's feeding time."

"That's right." Angela's nostrils dilated suddenly. "He's getting close to the door. Don't you smell him, doctor?"

Dr. Bachman sniffed once and snorted. "Certainly not. Now tell me about your father."

"Well," Angela began reluctantly, "he believed in reincarnation—"

"No, no," the psychoanalyst said impatiently. "The important things. How you felt about him when you were a little girl. What he said to you. How you hated your mother."

"I'm afraid there won't be time. He's got one of his hands on the door already."

Despite himself, Dr. Bachman glanced back over his shoulder. "The monster?" His beard twitched nervously. "Nonsense. About your father—"

"The door's opened!" Angela cried out. "I'm scared, doctor. It's feeding time!"

"I won't be tricked again," the psychoanalyst said sternly. "If we're to get anywhere with this analysis, I must have complete—"

"Doctor! Watch out! The fingers—Dr. Bachman! Doctor! Doc—!"

Angela sighed. It was a strange sigh, half hopelessness and half relief. She picked up her purse.

"Doctor?" she said tentatively to the empty room.

She stood up, sniffing the air gingerly. The odor was gone. So was Dr. Bachman.

She walked toward the door. "Doctor?" she tried once more.

There was no answer. There never had been an answer, not from seventeen psychiatrists, Aber through Bachman. There was no doubt about it. The monster did like psychiatrists.

It was a truly terrifying situation she was in, certainly through no fault of her own, and a girl had to do the best she could. She could console herself with the thought that the monster would never take her for food.

She was the trap door it needed into this world. Eat her, and feeding time was over.

She was perfectly safe.

As long as she didn't run out of psychiatrists.

29
Final Version

JOHN MORRESSY

"Property rights above all."

His days were full of work, but the life here was good.
Each day brought new discoveries. On his long, strong
legs he ranged far over this unfamiliar world, feeding a
curiosity that grew with each day's nourishment. The
woman, too, devoted her time to exploring, and between
them they had already learned much about their new
home.

After this long day of questing he returned hungry and
dusty, but in good spirits. She had come back before him,
and at the sight of him she brought out food. As they ate,
he told her of his day's findings.

"Did you see any new animals?" she asked.

"Some flying creatures. They're beautiful things."

"Take me with you tomorrow. I want to see them."

"You can name them. You're better at that than I am."

When they finished eating, he asked, "Did you find
anything new by the river?"

She smiled and shook her head, and the long waves of
her hair moved gently to brush first one side of her face,
then the other. She swept her hair back over her bare
shoulders and said, "I didn't go to the river. I went to the
mountain."

"To the top?"

"To the very top."

He had been reclining on an elbow. At her news, he sat up and reached out to her in a quick gesture, not of anger but of concern. "You know the law. At the top of the mountain . . . you should never go there. Not alone, certainly."

She rose lightly to her feet and tugged at his hand. "Come up with me, then, and see what I have to show you."

"The mountaintop is not a good place. Not even when we're together."

"There's no danger. I know there isn't."

He still did not move. "The light . . ." he said uncertainly.

"The light will be with us for a long time. Come." She tugged again, and he reluctantly arose and followed her up the gentle slope.

They reached the clearing on the mountaintop in a short time. He stopped, but she walked on, into the center of the clearing, where the bright bush stood alone, and picked two of the thumb-sized golden fruits. He cried out and rushed forward as she placed one in her mouth and bit down, but he was too late to stop her.

"Why did you do this? Remember the warning—if we eat this fruit, we die!" he said.

"I've eaten it before this, and I'm not dead. Try it," she said, extending the golden fruit to him.

"No, I can't."

"We were told, 'Eat this fruit and you die.' I've eaten it, and yet I live. Try it. Please."

"And if we die?"

"At least we die together. Would you rather live on here without me?"

That was a thought he could not bear. Without a word, he took the fruit from her fingers and placed it in his mouth. It burst at the pressure of his tongue, and rich sweet juice flooded his mouth with a savor unlike anything he had ever tasted before. He gave a little involuntary moan of delight at the sensation, and, without thinking, reached out to pluck one, two, then a handful more of the golden fruit, and the woman beside him laughed and did the same.

He turned to her, and another sensation swept through him at the sight of her. He was not sure how long they had been together, but since that first drowsy afternoon when he awoke and found her beside him, her head nestled in the crook of his outflung arm, he had never looked on her with the feeling he now felt. The glow of her smooth skin, the soft curves of her shoulders and breasts, the round smoothness of her belly, the long gentle line of her thighs were as new sights to him, and the look in her eyes drew him closer. He placed his hands on her shoulders and pulled her to him.

"You are the most beautiful of all things living. I never saw this before, but I see it now," he said.

They sank down on a soft bed of grass and explored together the wonder of their newly discovered bodies. They found a shared joy they had not dreamed of before, and they blessed the golden fruit that had awakened their sleeping senses.

Together, in the early twilight, they walked down the mountainside to their shelter. Her arm was around his waist, while he encircled her shoulder with his arm and drew her head against him. They walked in silence, slowly.

At the foot of the mountain they stopped. A light flickered and flared bright under the darkening sky and came to rest before them. He stepped forward in a protective stance as the light dimmed and took the form of one of the guardians of the place.

"What do you want here?" the man said.

The guardian's voice was like the rolling of great boulders down the mountainside. The rush of air from its pinions swept the fallen leaves past the man and blew the hair back from his face.

"You have broken the law," the guardian said.

The man was afraid. He wanted to fall back before that awesome figure. But he thought of the woman, and the punishment that might befall them, and anger rose in him stronger than the fear.

"What we have done is not your concern. Get out of our way," he said.

"Do you defy me?" the guardian roared, lowering a hand to the sword at its side.

"It is you who defy me, by intruding on the place that was given to me. Leave us," the man ordered, taking a step forward.

The guardian drew its sword. The man stooped, lifted a heavy stone from the ground, and hurled it with all his strength. It struck the guardian full in the chest, staggering it. The sword whirled free, glinting in the dying light. The woman sprang to snatch up the fallen blade.

"Now leave," she said to the stricken guardian. "And never intrude on us again."

The guardian hesitated, and seemed about to speak, but the man stepped forward and the woman brandished the sword, and the guardian faded away. The woman came to his side and put her arms around him. "You were brave," she said.

"Until now, I feared them."

"But no more."

"No, no more." He looked down at her, bemused. "Before I even raised my hand against the creature, I knew it was beaten."

"Do I make you so strong?"

"You've shown me why I must be strong."

He took the sword from her. Hand in hand, more watchful now, they descended the remainder of the way.

As they reached their shelter, the skies darkened. A wind rose, and its first faint whisper grew in an instant to a roar. Sudden drops of rain struck like flung pellets against their naked flesh. A peal of thunder shook the ground under their feet, and in a flash of lightning that seared the trees around them, their Creator appeared, his blazing face drawn into lines of wrath.

"What have you done?" He said in a voice that overbore the thunder.

The man stood fast before Him, the sword in his hand. "I drove out an intruder," he said.

"You have done more."

"Accuse me, then."

Thunder roared all around, and lightning lanced the ground at his very feet, but the man stood firm. At last came the accusation. "You have eaten the fruit of the knowledge of good and evil. This was forbidden you, and yet you did it. Now you must face My punishment."

"Why should I be punished?"

"Do you deny eating the golden fruit?" the voice of the Creator thundered.

"I deny doing wrong. You gave me this place, and told me I was master here. Why should anything be forbidden to me where I am master?"

"Do you feel no guilt? No shame?"

"I do not!" the man said, and took a step forward. "I will enjoy the fruits of my own garden as I choose. Send guardians to threaten me, and I'll treat them as I treated the first one."

"Would you attack Me, then?"

The man let the sword fall from his hand. "No, not You. Never You. I only defend what You gave me for my own."

The Creator raised His hand and pointed at the man, who steeled himself for a blast that did not come. Instead, in a solemn voice, like retreating thunder, the Creator said, "You have broken My law and struck down My servant, and you show no remorse. Will you kneel before Me and beg forgiveness?"

"No. I have done no wrong."

"I can destroy you."

"Then destroy me, and make a creature that will crawl before You," the man said.

"And a new companion for him," said the woman. She came to the man's side and placed her hand tight in his.

The wind fell, and the storm passed, and for a moment all was still. Side by side, the man and the woman awaited their doom.

"At last!" the Creator cried into the silence. "At last!" He cried again, and the darkness lifted. A joyous light shone forth from His countenance and illumined all around the man and woman and embraced them. "Over and over, on worlds beyond numbering, I have created you. On every world I put you to a test. And of all who take the test, none has yet had the courage to accept the consequences. Eat the fruit, and you can become as I. They could not bear this. When I faced them, they crawled before Me, and cringed, and whimpered for mercy. I demanded guilt and shame, and they gave it to Me, and they live in thrall to it forever. But you gave Me courage."

He stepped closer, and held out His arms. They came to Him, and He enfolded them in light and pressed them to Him. "On a million million worlds I have slaves and worshipers," He said softly. "But here, at last, I have My children."

30
Five Minutes Early

ROBERT SHECKLEY

"It takes a while to get your affairs in order."

Suddenly, John Greer found that he was at the entrance to Heaven. Before him stretched the white and azure cloud-lands of the hereafter, and in the far distance he could see a fabulous city gleaming gold under an eternal sun. Standing in front of him was the tall, benign presence of the Recording Angel. Strangely, Greer felt no sense of shock. He had always believed that Heaven was for everyone, not just for the members of one religion or sect. Despite this, he had been tortured all his life by doubts. Now he could only smile at his lack of faith in the divine scheme.

"Welcome to Heaven," the Recording Angel said, and opened a great brass-bound ledger. Squinting through thick bifocals, the angel ran his finger down the dense rows of names. He found Greer's entry and hesitated, his wing tips fluttering momentarily in agitation.

"Is something wrong?" Greer asked.

"I'm afraid so," the Recording Angel said. "It seems that the Angel of Death came for you before your appointed time. He *has* been badly overworked of late, but it's still inexcusable. Luckily, it's quite a minor error."

126

"Taking me away before my time?" Greer said. "I don't consider that minor."

"But you see, it's only a matter of five minutes. Nothing to concern yourself over. Shall we just overlook the discrepancy and send you on to the Eternal City?"

The Recording Angel was right, no doubt. What difference could five more minutes on Earth make to him? Yet Greer felt they might be important, even though he couldn't say why.

"I'd like those five minutes," Greer said.

The Recording Angel looked at him with compassion. "You have the right, of course. But I would advise against it. Do you remember how you died?"

Greer thought, then shook his head. "How?" he asked.

"I am not allowed to say. But death is never pleasant. You're here now. Why not stay with us?"

That was only reasonable. But Greer was nagged by a sense of something unfinished. "If it's allowed," he said, "I really would like to have those last minutes."

"Go, then," said the Angel, "and I will wait for you here."

And suddenly Greer was back on Earth. He was in a cylindrical metal room lit by dim flickering lights. The air was stale and smelled of steam and machine oil. The steel walls were heaving and creaking, and water was pouring through the seams.

Then Greer remembered where he was. He was a gunnery officer aboard the U. S. submarine *Invictus*. There had been a sonar failure; they had just rammed an underwater cliff that should have been a mile away, and now were dropping helplessly through the black water. Already the *Invictus* was far below her maximum depth. It could only be a matter of minutes before the rapidly mounting pressure collapsed the ship's hull. Greer knew it would happen in exactly five minutes.

There was no panic on the ship. The seamen braced themselves against the bulging walls, waiting, frightened, but in tight control of themselves. The technicians stayed at their posts, steadily reading the instruments that told them they had no chance at all. Greer knew that the Recording Angel had wanted to spare him this, the bitter end of life, the brief sharp agony of death in the icy dark.

And yet, Greer was glad to be here, though he didn't expect the Recording Angel to understand. How could a creature of Heaven understand the feelings of a man of Earth? Greer knew that he had been given a rare opportunity of saying goodbye to his home, and to do so without fear of what lay ahead. As the walls collapsed he was thinking of the beauties of the Earth, trying to remember as many as he could, like a man packing provisions for a long trip into a strange land.

31
Freedom

RICK NORWOOD

"Straight out of Don John."

The Grand Duke of Austria sat on his throne. A tall, clear-eyed man was brought before him in chains.

"This churl refuses to bow down to your hat, which we placed on display in the public square, as you commanded."

"I am a free Swiss," the man said. "I bow to no man, and to no man's hat."

"Take him out and hang him," said the Duke.

But as they were dragging the man away, the Duke cried out, "Wait! I know this fellow, and I will give him a sporting chance. Bring him and his son to the playing green behind the palace."

A few minutes later they were all gathered on the green, and the Duke explained the rules of the contest.

"You will be given a bowling ball and will stand at this end of the green. Your son will stand at the other end. If you can knock your son over with the bowling ball, you will go free. If you miss, you and your son both die."

A guard led the boy to the opposite end of the field.

"What's going on here!" the young man cried.

The guard, who had no doubt that the father's keen eye would save the day, bent to reassure the lad. "Ask not for whom the Tell bowls, he bowls for thee."

129

32
Garage Sale

JANET FOX

"Now if you could buy a garage *at one, you'd be safe."*

They were driving around the city on a steamy late-summer afternoon, two secretaries beating the heat of their inner-city walkup by cruising through suburbia. Here lawns lay crisp and green under a mist from sprinkler systems, the houses hermetically sealed to hold in the coolness breathed by air conditioners. Stella clacked as she drove, but only because she was addicted to plastic bracelets. She also liked to dye her hair different colors—though mercifully just one color at a time.

Jen was to Stella as the wren is to the cardinal, not noticeable beside the more flamboyant display, yet having a quiet style all her own.

"They got it made, huh?" said Stella. "Not having to bust their buns in a dumb office every day. House, hubby, and kids—the American dream, right?"

"I think you made a wrong turn."

"Where?"

"Back there. Some of these residential streets end in a cul-de-sac, and—"

"A cool de *what?*"

Jen subsided, since it was too late to get Stella going in

the right direction. Shadows of low-hanging foliage immersed the car, but only served to intensify the heat. The neat cookie-cutter ranches had given way to older residences in a variety of styles, most of them pretentious, spread more widely apart and set well back from the street.

"Or how about these? Woo-eee!"

As they passed a neo-Victorian horror, rife with gingerbread and flanked about with fountains and marble statues, both of them saw at once the hand-lettered sign poked into the funeral-grass lawn:

GARAGE SALE
TODAY ONLY

"Do you believe that?" giggled Stella, putting on the brakes so suddenly that Jen had to steady herself with a hand on the dash.

"What do you suppose they're selling, the Crown Jewels?" asked Jen.

"As long as it's a bargain," said Stella, her bracelets rattling as she climbed out of the car.

The house awed Jen a little as she walked toward it. Stella giggled and pointed as she passed a marble cupid relieving himself into an ornamental pool.

"I know you love these sales," said Jen, "but every time I go to one, I get talked into buying worthless junk."

"Never can tell. Today may be your day to find a treasure."

Jen looked furtively at the cupolas and the stained-glass windows. "A place like this—it could just be some kind of joke."

Stella gestured toward a cardboard sign tacked to the porch railing: GARAGE SALE IN BACK, with a scarlet arrow pointing the way.

There was a garage in back, though the builders had evidently not felt called upon to give it the ornateness they'd showered upon the house itself. Though the place was large inside, almost barnlike, they saw to their wonder that it was stacked wall to wall with a jumble of artifacts, furniture of all kinds and periods, clothing of several different eras, tools, household gadgets, and things that defied description.

"I think I just died and went to heaven," said Stella. She began to root contentedly about among the merchandise.

Jen nodded a greeting to the woman who seemed to be in charge of the sale. She sat behind a card table on a tattered chaise longue of violet brocade, most of her attention claimed by a cheap paperback romance. There was something odd about her, something Jen couldn't quite put her finger on, though certainly she might have been any housewife in faded jeans and a checkered shirt rolled to the elbows, a bandanna covering her head, the fat coils of hair rollers distending it.

"There's something funny about this place," she told Stella, who ignored her, rummaging through a trunk of musty-smelling garments, a moth-eaten feather boa draped about her shoulders. "Something funny," she muttered to herself, and began to move desultorily around the place, seeing an enormous moose head, the bottom half of a store-window mannikin and the photographs of generals Grant and Lee framed in what looked like the seat of a privy. "What an incredible collection of junk!" she said under her breath. Yet despite her incredulity, she began to be carried away by the sheer volume. What had Stella been saying about finding treasure?

She was poking about in a dim corner when she moved aside a Chinese silk screen patterned with tigers. As she did, she drew in her breath and hastily began to apologize. A man sat before her in a threadbare recliner, seemingly staring out at her, though with the reflection on his glasses she couldn't quite be sure. Her apology trailed off as she realized he wasn't moving.

"My God! Stella, he's dead! Stel—"

As she turned to run, she collided with someone she at first thought was her friend. It was the woman in charge of the sale; she smiled a small, secretive smile that made her angular, high-cheekboned face seem anything but ordinary, and she gripped Jen's arm to keep her from falling.

Jen opened her mouth to scream to Stella, but as she looked, by some trick of vision, her friend seemed small and far away, waltzing dreamily, a gown of blue voile held up before her.

"She can't hear you—not from here," said the woman calmly. Released from her grasp, Jen stood unsteadily before the strangely immobile man in the chair.

"Here? Where's here?"

"A juncture. A pivotal moment outside of time. Do you like him?" The woman removed the man's glasses with a proprietary gesture and cleaned them on the tail of her shirt. Jen saw that he had gentle myopic blue eyes.

"Do I like him?"

"I won't pretend he's like new. The hair's thinning on top, and he could lose a bit down here." She patted the obvious paunch beneath his white shirt. "But in many ways he was a good husband."

"He's your—No, you couldn't be selling—"

"Well, a person gets tired of things sometimes before they're quite worn out. You know how it is." A tiny dark questing head peeped from beneath the bandanna and slowly oozed its length down the woman's face: a snake as big around as a pencil with a minuscule tongue that darted out to taste the woman's cheek. Almost before the image registered, certainly before it was believed, the woman had swept it back under the bandanna with a casual gesture. Up close Jen could see the bulges beneath the cloth move, coiling and sliding.

"I guess so," said Jen, licking her lips and looking back toward the man in the chair. "He looks nice, but—" She hadn't noticed before, but there was a price written in grease pencil on his forehead. *$10.* "But why does he just sit there like that?"

"Since it's getting late," said the woman, lowering her voice conspiratorially, "and no one else has been interested, I'll let him go for half price."

"Is he dead or—"

"He's fully functional. I'll reanimate him when the time comes."

"Are you telling me you're some kind of . . . witch?"

"That's just a word, but I guess it'll do."

"They used to catch witches and burn them!"

The woman laughed, shaking her head until a darkly patterned tail slipped out onto her forehead and quickly slithered back under cover. "Not real witches, they didn't," she said.

"You must be crazy, and—" Jen looked desperately for Stella, but she was no longer there. A yellow plastic bracelet lay on the floor in a prosaic patch of sunlight.

"Don't expect corroboration from your friend. She was never here. Neither were you, if I don't make the sale."

"What if you do? Make the sale."

The woman smiled. "Yeah, I kind of thought you were interested. Well, you'll have a husband, that's all. Say you met him right after you finished business school."

"That's what I'll think?"

"That's what will have happened," said the woman, looking at her fingernails. They were very long fingernails, polished black, and the tips curved inward.

"Do we have . . . children?"

"For five dollars?"

Jen's fingers moved numbly, opening the catch of her purse. She didn't think she could just leave him there like that, staring into space and sitting in that ratty recliner for all eternity. And then, she hadn't had much luck getting a husband the usual way, so . . .

As she handed over the bill, the woman's eyes caught hers, cool amber eyes, steady-burning as lamps, the pupils a horizontal bar of darkness. Her whisper, grown low and sinister, hung in the air. "Tell you what, I'll even throw in the chair."

"Just look at me, Ben. Sometimes I think you're *glued* in that goddamned chair!"

Ben blinked up at her, his blue eyes so innocent, so vulnerable behind their panes of glass that she felt she could gladly throttle him. It was so predictable, so irritating. Screwing up his face with concentration, he did something to the TV's remote control, and the volume of the football game rose imperceptibly. "Really, Jen, I don't suppose you could come up with this overpowering desire to go out on any night except Monday. A man works hard, he deserves a chance to sit down once in a while." He twitched like a rabbit. "So what's for supper?"

"Oh, God!" A wisp of smoke curled through the kitchen door, and Jen ran to remove the smoking pan from the stove. She turned the water on it, half choking on the smell. Then she stood at the sink looking at the charred and drowned remains. "If I had it all to do over again," she said quietly, drawing a hand across her face and leaving a black smear. She sighed inaudibly, thinking that no one ever had a chance to do it over, no one. Never.

She busied herself in the kitchen for a few minutes, then returned to the living room, automatically picking up newspapers from the floor and an empty beer can that had left a ring on the coffee table.

"I burned the chops, so I put in a couple of TV dinners. I figured you'd like that, you like the damn TV so much anyway." For a moment she thought he hadn't heard her; he sat there immobile, like a graven idol, blue images from the screen flickering on his glasses.

At last he grunted. "That's just great," he said. "A

man works hard all day and comes home to TV dinners. Some wife I've found for myself.''

"Listen," she said, interposing herself between him and the set. "You're not that big a bargain yourself, mister." For some reason even she could not fathom, she found that vastly amusing, and repeated it. "No bargain," she said, and laughed until tears came to her eyes.

33
Getting Back to Before It Began

RAYLYN MOORE

"How fortunate the alphabet ends at Z."

For a long time the boy was alone, riding mile after mile at the back of the bus, watching the names of things pass by outside. Calumet, Feckless Joe's, Gillette, Gilbey's, Goshen, Gretna Estates, Kent, Lake Manahawkin, Lumberville, Miracle Whip, Northend Supply, Poor Old Frank's, Prudential.

At Sacktown the girl got on. Finding the seats up front all taken, she wandered back to where he was and sat beside him. Because he was a dreamy youth and not forward at all, he let the bus go through Saugus, Stickney, String City and Suquamish before he even spoke to her, and then he only said hello and how are you?

Since she was shy too, they traveled through Tioga, Transfer, Tribble and Troy before she answered. She said I'm fine and how far are you going?

He smiled and said I'm glad you asked. I've been riding this old bus a long time just hoping someone would inquire. You see, I'm an idealist and I have a theory, and people in my position need someone around to explain things to. (As is the case with many dreamy youths who are not forward, with this boy a little encouragement went a long way.)

137

He said I plan to ride to the absolute end of the line, past the place where the names stop. Out there everything will be unspoiled because it's unnamed. Haven't you ever noticed that once naming begins, ruin follows? Sometimes the destruction is fast, sometimes slow, but it comes. Inevitably.

She thought about it while they rode through Ulm, Uncompahgre, Underhill and Upper Black Eddy. When the bus stopped at Uz to let out some people, she said how much farther will you need to travel before you come to the place where the names run out?

I do like you very much, he said, because you ask all the right questions. And for other reasons too, he added, looking frankly for the first time at her plump round arms and cute knees and her light-bright long hair falling over the near velveteen collar of the coat around her shoulders. In answer I would say that all the evidence seems to indicate that it can't be much farther. For one thing, notice how lots of passengers are getting off now but no one is getting on.

She watched awhile with him and it was true. Riders debarked from the front of the bus in the towns of Value, Veach, Viroqua and Vultee, but in none of these places did anyone get on.

He said you will notice also that the billboards with the names of all the useless things in the world on them are getting fewer and farther between. Which is probably because these are all things one will not need to remember in the nameless country.

This was also true, the girl saw at once. The colored-up and lit-up names for tires, digestive aids, steakhouses, toothpaste, suntan oil, batteries, deodorants, household appliances and floor waxes appeared only sparingly in and near the villages of Walhonding and Wanilla, and not at all as the bus sped through Warshoal and Waverly Creek, where another clutch of passengers debarked but no one boarded.

Of course, the boy explained (eagerly now), the trick

will be for us to get well past the borderline, out where there's not even the dimmest concept of propernaming things and towns, because once one place has heard of another place, so to speak, and begins distinguishing it by a name, even a name like Other, the disease has already struck, you see. The rot has set in.

Us? she said, harking back to the beginning of his speech. *I'm* getting off this bus in Zerba where I plan to stay with an aunt and get a job in the ZigZag Pizza Palace.

The boy said quickly oh you can't do that. You must come with me.

Which just goes to show that by now he'd discarded his backwardness completely. But already the bus was rushing through Xelto heading for Yelvington, and he knew he didn't have time for a relaxed and orderly wooing.

It was touch and go for a while, but by Zelienopolis she had made up her mind, and as they whizzed right through Zerba without stopping, bus tires singing on the pavement because the hamlet was too small even for SLOW signs, she closed her delicate, trembling eyelids and bit hard into her berry-red lower lip, but she did not pull the cord to halt the coach.

Everyone else did though, many times over. By the time the bus reached Zincville there was only one other passenger left besides themselves, an elderly gentleman in a Borsalino hat, and he got off in Zooks Spur.

After that they rode on and on, finding out it was really true and becoming more and more excited. For out of the windows everything began looking unspoiled. There were a few sparse settlements, but evidently not having heard of one another, they had no names.

The names had truly run out. Been all used up. No more billboards loomed against the horizon. No more names on mailboxes and then finally no more mailboxes, nor utility poles, nor even fences, which would imply ownership, which would require naming of places.

They were trying to choose the ideal nameless spot for themselves when the driver's patience also ran out. He said what the hell's the matter with you two? You kids better shape up and snap to and make up your mind pretty quick. This bus doesn't go on forever, you know.

The boy, who would never be backward again, wasn't about to be intimidated by a mere bus driver, but it so happened that at this precise moment they saw an un-named place they both liked, a meadow with shade trees and fruit trees and a stream washing sunnily along be-tween mossy banks.

There would not be any troublesome traffic either be-cause several hundred yards ago the highway also had run out. In fact the bus had been having a rough go over the unspoiled earth. No wonder the driver was getting surly.

So they disembarked, not forgetting to take along the girl's handbag which contained a few items she thought she would need even here, and the boy's bedroll and rucksack of camping gear, which he swung enthusiastic-ally down from the overhead rack.

The bus turned around lumberingly and roared away in an acrid huff of inefficiently burning fuel. But after the cool fresh breezes of the nameless place had chased away the last of the bus smell, the couple settled down to be themselves and enjoy each other and celebrate their es-cape.

Everyone will think that it didn't last.

It will be suspected at once that in the girl's handbag was a supply of an indispensable facecream called Sof-Karess, and when this ran out, she begged to be taken back to the place where things have proper names so she could go into a store she remembered the name of and ask the clerk for more Sof-Karess.

Or it will be imagined that after the first joyful years and several babies, the couple tired of each other and quarreled and set up separate camps. So that the children, running to and fro between the camps, could tell one another and their parents where they were going, the settlements had to be named His and Hers.

It will be thought, in other words. that the girl and boy, being human, could not after all avoid either returning to what they were accustomed to, or bringing place names to their nameless place because the seeds of corruption were in themselves. For that's the way it always works in stories.

Unless it happens to be a story that proves the original rationale itself was a shuck. In which case it would turn out that one day the couple went for a walk and discovered, just on the other side of their unspoiled meadow, a highway with a string of towns called Aaronsburg, Absaraka, Acme Junction, and so on.

But none of this kind of thing happened. Not at all.

Instead, this devoted pair lived a richly satisfactory life, an ideal life. They had some lovely children. They stayed on their land and made whatever they needed with their own hands, though they found indeed that they required very little but each other and their own place.

Their only moments of anxiety came at rare intervals when they fancied they could hear distant rumblings and were afraid the gas tax money had piled up so relentlessly back where they'd come from that to get rid of it the highway department would be forced to extend the road into their nameless place, after which of course someone would have to name the place where the road led. Or when they imagined that some other person might have stumbled onto the same hypothesis the boy had worked out and would stay on the bus beyond the end of the line, making it necessary eventually to have two settlements named Ours and Theirs.

They needn't have given these possibilities a thought, however, for the bus never went that far out again.

34
The Giveaway

STEVE RASNIC TEM

"Be good, sweet maid—"

"If you don't cut that out something real bad's gonna happen to you!"

Six-year-old Marsha dropped the second handful of mud she was about to smear on seven-year-old Alice Kennedy's party dress. "Like what?"

Alice made a thinking face for a little while. "Well . . . I might tell your daddy about it and he just might give *you* away!"

"Uh-uh," Marsha grunted. She proceeded to gather another handful of mud. Some of it spattered onto her shoes and she had to twist each foot just so to wipe them in the grass. It was hard to do that and still hold onto the slippery mud. Then she walked carefully over to where Alice was sitting making mud pies and raised both hands.

"Stop it, Marsha! I told you what I'd do! I'll *tell* and he'll just give you away!"

Marsha didn't understand why Alice didn't want her to smear mud on the dress anyway; it was nice and cool and besides, Alice's dress was already muddy from making mud pies all afternoon. But she was even more confused about this giveaway stuff. She'd never heard of that before.

"What do you mean, give me away?"

"I'll tell him you've been real bad to me, Marsha, and he'll give you away to some other family, or even worse!"

Marsha just looked at her in confusion. "Moms and dads don't give their kids away," she said seriously.

Alice looked up from her mud pie and smiled. "That's what your daddy did with your brother Billy."

"That's not true, Alice Kennedy; Billy died and went to heaven!"

"How do you know? Did you see him go?"

"Well, no. But Daddy told me he did."

"They *have* to say that, stupid! They don't want you crying and making trouble."

"Don't call me stupid!" Marsha watched her shoes squishing into the mud. "Why did they give Billy away?" she asked softly.

"I heard your daddy tell my daddy that Billy was too small and that he'd never be very big, ever. He sounded real sad about that. So I guess he just gave him away so he can get a bigger boy later on."

Marsha nodded her head solemnly.

"Know who else got given away?"

"Who?"

"Johnny Parker."

"I 'member him! He was like a grownup 'cept he had something funny wrong with his head made him want to play with kids all the time. But he went to a special school! My aunt said so and she's a teacher!"

"Well, he was gonna go to one of them schools, but they gave him away instead. Know who else?"

"Uh-uh."

"Shelly Cox. She kept breaking things and being mad and real mean and one night her daddy had them take her away."

"Who's them?"

Alice looked back over her shoulder at the backyard of her house. "I don't know for *sure*. Guess who else?"

"Who?"

"*You*, Marsha, 'cause you got my party dress *all* muddy and my daddy's probably gonna want to give *me* away so I'm gonna have to tell on *you*."

"Tattletale!" Marsha cried, tears streaming down her face.

"Crybaby!" Alice yelled, running toward her house.

Marsha threw a handful of mud after Alice in frustration. "Uh-uh," she grunted as she began the long walk home.

There were loud voices coming from the kitchen when Marsha got home. She could hear her mother crying, her father shouting. He sounded real mad. Marsha hated it when they had a fight. She sat down in a chair in the living room, picked up one of her books, and pretended to read. But she could only pretend because they were too loud.

"Can't you do anything so simple as enter a check properly, Jennie? I bet Marsha could do that and she's only six years old!"

"I'm sorry, Ted. I just forgot! Will you leave me alone!"

"If I let you alone we'd be broke within the month! Last week you took out the grocery money twice and caused six checks to bounce! And you *say* you don't know what happened to the money! You're driving me crazy, Jennie! I can't take it! I tell you I can't take it any-more!"

"I've *tried* to be a good wife to you . . .'" Her mom started to cry and cough, and Marsha couldn't tell what she said anymore. She wanted to go in and see her mom, but she was too afraid. Her daddy was shouting louder than ever now.

"You haven't *been* a wife to me, Jennie, since Billy's been gone!"

Her mom was crying louder than before. Marsha could hardly understand her. "The doctor says . . . you know the doctor said I can't have *any more!*"

"You're lying, Jennie; you're lying through your teeth. I know that quack's nurse! You've been lying to me, lying all the time. You just *don't want to*, Jennie. *You just don't want to!*"

Marsha went upstairs until dinner. She thought her daddy noticed the dried mud on her shoes when she got up from the table, but he didn't say anything.

Marsha woke up with it still dark outside. Something told her she should go to the window. She was afraid, because it was real dark out there, but she thought she should probably go. She tiptoed as softly as she could, afraid she might wake up her dad.

A funny-looking car was parked out in front of the house. It was long and black, the longest and blackest car she had ever seen. And there was a long silver thing, jagged like lightning, that went from one end of the car to the other. This lightning was brighter than the streetlights and hurt her eyes.

The car windows were gray. They looked dirty. She couldn't see through them at all.

Marsha didn't want to see the big black car anymore, but she was more afraid not to see it. She didn't know why she was more afraid of not seeing it, but she was.

Marsha tiptoed down the stairs in her pajamas, scared to death that her father would catch her and maybe give her away like he had Billy. She went into the dark living room. The front door was wide open; she could see the long black car by standing in front of the open door.

She stepped carefully onto the front sidewalk and started walking to the car. She tried to be as quiet as a mouse like her aunt had told her once. She was scared of the car, but she had to keep walking toward it. She couldn't understand at all.

When she got to the side of the car she held her hands up to her eyes and leaned against the window, trying to see what was inside. But it was too gray, too dark. She started to walk around the front of the car and to the other

side to look in the windows there, when the tall man
stepped in front of her.

He was tall with black shadows all over him and he
had a big white bow tie and a big white flower on his
chest, but she couldn't see his coat, he was so black, so
she didn't know how the flower stayed on.

The tall man bent over. He had no face, just a head full
of white fog, like his face hadn't made itself yet.

Marsha began to cry in a soft voice, scared to death
she'd wake up her daddy and he'd give her away for
spoiling his sleep. But she couldn't help crying, and it
kept getting louder and louder until she was suddenly wet
and warm and knew she'd wet herself and he'd want to
give her away for that too.

She turned around to run back into the house.

Two men with no faces were standing there, carrying a
long thing between them. Marsha was so surprised she
stopped crying.

For some reason she wasn't so afraid now, so she
walked up to the long thing they were carrying to see
what it was.

Her mommy was tied to the thing and she was looking
up with her eyes all funny and her mouth open and oh she
knew her mommy was dead oh dead dead dead!

She ran screaming into the house and they grabbed her
and she was screaming and they put something into her
mouth—

Only "they" was her daddy. He was sitting on the
sofa now, looking all serious like when she'd done something real bad.

"You saw the car?"

She nodded her head tearfully.

"Your mommy went away in the car?"

"Ye-es," her voice broke and she cried a little.

"Okay, I want you to listen, Marsha." He held her
chin up and made her look into his eyes. "Your mommy
didn't do things right, Marsha; she wasn't *good* enough.
So you know what happened?"

Marsha nodded her head solemnly.

"I had to *give* your mommy *away*. That's what happens to people who mess up, Marsha. You've got to do your *best*, do your best for *me, all the time.*"

Again she nodded her head, but then her father was gone, as quickly as he had arrived, and she was alone on the couch in the darkened living room. She looked out the window but there was nothing there. She knew everything was all over, then.

Marsha sleepily climbed off the sofa and stumbled around trying to find a light switch. She couldn't find one so she had to make her way to the kitchen in the dark. She would have cried then, but she really didn't feel like crying anymore.

The kitchen light switch was too high, so she had to work in the dark. It was hard to find the pans or the turner in the dark, but she finally did. At least the refrigerator light let her see the eggs, and she kept the door open afterward so she could see better.

She knew she'd better start her daddy's breakfast now if she was to get it finished on time. The stove and the counters were real high for her, so it would take a long time for her to use them.

Daddy liked big breakfasts, and more than anything else in the whole wide world, she wanted to please her daddy.

35
Give Her Hell

DONALD A. WOLLHEIM

"You wouldn't think a punishment could fit that crime."

It's no good making a deal with the devil. He's a cheat. He's all they say he is and more. The effete modern books like to present him as a smiling red devil, all clean and slick. Or as some cagey, witty peddler, or a tophat-and-tails city slicker. But the monks of the Middle Ages knew better. They described him as a beast; a stinking, foul-breathed, corrupt, and totally loathsome abomination.

Take my word for it. He is. I know, for I was fool enough to make such a pact. I saw him and dealt with him and from beginning to end, it was never worth it.

I was desperate, and like all whom fate had played crooked, I was sore about it. Things were not going well with me, and it was all their fault. My wife and my daughter's. I refuse to take the blame in spite of what the devil may claim. I know when I'm right. My daughter had run away from my home—that was the shock that made me realize what was happening.

That girl ran away and she was only sixteen, and she'd stolen the contents of my wallet and took some of my wife's jewelry and ran away. My wife wasn't so shocked. She had the nerve to say it served me right. I didn't "understand the child."

What's to understand about a disobedient daughter who doesn't listen to her father, and who makes dates after eight o'clock at night, who sneaks magazines into her bedroom, actually talks to some of those uncouth kids from across the tracks, and has been seen in soda parlors after dark. Sure, I had to beat her. I've been doing that since she was seven. I've had to be stricter and stricter with her. Spare the rod and spoil the child—that's the slogan I was raised on and I did my best. But the girl was rotten—something from her mother's side of the family, no doubt—and she had the nerve to try to run away.

I called the police. I'm not going to be thought of as the father of a wild kid. I sent out an alarm. My wife objected, but I put her in her place. Slap across the face shut her up—I'd taught her long ago who was master. Me, the way it was meant to be. I locked her up in our bedroom, and later on I gave her a lesson with the strap, face down on the bed with her clothes off. Women know only one master. My mother never complained; she didn't dare, not even when she was dying after my father threw her down the stairs that night.

My father's ways were right and I was right. The cops brought the girl back to me the next day. I gave her a hiding she'd not forget, and then I arranged to have her committed to a corrective institution. One of those private sanitariums for disturbed children, you know. Exclusive, well-guarded, and well-disciplined. All right, they made life hell for her, but how else can you teach a wayward child how to do right. Better for the family name than to have her in public vision.

They had my orders and the extra payments I made were generous enough to enforce them—she'd not get out until she was good if they had to nearly kill her to do it. They kept her in a straitjacket for months at a time at my insistence, and in restraining cuffs and belts at all other times. A series of regular electric shocks taught her a few things. The doctor says now she's faking insanity, that she shrieks night and day, and they keep her by herself in a padded, locked cell. But I think she's faking. She's just a disobedient girl and she's got to learn who's master.

As for my wife, she had the nerve to leave me. She climbed out of the window the night I bribed the doctors to start my bad daughter's shock treatments. She ran to my business partner, that skunk, and he helped her hide. Next day he dared put it up to me. He said he thought I was the one who was cracking up. Me! The nerve of him.

Obviously he was scheming to steal my wife away from me. And he must have been double-booking my firm. I was sure of it. I could see it all from his faking, sly ways. He must have been plotting my ruin the way he must have been scheming after my wife.

So I took steps to sell him out. But the skunk had covered his tracks. He had acted first. He had an order taken out against me, charging me with deceit and having my wife charge me with mental cruelty and suing to get custody of my child and my business.

I could see I'd get no help from the courts and the lawyers. They're all corrupt, unable to see how a man must be stern with his own. These are decadent times. No wonder the world is going to hell.

I was in a jam. They'd cornered me, boxed me with legal chicaneries, tied up my funds. I was furious that night as I stalked up and down my house. The windows were shut and the shades were down. I don't stand for curious eyes. I was alone and the next day they'd be closing in from all directions. That's when I turned to Satan.

I figured if Satan had been maligned as much as I was, he must be all right. Just a victim of the same errors. I called on him. When you really mean it, the devil will come. I gave him a sacrifice—I tossed the Bible into the fire; I got hold of my wife's cat—that snarling, fuzzy beast—and I cut its throat on the living room rug and called Satan.

He stank. The place stank and he was there—a foul

sort of thing. He was crawly and slimy and toady. He belched rot, and his voice would give you the willies. But I don't go for appearances. I knew he had to have the stuff to stand up to all those dirty do-gooders and Gospel pounders.

I told him I wanted to get out of my jam. I wanted my wife back under my control, my daughter where I wanted her, and my partner in hell.

Satan agreed. He could do the first two things, and while the judgment of my partner would be up to That Other One, maybe he'd get his soul in the end, too. Anyway, he'd die, and what did he want of me?

My soul, of course. I'd trusted him for that. What good would it do him? I believe in reincarnation, anyway. I struck a hard bargain. I said first I had to have a chance to be reborn again and live a whole new life from the start. Then he could have my soul afterward.

Because if he got my whole soul but only gave me the last half of my life as I wanted it, that wasn't fair, was it? No. I drove a hard bargain. He had to give me an entire life from start to finish.

He whined and he threatened and he bellowed, but he agreed. On my deathbed, he said, he'd reappear and give me the word on the whole new life I was going to live. There were certain rules he had to go by in that sort of thing. Okay, I said, I trust you. You and me, we think alike, we think right. An iron hand in a velvet glove, that's the rule.

He stank, that no-good bum. He gave me his word, and I say he cheated, but he didn't think so.

My partner died that same night. His furnace exploded in his house. The place was a seething mass of flames. He tried to get down the stairs, got splashed with flaming oil, was scorched from head to foot, ran out in flames and died in agony. Served him right. The firm's ledgers were in his house for his auditors, and they burned up, too, putting me entirely in the clear.

He died in scandal, too, because my wife was caught

in his house. She had a room upstairs, and she jumped from the window and the newspapers snapped her picture in her torn nightgown on the lawn coming away from that man's house. That queered any divorce case for her. She came home, and she had to keep her mouth shut. There'd never be a chance for her to get custody of our runaway daughter or any divorce.

I've never let her forget the scandal, even though she claims there was nothing between them—he was just being hospitable. Ha! I showed her. She's not allowed out of the house now, and I beat her black and blue whenever she thinks of it. She hasn't got a legal leg to stand on, not after those newspaper photos and stories.

My daughter is still in the padded cell I arranged for her. If she's going to fake insanity, I'll make it so hot for her she'll learn the error of her ways. She's been there ten years now and the kid is stubborn. But the doc and his strongarms have been well paid. They use the leather mitts on her and the rubber sheets and the shocks. She'll stop her act or else.

Unfortunately I won't live to see it. I'm dying now, and I've arranged in my will to see that her cure and treatment continues. I got this cancer of the throat, from inhaling some kind of poison gases or something years ago. I think it was that evening with that stinking cheat. His bad smell burned my throat, it did. I told you he cheats.

And he's been back, just now. He's been back and he gave me the full dope on our deal. I'm to get a full life, from birth to maturity and eventually death. Only he's cheated.

He can't give me a life that hasn't been lived yet. He can't reincarnate me in a future year. No, he hasn't any control over future lives. He has only control over lives that have been lived, he said, the cheat—why couldn't he have said that when we first made the deal?

And it seems to be a rule in this kind of transaction that he can't take life over in the same sex. Something about positive and negative polarity in souls. If you live twice, then you got to see life from first one sex and then the other. Makes the soul rounded, he says, the cheat.

And it's also got to be somebody who's a blood relation, he tells me, the stinking, slimy no-good crook.

I'm dying, and in a few minutes more I'm going to be dead. And then I'll open my eyes again, a newborn baby, and start living through all the long, long years of another person's life. I got to experience everything, every darn, horrible, painful, frustrated, mean minute of it.

I'm going to be reborn as my own daughter.

It's going to be hell.

36
God's Nose

DAMON KNIGHT

"And you can't disprove that, either."

"God's nose," said my Zen Catholic friend, waving her expressive little hands, "to begin with, must be the biggest nose you can imagine. In fact, theology and mathematics teach us that it must be infinite in size. Just think—bigger than the Sun, bigger than comets, galaxies—and still . . . a nose."

The idea pleased her; she closed her eyes and smiled, squinting blindly up at the ceiling. Her neck was not quite clean. She was charming, black-haired, brown skinned, with a compact little body that was feminine without being unnecessarily soft. Her hands were like some small, friendly animal's—the palms wide, fingers and thumbs short, soft-padded, with sharp-pointed nails from which the red lacquer was peeling.

We were waiting in a friend's apartment for her lover to arrive, a man I had not met. We were sitting on cushions, tailor-fashion, since our absent friend owned no furniture. We had each had several glasses of Smirnoff's vodka mixed with orange soda. How the subject of God's nose had come up, I do not at this moment recall.

"Picture it in your mind," she said. "A good way is to begin to think of George Washington's nose."

"Washington's nose?"

"On Mount Rushmore," she answered impatiently. "That big sunlit stone nose, tall as a building, with a little man swinging on a scaffolding beside it—looking like a fly. Now: think of that nose, only enormously bigger, out there in the light of the stars—a nose so huge that our whole solar system would be like a wart." Eyes still closed, she shivered with pleasure.

"Does God's nose, then, have warts?" I asked her.

"No, evidently not, because a wart is an imperfection, and God's nose must be perfect. But pores? Hairs in the nostrils? Yes, obviously! And each pore, each hair, must be an absolutely perfect hair, or pore."

"I'm not sure I like the idea of God having a nose," I said.

"Then you're not getting the picture. Imagine being out there in a spaceship, near enough to see that nose looming over you—eternal, mysterious. You steer your spaceship parallel to the nose"—her hands showed me how—"trying to get from the tip to the bridge. But you know you never can, because it would take too long—you'd die of old age first."

She opened her eyes. "Doesn't that make you feel pretty humble?"

"It certainly does," I said. The tasteless vodka, or else the sickly sweet orange soda, had given everything in the room an unusual color and sharpness of outline. I felt that my Zen Catholic friend's words were nonsense, but a special, very valuable kind of nonsense which I must try to hang onto.

"People spend so much time worrying about the Creation," she said abruptly.

"I don't."

She made an impatient gesture. "People who think, I mean. Where did all the stars and planets come from, they ask? All the clouds of gas in the Milky Way? All the comets and meteorites?"

"Well, where did they come from?"

"Do you know what I think?" she asked intensely, leaning forward. I half expected to see that her eyes had slitted yellow pupils, like a cat's, but they were brown, so nearly black that you could not tell where the iris left off and the pupil began. They seemed all pupil—two enormous round black holes staring at me.

"I think," she said reverently, "that God sneezed."

There was a click and a sound of footsteps in the hall. My friend got to her feet in one eager motion. "Hello!" she called.

"Hello!" a deeper voice echoed. A man came into the room, smiling, dressed in a torn white shirt, sandals, faded dungarees.

My friend put her arm around him, smiling. "This is Godfrey," she said.

We shook hands, and I'm afraid I stared in fascination. Godfrey had the largest, most overbearing nose I have ever seen. It was nobly arched, thin, sensitive, with flaring nostrils. The rest of his face, with its pale brown mustache and beard, was hardly large enough to support it.

"We have to go now," my friend said, smiling, holding Godfrey's bicep with one possessive hand. After a few minutes, discovering that I did not want any more vodka or orange soda, I followed them down the stairs into the warm sunlight, thinking very curious and pleasant thoughts.

37
The Good Husband

EVELYN E. SMITH

"And a good man is hard to find."

When Ellen had been twenty, even twenty-five, she would never have considered John as a matrimonial prospect. He would have been too dull, too stuffy, and—for ten years was a great span of time then—too old. Now that she was thirty-three, forty-three didn't seem old at all, and John was, as far as she could determine, dependable and steady.

So she agreed to marry him. With a romantic impetuousness that she had thought him not capable of, he had insisted upon an elopement—not that there was anyone to care whether or not they lived in "sin." They were married one fall evening in a small town where marriages could be arranged hastily, and ever since then—six months it had been—they had been living in John's Greenwich Village apartment.

Once she had wondered whether she ever could grow fond of him. Now, looking at him as he sat reading near the fire, his bald spot shining, his rimless spectacles flickering with reflected flame, she wondered how she could ever do without him. Affectionately she got up and rearranged the muffler he wore indoors and out; he was always cold.

John looked up at her and smiled. His teeth were excellent, a feature she liked to dwell upon, because otherwise he was such a commonplace little man.

"You've been coming home later and later every evening," she remarked in a tone which she tried to keep from being querulous, rather bright and interested as if she wanted to know everything he did. Not that she knew anything—really. He never told her what his business was and she was afraid to press him, afraid of being thought a nagging wife, afraid of stretching the tenuous substance of her dearly won marriage.

But his coming home later and later had been hard on her, especially when he worked Saturdays and Sundays too. She had come to rely upon his company so much.

He sighed. "As I told you, dear, a lot of people are beginning to take their vacations, so I have to stay later to do their work."

She returned to her book, trying to give the appearance of satisfaction. But she was not satisfied. Poor John! Everybody pushed their work off on him—he was such a meek little fellow. Yet there was an undercurrent of strength in him too. She never could get him to answer her questions. Should she try again?

No. He was such a good husband. He never went out evenings by himself, although he often went for a walk late at night. Soon after their marriage, she had been startled to awaken, and find the bed empty. When he came back, however, he explained to her that he was subject to claustrophobia and sometimes had to get up and go out for air. Since he always did look much the better for his outings, she never complained.

Her friends, when they dropped in for bridge or a quiet evening, were almost openly contemptuous of John. Still, she would far rather have had him than Madge's handsome Bill, who chased after women, and had even been known to try to kiss Ellen herself in the kitchen . . . or Peter, Lillian's husband, who drank.

Moreover, John had his family tree. "Our branch of

the Carruthers family," he would inform guests in his dry, precise way, "has been in New York ever since the British took it from the Dutch. Some of my ancestors are buried out there."

And he would gesture toward the window that looked out on the graveyard. Behind the old brownstone was a forgotten little old cemetery. At first Ellen had thought the outlook macabre, but soon grew used to it. Moreover, the apartment was comfortable and furnished with handsome old pieces that gave John's claims for his family a solid foundation.

Her guests would smile when he gave his little talks; yet she resented neither their merriment nor his pompousness. He made her feel as if she belonged not only to him but to a whole tradition. Wanting to belong, to be part of something had been one of the major obsessions in her life.

And his prosiness was less objectionable than Madge's detailed narrative of her bouts with the doctor. Madge had a tendency to hypochondria. Recently she had added anemia to her ailments, and Lillian, always the copycat, had likewise professed a drop in her blood count.

When John went out to the kitchen for more ice, Madge would ask, slanting her eyes, "But just what does he do for a living, Ellen?" and Ellen would have to admit she had no idea.

Then Lillian would say, giggling and fingering one of the dog collars both she and Lillian had begun to affect, "Maybe he's a bookie."

And everyone would laugh, because the idea of John's being anything outside the law was so absurd.

But this night, brooding over her book, Ellen found her curiosity irrepressible. During fall and winter John had been a model husband. Now that spring was here, he was coming home later and later. "In the spring, a young man's fancy . . ." And in the spring all men thought they were young. Could there be another woman?

And, after all, what did John do during the day that he

was so reluctant to disclose? Didn't he know that she wouldn't mind even if he were a—a butcher?

When he got up very early the next morning, she got up too. She dressed quickly and quietly behind the closet door while he was putting on his rubbers and wrapping his muffler around his meager throat and tucking his umbrella under his arm.

On rubber-soled feet she crept downstairs behind him. He didn't go out into the street at all. He went into the narrow side alley and, with a big wrought-iron key from his pocket, opened the gate leading into the graveyard. There he went to a gravestone behind the big tree that concealed most of the cemetery from the overlooking windows and disappeared into the grave.

Not a minute too soon either, for dawn broke immediately afterward. There, in the watery light, was his umbrella leaning against the stone. Evidently he'd forgotten to take it in with him. She had thought he was getting a little absent-minded recently.

The inscription on the tomb said: "Sacred to the Memory of John Gaylord Carruthers, 1720–1763." He hadn't been lying about his family.

The thing to do, she knew, was to dig him up and plunge a stake through his heart. But she would find life lonely without John. Anyhow, now she knew he wasn't carrying on with another woman.

As she tenderly carried his umbrella upstairs, she thought of Madge's and Lillian's anemia—their dog collars—and laughed.

38
The Handler

DAMON KNIGHT

"And how many 'big' men have handles, I wonder?"

When the big man came in, there was a movement in the room like bird dogs pointing. The piano player quit pounding, the two singing drunks shut up, all the beautiful people with cocktails in their hands stopped talking and laughing.

"Pete!" the nearest woman shrilled, and he walked straight into the room, arms around two girls, hugging them tight. "How's my sweetheart? Susy, you look good enough to eat, but I had it for lunch. George, you pirate"—he let go both girls, grabbed a bald blushing little man and thumped him on the arm—"you were great, sweetheart, I mean it, really great. Now *hear this!*" he shouted, over all the voices that were clamoring Pete this, Pete that.

Somebody put a martini in his hand and he stood holding it, bronzed and tall in his dinner jacket, teeth gleaming white as his shirt cuffs. "We had a show!" he told them.

A shriek of agreement went up, a babble of did we have a *show* my God Pete listen a *show*—

He held up his hand. "It was a good show!"

Another shriek and babble.

"The sponsor kinda liked it—he just signed for another one in the fall!"

A shriek, a roar, people clapping, jumping up and down. The big man tried to say something else, but gave up, grinning, while men and women crowded up to him. They were all trying to shake his hand, talk in his ear, put their arms around him.

"I love ya *all!*" he shouted. "Now what do you say, let's live a little!"

The murmuring started again as the people sorted themselves out. There was a clinking from the bar. "Jesus, Pete," a skinny pop-eyed little guy was saying, crouching in adoration, "when you dropped that fishbowl I thought I'd pee myself, honest to God—"

The big man let out a bark of happy laughter. "Yeah, I can still see the look on your face. And the fish, flopping all over the stage. So what can I do, I get down there on my knees—" the big man did so, bending over and staring at imaginary fish on the floor. "And I say, 'Well, fellows, back to the drawing board!' "

Screams of laughter as the big man stood up. The party was arranging itself around him in arcs of concentric circles, with people in the back standing on sofas and the piano bench so they could see. Somebody yelled, "Sing the goldfish song, Pete!"

Shouts of approval, please-do-Pete, the goldfish song.

"Okay, okay." Grinning, the big man sat on the arm of a chair and raised his glass. "And a vun, and a doo— vere's de moosic?" A scuffle at the piano bench. Somebody banged out a few chords. The big man made a comic face and sang, "Ohhh—how I wish . . . I was a little fish . . . and when I want some quail . . . I'd flap my little tail."

Laughter, the girls laughing louder than anybody and their red mouths farther open. One flushed blonde had her hand on the big man's knee, and another was sitting close to him.

"But seriously—" the big man shouted. More laughter.

"No, seriously," he said in a vibrant voice as the room quieted, "I want to tell you in all seriousness I couldn't have done it alone. And incidentally, I see we have some foreigners, Litvaks, and other members of the press here tonight, so I want to introduce all the important people. First of all, George here, the three-fingered bandleader—and there isn't a guy in the world could have done what he did this afternoon—George, I love ya." He hugged the blushing little bald man.

"Next my real sweetheart, Ruthie, where are ya? Honey, you were the greatest, really perfect—I mean it, baby—" He kissed a dark girl in a red dress who cried a little and hid her face on his broad shoulder. "And Frank." He reached down and grabbed the skinny pop-eyed guy by the sleeve. "What can I tell you? A sweetheart?" The skinny guy was blinking, all choked up; the big man thumped him on the back. "Sol and Ernie and Mack, my writers, Shakespeare should have been so lucky." One by one, they came up to shake the big man's hand as he called their names; the women kissed him and cried. "My stand-in," the big man was calling out, and "my caddy," and "Now," he said, as the room quieted a little, people flushed and sore-throated with enthusiasm, "I want you to meet my handler."

The room fell silent. The big man looked thoughtful and startled, as if he had had a sudden pain. Then he stopped moving. He sat without breathing or blinking his eyes. After a moment there was a jerky motion behind him. The girl who was sitting on the arm of the chair got up and moved away. The big man's dinner jacket split open in the back, and a little man climbed out. He had a perspiring brown face under a shock of black hair. He was a very small man, almost a dwarf, stoop-shouldered and round-backed in a sweaty brown singlet and shorts. He climbed out of the cavity in the big man's body, and closed the dinner jacket carefully. The big man sat motionless and his face was doughy.

The little man got down, wetting his lips nervously. Hello, Harry, a few people said. "Hello," Harry called, waving his hand. He was about forty, with a big nose and big soft brown eyes. His voice was cracked and uncertain. "Well, we sure put on a show, didn't we?"

Sure did, Harry, they said politely. He wiped his brow with the back of his hand. "Hot in there," he explained, with an apologetic grin. Yes I guess it must be, Harry, they said. People around the outskirts of the crowd were beginning to turn away, form conversational groups; the hum of talk rose higher. "Say, Tim, I wonder if I could have something to drink," the little man said. "I don't like to leave him—you know—" He gestured toward the silent big man.

"Sure, Harry, what'll it be?"

"Oh—you know—a glass of beer?"

Tim brought him a beer in a pilsener glass and he drank it thirstily, his brown eyes darting nervously from side to side. A lot of people were sitting down now; one or two of them were at the door leaving.

"Well," the little man said to a passing girl, "Ruthie, that was quite a moment there, when the fishbowl busted, wasn't it?"

"Huh? Excuse me, honey, I didn't hear you." She bent nearer.

"Oh—well, it don't matter. Nothing."

She patted him on the shoulder once, and took her hand away. "Well, excuse me, sweetie, I have to catch Robbins before he leaves." She went on toward the door.

The little man put his beer glass down and sat, twisting his knobby hands together. The bald man and the pop-eyed man were the only ones still sitting near him. An anxious smile flickered on his lips; he glanced at one face, then another. "Well," he began, "that's one show under our belts, huh, fellows, but I guess we got to start, you know, thinking about—"

"Listen, Harry," said the bald man seriously, leaning forward to touch him on the wrist, "why don't you get back inside?"

The little man looked at him for a moment with sad hound-dog eyes, then ducked his head, embarrassed. He stood up uncertainly, swallowed and said, "Well—" He climbed up on the chair behind the big man, opened the back of the dinner jacket and put his legs in one at a time. A few people were watching him, unsmiling. "Thought I'd take it easy awhile," he said weakly, "but I guess—" He reached in and gripped something with both hands, then swung himself inside. His brown, uncertain face disappeared.

The big man blinked suddenly and stood up. "Well, *hey* there," he called, "what's a matter with this party anyway? Let's see some life, some action—" Faces were lighting up around him. People began to move in closer. "What I mean, let me hear that beat!"

The big man began clapping his hands rhythmically. The piano took it up. Other people began to clap. "What I mean, are we alive here or just waiting for the wagon to pick us up? How's that again, can't hear you!" A roar of pleasure as he cupped his hand to his ear. "Well come on, let me hear it!" A louder roar. Pete, Pete; a gabble of voices. "I got nothing against Harry," said the bald man earnestly in the middle of the noise, "I mean for a square he's a nice guy." "Know what you mean," said the pop-eyed man, "I mean like he doesn't *mean* it." "Sure," said the bald man, "but Jesus that sweaty undershirt and all . . ." The pop-eyed man shrugged. "What are you gonna do?" Then they burst out laughing as the big man made a comic face, tongue lolling, eyes crossed. Pete, Pete, Pete, the room was really jumping; it was a great party, and everything was all right, far into the night.

39
The Haters

DONALD A. WOLLHEIM

"You have to pay the price."

Council of Elders,
Village of Umbolo,
Twenty-five Miles Inland Along Third Rivulet Branching West Along River Congo Below Stanleyville,
Belgian Congo, Africa.

Reverend Sirs:

Inclosed you will find my check for one hundred dollars which you will be able to exchange at any branch bank in the nearest white center. This sum is, I understand, twice the amount you usually receive for a job of this sort. I have included extra because the distance of the field of operations may require extra energy on your part.

In exchange for this sum, you will hate to death the following person:

> Mr. Quentin W. Kelvin,
> 2574 King Charles Boulevard,
> Brooklyn, New York.

He is five feet, ten inches in height; hair, brown; eyes, brown; age, forty-six years and three months. I inclose a copy of his business letterhead, a sample of his handwriting, and a postage stamp he has licked.

I trust you can give me prompt service. For reasonable speed, I will be glad to donate an additional one hundred dollars to the Negro Aid Society of Harlem, or to any other charity, or organization, you may choose to name.

Yours very truly
EDWARD MANNIX

I read the letter twice, then handed it back to Mannix. "Are you nuts, Ed, or am I?"

He tried to throw another shot into his glass and missed. I grabbed the bottle, and put it out of his reach. "Not yet, sonny boy. Before you preserve your liver further, you tell me what this letter is all about."

"Ben," he croaked, "I am not a violent man, am I?"

"No!" I answered him.

"This person Kelvin has been my nemesis for years. We've been rivals ever since school days. I thought I'd done with him when graduation day came, but two years later, when I first met my wife, there he was again. And when I went into partnership with Jarvis, there was Kelvin managing a rival firm.

"Well, that's business. But after I took over, he began to get the edge. I do not particularly blame him because he thought of new angles before I did, because he managed to freeze me out over half of the time."

The waiter came by just then and wiped up the mess Mannix had made. Ed grabbed his arm. "Did you call the hospital?"

"Yes, sir. We have been making calls every fifteen minutes as you asked. And we gave them the message the first time; they understand."

"How . . . how is he?"

"The doctors say he is sinking fast, sir."

"Do they know what is wrong with him?"

"They are not sure."

Mannix turned to me with a we-are-lost-the-captain-shouted look. "There's nothing they can do."

I poured him a thimbleful. "Here, take it. And go on with the story."

He hunched over the glass. "Kelvin was better-looking than I. It was more or less of a surprise to me when Judy turned him down and married me instead. But he wasn't satisfied to let things stand. He's been constantly trying to turn her against me, playing up my failures and his own success. I think that is what finally made me decide to get him."

"So?"

"I had to do something. But I didn't know what. I knew, Ben, I could not get away with murder. Hate the sight of blood, and violence sickens me. Besides, I'm sure I'd give it all away no matter how airtight a defense I might be able to work out in advance. And I don't know any gangsters who might do the job for me.

"Then some time ago, I noticed a story in a Sunday supplement to the *Journal* about the witch doctors of Africa. It was more or less a general account of tribal magic, but one item in particular attracted me. It seems that one tribe there has made a study of hate. They have a method whereby men are trained from childhood in concentrating pure hate upon a single individual. So powerful was that concentration that the person selected would *rapidly fail in health and die.*"

The light began to break. "So you wrote this letter?"

"Yes. I checked up on it in the library and found that such a tribe does exist, and that the missionaries tell about people getting sick for apparently no reason at all and passing out. Permanently. Doctors have never been able to find any trace of disease in such cases, no traces of poison, injury, or deficiency in diet. The victim just begins to lose weight, to feel tired and ill, and finally to sink into a coma."

The light burst. "So that's why you're soaking in the

firewater. You're afraid it won't work after all? Or are you afraid of being a murderer in case it does?"

"I'm not afraid of being sent up for killing him, no. The laws of this State do not recognize witchcraft; this letter would not stand in any court. But I haven't told you the whole story, haven't told you why I'm afraid it *is* working.

"I'm broke, Ben. Kelvin cleaned me out a month ago.

"You know what that means? It means the check I sent to Africa is going to bounce. It'll take a couple of months before it does, because of the slowness of international banking. But when it does—"

The waiter was here again. "Mr. Mannix," he said, "the hospital just called; Mr. Kelvin died at 12:43."

"You see," groaned Mannix. "I was right. The Haters got him. What'll I do, Ben, when they find that check of mine is no good? What'll I do?"

40
The House

ANDRÉ MAUROIS

"The other side of dreaming."

"Two years ago," she said, "when I was so sick, I realized that I was dreaming the same dream night after night. I was walking in the country. In the distance, I could see a white house, low and long, that was surrounded by a grove of linden trees. To the left of the house, a meadow bordered by poplars pleasantly interrupted the symmetry of the scene, and the tips of the poplars, which you could see from far off, were swaying above the linden.

"In my dream, I was drawn to this house, and I walked toward it. A white wooden gate closed the entrance. I opened it and walked along a gracefully curving path. The path was lined by trees, and under the trees I found spring flowers—primroses and periwinkles and anemones that faded the moment I picked them. As I came to the end of this path, I was only a few steps from the house. In front of the house, there was a great green expanse, clipped like the English lawns. It was bare, except for a single bed of violet flowers encircling it.

"The house was built of white stone and it had a slate roof. The door—a light-oak door with carved panels—was at the top of a flight of steps. I wanted to visit the house, but no one answered when I called. I was terribly disappointed, and I rang and I shouted—and finally I woke up.

"That was my dream, and for months it kept coming back with such precision and fidelity that finally I thought: Surely I must have seen this park and this house as a child. When I would wake up, however, I could never recapture it in waking memory. The search for it became such an obsession that one summer—I'd learned to drive a little car—I decided to spend my vacation driving through France in search of my dream house.

"I'm not going to tell about my travels. I explored Normandy, Touraine, Poitou, and found nothing, which didn't surprise me. In October, I came back to Paris, and all through the winter I continued to dream about the white house. Last spring, I resumed my old habit of making excursions in the outskirts of Paris. One day, I was crossing a valley near L'Isle-Adam. Suddenly I felt an agreeable shock—that strange feeling one has when after a long absence one recognizes people or places one has loved.

"Although I had never been in that particular area before, I was perfectly familiar with the landscape lying to my right. The crests of some poplars dominated a stand of linden trees. Through the foliage, which was still sparse, I could glimpse a house. Then I knew that I had found my dream château. I was quite aware that a hundred yards ahead, a narrow road would be cutting across the highway. The road was there. I followed it. It led me to a white gate.

"There began the path I had so often followed. Under the trees, I admired the carpet of soft colors woven by the periwinkles, the primroses, and the anemones. When I came to the end of the row of linden, I saw the green lawn and the little flight of steps, at the top of which was the light-oak door. I got out of my car, ran quickly up the steps, and rang the bell.

"I was terribly afraid that no one would answer, but

almost immediately a servant appeared. It was a man, with a sad face, very old. He was wearing a black jacket. He seemed very much surprised to see me, and he looked at me closely without saying a word.

" 'I'm going to ask you a rather odd favor,' I said, 'I don't know the owners of this house, but I would be very happy if they would permit me to visit it.'

" 'The château is for rent, madame,' he said, with what struck me as regret, 'and I am here to show it.'

" 'To rent?' I said. 'What luck! It's too much to have hoped for. But how is it that the owners of such a beautiful house aren't living in it?'

" 'The owners did live in it, madame. They moved out when it became haunted.'

" 'Haunted?' I said. 'That will scarcely stop me. I didn't know people in France, even in the country, still believed in ghosts.'

" 'I wouldn't believe in them, madame,' he said seriously, 'if I myself had not met, in the park at night, the phantom that drove my employers away.'

" 'What a story!' I said, trying to smile.

" 'A story, madame,' the old man said, with an air of reproach, 'that you least of all should laugh at, since the phantom was you.' "

41
How Georges Duchamps Discovered a Plot to Take Over the World

ALEXEI PANSHIN

"It takes two to tango."

Georges was making love to Marie when he made his discovery. She was, in truth, a most piquant thing with black hair and black eyes and skin of pale ivory. But, it cannot be denied, she had a button in a most unusual place.

"What is this?" Georges said. "A button?"

"But of course," she said. "Continue to unbutton me."

"No, no," he said. "This button."

He touched it with a finger and she *chimed* gently.

"You are not human," he said.

She spread her hands, an enchanting effect. "But I feel human. Most decidedly."

"Nonetheless, it is apparent that you are not human. This is most strange. Is it, perhaps, a plot to take over the world?"

Marie shook her head. "I am sure I do not know."

Georges touched the button and she produced another bell-note, quiet, bright and clear. "Most strange. I wonder whom I should inform? If there is a plot to take over the world, someone should know.''

"But how could I be unaware?" Marie asked. "I am warm. I am French. I am loving. I am me."

"Nonetheless . . ." *Ding-g-g.* "It is incontrovertible."

Marie frowned. "Pardon," she said. "Turn again."
"Turn?"

"As you were. Yes." She stretched an inquiring finger, and touched. There was a deep and mellow sound like a pleasant doorbell.

"And what is this?" she asked.

"Mon Dieu!" he said in surprise. "Is that me?" He got up and went to look in the mirror, twisting somewhat uncomfortably, and sure enough, it was. He rang twice to make sure.

"In that case," he said, "it no longer seems important."

He kissed Marie and returned to the point of interruption. Skin of smooth pale beautiful ivory. I understand that if Georges receives the promotion he expects they are thinking of marriage in a year, or perhaps two.

42
The Human Angle

WILLIAM TENN

"Thank heaven for little girls."

What a road! What filthy, dismal, blinding rain! And, by the ghost of old Horace Greeley, what an idiotic, impossible assignment!

John Shellinger cursed the steamy windshield from which a monotonous wiper flipped raindrops. He stared through the dripping, half-clear triangle of glass and tried to guess which was broken country road and which was overgrown brown vegetation of autumn. He might have passed the slowly moving line of murderous men stretching to the right and left across country and road; he might have angled off into a side-road and be heading off into completely forsaken land. But he didn't think he had.

What an assignment!

"Get the human angle on this vampire hunt," Randall had ordered. "All the other news services are giving it the hill-billy twist, medieval superstition messing up the atomic world. What dumb jerks these dumb jerks are! You stay off that line. Find yourself a weepy individual slant on bloodsucking and sob me about three thousand words. And keep your expense account down—you just can't work a big swindle sheet out of that kind of agricultural slum."

So I saddles my convertible, Shellinger thought morosely, and I tools off to the pappy-mammy country where nobody speaks to strangers nohow "specially now, 'cause the vampire done got to three young 'uns already." And nobody will tell me the names of those three kids or whether any of them are still alive; and Randall's wires keep asking when I'll start sending usable copy; and I still can't find one loquacious Louise in the whole country. Wouldn't even have known of this cross-country hunt if I hadn't begun to wonder where all the men in town had disappeared to on such an unappetizing, rainy evening.

The road was bad in second, but it was impossible in almost any other gear. The ruts weren't doing the springs any good, either. Shellinger rubbed moisture off the glass with his handkerchief and wished he had another pair of headlights. He could hardly see.

That dark patch ahead, for instance. Might be one of the vampire posse. Might be some beast driven out of cover by the brush-beating. Might even be a little girl.

He ground into his brake. It was a girl. A little girl with dark hair and blue jeans. He twirled the crank and stuck his head out into the falling rain.

"Hey, kid. Want a lift?"

The child stooped slightly against the somber background of night and decaying, damp countryside. Her eyes scanned the car, came back to his face and considered it. The kid had probably not known that this chromium-plated kind of post-war auto existed. She'd certainly never dreamed of riding in one. It would give her a chance to crow over the other kids in the 'tater patch.

Evidently deciding that he wasn't the kind of stranger her mother had warned her about and that it would be less uncomfortable in the car than walking in the rain and mud, she nodded. Very slowly, she came around the front and climbed in at his right.

"Thanks, mister," she said.

Shellinger started again and took a quick, sidewise glance at the girl. Her blue jeans were raggedy and wet. She must be terribly cold and uncomfortable, but she wasn't going to let him know. She would bear up under it with the stoicism of the hill people.

But she was frightened. She sat hunched up, her hands folded neatly in her lap, at the far side of the seat right up against the door. What was the kid afraid of? Of course, the vampire!

"How far up do you go?" he asked her gently.

" 'Bout a mile and a half. But that way." She pointed over her shoulder with a pudgy thumb. She was plump, much more flesh on her than most of these scrawny, share-cropper kids. She'd be beautiful, too, some day, if some illiterate lummox didn't cart her off to matrimony and hard work in a drafty cabin.

Regretfully, he maneuvered around on the road, got the car turned and started back. He'd miss the hunters, but you couldn't drag an impressionable child into that sort of grim nonsense. He might as well take her home first. Besides, he wouldn't get anything out of those uncommunicative farmers with their sharpened stakes and silver bullets in their squirrel rifles.

"What kind of crops do your folks raise—tobacco or cotton?"

"They don't raise nothing yet. We just came here."

"Oh." That was right: she didn't have a mountain accent. Come to think of it, she was a little more dignified than most of the children he'd met in this neighborhood. "Isn't it a little late to go for a stroll? Aren't your folks afraid to let you out this late with a vampire around?"

She shivered. "I—I'm careful," she said at last.

Hey! Shellinger thought. Here was the human angle. Here was what Randall was bleating about. A frightened little girl with enough curiosity to swallow her big lump of fear and go out exploring on this night of all others. He didn't know how it fitted, just yet—but his journalistic nose was twitching. There was copy here; the basic, colorful human angle was sitting fearfully on his red leather seat.

"Do you know what a vampire is?"

She looked at him, startled, dropped her eyes and studied her folded hands for words "It's—it's like some-one who needs people instead of meals." A hesitant pause. "Isn't it?"

"Ye-es." That was good. Trust a child to give you a fresh viewpoint, unspoiled by textbook superstition. He'd use that— "People instead of meals." "A vampire is supposed to be a person who will be immortal—not die, that is—so long as he or she gets blood and life from living people. The only way you can kill a vampire—"

"You turn right here, mister."

He pointed the car into the little branchlet of side road. It was annoyingly narrow; surprised wet boughs tapped the windshield, ran their leaves lazily across the car's fabric top. Once in a while, a tree top sneezed collected rain water down.

Shellinger pressed his face close to the windshield and tried to decipher the picture of brown and mud amid weeds that his headlights gave him. "What a road! Your folks are really starting from scratch. Well, the only way to kill a vampire is with a silver bullet. Or you can drive a stake through the heart and bury it in a crossroads at midnight. That's what those men are going to do tonight if they catch it." He turned his head as he heard her gasp. "What's the matter—don't you like the idea?"

"I think it's horrid," she told him emphatically.

"Why? How do you feel—live and let live?"

She thought it over, nodded, smiled. "Yes. Live and let live. Live and let live. After all—" She was having difficulty finding the right words again. "After all, some people can't help what they are. I mean"—very slowly, very thoughtfully—"like if a person's a vampire, what can they do about it?"

"You've got a good point there, kid." He went back

to studying what there was of the road. "The only trouble's this: if you believe in things like vampires, well, you don't believe in them good—you believe in them nasty. Those people back in the village who claim three children have been killed or whatever it was by the vampire, they hate it and want to destroy it. If there are such things as vampires—mind you, I said 'if'—then, by nature, they do such horrible things that any way of getting rid of them is right. See?"

"No. You shouldn't drive stakes through people."

Shellinger laughed. "I'll say you shouldn't. Never could like that deal myself. However, if it were a matter of a vampire to me or mine, I think I could overcome my squeamishness long enough to do a little roustabout work on the stroke of twelve."

He paused and considered that this child was a little too intelligent for her environment. She didn't seem to be bollixed with superstitions as yet, and he was feeding her *Shellinger on Black Magic*. That was vicious. He continued soberly, "The difficulty with those beliefs is that a bunch of grown men who hold them are spread across the countryside tonight because they think a vampire is on the loose. And they're likely to flush some poor hobo and finish him off gruesomely for no other reason than that he can't give a satisfactory explanation for his presence in the fields on a night like this."

Silence. She was considering his statement. Shellinger liked her dignified, thoughtful attitude. She was a bit more at ease, he noticed, and was sitting closer to him. Funny how a kid could sense that you wouldn't do her any harm. Even a country kid. Especially a country kid, come to think of it, because they lived closer to nature or something.

He had won her confidence, though, and consequently rewon his. A week of living among thin-lipped ignoramuses who had been not at all diffident in showing *their* disdain had made him a little uncertain. This was better. And he'd finally gotten a line on the basis of a story.

Only, he'd have to dress it up. In the story, she'd be an ordinary hillbilly kid, much thinner, much more unapproachable; and the quotes would all be in 'mountain' dialect.

Yes, he had the human interest stuff now.

She had moved closer to him again, right against his side. Poor kid! His body warmth made the wet coldness of her jeans a little less uncomfortable. He wished he had a heater in the car.

The road disappeared entirely into tangled bushes and gnarly trees. He stopped the car, flipped the emergency back.

"You don't live here? This place looks as if nothing human's been around for years."

He was astonished at the uncultivated desolation.

"Sure I live here, mister," her warm voice said at his ear. "I live in that little house over there."

"Where?" He rubbed at the windshield and strained his vision over the sweep of headlights. "I don't see any house. Where is it?"

"There." A plump hand came up and waved at the night ahead. "Over there."

"I still can't see—" The corner of his right eye had casually noticed that the palm of her hand was covered with brown hair.

Strange, that.

Was covered with fine brown hair. Her palm!

"What *was* that you remembered about the shape of her teeth?" his mind shrieked. He started to whip his head around, to get another look at her teeth. But he couldn't.

Because her teeth were in his throat.

43
The Importance of Being Important

CALVIN W. DEMMON

"They also serve who only—"

Once upon a time there was a little boy who lived all by himself in the Big City. He lived in an apartment which looked down upon a Very Busy Street, and he had a television and a record player and there were blue curtains on his windows.

His name was Stanley Scheer, and he was about eight or nine.

Stanley Sheer believed himself to be the most important person in the world. He believed that everybody else in the whole world had been put there to help Stanley Scheer. And, worst of all, he thought they all *knew* about it. For Stanley Scheer thought that everything that happened to him was of great importance to everybody else, and that a whole lot of what happened to him had been planned by everyone else. He thought that all the world was a stage, and he was doing an important monologue under the direction of Them.

For example, Stanley Scheer firmly believed that if he really needed to do something, They would make provision for it. He believed that if he needed an elevator in a Hurry to take him down to the garage below They would make sure that one was waiting on his floor. He believed that if he wanted broccoli for lunch in the cafeteria downtown and there was only enough broccoli for one person left They would save it for him. And he believed that if he needed a parking place someone unimportant would get a Message or something from Them and pull out right in front of Stanley Scheer.

The fact that he didn't always get his elevator or his parking space or his broccoli seemed to *prove* to Stanley Scheer that They had some sort of Mysterious Plan for him. Because he was the most important man in the world They had to watch out for him, and make sure that he carried out his ultimate purpose. This Stanley Scheer was sure of, and this he believed. They had some sort of Ultimate Purpose in mind for him, and it was up to Them to make sure that nothing happened to him until he fulfilled it, because he was the Most Important Man in the World.

It got so that Stanley Scheer was devising little Tricks for them. He would get his bankbook down from the shelf and take his car downtown and walk toward the bank and then, instead of entering the bank, he would dart into the cafe next door to see if he could surprise Them before they had everybody bustling around again. He would suddenly turn right on his way to work instead of turning left, hoping to catch Them with their automobiles stopped and their streetlights turned off. He would jump up in the middle of a television program and spin to another channel to see what They were watching in the evening. He never caught Them at anything, but that didn't shake his faith in Them. "You can't see Radio Waves, either," he would say to himself.

One day Stanley Scheer got his bankbook down from the shelf, took the waiting elevator down to the garage, and drove to the bank. As he pulled into the crowded parking lot, a car pulled out of a parking place directly in front of him, leaving him a vacant space. It was the only vacant space on the lot. Stanley Scheer smiled, drove into the space, stopped his car, and got out. He walked into the bank, deposited his paycheck, walked back to the parking lot, entered his car, and started it up. Then he dropped it into reverse and spun out of the parking space barely missing a car which was waiting behind him. He mashed the accelerator to the floor and roared out of the parking lot, careening wildly around corners and rocketing down the street with smoke pouring from his exhaust pipe.

In the bank parking lot, the car which had been waiting behind Stanley Scheer pulled into the space. The Most Important Man in the World got out, shook his head, smiled sadly, and walked towards the bank.

Stanley Scheer, who was killed in a head-on collision on his way home, had fulfilled his Ultimate Purpose.

44
Interview with a Gentleman Farmer

BRUCE BOSTON

"What else would a gentleman farmer raise."

Mr. Dixon's farm occupies 130 acres of New Hampshire countryside, where streams abound and hillsides are lush. He first took up his profession nearly thirty years ago, after returning from World War II where he served in the Pacific under MacArthur and was thrice decorated. Today, many of his competitors consider him one of the finest breeders in the business.

I arrived at the Dixon farmhouse, a salmon pink ranch-style, early in the afternoon. Mrs. Dixon, a plumpish, merry-faced woman, met me at the door, wiping soapy hands upon her apron. She informed me that her husband was "out back aworkin'." As she led me through the living room and kitchen, which were modestly, even severely, furnished, I asked her a number of questions without success.

"I really can't tell you a thing," she pleaded, "I leave all the gentlemen to my husband."

To the rear of the house there were several other buildings, including an immense barn, bright red and criss-crossed by strips of white planking. Beyond the gently rolling fields, green hills rose up on every side. In the midst of this picture-postcard setting, Mr. Dixon emerged from an open doorway, wrestling with a large bale of chicken wire. As we approached, he took off his hat, a simple blue baseball cap, and with one forearm wiped the sweat from his brow. He was a tall, large-boned man with narrow eyes. His salt-and-pepper hair, barely receding, was crewed closely to the skull.

We exchanged greetings. Since he had "a good deal o'work to do," he suggested we get right down to the interview. "Might as well stretch our legs a bit while we're at it," he added. Screwing his cap back on he took off at a brisk pace. I fumbled with pad and pencil from my coat pocket and went after him. Mrs. Dixon, seemingly unnoticed by her husband, turned back to the house.

"What impact have recent economic trends had on your work?" I began.

"They're no skin off my nose," Mr. Dixon informed me. "If you're a gentleman farmer you never have to worry." He nodded curtly. "There'll always be a demand for good gentlemen."

I saw a small herd of gentlemen, perhaps twenty, grouped at the far end of the field we were passing. I noticed that they were all naked.

"A true gentleman is always a gentleman whether he has any clothes on or not," Mr. Dixon explained. "I remember a few years back, one of them larger concerns . . . the combines, we call them . . . brought in some Australian stock. Tried to flood the market, drive the price down so they could force fellas like me out of business." Mr. Dixon stopped abruptly and turned to face me. His eyes narrowed still further, glinting silvery in the afternoon sun; then he broke into rickety laughter and slapped his knee. "They dressed 'em up in silk suits, cravats, fancy boots, the whole shebang! Then they had a show over in Portsmouth of all places. Made complete fools of themselves, that's what they did. Some gentlemen! Why those damn Aussies didn't even know which

fork to use on their salads.'' He laughed again, dabbing
tears from his eyes with a checkered bandanna.

I asked if I might take a closer look at some of the
herd, and Mr. Dixon proceeded to instruct me in the
proper method of summoning gentlemen. Taking out his
wallet, he removed several bills and began rubbing them
between thumb and forefinger. ''Money,'' he called, his
voice rising yodel-like on the second syllable, ''Mon-ey!
Mon-ey! Mon-ey!''

The gentlemen came bounding across the field in
groups of twos and threes to gather on the opposite side
of the fence. Mr. Dixon dug into his pocket and came up
with a handful of coins, which he tossed into their midst.
As the gentlemen scrambled for them, he pointed out his
fields to me. ''Pure dichondra,'' he said, ''I raise all of
my gentlemen on beefsteak and dichondra. When people
complain to me about the price of gentlemen, I say 'Look
at the price of beefsteak. Look at the price of dichondra.'
One thing you can be sure of. When you deals with me,
you gets what you pay for.''

By this time the gentlemen had settled down and were
eyeing us expectantly. They were all young bucks and
looked like a healthy lot, but I also noticed that they were
quite pale. I asked Mr. Dixon about this.

''Pure Anglo stock,'' he beamed. ''No wops or spics
for me. I can only afford to let them out for a couple of
hours each day. A true gentleman will always burn before he tans.''

Mr. Dixon then proceeded to engage his gentlemen in
conversation. In the space of a few minutes they covered
a wide variety of subjects. Not only salad forks, but entering and exiting elevators, the fine points of hat tipping,
tracking lions at the Bronx Zoo, and tea bags versus mustache cups as methods of imitating the Queen. Mr. Dixon
was right about one thing. The carriage, manner, and
enunciation of his stock were so uniformly flawless that I
soon forgot they were without clothes.

Mr. Dixon glanced at his watch and quickly called the

conversation to a halt. He took me by the arm and began
guiding me back in the direction we had come. "I imagine you'll want a look at one of the breeding pens before
you go," he said. I had hoped for a much longer interview, but I could see that I was confronting a man truly
committed to his work—in his own way, perhaps something of an artist—and I felt thankful for the time which I
had been allotted. Mr. Dixon's gentlemen followed us
along the fence line until they reached the perimeter of
their enclosure.

"Good day, sirs," they called out in a ragged, yet
hardy and melodious chorus.

With amazing agility for a man of his age, Mr. Dixon
clambered up the side of a concrete bunker, painted the
same bright cherry red as the barn. He reached down a
hand and hoisted me up next to him. We walked across
the roof to a wooden trapdoor. First sliding a bolt, Mr.
Dixon lifted the door by means of an iron ring embedded
in its surface. It fell back heavily against the roof.

A shaft of sunlight shot into the depths of the pit below
us. I glimpsed a confused tangle of white limbs, shoulders, patches of hair, before they shifted quickly back
away from the light into darkness, leaving only a small
rectangle of straw-strewn dirt. The sounds of grunting,
gasping, and cooing issued forth from within. I leaned
back away from the opening and gulped fresh air. Mr.
Dixon shook his head.

"Although a gentleman is the cleanest of all God's
creatures," he proclaimed, "he likes his sex dirty. Lots
of gentlemen farmers don't seem to understand that, and
that's why they fail. You have to have a stomach for
work like mine." He crinkled his nose as he leaned forward and let the trap door fall shut. "But even I can't take
that for very long."

Mr. Dixon accompanied me to my car. As I thanked
him for the interview, he placed a hand on my shoulder.

"My pleasure, young man, my pleasure." His hand

slipped lower, kneading the bicep. "You're a sturdy fellow, aren't you?" He eyed me speculatively. "You know, it's never too late to think about becoming a gentleman. What did you say your ancestry was?"

I assured him that my mother was a full-blooded Magyar Jewess, slammed the car door on his fingers, and as he hopped off across the fields yelling, hastily made good my departure.

45
Judgment Day

JACK C. HALDEMAN II

"Actually, we'd stand a better chance in that situation."

They were coming.

I woke up knowing that, just as I knew they wouldn't take me. There are many things in my life I am ashamed of. They might take Laura, though. She's the one truly good person I know. I nudged her awake.

"I had the strangest dream," she said, sleepily, brushing the hair from her face.

"I know," I said. "I had it too."

She looked at me with that half-awake way that she has. I could tell she understood.

"They won't take me either," she said. There was sadness in her voice.

"They might. You've never hurt anyone in your life. You're a kind and good person."

She shook her head. "I'm not good enough," she said. "Not for them."

It was true and we both knew it in our hearts. They wanted perfection, nothing less.

Laura shivered and I held her close. The bedroom was dark and we shared a secret the whole world knew. I listened to the clock tick. There wasn't much to say. We stayed that way all morning and I didn't go to work.

Everything stopped that day. No wars, no work, no play; it wasn't a day for that. Men and women around the world looked to the stars and into their hearts. They saw the darkness, the shortcomings. Each in their own way grieved for what man had become. It had come to this; all the promise, all the hopes. There was nothing to do but wait. They were coming.

The dream had a billion voices and it touched us all. The powerful and the poor got the same message. When night had passed we all understood. They wanted the best.

It was fair, no one could dispute that. They weren't interested in the ones who held power, or the wisest, or the richest people in the world. They wanted the best that Earth had to offer. Nothing less would do. In the night they touched our minds they had also made their decision. There was nothing to do but wait for them to come and see who they had chosen.

It wouldn't be the smoothest talker who would speak for Earth. The wisest men wouldn't plead our case before the collective minds of a thousand planets. They weren't interested in words or great deeds, what they wanted was kindness and compassion and I wondered where they'd find it.

They were giving us the best chance that Earth could have. There would be no deceit, no lies, no misunderstandings. They would take two—they had chosen two—and they would speak for Earth. There would be no others, there would be no second chance. We waited and wondered.

Everything stood still. Even the pulpits were quiet. What we had seen that night had made us look deep into our souls and we all fell short. We looked at what we could have been and measured it against what we had become. It was a dark pain and we all felt it. Then they came.

They came in a silver ship and said nothing. There was nothing to say, they had said it all that night. Silently they went to those they had chosen and then they left.

They took to the stars two dolphins, a mated pair.

We are waiting for their decision.

46
Just One More

EDWARD D. HOCH

"Maybe that explains Rin Tin Tin and Lassie."

Once he had the lights just right, Art Mueller checked the
art director's layout one last time. Then he moved
quickly with the small motorized camera, snapping pictures with the speed and efficiency of a top fashion photographer.

"That's it! Look this way, look this way! One more,
one more!"

Mueller always talked while he worked, even though
his subjects rarely paid attention. He'd convinced himself long ago that the sound of his voice was soothing to
his models. Whether or not that was true, his constant
motion and talking never failed to impress the visiting art
directors who paid their bills.

"Think you've got enough?" Jeanne asked. She
was his assistant, handling everything from account-
ing to darkroom chores. Occasionally she slept with
Mueller too, but he didn't consider that one of her office duties.

"Maybe just one more. I'd like to move that dish a
little to the left."

"That's not the way the layout is," she told him.

"I know, I know." He turned to a gray-haired man

standing behind the lights. "Felix, get the mutt's nose out of the dish for a minute, will you?"

Felix Trenton stepped forward, unsmiling. "I'd hardly call the highest-paid dog in the country a mutt, Art. Rainbow probably makes as much in a year as you do."

"But you keep the cash and he gets the dog biscuits—right, Felix?"

"What's wrong with that? I taught him everything he knows." He pulled Rainbow back from the dish of Frisky-Pups while Mueller bent to move it.

"Yeah, Felix. You're starting to look a little like him, you know? A bit long in the tooth."

The agency's art director, a tight little man named Jenkins, hurried over. "What's all this? Why are you moving the dish?"

"Get more light on the food. Make it look better."

"That's not the way my layout shows it."

"Let's give it a try."

"They bought the ad from my layout, you know."

"Sure, sure." Mueller glanced over at Jeanne. "Get me another roll of film, will you?"

She opened the refrigerator door and took out a box, opening it as she brought it to him. He snapped it into the camera and closed the back. But the pause had made Rainbow restless and Trenton was having trouble with him. Mueller put down the camera. "Let me do it, Felix. I've got a way with animals."

The older man snorted and stepped aside. He was one of the best trainers around, but Mueller never credited him with much knowledge of what went on inside an animal's head.

"Settle down, boy! Settle down now! Just one more. I'm only going to take one more and then you can forget this crap and have some real bones. You'd like that, wouldn't you, boy?" He nuzzled the big furry dog for a moment and then released him, going back to his camera.

As he was about to start shooting he heard the bell on the studio door tinkle. "Damn! See who that is, will you,

Jeanne?'' Then he bent to his task. ''All right, boy! Look this way! One more! That's it, that's it! One more!''

The art director sighed with relief when he'd finished. ''Is that it, Art?''

''That's it. I'll have a sheet of contact prints for you in the morning.''

He unloaded the camera and placed the exposed film in Jeanne's darkroom tray for developing. Then he went out to see who their visitor was.

''Art, this gentleman wants to hire you if you're available.''

Mueller looked the man over. He was middle-aged, with a neatly trimmed beard and piercing eyes. Jeanne handed over a card that announced him as Professor John Hasty. Mueller tapped the card and said, ''I'm an animal photographer, you understand. Mainly commercial work for ad agencies and such.''

''I know you're an animal photographer,'' Professor Hasty said. ''That's why I've come to you.''

''What sort of animal would you like me to photograph?''

The bearded man hesitated and then said, ''A werewolf.''

''Oh, come on now!''

''I'm quite serious.''

Mueller turned back to Jeanne. ''Help them pack up their dog food, will you? I'll speak to the Professor in my office.'' He led the way into the cork-lined room where he could be surrounded by blow-ups of dogs and cats and horses. Behind his desk, over his chair, there was even his favorite picture of an elephant standing on the roof of a little imported car.

''Very impressive,'' Hasty said. ''Your reputation is well deserved.''

''Not a werewolf among them, you'll notice.''

''I wouldn't be too sure about that, Mr. Mueller.''

''Oh?''

''That's exactly why I've come to you. I've devoted

most of my adult life to a study of lycanthropy in all its guises. I can tell you that werewolves *do* exist!''

"I'm sure," Mueller responded, already growing bored with the bearded man.

"But they have not been fully understood until now. Humans are not the only species capable of transforming themselves into wolves. I believe that certain forms of coyote, hyena and the like also have the power.''

"Probably any animal with a *y* in its name," Mueller muttered.

"What?"

"Nothing. Go on."

"I also believe that the physical changes brought about during metamorphosis may be visible in their early stages—visible to the camera, if not to the naked eye."

"Look," Mueller interrupted. "I've given enough of my time. Exactly what do you want me to do?"

"Please be patient. I can sense you're skeptical."

"You might say that."

"Animals are instinctive creatures—far more so than humans. When I'm near a creature capable of changing into a werewolf, the metamorphosis often begins in its early stages before the animal can control it. The teeth grow longer, the ears more pointed. The process is usually arrested before becoming noticeable, but a skilled photographer could capture it on film. I'd like to begin out at the Bronx Zoo, visiting the cages while you snap away."

"You don't need me for this. Take along an Instamatic or a Polaroid and do it yourself."

"I've tried that," Professor Hasty insisted. "The pictures aren't sharp enough, or close enough. I need a professional photographer using a telephoto lens to get me a closeup of the animal's head."

"Sorry, I'm not your man."

"I have research funds available—"

"Sorry."

"Will you at least think about it?" He seemed to be almost pleading. "Could you phone me tomorrow?"

"You can phone me if you want, but I doubt if I'll change my mind."

"Think about it. That's all I ask. One photograph—the right photograph—could make us both famous."

Mueller saw him to the door. "If they can sense you're after them, you'd better watch your step, Professor."

"I have been. I never leave the house unarmed."

Mueller closed the door behind his visitor and shook his head. One never knew what was coming next. He walked back into the studio and saw that the agency people were gone. Felix Trenton had the leash on Rainbow and was leading him out. He smiled when he saw Mueller.

"Did I hear that man say he wanted you to photograph werewolves?"

"You heard right. Damned crazy world."

"You get them all." Trenton tugged on Rainbow's leash. "Shake hands with Art and thank him like a good dog."

Mueller smiled as he accepted Rainbow's paw and arf. "Good boy. Give him an extra bone tonight, Felix, from your bank account."

After they'd gone, Mueller went in search of Jeanne. She was just coming out of the darkroom. "Can you make the contact prints tonight, Art? I've got a heavy date."

"Someone besides me?"

"Are you kidding? This is a guy who doesn't want to take pictures of me in bed."

He swatted her rear. "Go on. I'll finish up here."

When he was alone, he switched the telephone to the answering machine and went into the darkroom. Before long he'd printed two sheets of the contacts and they looked good. That damned dog was a real star!

He was especially interested in the last set of pictures, using the camera angle he'd devised, with the food dish up front. The Frisky-Pups looked better, all right, but for some reason Rainbow wasn't quite so photogenic.

He put them under his magnifier to look closer.

Odd.

Why did his teeth look longer in those final pictures? And his ears—

Then he remembered what had happened while he was shooting those last photos. Professor Hasty had entered the studio.

It wasn't possible, was it?

Was it?

He heard the tinkle of the bell again and knew that someone had entered the studio. "Who is it?" he called out from the darkroom door. When no one answered he sighed and started out to the office.

That was when he saw Rainbow.

Rainbow, the highest-paid dog in America.

Rainbow, who could turn a doorknob with his teeth.

But he was different now—larger, uglier.

Mueller felt his heart thudding as he made for the extra camera on his filing cabinet. If he could get a picture of this—

"Down boy! Down! One more picture! Just one more!"

His fingers reached the camera in the same instant that Rainbow's jaws reached his throat.

47
The Lady and the Merman

JANE YOLEN

"Wheresoever love goes, the lover follows."

Once in a house overlooking the cold northern sea a baby was born. She was so plain, her father, a sea captain, remarked on it.

"She shall be a burden," he said. "She shall be on our hands forever." Then without another glance at the child he sailed off on his great ship.

His wife, who had longed to please him, was so hurt by his complaint that she soon died of it. Between one voyage and the next, she was gone.

When the captain came home and found this out, he was so enraged, he never spoke of his wife again. In this way he convinced himself that her loss was nothing.

But the girl lived and grew as if to spite her father. She looked little like her dead mother but instead had the captain's face set round with mouse-brown curls. Yet as plain as her face was, her heart was not. She loved her father but was not loved in return.

And still the captain remarked on her looks. He said at every meeting, "God must have wanted me cursed to give me such a child. No one will have her. She shall never be wed. She shall be with me forever." So he called her Borne, for she was his burden.

Borne grew into a lady and only once gave a sign of this hurt.

"Father," she said one day when he was newly returned from the sea, "what can I do to heal this wound between us?"

He looked away from her, for he could not bear to see his own face mocked in hers, and spoke to the cold stone floor. "There is nothing between us, daughter," he said. "But if there were, I would say *Salt for such wounds.*"

"Salt?" Borne asked.

"A sailor's balm," he said. "The salt of tears or the salt of sweat or the final salt of the sea." Then he turned from her and was gone next day to the farthest port he knew of, and in this way he cleansed his heart.

After this, Borne never spoke of it again. Instead, she carried it silently like a dagger inside. For the salt of tears did not salve her, and so she turned instead to work. She baked bread in her ovens for the poor, she nursed the sick, she held the hands of the sea widows. But always, late in the evening, she walked on the shore looking and longing for a sight of her father's sail. Only less and less often did he return from the sea.

One evening, tired from the work of the day, Borne felt faint as she walked on the strand. Finding a rock half in and half out of the water, she climbed upon it to rest. She spread her skirts about her, and in the dusk they lay like great gray waves.

How long she sat there, still as the rock, she did not know. But a strange pale moon came up. And as it rose, so too rose the little creatures of the deep. They leaped free for a moment of the pull of the tide. And last of all, up from the deeps, came the merman.

He rose out of the crest of the wave, seafoam crowning his green-black hair. His hands were raised high above him, and the webbings of his fingers were as colorless as air. In the moonlight he seemed to stand upon his tail. Then, with a lick of it, he was gone, gone back to the deeps. He thought no one had remarked his dive.

But Borne had. So silent and still, she saw it all, his beauty and his power. She saw him and loved him, though she loved the fish half of him more. It was all she could dare.

She could not tell what she felt to a soul, for she had no one who cared. Instead she forsook her work and walked by the sea both morning and night. Yet, strange to say, she never once looked for her father's sail.

That is why one day her father returned without her knowing. He watched her pacing the shore for a long while through slotted eyes, for he would not look straight upon her. At last he said, "Be done with it. Whatever ails you, give it over." For even he could see this wound.

Borne looked up at him, her eyes shimmering with small seas. Grateful for his attention, she answered, "Yes, Father, you are right. I must be done with it."

The captain turned and left her then, for his food was cold. But Borne went directly to the place where the waves were creeping onto the shore. She called out in a low voice, "Come up. Come up and be my love."

There was no answer except the shrieking laughter of the birds as they dived into the sea.

So she took a stick and wrote the same words upon the sand for the merman to see should he ever return. Only, as she watched, the creeping tide erased her words one by one. Soon there was nothing left of her cry on that shining strand.

So Borne sat herself down on the rock to cry. And each tear was an ocean.

But the words were not lost. Each syllable washed from the beach was carried below, down, down, down to the deeps of the cool, inviting sea. And there, below on his coral bed, the merman saw her call and came.

He was all day swimming up to her. He was half the night seeking that particular strand. But when he came, cresting the currents, he surfaced with a mighty splash below Borne's rock.

The moon shone down on the two, she a grave shadow perched upon a stone and he all motion and light.

Borne reached down her white hands and he caught them in his. It was the only touch she could remember. She smiled to see the webs stretched taut between his fingers. He laughed to see hers webless, thin, and small. One great pull between them and he was up by her side. Even in the dark she could see his eyes on her under the phosphoresence of his hair.

He sat all night by her. And Borne loved the man of him as well as the fish, then, for in the silent night it was all one.

Then, before the sun could rise, she dropped his hands on his chest. "Can you love me?" she dared to ask at last.

But the merman had no tongue to tell her above the waves. He could only speak below the water with his hands, a soft murmuration. So, wordlessly, he stared into her eyes and pointed to the sea.

Then, with the sun just rising beyond the rim of the world, he turned, dived arrow slim into a wave, and was gone.

Gathering her skirts, now heavy with ocean spray and tears, Borne stood up. She cast but one glance at the shore and her father's house beyond. Then she dived after the merman into the sea.

The sea put bubble jewels in her hair and spread her skirts about her like a scallop shell. Tiny colored fish swam in between her fingers. The water cast her face in silver, and all the sea was reflected in her eyes.

She was beautiful for the first time. And for the last.

48
The Last Unicorns

EDWARD D. HOCH

*"And griffins, and cockatrices, and
rocs, and—"*

The rain was still falling by the time he reached the little
wooden shack that stood in the center of the green, fertile
valley. He opened his cloak for an instant to knock at the
door, not really expecting a reply.

But it opened, pulled over the roughness of the rock
floor by great hairy hands. "Come in," a voice commanded him. "Hurry! Before this rain floods me out."

"Thank you," the traveler said, removing the soggy
garment that covered him and squeezing out some of the
water. "It's good to find a dry place. I've come a long
way."

"Not many people are about in this weather," the man
told him, pulling at his beard with a quick, nervous gesture.

"I came looking for you."

"For me? What is your name?"

"You can call me Shem. I come from beyond the
mountains."

The bearded man grunted. "I don't know the name.
What do you seek?"

Shem sat down to rest himself on a pale stone seat. "I

hear talk that you have two fine unicorns here, recently brought from Africa.''

The man smiled proudly. ''That is correct. The only such creatures in this part of the world. I intend to breed them and sell them to the farmers as beasts of burden.''

''Oh?''

''They can do the work of strong horses and at the same time use their horns to defend themselves against attack.''

''True,'' Shem agreed. ''Very true. I . . . I don't suppose you'd want to part with them . . . ?''

''Part with them! Are you mad, man? It cost me money to bring them all the way from Africa!''

''How much would you like for them?''

The bearded man rose from his seat. ''No amount, ever! Come back in two years when I've bred some. Until then, begone with you!''

''I *must* have them, sir.''

''You *must* have nothing! Begone from here now before I take a club to you!'' And with those words he took a menacing step forward.

Shem retreated out the door, back into the rain, skipping lightly over a rushing stream of water from the higher ground. The door closed on him, and he was alone. But he looked out into the fields, where a small barnlike structure stood glistening in the downpour.

They would be in there, he knew.

He made his way across the field, sometimes sinking to his ankles in puddles of muddy water. But finally he reached the outbuilding and went in through a worn, rotten door.

Yes, they were there . . . Two tall and handsome beasts, very much like horses, but with longer tails and with that gleaming, twisted horn shooting straight up from the center of their foreheads. Unicorns—one of the rarest of God's creatures!

* * *

He moved a bit closer, trying now to lure them out of the building without startling them. But there was a noise, and he turned suddenly to see the bearded man standing there, a long staff upraised in his hands.

"You try to steal them," he shouted, lunging forward.

The staff thudded against the wall, inches from Shem's head. "Listen, old man . . ."

"Die! Die, you robber!"

But Shem leaped to one side, around the bearded figure of wrath, and through the open doorway. Behind him, the unicorns gave a fearful snort and trampled the earthen floor with their hoofs.

Shem kept running, away from the shack, away from the man with the staff, away from the fertile valley.

After several hours of plodding over the rain-swept hills, he came at last upon his father's village, and he went down among the houses to the place where the handful of people had gathered.

And he saw his father standing near the base of the great wooden vessel, and he went up to him sadly.

"Yes, my son?" the old man questioned, unrolling a long damp scroll of parchment.

"No unicorns, Father."

"No unicorns," Noah repeated sadly, scratching out the name on his list. "It is too bad. They were handsome beasts . . ."

49
The Last Wizard

AVRAM DAVIDSON

"Sometimes you get more in the answer than the question holds."

For the hundredth time Bilgulis looked with despair at the paper and pencil in front of him. Then he gave a short nod, got up, left his little room, and went two houses up the street, up the stairs, and knocked on a door.

Presently the door opened and high up on the face which looked out at him were a pair of very pale gray-green eyes, otherwise bloodshot and bulging.

Bilgulis said, "I want you to teach me how to spell. I pay you."

The eyes blinked rapidly, the face retreated, the door opened wider, Bilgulis entered, and the door closed. The man said, "So you know, eh? How did you know?"

"I see you through window, Professor," Bilgulis said. "All the time you read great big books."

" 'Professor,' yes, they call me that. None of them know. Only you have guessed. After all this time. I, the greatest of the adepts, the last of the wizards—and now you shall be my adept. A tradition four thousand, three hundred and sixty-one years old would have died with me. But now it will not. Sit there. Take reed pen, papyrus, cuttlefish ink, spit three times in bottle."

Laboriously Bilgulis complied. The room was small, crowded, and contained may odd things, including smells. "We will commence, of course," the Professor said, "with some simple spells. To turn a usurer into a green fungus: *Dippa dabba ruthu thuthu*—write, write!—*enlis thu*. You have written? So. And to obtain the love of the most beautiful woman in the world: *Coney honey antimony funny cunny crux*. Those two will do for now. Return tomorrow at the same hour. Go."

Bilgulis left. Waiting beside his door was a man with a thick briefcase and a thin smile. "Mr. Bilgulis, I am from the Friendly Finance Company and in regard to the payment which you—"

"Dippa dabba ruthu thuthu enlis thu," said Bilgulis. The man turned into a green fungus which settled in a hall corner and was slowly eaten by the roaches. Bilgulis sat down at his table, looked at the paper and pencil, and gave a deep sigh.

"Too much time this take," he muttered. "Why I no wash socks, clean toilet, make big pot cheap beans with pig's tail for eat? No," he said determinedly and once more bent over the paper and pencil.

By and by there was a knock on his door. Answering it he saw before him the most beautiful woman in the world. "I followed you," she said. "I don't know what's happening . . ."

"Coney honey antimony," said Bilgulis, *"funny cunny crux."*

She sank to her knees and embraced his legs. "I love you. I'll do anything you want."

Bilgulis nodded. "Wash socks, clean toilet," he said. "And cook big pot cheap beans with pig's tail for eat." He heard domestic sounds begin as he seated himself at the table and slowly, gently beat his head. After a moment he rose and left the house again.

Up the street a small crowd was dispersing and among the people he recognized his friend, Labbonna. "Listen, Labbonna," he said.

Labbonna peered at him through dirty, mended eye-glasses. "You see excitement?" he asked, eager to tell. "I no see."

Labbonna drew himself up and gestured. "You know Professor live there? He just now go crazy," he said, rolling his eyes and dribbling and flapping his arms in vivid imitation. "Call ambulance but he drop down dead. Too bad, hey?"

"Too bad." Bilgulis sighed.

"Read too much big book."

Bilgulis cleared his throat, looking embarrassed. "Listen, Labbonna—"

"What you want?"

"How long you in country?"

"Torty year."

"You speak good English."

"Citizen."

Bilgulis nodded. He drew a pencil and piece of paper from his pocket. "Listen, Labbonna. Do me big help. How you make spell in English, *Please send me your free offer?* One 'f' or two?"

50
Letters from Camp

AL SARRANTONIO

"Fulfilling a vital need."

Dear Mom and Dad,
   I still don't know why you made me come to this dump
for the summer. It looks like all the other summer camps
I've been to, even if it is "super modern and computer-
ized," and I don't see why I couldn't go back to the one I
went to last year instead of this new one. I had a lot of fun
last summer, even if you did have to pay for all that stuff
I smashed up and even if I did make the head counselor
break his leg.
   The head counselor here is a jerk, just like the other
one was. As soon as we got off the hovercraft that
brought us here, we had to go to the Big Tent for a "pep
talk." They made us sit through a slide show about all
the things we're going to do (yawn), and that wouldn't
have been so bad except the head counselor, who's a
robot, kept scratching his metal head through the whole
thing. I haven't made any friends, and the place looks
like it's full of jerks. Tonight we didn't have any hot
water and the TV in my tent didn't work.
   Phooey on Camp Ultima. Can't you still get me back
in the other place?

* * *

Dear Mom and Dad,

Maybe this place isn't so bad after all. They just about let us do whatever we want, and the kids are pretty wild. Today they split us up into "Pow-wow Groups," but there aren't really any rules or anything, and my group looks like it might be a good one. One of the guys in it looks like he might be okay. His name's Ramon, and he's from Brazil. He told me a lot of neat stories about things he did at home, setting houses on fire and things like that. We spent all day today hiding from our stupid robot counselor. He thought for sure we had run away, and nearly blew a circuit until we finally showed up just in time for dinner.

The food stinks, but they did have some animal type thing that we got to roast over a fire, and that tasted pretty good.

Tomorrow we go on our first field trip.

Dear Mom and Dad,

We had a pretty good time today, all things considered. We got up at six o'clock to go on our first hike, and everybody was pretty excited. There's a lot of wild places here, and they've got it set up to look just like a prehistoric swamp. One kid said we'd probably see a Tyrannosaurus Rex, but nobody believed him. The robot counselors kept us all together as we set out through the marsh, and we saw a lot of neat things like vines dripping green goop and all kinds of frogs and toads. Me and Ramon started pulling the legs off frogs, but our counselor made us stop and anyway the frogs were all robots. We walked for about two hours and stopped for lunch. Then we marched back again.

The only weird thing that happened was that when we got back and the counselors counted heads, they found that one kid was missing. They went out to look for him but couldn't find anything, and the only thing they think might have happened is he got lost in the bog somewhere. One kid said he thought he saw a Tyrannosaurus

Rex, but it was the same kid who'd been talking about
them before so nobody listened to him. The head counselor went around patting everybody on the shoulder,
telling us not to worry since something always happens to
one kid every year. But they haven't found him yet.

Tonight we had a big food fight, and nobody even
made us clean the place up.

Dear Mom and Dad,

Today we went out on another field trip, and another
stupid kid got himself lost. They still haven't found the
first one, and some of the kids are talking about Tyrannosaurus Rex again. But this time we went hill climbing and
I think the dope must have fallen off a cliff, because the
hills are almost like small mountains and there are a lot of
ledges on them.

After dinner tonight, which almost nobody ate because
nobody felt like it, we sat around the campfire and told
ghost stories. Somebody said they thought a lot of kids
were going to disappear from here, and that made everybody laugh, in a scary kind of way. I was a little scared
myself. It must have been the creepy shadows around the
fire. The robot counselors keep telling everyone not to
worry, but some of the kids—the ones who can't take it—
are starting to say they want to go home.

I don't want to go home, though; this place is fun.

Dear Mom and Dad,

Today we went on another trip, to the far side of the
island where they have a lake, and we had a good time
and all (we threw one of the robot counselors into the
lake but he didn't sink), but when we got off the boat
and everybody counted we found out that eight kids
were gone. One kid said he even saw Harvey get
grabbed by something ropy and black and pulled over
the side. I'm almost ready to believe him. I don't know
if I like this place so much any more. One more field

trip like the one today and I think I'll want to come home.

It's not even fun wrecking stuff around here any more.

Dear Mom and Dad,

Come and get me right away, I'm *scared*. Today the robot counselors tried to make us go on another day trip, but nobody wanted to go, so we stayed around the tents. But at the chow meeting tonight only twelve kids showed up. That means twenty more kids disappeared today. Nobody has any idea what happened to them, though I do know that a whole bunch of guys were playing outside the perimeter of the camp, tearing things down, so that might have had something to do with it. At this point I don't care.

Just get me out of here!

Mom and Dad,

I think I'm the only kid left, and I don't know if I can hide much longer. The head counselor tricked us into leaving the camp today, saying that somebody had seen a Tyrannousaurus Rex. He told us all to run through the rain forest at the north end of the camp, but when we ran into it, something horrible happened. I was with about five other kids, and as soon as we ran into the forest we heard a high-pitched screeching and a swishing sound and the trees above us started to lower their branches. I saw four kids I was with get covered by green plastic-looking leaves, and then there was a gulping sound and the branches lifted and separated and there was nothing there. Ramon and I just managed to dodge out of the way, and we ran through the forest in between the trees and out the other side. We would have been safe for a while but just then the robot counselors broke through the forest behind us, leading a Tyrannosaurus Rex. We ran, but Ramon slipped and fell and the Tyrannosaurus Rex was suddenly there, looming over him with its dripping jaws and rows of sharp white teeth. Ramon took out his box of matches but the dinosaur was on him then and I didn't wait to see any more.

I ran all the way back to the postal computer terminal in the camp to get this letter out to you. Call the police! Call the army! I can't hide forever, and I'm afraid that any second the Tyrannosaurus Rex will break in here and

Dear Mr. and Mrs. Jameson:

Camp Ultima is glad to inform you of the successful completion of your son's stay here, and we are therefore billing you for the balance of your payment at this time.

Camp Ultima is proud of its record of service to parents of difficult boys, and will strive in the future to continue to provide the very best camp facilities.

May we take this opportunity to inform you that, due to the success of our first camp, we are planning to open a new facility for girls next summer.

We hope we might be of service to you in the future.

51
L is for Loup-Garou

HARLAN ELLISON

"Blame the wise guys at the treasury."

Had Šaša Nováček's parents come to America from Ireland or Sweden or even Poland, he would not have realized that the woman next door was a werewolf. But they had come from Ostrava, in Czechoslovakia, and he recognized the shape of the nostrils, the hair in the palms of her hands when she loaned him a cup of non-dairy creamer, the definitive S-curve of the spine as she walked to hang her laundry. So he was ready. He had bought a thirty-ought-six hunting rifle and he had melted down enough twenty-five-cent pieces to make his own silver bullets. And on the night of the full moon, when the madness was upon her, and she burst through the kitchen window in a snarling strike of fangs and fur, he was ready for her. Calmly, with full presence, and murmuring the names of the very best saints, he emptied the rifle into her. Later, the coroner was unable to describe the condition of Šaša Nováček's body on a single form sheet. The coin of the United States of America, notably the twenty-five-cent piece, the quarter, has less than one percent pure silver in it. Times change, but legends do not.

52
Love Filter

GREGG CHAMBERLAIN

"Little things mean a lot!"

Old Mob lived alone, except for her aged cat, Corif, in a shanty near the desert's edge. The nearest village was a morning's walk or a day's hobble away. Mob sometimes went there to trade what she had for what she wanted.

Daily she and Corif followed the caravan trails. He hobbled about his business in the sand while she poked the sands with her stick, looking for stuff fallen along the trail that she could use to sell.

One day Corif uncovered a wine amphora with the seal still intact. Mob looked the jug over carefully, thinking of the silver it would bring at the village inn. I could stand a little wine myself, she thought. Should check the contents anyway.

The seal was old clay and broke easily. She looked inside. Empty. She held the amphora upside down. Nothing.

Nothing inside except air that was so old and stale it was green. It poured out of the jug. And out, and out, forming a little green cloud above Mob's head. And in the cloud was a face.

"Blessings on you, O ancient crone, for freeing me from my prison. Name your reward and I shall grant whatever you wish, if it lies within my power to do so."

Old Mob licked her gums. "What I want is to be young and beautiful again and know the love of a handsome, lusty young man. Make me again the woman I was at eighteen and make my cat," she said, pointing at a shivering Corif, "a strong, handsome young man."

"Done! Come tomorrow's dawning you shall have your wish." The cloud thinned and was gone.

Mob clapped her wrinkled hands and, muttering excitedly to herself, hobbled home where she cooked a hasty supper and then tucked herself and the cat in bed.

In the morning when Mob awoke, she immediately remembered the jinn's words. She felt no aches and pains such as had plagued her lately in the morning. Tentatively her hands explored beneath the thin blanket. And found round, firm breasts thrusting up against the coarse wool, a flat, smooth belly untouched by childbirth, and soft, sleek thighs unmarked by ugly blue veins.

Then she thought of Corif. She turned and saw a godling lying on his side next to her. Head propped on his right hand, he looked into her eyes and smiled.

Oh, goddess of love, Mob thought. A warrior, a titan, a Man! Smiling, she reached out and pulled him to her.

Corif grinned and sang in a sweet soprano, "Aren't you sorry now you took me to the village surgeon for that little operation?"

53
The Maiden's Sacrifice

EDWARD D. HOCH

"And the purpose of capital punishment?"

Now it came to pass that Cuitlazuma, a wise man of science, became ruler of the great Aztec nation. He had labored long among the scholars of the kingdom, helping to perfect their regulatory calendar and to bring a high degree of development to the educational methods of the temple. Now, in the prime of his life, he was able to lead his people to even greater levels of accomplishment.

"Tell me, Monto," he asked one day, strolling with his aide near the great temple of Quetzalcoatl, "do you think others live beyond the jungles, across the waters?"

"Surely, yes, Cuitlazuma," the younger man replied. "A whole race of men who will someday come to our shores."

"And destroy all that we have built?"

"Perhaps."

The conversation saddened Cuitlazuma, for he had seen the Aztec nation grow in his own lifetime to its present peak of learning. The highly developed social life of the community was matched by superior educational methods and learned studies in astronomy. The great calendar stones that surmounted their temples—upon which Cuitlazuma himself had labored—gave mute evidence of the progress of civilization. And yet, the ruler was troubled.

"Monto, we must build against that day—against the day when all this is threatened, when our way of life crumbles." They had climbed to the top of the wide temple steps, and the ruler said, "Look here at what we have—streets and shops and buildings being constructed on every side, the flow of traffic regulated to a high degree. We take a census of our people, and govern them with a wise hand. Are we—and they—to lose all this?"

"Our generations will pass. Our children will die."

"But do they have to, Monto? Do they really have to?" The idea, only now beginning to form, excited him to a high degree. "Monto, call me a council of our wisest priests and men of science. I wish to speak to them."

"On what topic, Cuitlazuma?"

"Ah, on the topic of eternal life, of course."

And so they gathered to speak of it, and the most learned of the Aztec men of science were heard from. After two days of discussing the problem, with all its religious and medical implications, a decision was reached. Their people died because the heart stopped beating within them. Find a way of keeping the heart alive, and the eternal life they dreamed of would be possible. And with eternal life would go the hope of maintaining the Aztec civilization for all days to come, even against the enemy from across the sea.

"The heart, the heart," Cuitlazuma said. "That is the key to everything. Go among the people, especially the younger people, and find those willing to help us with our experiments."

And after some days a young girl was shown into Cuitlazuma's chamber. She was called Notia and she was very beautiful. "They have explained to you what is needed?" he asked.

"It is an honor to serve my ruler, oh sir."

"You are only a maiden. Do you realize what it is you will be sacrificing?"

"Of course, oh sir."

"Very well."

And so a place was prepared, at the very top of the temple steps where all could see—because Cuitlazuma would not do this thing in secret. The girl Notia was prepared, dressed all in a gown that billowed behind her as she walked.

And on the day when it was to happen, Cuitlazuma spoke with the doctors and the medical men. And then they went together to visit old Quizal, the woman who was dying. "My heart is worn, oh sir," she murmured from her pallet.

"Woman, we will try to remedy that today."

And later the doctors spoke to Cuitlazuma, because they feared this thing he was about to do. "What if it fails?" they asked.

"Then we will try again. And again."

The doctor nodded. There was nothing more to be said.

And later Monto came to his leader's quarters. "The maiden is prepared. Old Quizal is prepared. You will do it?"

Cuitlazuma picked up the sharpest of his knives, the ceremonial dagger he had never used. "I will do it. Only I should have the responsibility."

"How will you do it?"

Cuitlazuma leaned against the cold wall, resting his forehead for a moment against his arm. "I will cut into her chest as she lies there, and remove the living heart from her body. Then I will place it in the chest of old Quizal, to give her more years of life. The doctors will be there to connect the heart and close the wound."

"If you succeed, Cuitlazuma, it will be the beginning of eternal life for our people."

Cuitlazuma nodded and picked up the dagger. It was time to go, to meet with the maiden Notia on the temple steps. "And if I fail what we begin here today . . ."

"If you fail?"

"If I fail, there will be only the deed to be remembered, and not its purpose. And centuries from now some writer of histories will look back and say that the Aztecs practiced human sacrifice."

54
Malice Aforethought

DONALD A. WOLLHEIM

"Serve him right."

It was bad enough that people always mistook Allen San Sebastian for the writer Marvin Dane. It was worse how the society of the literary world kept shoving the two together until, having met at so many parties and people's homes, they were regarded by the outside world as being friends.

Actually neither liked the other very much—that is always the curse of similarity in competitors. They would have avoided each other if they could, but they couldn't, not without snubbing too many valuable intermediaries. Both wrote stories for the same magazine, both did their best to toady up to the impossible boor who was its editor.

LeClair B. Smith, who was owner and editor of *Grimoire: The Magazine of Spectral Fiction,* was a sharp-dealing, coarse-tongued, self-educated business-man who knew nothing about literature, had a Sunday supplement taste in art, but knew just about everything when it came to squeezing the pennies from the news-dealers and the trusting public. That *Grimoire* was such a success was due to that grim jest of fate that made Smith capable of enjoying a good horror tale when he read one.

Possibly it was a subconscious reflection of the sadism that makes so many successful men scornful of the feelings of others. Certainly his handling of his authors instilled horror in those who had perforce to deal with him.

For it was good business to stay in his favor, as San Sebastian well knew, and when you had to depend on Smith's checks for your living, it became a matter of life and death.

San Sebastian had left his parental farm, somewhere in the Middle West, after selling several stories, and had made himself live in the intellectual slums of the big city. It was good business; besides, he could concentrate better where there were no infernal roosters to rouse him from bed at half-past four, and he could stay up as late as he pleased with decent conversations and a half-gallon of thick sweet muscatel to sip from. The fly in his ointment was Marvin Dane.

They looked alike, both tall, gaunt, dark-haired. Both had a tendency to squint, both had the same dry sense of humor. But there, insisted San Sebastian, the resemblance ended. He could write and Dane couldn't. Smith, their god and judge, didn't share San Sebastian's opinion. He thought they could both write—and also happened to think that San Sebastian was slipping and Dane was coming up.

San Sebastian had begun to realize the horrible truth himself when three stories in a row were rejected as being too similar to material bought just previously. He didn't know what this material was until two months later when he saw a story of Dane's in the latest *Grimoire* that shook him to the core. It was quite identical, plot, writing and all, to one of his stories.

Dane a plagiarist? Hard to see how. San Sebastian, after overcoming his first fit of fury and black anger, found himself lost in a reflex of puzzlement. Nobody, but nobody, saw San Sebastian's stories until he'd written them out, rewritten them, pecked out a copy painfully on his

typewriter and then, after waiting a week or so to reread
them again, made his further corrections.

Dane couldn't possibly have seen the stories before; he
couldn't possibly have sneaked into San Sebastian's
rooms to copy his tales; and besides San Sebastian never
discussed plots with any of his friends. Yet there it was.

By the time the third familiar story of Dane's had appeared in print and two other tales of San Sebastian's had
been rejected by Smith with the cutting insinuation that
San Sebastian must have peeked at Dane's red hot typewriter, Allen San Sebastian was in a state bordering on
madness. He could, of course, try to sell his rejected tales
to a competitor magazine. But besides the fact that he
didn't go over as well with the other editors, they might
holler bloody murder when Dane's duplicates hit the
stands first.

San Sebastian finally took a friend into his confidence.
A rather older man, Carlton Vanney was more steady in
his ways, with a bent for the psychological and the occult. He discussed the matter, showed this friend Dane's
published stories and his own originals. It was, he insisted, not possible for either writer to have seen the
other's work in production.

Vanney, a man of considerable experience, after giving the matter much thought, pointed out that the coincidence of ideas was not precisely new in history. It
happened before, it happened often in fact with creative
minds that two persons would think of the same thing at
the same time. It seems, Vanney said, that the universe
moved at a certain pace, and then when conditions were
ready for certain ideas, they developed spontaneously to
the first minds that bothered to look for them.

For instance when the science of mathematics had
reached an impasse in the old arithmetics, Newton and
Leibnitz, separated in two different nations, without
knowledge of each other, individually invented and
worked out the system of calculus. Again the planet Nep-
tune had been seen by two different astronomers almost

simultaneously. Again and again, inventions were duplicated, sometimes at half a world's distance, by minds of similar caliber.

It was as if there were an invisible telegraphic network linking all the minds of the world. So that when a Frenchman named Ader made a wild short flight in a crazy apparatus of canvas and propellers in 1898, two young mechanics in Ohio could conceive a mad inspiration for a miracle that would mature at Kitty Hawk a few years later.

Now, reasoned Carlton Vanney, was it not logical that when two minds as similar as Dane's and San Sebastian's were living within a few blocks of each other, were simultaneously trying to determine the demands of the same mind, LeClair B. Smith's, in the same specialized style of writing, *Grimoire*'s, that one should telegraph his ideas to the other, just as a powerful sending station transmits instantly to the receivers of a waiting set? Who is to say which of the two originated the ideas of these stories? It may be San Sebastian glimpsing them from Dane's mind, or vice versa. No personal guilt could be placed.

The reason, the only reason, why Dane was winning was that he was the faster writer. Dane wrote by typewriter the first time and never rewrote. Once he tore his first draft from the keys of his machine, it went within hours to Smith's desk. And it would not be for two weeks before San Sebastian's tortoise-paced prose would reach that same destination.

Marvin Dane was clever, enough, beyond doubt. He had often irked San Sebastian by his boasting that he never cluttered his imagination with the stories of others. He never read other writers' efforts and he never relied on the classics and anthologies for inspiration. His mind was very probably wide open for stray plots coming over the telepathic ether.

This answer satisfied San Sebastian's curiosity, but left him in an even grimmer plight than before. Was he doomed always to lose out in this ghastly race? Did this spell his end as a writer?

For several days Allen San Sebastian wandered the streets of the big city lost in wonder and despair. There must be an answer, but what, but how? This was to be a struggle to the death—for it was clear that the only obvious course that would clear his future would be Dane's incapacitation.

He could, for instance, break into Dane's apartment and smash his typewriter with an axe. By the time Dane could borrow or buy another machine, San Sebastian would have at least one new story on Smith's desk first. But this was obviously an impractical solution. He could pay someone to beat up Dane and put him in the hospital. This too did not exactly appeal to him. Besides, it invited a host of trouble; whom would he get to do it and how could he keep himself from being blackmailed thereafter? As for murder, the idea didn't appeal to him at all.

Then, one afternoon, the idea came to him. Almost in a fever flush, San Sebastian made his way home, closed and locked the door behind him, and dashed to his bookcase. Pulling out a volume therein, he seated himself at his desk, took pen in hand and began transcribing the pages of the book that he had opened. Carefully he bent himself to his task.

In two hours he had completed the first writing. Setting the manuscript aside, he waited. The next day he again repeated the process, laboriously copying out the printed pages for a second time. Yet a third day he worked on it, then set up his typewriter and began typing out the pages slowly in his usual painstaking manner. He drew out the work as long as possible.

On the fourth day, upon typing *finis* to the last page, he clipped all the completed pages together, read through them very carefully once more, and then, taking the various manuscripts into his little kitchenette, burned them each and every one over a jet of his gas stove.

Then he took a rest from literary work for two months.

Now LeClair B. Smith was, as has been said, pretty much of a nonliterary businessman, self-educated and self-opinionated. He knew a good horror story when he saw one; and when Marvin Dane submitted a humdinger to him, he bought it on that same day and fitted it into his magazine's schedule. Dane, as has also been said, had the not unadmirable quality of keeping his mind clear of other horror writers' works.

It was very embarrassing when a host of discerning readers and fans flooded the magazine with angry letters for publishing H. P. Lovecraft's "The Rats in the Walls" under the title of "The Mumbling Vermin of Oxham Priory" by Marvin Dane—"A gripping tale of ancestral doom, written especially for *Grimoire* by a modern de Maupassant." It was disastrous for Marvin Dane when Smith not only threw him out of his office but sued him for the return of the money and damages.

And it didn't do Allen San Sebastian any harm when Dane's new stories were constantly returned to him by the office boy unopened, as per editorial orders. You could be sure to find San Sebastian's name in any table of contents in any new issue of *Grimoire*. As for Dane, after that ruinous climax to his literary career, for which he was unable to blame anyone but himself and his sizzling typewriter, he became a moderate sort of success as the clerk in a small but select bookstore catering to obscurantist prosody.

55

The Man Who Sold Rope
to the Gnoles

MARGARET ST. CLAIR

"Salesmen deserve it, perhaps."

The gnoles have a bad reputation, and Mortensen was
quite aware of this. But he reasoned, correctly enough,
that cordage must be something for which the gnoles had
a long unsatisfied want, and he saw no reason why he
should not be the one to sell it to them. What a triumph
such a sale would be! The district sales manager might
single out Mortensen for special mention at the annual
sales-force dinner. It would help his sales quota enormously. And, after all, it was none of his business what
the gnoles used cordage for.

Mortensen decided to call on the gnoles on Thursday
morning. On Wednesday night he went through his *Manual of Modern Salesmanship*, underscoring things.

"The mental states through which the mind passes in
making a purchase," he read, "have been catalogued as;
1) arousal of interest 2) increase of knowledge 3) adjust-
ment to needs . . ." There were seven mental states
listed, and Mortensen underscored all of them. Then he
went back and double-scored No. 1, arousal of interest,
No. 4, appreciation of suitability, and No. 7, decision to
purchase. He turned the page.

"Two qualities are of exceptional importance to a salesman," he read. "They are adaptability and knowledge of merchandise." Mortensen underlined the qualities. "Other highly desirable attributes are physical fitness, a high ethical standard, charm of manner, a dogged persistence, and unfailing courtesy." Mortensen underlined these too. But he read on to the end of the paragraph without underscoring anything more, and it may be that his failure to put "tact and keen power of observation" on a footing with the other attributes of a salesman was responsible for what happened to him.

The gnoles live on the very edge of Terra Cognita, on the far side of a wood which all authorities unite in describing as dubious. Their house is narrow and high, in architecture a blend of Victorian Gothic and Swiss chalet. Though the house needs paint, it is kept in good repair. Thither on Thursday morning, sample case in hand, Mortensen took his way.

No path leads to the house of the gnoles, and it is always dark in that dubious wood. But Mortensen, remembering what he had learned at his mother's knee concerning the odor of gnoles, found the house quite easily. For a moment he stood hesitating before it. His lips moved as he repeated, "Good morning, I have come to supply your cordage requirements," to himself. The words were the beginning of his sales talk. Then he went up and rapped on the door.

The gnoles were watching him through holes they had bored in the trunks of trees; it is an artful custom of theirs to which the prime authority on gnoles attests. Mortensen's knock almost threw them into confusion, it was so long since anyone had knocked at their door. Then the senior gnole, the one who never leaves the house, went flitting up from the cellars and opened it.

The senior gnole is a little like a Jerusalem artichoke made of India rubber, and he has small red eyes which are faceted in the same way that gemstones are. Mortensen had been expecting something unusual, and when the gnole opened the door he bowed politely, took off his hat, and smiled. He had got past the sentence about cordage requirements and into an enumeration of the different types of cordage his firm manufactured when the gnole, by turning his head to the side, showed him that he had no ears. Nor was there anything on his head which could take their place in the conduction of sound. Then the gnole opened his little fanged mouth and let Mortensen look at his narrow, ribbony tongue. As a tongue it was no more fit for human speech than was a serpent's. Judging from his appearance, the gnole could not safely be assigned to any of the four physio-characterological types mentioned in the *Manual;* and for the first time Mortensen felt a definite qualm.

Nonetheless, he followed the gnole unhesitantly when the creature motioned him within. Adaptability, he told himself, adaptability must be his watchword. Enough adaptability, and his knees might even lose their tendency to shakiness.

It was the parlor the gnole led him to. Mortensen's eyes widened as he looked around it. There were whatnots in the corners, and cabinets of curiosities, and on the fretwork table an album with gilded hasps; who knows whose pictures were in it? All around the walls in brackets, where in lesser houses the people display ornamental plates, were emeralds as big as your head. The gnoles set great store by their emeralds. All the light in the dim room came from them.

Mortensen went through the phrases of his sales talk mentally. It distressed him that that was the only way he could go through them. Still, adaptability! The gnole's interest was already aroused, or he would never have asked Mortensen into his parlor; and as soon as the gnole saw the various cordages the sample case contained he would no doubt proceed of his own accord through "appreciation of suitability" to "desire to possess."

Mortensen sat down in the chair the gnole indicated and opened his sample case. He got out henequen cable-laid rope, an assortment of ply and yarn goods, and some superlative slender abaca fiber rope. He even showed the gnole a few soft yarns and twines made of cotton and jute.

On the back of an envelope he wrote prices for hanks and cheeses of the twines, and for 550-foot lengths of the ropes. Laboriously he added details about the strength, durability, and resistance to climatic conditions of each sort of cord. The senior gnole watched him intently, putting his little feet on the top rung of his chair and poking at the facets of his left eye now and then with a tentacle. In the cellars from time to time someone would scream.

Mortensen began to demonstrate his wares. He showed the gnole the slip and resilience of one rope, the tenacity and stubborn strength of another. He cut a tarred hemp rope in two and laid a five-foot piece on the parlor floor to show the gnole how absolutely "neutral" it was, with no tendency to untwist of its own accord. He even showed the gnole how nicely some of the cotton twines made up in square knotwork.

They settled at last on two ropes of abaca fiber, $\frac{3}{16}$ and $\frac{5}{8}$ inch in diameter. The gnole wanted an enormous quantity. Mortensen's comment on these ropes' "unlimited strength and durability," seemed to have attracted him.

Soberly Mortensen wrote the particulars down in his order book, but ambition was setting his brain on fire. The gnoles, it seemed, would be regular customers; and after the gnoles, why should he not try the Gibbelins? They too must have a need for rope.

Mortensen closed his order book. On the back of the same envelope he wrote, for the gnole to see, that delivery would be made within ten days. Terms were 30 percent with order, balance upon receipt of goods.

The senior gnole hesitated. Slyly he looked at Mortensen with his little red eyes. Then he got down the smallest of the emeralds from the wall and handed it to him.

The sales representative stood weighing it in his hands. It was the smallest of the gnoles' emeralds, but it

was as clear as water, as green as grass. In the outside
world it would have ransomed a Rockefeller or a whole
family of Guggenheims; a legitimate profit from a transaction was one thing, but this was another; "a high ethical standard"—any kind of ethical standard—would
forbid Mortensen to keep it. He weighed it a moment
longer. Then with a deep, deep sigh he gave the emerald
back.

He cast a glance around the room to see if he could find
something which would be more negotiable. And in an
evil moment he fixed on the senior gnole's auxiliary
eyes.

The senior gnole keeps his extra pair of optics on the
third shelf of the curiosity cabinet with the glass doors.
They look like fine dark emeralds about the size of the
end of your thumb. And if the gnoles in general set store
by their gems, it is nothing at all compared to the senior
gnole's emotions about his extra eyes. The concern good
Christian folk should feel for their soul's welfare is a
shadow, a figment, a nothing, compared to what the thoroughly heathen gnole feels for those eyes. He would
rather, I think, choose to be a mere miserable human
being than that some vandal should lay hands upon them.

If Mortensen had not been elated by his success to the
point of anaesthesia, he would have seen the gnole
stiffen, he would have heard him hiss, when he went over
to the cabinet. All innocent, Mortensen opened the glass
door, took the twin eyes out, and juggled them sacrile-
giously in his hand; the gnole could feel them clink.
Smiling to evince the charm of manner advised in the
Manual, and raising his brows as one who says, "Thank
you, these will do nicely," Mortensen dropped the eyes
into his pocket.

The gnole growled.

The growl awoke Mortensen from his trance of eupho-
ria. It was a growl whose meaning no one could mistake.
This was clearly no time to be doggedly persistent. Mortensen made a break for the door.

The senior gnole was there before him, his network of tentacles outstretched. He caught Mortensen in them easily and wound them, flat as bandages, around his ankles and his hands. The best abaca fiber is no stronger than those tentacles; though the gnoles would find rope a convenience, they get along very well without it. Would you, dear reader, go naked if zippers should cease to be made? Growling indignantly, the gnole fished his ravished eyes from Mortensen's pockets, and then carried him down to the cellar to the fattening pens.

But great are the virtues of legitimate commerce. Though they fattened Mortensen sedulously, and, later, roasted and sauced him and ate him with real appetite, the gnoles slaughtered him in quite a humane manner and never once thought of torturing him. That is unusual, for gnoles. And they ornamented the plank on which they served him with a beautiful border of fancy knotwork made out of cotton cord from his own sample case.

56
Miranda-Escobedo

JAMES SALLIS

"Well, if that doesn't beat hell."

I'd been on beat patrol in the East Village for four days when I came across the motorbike accident.

"I want to go where the action is," I'd told the loot. And I hadn't done bad: four Positives and ten Probables—I'd had to fight for those Probables. There was even talk of a citation, though it was really too early for something like that.

I was walking down the street kind of slow, looking around me, thinking of all the years I'd wasted in Identification comparing loops, whirls, ridges, auras. But this, I was thinking (I'd picked up some of the street talk around me), was where it was at!

The accident had taken place outside a bookstore; copies of *The Exorcist* were highlighted in the window. A youngish man on a motorbike had come flashing down the street and plowed into the back of a '55 Chevy driven by an elderly schoolteacher. ("I tried to get out of his way," she was telling the cops, sobbing hysterically.)

The young man was obviously gone. Both legs were bent back under him at odd angles, his chest was crushed, and one eye had been torn out.

He was standing there looking down at his body.

I took one look at the aura and said, "Come on, buddy, let's go."

At first he didn't hear me. They always take it hard; we have trauma centers for those who take it *really* hard. So the manual says: At separation, give them a few minutes.

It didn't take that long. I guess he sensed me standing beside him. Anyway, he looked around, and I knew I didn't have to repeat what I'd said; he *knew* what I was doing there. They usually do.

"Now wait a minute, man," Number Fifteen said. "You ain't got nothing on me."

"No? Well let me tell you something, punk. I've got Probable Cause—your aura's obviously damaged—and that's enough. We'll let Identification take it from there, okay? But you're coming with me."

I had a momentary vision of my prior colleagues down in I.S. receiving the request, marked, of course, Rush/Urgent. *All* the requests were marked Rush/Urgent.

I got the bell jar out of my pocket and held it out toward him, but I kept the top on. Still, the little foil leaves trembled. And *that's* when most of them break down, pack it in.

I could see from the way he looked down briefly, then back up, that this guy was going to be a hassle.

"Hey, now, man," Number Fifteen said. "Look, you check, you'll see I've got an in. I made a payment, three of them, just last week . . ."

So he was a pimp and a dealer. My Probable Cause was looking better every minute.

". . . You can't touch me, man."

"Like *hell* I can't," I said. And that shook him.

"But I—"

He looked around nervously. But *I* was a little shook too, a little worried; this collar was taking too long, and the others weren't usually too far behind us.

Suddenly, he looked up and grinned.

"Man, you didn't read me my rights," he said.

So *I* looked up, and there he was.

He was standing at the edge of the crowd, wearing the usual white linen suit, which (plainclothes) meant he had a lot more experience than I, and I knew I'd blown it. Still, *some*thing might be salvaged. Plea bargaining doesn't take place just in the courtrooms.

"You stay right where you are," I said to the suspect, and went over to the detective.

"Egan," I said. "Fourteenth Precinct."

"McBain, 87th."

"Well, what do you think?" I said after a while.

"Well . . ." He looked at the bookstore window. "You read that?"

"What?"

"That book. You read it?"

"No. Meant to, but—well, you know how it is, with the job and all."

"Good book," he said. *"Damned* good book."

He took out a handkerchief and blew his nose. Well, that figured; it was winter, and they didn't keep it as warm as we did.

"Well, what do you think?" I said again.

"Well . . ." He looked the suspect over, up and down. "The aura's obviously damaged."

"Right," I said.

"But there's the matter of the agreement with you people."

"You know as well as I do," I said, "that that's not exactly a binding legal contract."

"Of course . . ." He looked back at the suspect. I wondered if he had his Identification people running a check. Probably not, at this point. "There's also the matter of your failure to give him his rights."

I shrugged. He was right, of course. The collar'd probably get tossed out for not following the proper procedure.

"Look," he said. "I mean, I'd give him to you. We don't have much space, not near as much as you . . ."

I wanted to holler I'll take him, I'll take him. But I restrained myself, maintaining the "poker face" the manual advised for such times.

". . . but I haven't filled my quota for the week," he said.

My spirits, as they say, sank.

"And I'm up for promotion next month," he said.

Which pretty much cinched it.

"Okay, okay," I said. "He's yours."

He nodded, took out the bell jar, and went over to the suspect. He held it out, took the top off. There was a quiet *pop*, and the foil leaves danced.

He walked past me on his way back up the street.

"God save me from street-wise punks," I muttered.

"What the hell," he said, walking on.

I finished the shift and, the next day, put in for a transfer to Central Holding, a joint service. Just a lot of paperwork and PR, but like the man said:

What the hell.

57
Mr. Wilde's Second Chance

JOANNA RUSS

"Design for living."

*This is a tale told to me by a friend after the Cointreau
and the music, as we sat in the dusk waiting for the night
to come:*

When Oscar Wilde (he said) died, his soul was found
too sad for heaven and too happy for hell. A tattered spirit
with the look of a debased street imp led him through
miles of limbo into a large, foggy room, very like (for
what he could see of it) a certain club in London. His
small, grimy scud of a guide went up to a stand something like that used by ladies for embroidery or old men
for chess, and there it stopped, spinning like a top.

"Yours!" it squeaked.

"Mine?"

But it was gone. On the stand was a board like the kind
used for children's games, and nearby a dark lady in
wine-colored silk moved pieces over a board of her own.
The celebrated writer bent to watch her—she chanced to
look up—it was Ada R——, the victim of the most celebrated scandal of the last decade. She had died of pneu-
monia or a broken heart in Paris; no one knew which. She
gave him, out of the corner of her black eyes, a look so
tragic, so shrinking, so haunted, that the poet (the most

courteous of men, even when dead) bowed and turned away. The board before him was a maze of colored squares and meandering lines, and on top was written "O. O'F. Wilde" in coronet script, for this was his life's pattern and each man or woman in the room labored over a board on which was figured the events of his life. Each was trying to rearrange his life into a beautiful and ordered picture, and when he had done that he would be free to live again. As you can imagine, it was both exciting and horribly anxious, this reliving, this being down on the board and at the same time a dead—if not damned—soul in a room the size of all Etna, but queerly like a London club when it has just got dark and they have lit the lamps. The lady next to Wilde was pale as glass. She was almost finished. She raised one arm—her dark sleeve swept across the board—and in an instant her design was in ruins. Mr. Wilde picked up several of the pieces that had fallen and handed them back to the lady.

"If you please," she said. "You are still holding my birthday and my visits to my children."

The poet returned them.

"You are generous," said she. "But then everyone here is generous. They provide everything. They provide all of one's life."

The poet bowed.

"Of course, it is not easy," said the lady. "I try very hard. But I cannot seem to finish anything. I am not sure if it is the necessary organizing ability that I lack or perhaps the aesthetic sense; something ugly always seems to intrude . . ." She raised her colored counters in both hands, with the grace that had once made her a favorite of society.

"I have tried several times before," she said.

It was at this point that the poet turned and attempted to walk away from his second chance, but wherever he went the board preceded him. It interposed itself between him and old gentlemen in velvet vests; it hovered in front of ladies; it even blossomed briefly at the elbow of a child.

Then the poet seemed to regain his composure; he began to work at the game; he sorted and matched and disposed, although with what public in view it was not possible to tell. The board—which had been heavily overlaid in black and purple (like a drawing by one of Mr. Wilde's contemporaries)—began to take on the most delicate stipple of color. It breathed wind and shadow like the closes of a park in June. It spread itself like a fan.

O. O'F. Wilde, the successful man of letters, was strolling with his wife in Hyde Park in the year nineteen-twenty-five. He was sixty-nine years old. He had written twenty books where Oscar Wilde had written one, fifteen plays where the degenerate and debauché had written five, innumerable essays, seven historical romances, three volumes of collected verse, and had given public addresses (though not in the last few years), and had received a citation (this was long in the past) from Queen Victoria herself. The tulips of Hyde Park shone upon the Wildes with a mild and equable light. O. O'F. Wilde, who had written twenty books, and—needless to say—left two sons an unimpeachable reputation, started, clutched at his heart, and died.

"That is beautiful, sir, beautiful," said a voice in the poet's ear. A gentleman—who was not *a gentleman*—stood at his elbow. "Seldom," said the voice, "have we had one of our visitors, as you might say, complete a work in such a short time, and such a beautiful work, too. And such industry, sir!" The gentleman was beside himself. "Such enthusiasm! Such agreeable docility! You know, of course, that few of our guests display such an excellent attitude. Most of our guests—"

"Do you think so?" said Mr. Wilde curiously.

"Lovely, sir! Such agreeable color. Such delicacy."

"I see," said Mr. Wilde.

"I'm so glad you do, sir. Most of our guests don't. Most of our guests, if you'll permit me the liberty of saying so, are not genteel. Not genteel at all. But you, sir—"

Oscar Wilde, poet, dead at forty-four, took his second

chance from the table before him and broke the board across his knee. He was a tall, strong man for all his weight, nearly six feet tall.

"And then?" I said.

"And then," said my friend, "I do not know what happened."

"Perhaps," said I, "they gave him his second chance, after all. Perhaps they had to."

"Perhaps," said my friend, "they did nothing of the kind . . .

"I wish I knew," he added. "I only wish I knew!"

And there we left it.

58
Mortimer Snodgrass Turtle

JACK C. HALDEMAN II

"It doesn't matter what you do as long as you do it best."

It was a beautiful, cool morning in the forest. Drops of dew hung to the undersides of the broad fern leaves like small suspended diamonds. On the musty forest floor animals were beginning to stir. It was the dawn of another day in the life of the turtles.

Steadily, slowly, the turtles started their daily forage for food. Heads forward, necks straining, feet outstretched, they padded along the moss-covered ground, looking for berries and other fine tidbits. Such was the fate of all turtles, the daily search for food.

But was that all there was to life? It would appear so, for all the turtles seemed content with their lot. All, that is, except one—Mortimer Snodgrass Turtle, known far and wide for his strange behavior and weird ideas. In short, Mortimer was a troublemaker and a pain in the shell to his elders.

After all, hadn't it been Mortimer who suggested that they forage at night when it was cooler and there weren't so many big animals around? A lot of good that suggestion did. Somebody forgot to tell Mortimer that turtles don't see too well in the dark, and he had walked right over the edge of the river and floated so far downstream that it took him three weeks to walk back. No doubt about it, Mortimer was trouble.

"Hey, Mort," said Fred, one of Mortimer's hatchlings. "Get a move on. Time to forage for food."

"Not interested."

"What do you mean? What else is there besides eating and sleeping?"

"There are higher things a turtle can aspire to," replied Mortimer, stifling a yawn. Truth is, he was tired and really didn't feel like foraging.

"What higher things can a turtle do? I guess it's possible to be made into soup or stuffed and used as a paperweight, but somehow that doesn't appeal to me."

"I'm going to think of something," replied Mortimer.

"Thinking doesn't fill your stomach, foraging does. See you around."

Mortimer nodded and settled back to do some serious thinking about the higher purposes of being a turtle.

It was a difficult job. The life of an average turtle was a quiet one, not easily given to activities of the sort usually referred to "higher purposes." They were hatched, grew up through a lifetime of sleeping and foraging, and perhaps produced a new generation of turtles before they died. Not a very noteworthy existence—perhaps suitable for his hatchlings, but not nearly enough for the adventurous Mortimer.

If only he had been born a sea turtle. Ah, for the freedom of the sea, the limitless expanse of streams and oceans. Swimming, that was something a turtle could really excel in. However, the brief encounter with water the time he fell into the stream had convinced him that he was not cut out for the aquatic life. So swimming was out, and the only comparable activity for a land turtle was walking, and everybody did that about the same.

Maybe that was the idea. If everyone walked the same, he would do it differently, yes, better! Best! The only outstanding characteristic of a turtle's walk was that it was slow. That was it! He would be the slowest walking turtle around. He would go slower than any turtle had dared go before!

As quickly as the thought came to Mortimer, he realized that this was no mere trick he could perform without training his body to perfection. For the next few weeks he ate heavily to build his strength and practiced walking slowly. Often on his training walks he would be passed by his fellow hatchlings.

"What are you doing, Mort?" they would ask.

"I'm going to be the slowest turtle in the world," he would reply.

"You're getting there," they would say, passing him by in search of berries.

And so he was, for with each succeeding day he would grow slower and slower. Ah, this was a turtle's highest purpose. Often his elders would walk past.

"What are you doing, crazy Mortimer?" they would ask.

"I'm going to be the slowest turtle in the world," he would reply.

"You're getting there," they would say, shaking their heads.

Soon he was ready for the big day. He would show them that a turtle was not limited to the artificial bounds imposed upon him. It was possible to go past the turtle's world into the dizzy realm of the snails—and, yes, even beyond; perhaps even to the world of a rock or a piece of moss. There were no limits to how slow he could go.

In spite of warnings from their elders, many of Mortimer's hatchlings were gathered the morning he attempted his feat. They held back, half hiding in the ferns, waiting for him to start. They waited and waited. Several grew bored and left before they realized he had actually started. He was moving so slow they had thought he was asleep.

Every muscle straining, he lifted his right front leg

ever so slowly. A snail paused to watch him and then went on, leaving Mortimer in a cloud of dust.

The rest of the hatchlings milled around for a while, eating ferns and making rude comments. After a while, they all left. It was the most boring thing they had ever seen.

Let them leave, it didn't bother Mortimer. If they failed to understand his mission, it was their fault, not his. He grew dizzy and drifted off into visions of slowness. In his dreams, a giant turtle came to him and told him he would die and be reborn even slower than before. He wept at the vision. Slowly.

For six days he remained in approximately the same spot. Fellow hatchlings occasionally came by to see if he had moved, but soon they quit coming, and on the seventh day a deranged armadillo came along and ate him.

He was reborn as a rock. Some folks never learn.

59
Mouse-Kitty

RICK NORWOOD

"Find the man in the Mire 'n' Ask."

After the unsuccessful colonial revolt, the British colonies in the New World were organized into the United States of Canada. In time, this vast and peaceful nation grew to include the entire North American continent. One of its most famous heroes was the Cisco Kid of the Royal Canadian Mounted Police.

Strange reports were coming in from prospectors in the Yukon. A new animal had been seen, a swift, elusive beast which the miners called a mouse-cat.

What made the reports so remarkable was the news that the mouse cat, unique among mammals, had three ears. The Cisco Kid was sent to investigate.

The Cisco Kid returned from the Yukon empty-handed. The mouse-cat had proved too shy and clever to be captured. He had, however, observed the little animals closely, and he could vouch for the fact that they had not three ears but four!

The controversy was referred to the Science Court, and in short order they handed down a verdict in favor of bilateral symmetry. "For," said the Chief Justice, "who are we to believe, the three mouse-cat ears or the count of Mounty Cisco?"

60
Naturally

FREDRIC BROWN

"Nonsense! A hexagram is the Star of David."

Henry Blodgett looked at his wrist watch and saw that it was two o'clock in the morning. In despair, he slammed shut the textbook he'd been studying and let his head sink onto his arms on the table in front of him. He knew he'd never pass that examination tomorrow; the more he studied geometry the less he understood it. Mathematics in general had always been difficult for him and now he was finding that geometry was impossible for him to learn.

And if he flunked it, he was through with college; he'd flunked three other courses in his first two years and another failure this year would, under college rules, cause automatic expulsion.

He wanted that college degree badly too, since it was indispensable for the career he'd chosen and worked toward. Only a miracle could save him now.

He sat up suddenly as an idea struck him. Why not try magic? The occult had always interested him. He had books on it and he'd often read the simple instructions on how to conjure up a demon and make it obey his will. Up to now, he'd always figured that it was a bit risky and so had never actually tried it. But this was an emergency and

245

might be worth the slight risk. Only through black magic could he suddenly become an expert in a subject that had always been difficult for him.

From the shelf he quickly took out his best book on black magic, found the right page, and refreshed his memory on the few simple things he had to do.

Enthusiastically, he cleared the floor by pushing the furniture against the walls. He drew the pentagram figure on the carpet with chalk and stepped inside. He then said the incantations.

The demon was considerably more horrible than he had anticipated. But he mustered his courage and started to explain his dilemma. "I've always been poor at geometry," he began . . .

"You're telling *me,*" said the demon gleefully.

Smiling flames, it came for him across the chalk lines of the useless hexagram Henry had drawn by mistake instead of the protecting pentagram.

61
Night Visions

JACK DANN

"A fate worse than death."

Martin steps on the accelerator of his Naples-yellow coupe and prepares to die. It will be a manly death, he thinks, although he is somewhat saddened by the thought of his beautiful car lying wrecked in a ditch. He glances at the rectilinear information band that stretches across the instrument panel: the speedometer needle is resting neatly between the nine and the zero.

He feels a delicious anticipation as he cruises through the darkness and low-lying mountain fog. The high beams turn the trees preternaturally green; the moon changes shape to accommodate the clouds boiling above.

As the speedometer needle reaches one hundred, Martin closes his eyes and turns the steering wheel to the left. He envisions his car moving diagonally across the highway, then over the embankment, taking with it several guardrails, and plunging into the ghostly arms of fog below. He does not brace himself for the coming crash. Relaxed, he waits for the car to leave the highway and the events of his life to rush before him as if in a newsreel. Surely time will distend like a bladder, filled with the insights and profound despair that must attend the last instants of consciousness.

Martin resolves to keep his eyes closed; he *will* meet his destiny. But the car remains on the highway, as if connected to an overhead line like a trolley. The radial tires make a plashing sound as they meet each measured seam in the pavement. Curious as to why he has not yet crashed and died, Martin dreams of the splintering of bone, the blinding explosion of flesh, the truly cosmic orgasm.

Then, just as the left front and rear tires finally slip off the road, a siren sounds. Surprised, Martin opens his eyes to find that the car, as if under the influence of a bewitched gyroscope, has regained the highway.

A police car overtakes him; and Martin pulls over beside an illuminated glen of evergreen to accept his speeding ticket as if it were a penitent's wafer.

It is unfair that I should have to kill myself, Martin thinks, as his car dips in and out of the fog like a great warship on a desolate sea. Ahead, he can see the gray lights of the medium-sized city that is nestled between black hills. He muses in the darkness; soon the highway will become elevated and illuminated.

Martin regrets his life. What has he to show for it but one hundred and thirty-eight hack novels, two children, and a wife he does not love? He considers himself still a virgin, for he has never had sex with anyone but his wife. At thirty-nine years of age, he is still obsessed with sex. He has written thirty-five pornographic novels, yet never gone down on a woman. He thinks of himself as a writing machine, and machines don't have experiences. They have no free will, they don't love or get laid. They just operate until they are turned off or break down.

He slows down behind a small, foreign car. The highway is suddenly crowded, and Martin experiences a familiar claustrophobia: he remembers the Long Island Expressway during the rush hour, the hypnotic seventy-mile-per-hour ritual of tailgating, the mile-long bumper-to-bumper traffic jams.

There can be no car-crashing here, for Martin does not wish the death of others on his conscience.

He passes a late-model convertible. A young man is driving, his arm around a pretty girl. Now, that would be a perfect car for an ending, Martin thinks—the wind whistling in your ears, drying your eyes, and no hard roof to protect skull from pavement.

Saddened by the thought that convertibles are no longer being made, he drives carefully onward. Safety poles whiz by him like teeth in some infernal machine; one wrong turn, a slight pull on the steering wheel, and the car would be smashed to scrap. But, always considerate of others, he keeps to the road. He passes a series of midtown exits, sees the blinking lights of a plane coming in from the east, and then the city and its dull glow of civilization is behind him. Ahead is a sliver of gray highway cutting through mountains, a low wall of nightfog, and heavy clouds hanging below an angry red moon.

Now Martin thinks he will slip into darkness, which will absorb the impact of flesh and metal; and he will simply drift away like a ghost on the morning mist.

The highway becomes a two-lane road for the next few miles and follows the contours of the land. Martin's throat tightens in joyful anticipation as he closes his eyes and presses the accelerator to the floor.

He dreams of flight and concussion; he dreams that time is made of rubber and he is pulling it apart. As he waits for his past to unfold, he repeats a mantra that his elder daughter taught him.

He tries to visualize his wife, Jennifer. Although Martin knows her intimately and can describe her in minute detail, he can no longer *see* her. He remembers her now as an equation, as numbers complemented by an occasional Greek letter to signify a secret part of her psyche.

She is probably phoning the police, calling the neighbors, making a fuss and waking the children.

He pulls another band of time taut and dreams about his funeral. His closest friends will all stand about the grave, then toss a few clumps of earth into the hole; his children will be crying loudly while Jennifer looks on quietly. All in all, a fine despair; a fitting end.

Martin wonders how long he has been daydreaming. Probably only an instant, he thinks. He remembers his childhood.

And he turns the steering wheel hard to ensure his death. He screams, anticipating the shattering pain and subsequent numbness.

But nothing happens.

He waits several more beats, then opens his eyes, only to find himself negotiating a cloverleaf turnoff. He has unwittingly turned onto an exit ramp and is now shooting back to the highway, heading in the opposite direction.

He strikes the wood-inlaid steering wheel.

"Dammit, Jennifer, I'm not coming home . . ."

There is very little time left; the sky is already becoming smudgy. Dawn is not far away, and the thought of driving into a bleeding sunrise does not escape him.

It must be done while it is still dark, he thinks; the sunlight would expose him to the world.

Shale palisades rise on either side of the highway like ruined steps. But this time Martin does not shut his eyes. There is no time to dream.

He turns the wheel sharply, once again preparing for the bright explosion of death.

But the car runs smoothly forward, as if Martin had never turned the wheel. The car follows the gentle curve of the highway. Martin is only a passenger.

"No," he screams as he turns the steering wheel again. The car does not respond. He steps on the brake, but the car maintains its speed. Although he is screaming—long, sharp streamers of sound—he hears only engine noise. Perfect rows of numbers pass through his mind: all the coupe's specifications he had once memorized.

Half a mile to the next exit, the car decelerates, turns

into the right-hand lane, and then into the thirty-mile-per-hour exitway. It rushes toward the sunrise, which is first a bleeding then a yellow-butter melting beyond the gray hills.

Home is only about twenty miles away.

Martin feels himself running down. He can barely move, for he is as heavy as the car. His hands rest upon the steering wheel as if he were in control. The air-conditioner blows a steady stream of cold air at his face. Numbers pass through his mind.

It is becoming a gritty day. Long, gray clouds drift across the sky, and Martin dreams that the sky is made of metal. He dreams that the world is made of metal, that he is made of metal.

In one last burst of strength, hope, and will, Martin commands his foot to press the accelerator to the floor. Once more, he dreams of the lovely shock of body and brain being pulped.

But the coupe maintains its speed.

Martin is almost home.

62
Once Upon a Unicorn

F. M. BUSBY

"They can always tell."

Seventeen years old and washed up. I still can't believe it. It's a bitch, that's what; a bull bitch on wheels.

Rillo used to tell me, "Don't talk so rough. You'll ruin your goddamned image." He's washed up too; the hell with him. It wasn't all my fault.

That's right: Rillo Furillo, my husband the star. You know him, all right, with his big beautiful bod and male-chauvinist-pig smile. What you don't know is, he's playing with a thirty-eight-card deck.

You know me, too—sweet little Wendine Thorise, veteran Child Star, with the big blue eyes and long blond hair down to keep your hands to yourself. Sweet sixteen and never been kissed. Well, there has to be some place I'd never been kissed; the tonsils maybe? Though some have tried.

Last fall we'd just wrapped up the third made-for-TV movie starring sweet little me. I was in big. I was also in bed with Arnie Karaznek, being produced just like his movies, with pauses for commercials. About when you'd expect, the phone rang. I said, "Oh, balls!" for what that was worth; he answered it anyway.

"Hello? Oh, Phil. Yeah. Yeah, go ahead. I'm not busy."

"You're sure not, you bastard. Phil who?"

"Shut up. Not you, Phil. Phil Sparger, you dumb-dumb. No, not you, Phil! Dammit Wendine, shut up or I'll belt you one. Forget you heard that, Phil. Okay?"

"All right, Phil, what is it? . . . No. Oh God, no! In the showers? At a *Junior* High School? All right, Phil; all right. Now here's what you do . . ."

That's when I quit listening, because Arnie was always good for maybe an hour on "now here's what you do." I wiggled the rest of the way loose and went to the toity and read Cleveland Amory in *TV Guide* some more. I was pretty sure he liked my series "The Wendings of Wendine," but he's sneaky.

I was into my third reading when Arnie banged on the door. "Come on out of there, willya? You'll wear out the batteries in that vibrator." Dumb Arnie. The batteries were already dead from the last time he'd answered the phone in the middle. But I came out, anyway.

"I don't have to ask about *your* batteries, though; do I, Arnie? Already plugged back into the studio, solid. I wish to hell you'd just once . . ."

"Come on, can it, Wendine. This is serious."

"Yeah? So am I. Oh well, go ahead; who blew it this time?"

"Rillo. Only thank God he didn't, really. They just thought he would."

I didn't say anything; what was there to say about Rillo? I poured myself a short shot and lit a smoke, waiting for Arnie to get it off his mind. Maybe there was hope yet.

"I told Phil how to fix it this time, but we've got to do something permanent about Rillo's problem. I think I've got it figured. I can count on you, now, can't I, Wendine?"

I didn't like it already but I had to ask. "Such as for what?"

"It's the romance of the century!"

"What is?" I knew all right but I had to hear it to believe it.

"You and Rillo. What did you think?"

I threw the shot glass, but Arnie ducks better than I
throw. All I broke was one of his dumb ceramics over the
fireplace. It was better than nothing.

"I am not marrying any goddamned queer!"

"Look, chickie; Rillo isn't queer. He's just curious, is
all."

"*Damn* curious. The answer is still go shove it,
Arnie."

It was a beautiful wedding in all the magazines. I cannot
convey, I really can't, the depth of my girlish emotions
when Rillo and I were at last alone with our great love, I
said for publication. There we were, all right, he was
with great bod, his manly smile, his limpid eyes and pas-
sionate voice. I was there too, sort of.

We really were a top news sensation; for three straight
months I didn't see Jackie on a magazine cover. The climax, if you'll pardon the expression, came when Rillo
and I made our movie together—a real live honest not-
for-TV movie, with no commercials.

We made it damn fast, as a matter of fact, because I
was expecting what they still call a blessed event in spite
of population pollution. It had to be Arnie; the timing
was wrong for that cute cameraman. Probably the week
Arnie's phone was out of order. So in a way it was lucky
Rillo and I got married when we did.

It's too bad that the movie is down the flush now. It was
a horn of corn but kind of cute, a fantasy fairy-tale thing.
Semi-adult Disney. Actually it was all Arnie's boss's idea,
including keeping the whole production under wraps until
he could spring the story on TV for crash effect.

Arnie Karaznek's boss goes by his initials only, ever
since he read a Harold Robbins book. The initials sound a
little suggestive but he doesn't seem to mind. Would you

believe Franklin Ulysses? Anyway, old F.U. ran into a scientific thing in the papers, and halfway understood it for once.

I'm not stupid, you know; just dumb. I catch a lot that goes on; sometimes I don't use it right, is all. I'll bet I understood as much as Arnie's boss did, about some zoo groups were breeding present-type animals back to earlier forms that went extinct. Like you could take a cage of lizards and go for dinosaurs. Well, maybe not quite that—but West Berlin does have a corral full of Stone Age supercows. Aurochs, they call them.

Arnie's boss read where somebody in Africa had bred back to unicorns. You've heard of unicorns; there weren't any, really—not one-horned horses, anyway. There isn't any such thing as a one-horned animal: rhinoceroses have a mustache with a permanent hard-on and narwhals are freak porpoises with one long tooth each. I remember that from high school before I dropped out, to put the best face on that change in my life-style. But it seems there used to be an antelope with its horns twisted together so tight in front that it looked like one horn. And this African outfit had bred antelopes back to that model.

Arnie's boss wanted to cash in, some way. The movie was called "The Lure of the Unicorn." Old F.U. paid a real bundle to get us an antelope in a hurry.

Too bad it won't go, now. The antelope was dumb and had a face like a camel's understudy, but it was *nice*-dumb, even if it didn't learn tricks too well. Gee, when I saw on the screen, the shot where it came and laid its head in my lap, I forgot about the lump of sugar it was really after, and cried all over hell. For a minute there, I almost thought that unicorn was right.

We got all the film in the can before I began to show much. Rillo and I did a good job, we thought; so did Arnie and even Franklin Ulysses. I figured we had it all on ice. Then F.U. got another one of his great ideas.

"A TV show, a Special, *live!* That's how we'll flack this flick," he said. "How can it miss?" By this time I was getting a little big in the gut, but everyone said it wouldn't matter.

"The added touch of your pregnancy will make the situation all that much more piquant," Arnie said at a P.R. meeting. Arnie has a lot of tact, around P.R. people. Without them he'd have said "Just do like I say, you dumb broad!" I wish to hell the kid were going to be the cameraman's.

At first reading the TV script didn't look too bad. After the taped lead-in somebody would lay the unicorn legend onto Mr. Nielsen's sheep, heavy on the whipped cream. Rillo was supposed to do that bit but he was having a little problem with uppers and downers—nothing really serious. So Milan Banfield, the second lead, had to take it.

Then Rillo and I would do the part of our big scene where the unicorn did its trick. All I had to do was sit still and mug right, and all Rillo had to do was sit alongside me and not twitch too much while we spoke our lines. No big problem.

One thing bothered me. "Look, Arnie," I said one time. "Everybody knows I'm married; right? And some of the magazines are spilling it that I'm knocked up now. So we do this thing. What kind of klutz is going to believe that this freak antelope knows what the hell it's doing?"

"The kind of klutz that watches this kind of TV show and buys tickets for this kind of movie." I couldn't argue; sometimes Arnie does know his business.

So we went out and did it. It was pretty for the camera, sunshine on sparkling dew. The wet grass was freezing my butt. I kept smiling, though; it couldn't last forever. Rillo's smile must be a silicone-implant, I thought; I'd never seen anything shake it.

When it came our turn to help sell tickets, Rillo and I started through our lines; it all seemed to be working okay, until the camera was ready for the unicorn. It was too far back, out of the shot; somebody had blown the timing. I can ad-lib; I threw in a few lines to keep things moving. Rillo can't; half the time I had to answer myself.

Someone finally shoved the unicorn on-camera. About time. And then it all went absolutely to hell in a bucket.

The damn beast cut me dead. Up front of about ten million people who had just had the unicorn story laid on them with a double scoop, that goddamned creature ambled up, sniffed, and laid its head in *Rillo's* lap.

I guess even a freak antelope has to be right once in a while.

63
$1.98

ARTHUR PORGES

"I can think of no greater bargain."

That morning Will Howard was taking a Sunday stroll
through the woods, a pleasure which lately had been
shared and intensified by Rita Henry. Not even the bright
sun, the bracing air, the unique song of a canyon wren,
could lighten Will's dark thoughts. Right now she was
out riding with Harley Thompson at an exclusive country
club. Will couldn't blame her. Harley was six feet two, a
former Princeton tackle; ruggedly handsome, full of
pleasant small talk; the young-executive-with-a-big-
future. And he, Will Howard, a skinny, tongue-tied
fellow—

At that moment he felt something tug feebly at one
trouser cuff, and looked down to see a tiny field mouse
pawing frantically at the cloth. Gaping, Will studied the
palpitating animal, completely baffled by such strange
behavior on the part of so timid a creature. Then the
springy, leaping form of a weasel, implacable, fearless
even of man, appeared on the trail.

Quicky Will scooped the terrified rodent into one
palm. The weasel stopped, making a nasty, chikkering
sound, eyes red in the triangular mask of ferocity that
was its face. For a heartbeat it seemed about to attack

258

its giant opponent, but as Will stepped forward, shouting, the beast, chattering with rage, undulated off the path.

"You poor little devil," Will addressed the bright-eyed bit of fur in his hand. A crooked smile touched his lips. "You didn't have a chance—just like me and Thompson!" Stooping, he deposited it gently in the underbrush. Then he stared, his jaw dropping. In place of the mouse, there appeared suddenly a chubby, Buddha-like being, some two inches tall. Actually, as measurement would have revealed, it stood precisely one and ninety-eight hundredths inches.

In a voice which although faint was surprisingly resonant, the figure said: "Accept, O kindly mortal, the grateful thanks of Eep, the God. How can I reward you for saving me from that rapacious monster?"

Will gulped, but being an assiduous reader of Dunsany and Collier, he recovered promptly. "You—you're a god!" he stammered.

"I am indeed a god," the being replied complacently. "Once every hundred years, as a punishment for cheating in chess, I become a mouse briefly—but no doubt you've read similar accounts to the point of excessive boredom. Suffice it to say, you intervened just in time. Now I'm safe for another century—unless, of course, I succumb to temptation again and change a pawn to a bishop. It's hard to resist," he confided, "and helps one's end game immensely."

Will thought of Harley Thompson, the heel that walked like a man. The fellow who laughed at fantasy, who ribbed him for reading the *Magazine of Not-Yet but Could-Be*. Well he knew that behind Thompson's personable exterior was a ruthless, self-seeking, egotistical brute. Rita could never be happy with a man like that. Here was a chance to gain his first advantage over Harley. With the help of a grateful god, much could be achieved. That Dunsany knew the score, all right. Maybe three wishes—but that was tricky. Better let the god him-self choose . . .

"You mentioned a—a reward," he said diffidently.

"I certainly did," the god assured him, swinging on a dandelion stem and kicking minute bare feet luxuriously. "But, alas, only a small one. I am, as you see, a very small god."

"Oh," Will said, rather crestfallen. Then bright-ening: "May I suggest that a *small* fortune—?" Truly the presence of an immortal was sharpening his wits.

"Of course. But it would have to be exceedingly small. I couldn't go above $1.98."

"Is that all?" Will's voice was heavy with disappoint-ment.

"I'm afraid it is. We minor gods are always pinched for funds. Perhaps a different sort of gift—"

"Say," Will interrupted. "How about a diamond? Af-ter all, one the size of a walnut is actually a small object, and—"

"I'm sorry," the god said regretfully. "It would have to be tiny even for a diamond. One worth, in fact, $1.98."

"Curse it!" Will groaned. "There must be something small—"

"There should be," the little god agreed good-naturedly. "Anything I can do, up to $1.98, just ask me."

"Maybe a small earthquake," Will suggested, without much enthusiasm. "I could predict it in advance. Then perhaps Rita—"

"A small earthquake, yes," Eep replied. "I could manage that. But it would be the merest tremblor. Doing, I remind you, damage only to the amount of $1.98."

Will sighed. "You sound like a bargain basement," he protested.

"Of course," the god mused aloud, as if sincerely seeking a solution, "by taking the money in a different currency—say lira—it would *seem* like more; but the value would actually be the same.''

''I give up,'' Will said. Then, in a more kindly voice, as Eep looked embarrassed, ''Don't feel bad. I know you'd like to help. It's not your fault that money's so tight.'' Glumly he added: ''Maybe you'll think of something yet. I'm selling now, or trying to—I'm not much of a salesman. Once the client sold *me* his office furniture. But if you could arrange a good sale—''

''It would bring in only $1.98.''

''That wouldn't be easy,'' Will told him, smiling wryly. ''Right now I'm handling diesel locomotives, office buildings, and abandoned mines. And I'm vice-president in charge of dry oil wells.''

''Any luck so far?'' the little god demanded, kicking a grasshopper, which soared off indignantly.

''I almost sold an abandoned copper mine to a wealthy Californian for an air-raid shelter, but Thompson nosed me out—again. He showed him how one gallery in another mine could be made into the longest—and safest—bar in the world. It killed my sale; the man bought Thompson's mine for $67,000. That infernal Harley!'' he exclaimed. ''I wouldn't mind his getting the supervisor's job instead of me; I'm no good at giving orders, anyhow. Or his stealing my best customers. Even his lousy practical jokes. But when it comes to Rita—! Just when she was beginning to know I'm alive,'' he added bitterly.

''Rita?'' the god queried.

''Rita Henry—she works in our office. A wonderful girl. So sweet, so—alive, and with the most marvelous greenish eyes—''

''I see,'' Eep said, thumbing his nose at a hovering dragonfly.

''That's why I could use a little help. So do what you can, although it can't help much with a ceiling of—''

''—$1.98,'' the god completed his sentence firmly. ''I shall spend the afternoon and evening here contemplating the place where my navel would be if I were not supernatural. Trust the Great (although small) God Eep. Farewell.'' He walked into the grass.

Much too depressed for any amusement, Will spent the evening at home, and at eleven went gloomily to bed, convinced that a mere $1.98 worth of assistance, even from a god, was unlikely to solve his problem.

In spite of such forebodings, he was tired enough from nervous strain to fall asleep at once, only to be awakened half an hour later by a timid rapping at the apartment door.

Blearily, a robe over his pajamas, he answered it, to find Rita standing on the threshold. She gave him a warm smile that was bright with promise.

"Rita!'' he gasped. "Wha—?"

One finger on her lips, she slipped in, closing the door softly behind her. Then she was in his arms, her lips urgent, her body melting.

"Rita,'' Will murmured, "at last . . .''

She gazed up at him. Was there just a hint of puzzlement, of bewilderment in those green eyes? "Something just seemed to force me . . . I had to come . . .'' She took his hand and led him to the bedroom. There, in the warm darkness, he heard the whispery rustle of silk. "I had to come,'' Rita said again. "We're just right for each other . . . I know . . .''

The bed creaked and, on reaching out one yearning hand, Will touched skin like sun-warmed satin.

The next morning, when she picked up the wispy panties from the floor where they had been tossed in flattering haste, a scrap of paper dropped from the black nylon.

Wondering, Will picked it up. It was a newspaper clipping. Someone had written in the margin in a tiny, flowing script: "A gratuity from the grateful (up to $1.98) God Eep."

The clipping itself, a mere filler, read: "At present prices, the value of the chemical compounds which make up the human body is only $1.98."

64
Opening a Vein

BILL PRONZINI
and BARRY N. MALZBERG

"And that's the purpose of it all."

The last man on Earth was a vampire.

So he rummaged around in the ruins until he came upon a copy of *The Rites of Goetic Theurgy,* and then he conjured up the Devil.

"Listen," the vampire said, wrinkling his nose at the smell of sulphur and brimstone that surrounded Lucifer, "I summoned you here because I'm the last living thing on Earth, as if you didn't know, and I want to make a deal for some blood."

The Devil laughed mockingly. "A deal?" he said. "Vampires have no souls, so what could you possibly bargain with?"

"We could work out something—"

"Even if you *had* a soul," the Devil said fetchingly, "I wouldn't bargain with the likes of you. Now that the Final War has wiped the globe clean, I have all the souls I need to last me through Eternity."

"But you've *got* to help me," the vampire pleaded. "I'm starving here all alone!"

"That's your problem," the Devil said and prepared to depart, then hesitated. "The trouble is that I'm a sentimental fool," he said. "It must be my origins." He lifted his head proudly, considering the abysmal landscape. "One taste," he said. "That's all."

"Of *you?*"

"As you pointed out," the Devil said, "your choice is limited."

The vampire sighed. Not unsophisticated in the ways of temptation he suspected the Devil's ploy was to allow him only enough blood to exacerbate desire, sentencing him to an eternity of even greater torment. On the other hand, his desires were immediate and it was perhaps unwise to take the long view. Considering all of this, the vampire leapt upon the Devil (who received him willingly) and drained a considerable amount of blood from the old tempter, finding it to his surprise to be quite fresh and of no noxiousness whatsoever.

The Devil made no effort to fend him off and the vampire was able to feast, if that is the word, at leisure. At length, sated, he withdrew to find that the Devil was a thin and shriveled figure upon the ground, utterly drained of life or fluids.

I've killed the Devil, the vampire thought. It was a pity, under all the circumstances, that there were no witnesses. In simpler times, he thought, he would at least have gotten a medal.

In the abysmal chaos however there were neither medallions nor presenters. There was merely the large meal lingering within him and a vague feeling of regret which the vampire, soon enough, interpreted as boredom. There was not even the hope of further meals, now, and an intolerable eternity of solitude.

Thinking this and other despairing thoughts he looked out upon the formless void. Perhaps there was something he could do about that anyway, he thought.

Energized by the blood of the practical Devil he set about doing it.

He waited awhile before creating the swimming and crawling things. No sense in haste. Time and his powers made him easeful.

In due course, the game would come.

65
The Other

KATHERINE MACLEAN

"Physician, heal thyself."

Tree shadows moved on the gray linoleum of the hospital floor, swaying like real leaves and twigs. Joey blurred his eyes to make the leaf shadows green.

The floor quivered slightly to foam-padded footsteps, and a man-shaped shadow appeared across the sunlight. That was Dr. Armstrong. He was kind. He always walked softly and then stood and shuffled when he hoped you would notice him.

The feet shuffled hopefully. When Joey concentrated on the doctor's shadow he could turn the head part pink, like a face.

Dr. Armstrong's voice said something. It was a pleasant light tenor voice, a little anxious.

"What did he say?" Joey asked the other, the one in his head who listened and calculated and explained.

"He asked *How are you?*"

"What did he mean?"

"He wants you to get up and be busy, like him," said the cool advice of his Other, his guardian and advisor. "That's what they all want."

"Not right now. I am watching the leaves. What shall we tell him?"

266

"Tell him, *Just about the same.*"

Joey made the effort, and spoke, hearing his own voice very close to his ears. He was ready to turn and look out the window now, but the doctor's feet were beside him, anxiously demanding his attention, afraid he would turn away.

"What did he say?" Joey asked the Other.

There was a pause, a barrier, a reluctance to speak, then the cool voice answered. "He asked about me."

"Was he—" Joey was alarmed. People meddled, people said things which got inside and hurt. And yet Dr. Armstrong had always been nice; he never criticized so far. "No—I don't want to know. Well—tell me a little."

The voice was indistinct. "Asked who you talk to—when you . . . before talking outside to him."

"Tell him it's you," Joey said, confident and warm. The voice was his friend, and Dr. Armstrong was his friend. They should know each other. The voice helped Dr. Armstrong. "Tell him it's you."

"What name? Authority people need names for existing things. They don't understand without names."

"What are you?"

"I am a construct. You made me."

"We can't tell him that. People punish me for making up people." Joey felt pain in his middle, near stomach and heart. It was hard to breathe. "Mommee shouted and cried."

"We won't tell him that," the voice agreed.

Joey felt calmer. The voice was good; there had to be a good name for it, one that the outside others would approve. "We can find a name for you. There are so many words. What else are you?"

"I am part your mother and your father and little parts and feelings of anyone who ever worried about you and wanted you to stop doing things so that you would be all right and strangers would not be angry at you. And you made me into a grownup to talk to you. Many years. I've grown wise, Joey. I worry about you and want you to stop . . .''

"Don't bother me about that now," Joey said, withdrawing himself in his head so that the voice was far away where he would not have to listen. "You explain to Dr. Armstrong that you are on his side, that you are grownup like him, and tell me what to do. I wouldn't know when to get up, or what people want . . . They would be angry."

"Doctors don't want to talk to me. They want to talk to you, Joey. They don't ask how to do something: they ask what do you feel."

"I can't talk. They'd see me. I'd cry, and want to touch arms and rub cheeks. Talk for me. Tell them you're a doctor. Use their words."

Joey heard his voice close but too quiet and mumbly. He forced it louder. ". . . *father image, Dr. Armstrong. He tells me what is right to say. He is strict, so it is all right.*''

That sounded good. That sounded safe to say. Joey heard the musical tenor of Dr. Armstrong's anxious, well-intentioned voice. It would be praise.

Don't listen to it, Joey. It's not—

Pain and grief struck him in the middle, curling him over. Got to get away quickly or die. Make it not happen. Into the past, in the dark, in the comforting dark, before people could take away their love. He was lying on the floor, curled up, and the warm dark was wrapping around like a blanket.

But the feet still stood by, shuffling nervously. That past event must be finished before it could be forgotten. Joey took a deep breath, made a shouting effort, heard his distant scream and left it behind, screaming forever like a soundless sign on the wall of a deserted train station, at a distant place in time.

"He said the wrong thing. Tell him to go away."

Outside-people do not know the roads and paths inside the world of image, memory, and dream: they stumble, blunder and destroy among the fragile things. He decided that he should not have listened and replied. When time came around to return from darkness to the world of light, he would be silent.

Dr. Armstrong, twenty-four years old, successful and considered brilliant, walked into his small office in the hospital. He carefully shut the door behind him and made sure his latch had caught before sitting at his desk.

He put his face down into his hands. *(He said the wrong thing. Tell him to go away.)* The article about Rosen's techniques had said that Rosen talked freely with his patients, discussing their fantasy worlds with them as if they were real, and explaining the meaning of the symbols to them. Perhaps he should see it demonstrated before trying it again.

God! Joey had fallen from the chair and hit the floor already curled up, knees to chin, eyes shut, as if stunned and dead. Maybe he would be all right. Tomorrow, casual inquiry to the nurses . . . The nurses might blame him for Joey. How many other mistakes did they blame him for already?

Why was he sitting like this with his face in his hands? *I'm tired,* he thought. *Just tired.*

Dr. Armstrong leaned his face more heavily into his hands, his elbows braced on the desk as though he were tired. Tears trickled down between his spread fingers and splashed on the psychiatric journal on his desk.

It is not I who is weeping, he thought. *I am the cool and logical student, the observer of human actions. I can observe myself also, which proves that my body weeps. This wastes time I could use to study and to think.*

Tears trickled down between his spread fingers and splashed on the psychiatric journal.

It is not I who is weeping, he thought. *It is that other, the childish feeling in me, who can be wounded by love and hope, and pity and confusion, and being alone. I am an adult, a scientist. It is the other who weeps, the ungrown-up one we must conceal from the world.*

"*No one sees you,*" he said to the Other. "*You can weep for five minutes. This spasm will pass.*"

66
The Other One

RICK NORWOOD

"There's nothing sure—mostly."

The man in Black! There, standing in the shadows!

Like a creature from the pages of an EC horror comic, he dogs my steps.

Nothing's sure. I don't think *anyone* knows. Nothing's really sure, but . . .

Ever since that awful day—that wonderful, awful day—he has been there. Everywhere I go! The Man in Black!

I remember. I plunged my arms, up to the elbows, into the brown paper bag full of beautiful green money. And suddenly, like a surgeon, I was thrusting my arms into a wound in the old man's chest. I don't think that really happened, but nothing's sure.

The Man in Black! Does he know? How *can* he know? I haven't spent the money. ("This money is stained," they would say. "What are these dark stains?")

Sometimes I draw the curtains tightly and take great handfuls of money and throw it into the air. Then, quick, quick, on hands and knees, I gather it up and stuff it in the sack. Can the Man in Black see through drawn curtains? Nothing's sure.

Why does he follow me now, where the light from the

street lamps pools like blood on the dark sidewalks? From lamp to lamp I run, deeper into the forest. But never far behind . . . the Man in Black.

Into a tunnel! This must be the lair of some animal. By its smell, I can identify the beast that dwells here. Its name is Subway. I will flee on its back. It will carry me away on its back.

But no! The station is deserted. I hear footsteps on the stairs.

At the far end of the platform, the posters and graffiti melt like paint. He's coming!

I think I am ready for him now. He is here.

"Are you . . ." I say, leaning close. "Are you . . ." (Nothing's sure but—) "Are you . . . Death?"

He shows me the silver letters on his briefcase: IRS.

"No," he says. "I'm the other one."

67
The Other Train Phenomenon

RICHARD BOWKER

"Come on, you know *he's right."*

The subway train had broken down in the tunnel. I was
standing up, my back was aching, and I was late. The air
conditioning had gone off when the train broke down,
and little rivulets of sweat were running down my body,
seeking out the routes that would cause me the most dis-
comfort. Then a nut started talking to me.

He was one of those thin, hollow-eyed, intense fellows, the kind who sells his poetry on street corners or
runs off revolutionary manifestos on the mimeograph in
his basement. He was wearing sneakers, dirty chinos,
and, despite the heat, a flannel shirt with the collar button
buttoned. Not someone I wanted to pass the time of day
with.

"These trains are a disgrace. Aren't they?" he demanded. His voice was thin and quavering. His beady
black eyes were constantly in motion, scanning the faces
around him suspiciously.

"Um," I replied noncommittally, getting ready for a
tirade against the imperialist regime that let our subways
rot while it suppressed the aspirations of freedom-loving
peoples around the world.

"You ride the subway often?"

"Um, uh-huh."

This was evidently the right answer. He approved. "So do I," he said, his eyes darting here and there. That made us soulmates, I guess. His eyes suddenly focused intensely on mine. "When you were waiting for this train, did you happen to notice—did a train come in from the other direction first?"

I felt stupid having to answer, but the intensity of his interest made me think back to when I was waiting in the station. "Well, I guess so," I replied. "The other train always comes first."

He nodded emphatically. "That's right, that's right. It always happens. The other train always comes first. But why should that be? According to the so-called Laws of Probability, if the trains run as often in both directions, and your time of arrival is random with respect to their schedules, your train should come first about half the time. Right?"

"Well," I offered, somewhat puzzled, "maybe it just *seems* as if—"

"Aha!" he cried triumphantly, his black eyes flashing. "That's what *they* would say. *They'd* like you to believe that. But I have *facts*. Facts which *they* cannot dispute. For five years I have noted which train came first whenever I used the subway. Here are the facts. Right here!" He brandished a thick notebook that I hadn't noticed before. He flipped through the pages. They were filled with pencil markings and scrawled figures. "I have recomputed the results as of last Thursday. Eighty-two percent of the time the other train came first. Eighty-two percent! Do you know the odds against that figure arising by chance?"

Offhand I didn't.

"One in ten million!" he shouted, causing a few people to look up from their *National Enquirers.* He glanced around nervously and continued in a lower tone. "Does that sound like the so-called Laws of Probability are holding in this case?"

I had to admit it didn't.

"Of course not. Well then, there must be an explanation. A new theory must be proposed. One that takes into account the fact that the train I am waiting for is far less likely to arrive before the corresponding train in the opposite direction."

My heart sank. He was going to explain his theory.

"Bad luck, good luck, these terms are meaningless in Probability," he went on. "It is all supposed to even out in the end. But obviously it doesn't for some people. I am one of those people. A loser. An outcast. Nothing has ever gone right for me. Clearly nothing ever will. Just your imagination, some people say. Untrue. Eighty-two percent. That is proof. Statistical proof of my bad luck.

"But I'm not the only one who is subject to what I call the 'Other Train Phenomenon.' You noticed it. All regular subway riders notice it. Are other subway riders like me: losers, failures? Of course they are. If they were successful they wouldn't ride the subway every day. They'd drive to work, or better still, they wouldn't go to work at all. Take a look around you. These people are losers."

I did. They were.

"My theory, then, is that the Laws of Probability do not hold at the human level. Oh, they work for most things—for height and weight and predicting the number of dog bites in New York City. But in these little everyday events—the things that really matter to people—bad luck tends to occur more often for certain people . . . those who ride the subway regularly."

Well, it had a surface plausibility, but I certainly wasn't the one to judge. "Have you published anything about this theory of yours?"

His eyes stopped moving long enough to glare at me. The wrong question. He extracted a sheaf of soiled letters from the notebook and waved them at me. I caught sight of a couple of lines: "However, we do not think the subject matter is quite . . ." "Since you lack any credentials for the field you are . . ."

"This," he said, "is what *they* think of my theory. No journal would touch it. I applied for grants. I wanted to do a study of other subway riders, to see if their percentages were similar to mine. None of the foundations were interested. What does that suggest to you?"

I was surprised by the question. I knew what it suggested to me, but I knew that wasn't what he wanted to hear. I shrugged uncomfortably.

His eyes swept the car and he sidled up closer to me. "A conspiracy," he whispered. His breath smelled of onions. He raised one eyebrow, to signal that he was zeroing in on something important. "Do you think," he asked, "that the people who run the academic journals and big foundations take the subway very often?"

I shook my head. I supposed they didn't.

"Of course not," he snapped. "They're not losers. They work in plush offices. They have comfortable, tenured jobs. They're chauffeured to work, or maybe walk along tree-lined paths through their campuses. They wouldn't be caught dead squeezing into one of these broken-down trains at rush hour day after day.

"Do you see what I'm getting at?" he demanded excitedly. *"They know!"* He shouted that out, which made him whirl around in fear; then he got control of himself and continued in a lower tone. "They know, all right, but they keep it a secret. It follows, doesn't it? If there are losers, there should be winners, too. People who don't have to wait for trains. People who get tables in crowded restaurants, whose cars break down right next to all-night gas stations, whose babies get born late in December so they can claim them as tax deductions for the whole previous year. *The people who run things.*

"They know," he said, and I could see the control slipping away again. "Part of being a winner is knowing about the losers, about the so-called Laws of Probability. They talk about it in their clubs when the waiters aren't listening, you know, they joke about it in board meetings and executive washrooms. At the country club, by the swimming pool. All the places where you and I can never go. 'Isn't it nice that we are the winners,' they say. 'Isn't it nice that the losers don't realize it. By the way, I hear that some loser is nosing around about the Other Train Phenomenon. Written an article or something. It must not appear. That wouldn't do. He must be stopped.' "

The train suddenly lurched forward, and the nut grabbed my arm, his eyes wide with fear. "They're after me!" he screamed. "I have broken the unwritten law. I have uncovered their secret manipulations of the universe. And they will destroy me for it! They will destroy me!"

The wheels of the train started to squeal as it rounded the curve into the next station, and the noise drowned out the rest of what he had to say. By the time we slowed down he was sobbing. "Help me. They're after me. You must help me."

"This is my stop," I said, even though it wasn't, and I disengaged my arm as quickly as I could. He seemed to be too weak to resist.

I turned to leave, and bumped into two young men who had evidently walked up from the other end of the car. They were both wearing dark three-piece pin-striped suits and were carrying folded *Wall Street Journals*. They didn't look like they rode the subways very often. "Pardon me," they both said politely, although I was the one who had bumped into them. I rushed past them and got off the train.

I noticed them start talking to the nut, who was still in pretty bad shape. They both appeared interested in him, however. One of them had taken the nut's notebook and was leafing through it quickly. He closed it and placed it neatly inside his *Wall Street Journal* as the train pulled out.

A train came in the station from the other direction, and after a few minutes another train heading my way appeared. The air conditioning was working, thank God.

Subway riders must be grateful for small favors.

68

The Painters Are Coming Today

STEVE RASNIC TEM

"And what does the second coat do?"

"What was that?" He lowered his newspaper, exposing two bloodshot eyes. Marcia noted his thinning hair almost with surprise.

She stared down at her knitting. "I said that the painters are coming today."

He laid his newspaper into his lap and twisted his body around to face her chair. "What painters?"

"I don't know, Walter; you hired them."

"What the hell are you talking about?"

Marcia looked at him quizzically. "They called this morning, said they'd be out to paint the outside of the house this afternoon. You didn't hire them?"

"I didn't hire them, Marcia."

"I thought you hired them."

"I *didn't* hire them!"

"*You* are a very irritable person, Walter McKensie."

The painters arrived in the middle of the afternoon. Walter watched them through the thin lace curtain.

"What are you doing, Walter?"

"I'm trying to figure out what they're up to, exactly what their game is."

"What are they doing now?"

"Well, they're removing several buckets of paint from their truck, some brushes, and one of them just unbolted a ladder."

"Then I guess they're going to paint the house, Walter."

Walter stared at her sullenly.

One of the painters had already leaned a ladder against the side of the house before Walter went outside. The other painter was down on his knees mixing paint, and Walter almost tripped over the kneeling form as he came down the sidewalk.

"Watch it, buddy."

"Now see here, just what do you . . ."

"It isn't a difficult job," the man on the ground interrupted, "I would say no more than a couple of hours."

"I didn't hire any painters."

"Of course, we want to do a careful job, want to make sure it's of an even thickness, no lumps or runs. Say, two coats to start with."

"Is this some kind of con? I didn't hire any painters!"

The painter by the ladder had walked over. He appeared to Walter to be quite tall. "We *ain't* just ordinary painters, Mac."

"I don't care. I didn't call any . . ."

"In fact we're pretty special."

"I'm not going to pay for . . ."

"We were *sent.*"

"You were . . ."

"We were *sent;* it's our job."

"But who . . ."

"Oh, I think cerulean would be a nice color, don't you, Walter?" Marcia had come out of the house. She was standing behind him.

"Marcia!"

"Sky blue, ma'am? Fine color."

"Marcia, we're not going to let these crooks . . ."

"Of course, Mrs. McKensie is it? Of course, I've always been partial to robin's-egg blue."

"I don't care if . . ."

"Well, you do know your business, don't you, Mr.
. . . Painter? I'd be glad to let you . . ."

"WILL SOMEBODY LET ME FINISH A SEN-
TENCE AROUND HERE?"

They all stared at Walter.

He took a deep breath. "I didn't call you two jerks. I
didn't want my house painted. I'm *not going* to have my
house painted!"

"Walter, you just have no sense of the, the . . .
nice!" Marcia stamped her foot. "Is this what we've
come to, Walter? Evenings at home, the newspaper, your
irritability, ugly old paint?"

Out of the corner of his eye Walter could see one of the
painters swiping at the side of the house with a paint-
brush. "Hey you! Just a darn . . ."

Walter stared at the house. He opened his mouth, but
couldn't speak.

Where the painter had brushed there was nothing. No
wall. Not even the living room beyond the wall. Walter
could see grass, dirt, and the tree behind the house.

"There's nothing . . ."

"There are painters and there are painters, you know."
The shorter of the two was speaking.

"I can't see . . ."

"Take Frederick Mason now. *There* was a house
painter."

"Where did the house . . ."

"Originated the 'minimal' school of house painting
you see."

"It just vanished where he . . ."

"Mason felt that it was what you *couldn't* see, what
was suggested, that was important. More than what you
could see."

"We *ain't* your ordinary painters," the tall one said.

"We were *sent*. It's our job," the shorter one said.

Walter was sputtering now, Marcia slapping him on
the back. "Walter? Speak up, now."

He turned suddenly and grabbed her by the arms. "I tell you it's *disappearing!* What are they *doing* here?"

Marcia pushed his hands away and stepped back, eyeing Walter suspiciously. "Walter, *please.*"

Walter turned to the painters angrily. "What *are* you?"

"It's our job. We were *sent,*" they chimed.

Walter made a lunge for the tall man's brush, and grabbed the bristle end.

Four fingers disappeared. Walter examined his hand silently.

Marcia noticed the chunk missing out of Walter's hand. "Oh . . . *good,*" she said, her fingers to her lips.

The shorter painter walked over to Walter, who stood statuelike in the middle of the lawn looking at his now-absent hand. The painter began brushing his clothes, his other hand, his exposed throat. Walter was slowly disappearing.

"Oh, let me try." Marcia took the brush and finished Walter up to his head. Walter stared at her sullenly.

"Oh . . . *good,*" Marcia said as she removed her husband's ears. Then his nose. Then his balding pate. She tweaked the remaining fatty cheeks. The eyes winced.

Marcia finished Walter off.

"Oh, that was fun," she said.

She whirled around giddily, and danced over to examine the house. She could see the sky through a wide brush stroke near the top of the painters' ladder. "Hmmm, cerulean."

Marcia looked down at the painter tickling her legs with his brush. Half gone. She smiled at the painters. "Me too?"

"We were *sent.* It's our job."

She looked around her. Dozens of painters' trucks were parked at her neighbors' houses. Painters were setting up their equipment, removing wide swatches of house with each brush stroke.

"We were *sent.* It's our job."

She suddenly grinned at the painters. "Oh . . . Okay."

Both of the painters worked together, finishing her off in seconds.

"Good job," the shorter one said.

"Sure was. Gettin' better all the time," the tall one added.

They finished off the house. They wiped away the tree in the McKensies' backyard.

Then they started on the lawns, a thousand painters humming as they worked.

69
Paranoid Fantasy #1

LAWRENCE WATT-EVANS

"Better they should get you, and have it all over with."

The alarm went off and Nathan woke up.

He glanced out through the bulletproof glass of the window by his bed; seeing no obvious danger, he unstrapped himself, sat up, and turned off the burglar alarm, muttering the charm, "Rabbit, rabbit," as he did so. He took the silver cross from around his neck and dressed for the day, starting with chainmail undershirt and lead-lined jockey shorts.

After replacing the garlic at each window he burned a cone of incense, with the appropriate prayers, to placate the gods. Carefully, his hands protected by rubber gloves, he took his defanged white mouse, Theodosius, from its massive cage, then headed down to the corner restaurant for breakfast, being certain to lock the door behind him, both the three regular locks and the special one the police couldn't open. Always watching for the things that come through the walls, he ate heartily, after feeding a little of everything to Theodosius to check for poison.

Shortly thereafter, Nathan, briefcase in hand, was off to his downtown office. As if from nowhere, his obnoxious neighbor Eddie appeared before him. Nathan had been too busy not stepping on the cracks in the sidewalk to see him coming.

Eddie cried out, "Hi, Nathan! How's business?"

Nathan made a sign to ward off the evil eye, glanced about for other menaces, then muttered something about being late.

"Aw, hell, Nathan, so you'll be a few minutes late! I missed the entire day, yesterday, and nothing's happened to me! You worry too much, you know that? Why are you always . . . hey! What's that? Hey! Help!" This last was said as several large trolls and assorted gargoyles suddenly leaped out of the nearby shrubbery. With nasty giggles and remarks about foolhardiness, they grabbed Eddie, trussed him up tightly, and carried him off.

Nathan watched them go, then continued on his way to the bus stop, unconcerned. *He* was safe from *that* bunch. It was the Others that worried him, and *they* only come out at night.

70
Perchance to Dream

KATHERINE MACLEAN

"Where fantasy is bliss—"

He decided it was time to return.

And awoke stiffly in a body that was shaking with chill, feeling weak and mechanical, walking down a usual street to the usual train, to go to the usual job.

Houses that he passed looked empty, with dusty windows and curtains askew. There was a sick faint smell in the air that he recognized as the stench of decaying meat. He could not remember getting up or dressing, and he was not sure it was morning, but he kept on walking.

Grass trimmed neatly on each square lawn. Bits of a doll across one lawn which had perhaps been run over by the lawn mower. Hedges trimmed square and low. One hedge finished at a slant, a constantly descending height that cut the roots of the last bush in the line.

A dog ran by in a lope that was low to the ground, head low and flat, like a wild thing. It threw him an indifferent, yellow-eyed glance as it passed, then circled him at the same speed, then suddenly changed, and happy, tailwagging, and timid, the dog approached him to be petted, frantically signaling joy and submission.

Charles stroked its head and looked around. Across the street Harold Stevenson was walking briskly along in his

usual style to catch the same train. There was something
wrong about the cut of his suit. It hung on him, with too
much extra material. Charles looked at his hand that was
patting the dog. It had a narrow, skinny wrist with bones
showing through pale skin.

Harold walked nearer and was opposite him, swinging
his briefcase briskly, looking sharp-angled and neat, a
man drawn from straight lines. He always had been precise and meticulous, a man of efficient habits.

"Hi, Harold," Charlie called to him, moved by a
hesitating impulse.

"Hi, Charlie. See you at the station." Harold waved
stiffly and kept moving; he circled to pass a man sitting
on the sidewalk, and went on. The form on the sidewalk
sat crosslegged in a yogi pose with its eyes open and did
not move. It was fully clothed, but its face was skeletal.

Charlie looked down again to see the dog under his
petting hand, but the dog had run off silently. Charlie
straightened, put his unused hand in his pocket and
walked along toward the railway station, swinging his
briefcase. He began to be impatient with the monotony.

He went with his body as far as the railway station, sat
down on a waiting bench, unfolded a newspaper he found
in his pocket and held it before his face to pretend to be
reading. Others sat separately along the benches, holding
reading material in front of their faces, not moving or
turning pages.

Charlie returned inside his head to the other country.
Mellow warm winds across his naked skin suddenly,
braced on top of a peaked hill, leaning into the wind almost with a feeling of a bird about to take off. He leaned
farther forward, feeling his feet grip the rock and hard
dry dirt, then with a burst of effortless bounding speed he
ran down the slope and arrived at a wet sand beach still
running. He swerved, making S-shaped deep tracks of
his running feet as he slowed then stopped with a hop in
front of two men crouched over a surfboard painting a design.

"The pattern of a symbol shapes our thoughts and our thoughts shape the curl of the beach," said one to the other.

Charlie put his hand on a tanned shoulder, half feeling the contact. It was warm, but far away and long ago, as if he could not fully return to where they were. "Jim," he said. "Jim, important."

Jim rose and faced him, a wide expanse of sun-tanned chest, sun-lightened blond hair. Behind him in the distance on the sand lay the long-legged girl that was his, who was probably his fat wife at home in the suburb. "What . . . ?"

"Jim, everyone must wake up and go back to business, and make it move. It's all stopping. Our bodies are dying. We can't leave them alone like that."

"Our bodies are in fine shape," Jim said, looking down at his own sleek oiled expanse of chest. "We brought them with us." He was wearing blue swim trunks.

"But it's not real. We have to return to reality."

"What's reality?" Jim said. He pinched his bicep and grinned. "See," said his receding voice, becoming distant. "It hurts. The pattern we paint shapes the line of the picture, like the fate line in the palm or your cloud road to the sky." The distant voice faded out.

Charlie awoke to find himself on the train. The train was stopped between stations. He looked out of the window and saw green weeds growing alongside the railway tracks and up a steep embankment like a sloped gravel garden beside the train.

The direction of the sun reminded him of afternoon. He called to a man reading on the seat across the aisle and noticed that there were few people in the train, not the crowds he remembered.

"Where are we?" Charlie asked.

"Inefficient service," the man said seriously. "High taxes. Too much crookedness." He tapped his newspaper. "Investigation." He began again to read. His

glasses had fingerprint marks fogging them and the paper
was yellowing and folded with many crease marks.

A conductor came through. "Slight delay in service,"
he said in a singsong voice. "Slight delay in service."

71
Personality Problem

JOE R. LANSDALE

"Monstrous! Monstrous!"

Yeah, I know, Doc, I look terrible and don't smell any better. But you would, too, if you stayed on the go like I do, had a peg sticking out of either side of your neck and this crazy scar across the forehead. You'd think they might have told me to use cocoa butter on the place after they took the stitches out, but naw, no way. They didn't care if I had a face like a train track. No meat off *their* nose.

And how about this getup? Nice, huh? Early wino or late drug addict. You ought to walk down the street wearing this mess, you really get the stares. Coat's too small, pants too short. And these boots, now, they get the blue ribbon. You know, I'm only six five, but with these on I'm nearly seven feet! That's some heels.

But listen, how can I do any better? I can't even afford to buy myself a tie at the Goodwill, let alone get myself a new suit of clothes. And have you ever tried to fit someone my size? This shoulder is higher than the other one. The arms don't quite match, and . . . well, you see the problem. I tell you, Doc, it's no bed of roses.

Worst part of it is how people are always running from me, and throwing things, and trying to set me on fire.

289

Oh, that's the classic one. I mean, I've been frozen for a while, covered in mud, you name it, but the old favorite is the torch. And I *hate* fire. Which reminds me, think you could refrain from smoking, Doc? Sort of makes me nervous.

See, I was saying about the fire. They've trapped me in windmills, castles, and labs. All sorts of places. Some guy out there in the crowd always gets the wise idea about the fire, and there we go again, Barbecue City. Let me tell you, Doc, I've been lucky. Spell that L-U-C-K-Y. We're talking a big lucky here. I mean, that's one reason I look as bad as I do. These holes in this already ragged suit . . . Yeah, that's right, bend over. Right there, see? This patch of hide was burned right off my head, Doc, and it didn't feel like no sunburn either. I mean it hurt.

And I've got no childhood. Just a big dumb boy all my life. No dates. No friends. Nothing. Just this personality complex, and this feeling that everybody hates me on sight.

If I ever get my hands on Victor, or Igor, oh boy, gonna have to snap 'em, Doc. And I can do it, believe me. That's where they crapped in the mess kit, Doc. They made me strong. Real strong.

Give me a dime. Yeah, thanks.

Now watch this. Between thumb and finger. *Uhhhh.* How about that? Flat as a pancake.

Yeah, you're right. I'm getting a little excited. I'll lay back and take it easy.

Say, do you smell smoke?

Doc?

Doc?

Doc, damn you, put out that fire! Not you, too? Hey, I'm not a bad guy, really. Come back here, Doc! Don't leave me in here. Don't lock that door!

72
Pharaoh's Revenge

C. BRUCE HUNTER

"Something was lost in the translation."

Geoffrey glanced once more at the dusty papyrus scroll he had spread out beside a candle on the display case. He didn't need to read it again, of course. He had translated it a half-dozen times to be sure there was no mistake, and by now he knew its contents by heart. There were the obligatory prayers to Osiris and Ra, a list of ingredients, instructions for their preparation, and the promise of eternal life and unlimited power. And a cartouche at the end he hadn't been able to translate, but he didn't have to know its meaning. He had already deciphered all the important information in the scroll.

Luckily all the ingredients still existed, though researching their modern names had taken three months, and assembling them had meant another month of exploring chemist shops, spice companies, and industrial manufacturers. But he had finally completed the task, and the reward for his labors now effervesced in a beaker in front of him.

He took a deep breath and reached for the long-forgotten alchemist's formula that would soon catapult him from the lowly status of junior Egyptologist to king of the world. Closing his eyes, he gulped the dark, astringent liquor.

It burned slightly going down and Geoffrey exhaled

abruptly. The burning became a pain in the center of his chest, then spread slowly through his body. He gasped for air, but the pain turned into the searing heat of desert air too hot to breathe.

He gritted his teeth and groped for something . . . anything to squeeze his hands against. He stumbled into the display case, knocking over the candle and thrashing wildly. Then, in one final, excruciating moment, an abject darkness invaded his head.

Outside the room, a shuffle of footsteps echoed down the hallway.

"I'm sure I heard a noise in here," said a muffled voice that was quickly followed by a jiggle of the door-knob and the rasp of a key in the lock. The door swung open and the curator stepped into the darkened room.

"Turn on the lights, will you, Smyth," he said, and when the overhead bulb flashed on and he saw the body crumpled on the floor, he exclaimed, "Good Lord, Smyth, isn't this one of the assistants in your section?"

"Why, yes. That's young Jones," Smyth replied. "What happened to him?"

"Looks like he may have done himself in." The curator pried open the youth's fingers to free the crumpled paper clutched in his fist.

"What's that?" the other asked.

"It appears to be one of the scrolls from the storeroom. Jones here must have been translating it."

"Ah, yes," Smyth said, taking the scroll from his colleague's hand to examine it. "It's one of those formulas that's supposed to give life and power to its users. The museum has a number of them in storage; they're historically unimportant, really. Funny thing, though, I've never been able to make out this cartouche that comes at the end of some of them."

"Let me see," the curator said, peering at the crumpled document. "Oh, that's just a warning. It translates roughly, 'for external use only.' "

73
Pick-up for Olympus

EDGAR PANGBORN

"They still perk!"

This was Ab Thompson—you might have seen him if you were around there in the 1960s: thin nose, scant chin, hair sandy to gray, pop eyes, and a warm depth of passion for anything with wheels. If it had pistons, wheels, some kind of driving shaft, Ab could love it. When the old half-ton bumbled into his filling station, the four cylinders of his lonesome heart pounded to the spark; the best of many voices within him said tenderly: *Listen how she perks!* The bearded driver leaning from the cab had to ask him twice: "Is this the right road for Olympus?"

A genuine 1937 Chevvy, sweet as the day she was hatched. Oh—little things here and there, of course. Ab pulled himself together. "Never heard of it. You're aimed for N'York—might be beyond there somewheres." The muddy hood stirred his longing; when this thunder-buggy was made, streamlining wasn't much more than the beginning of a notion. "Water? Check the oil, sir?"

"Yes, both. Got enough gas, I think." The driver's voice was fatigued, perhaps from the June heat. Ab Thompson raised the hood and explored. Rugged, rugged . . . "They don't make 'em like this nowadays."

"I guess not." In the back of the truck a drowsy-eyed woman in a loose gown of white linen scratched the head of a leopard and kept watch of half a dozen shy little goats.

Ab marveled: it was like the dollar Ingersoll his pop used to brag about—and oh, dear Lord, how long ago was that? Before what they called the Second World War?—Ab couldn't just remember. Naturally this old girl was beat up—beat up bad, and almost thirty years old. But she ticked away. She perked. Needed a new fan belt. Leak in the top of the radiator—dump in some ginger, maybe she'd seal herself up. And the valves . . . He showed the driver the spot of dirty oil on the measuring rod. "She'll take a quart, maybe two."

"All right," said the bearded man. The woman murmured reprovingly to the leopard and tied a short rope to the grass collar on his neck. When the oil was in, the driver said apologetically: "Seems very noisy."

"That's your valves, mister. I could tighten 'em some. You got one loose tappet, I dunno—I could tighten 'er some only not too much on account if I make her too tight you don't get the power is all."

"Well—" the driver scratched the thick curls tumbling over the horns on his forehead. "Well, suppose you—"

"She ain't had a real valve job in quite some time, am I right, mister? I ain't equipped for a valve job is the hell of it. But I could look her over, give you an idea, won't cost you nothing, glad to do it. Understand, that there ticking don't hurt nothing, it's just your tappet, but them valves—" Ab spat in embarrassment.

"Yes, look her over. I'd be much obliged."

"Kind of like a good watch, mister—got to keep her cleaned up."

"Yes. Look her over, give me an idea."

Ab sighed in happiness. "Okay. Twenty minutes, say . . ."

You could pound the daylights out of them, he thought—they'd still perk. Bet she could take a 10-

percent grade in high, even now. Actually the valves weren't bad, he saw—sighing over the leaf-gauge, wishing in a brief sorrow like the touch of wings that somehow, somewhere, it might be possible to set up the right kind of shop. Suppose you could stretch the money as far as hiring an assistant—then maybe an addition on the south side, with room for a lift—nuts: no use dreaming . . . The valves weren't bad—bit of maladjustment, natural after neglect. She'd perk. They never made them like this nowadays—

The woman in white was exercising the leopard on the rope, in the open space around the gas tanks; a goat bleated peevishly.

Not that there was anything wrong with the new cars, Ab thought—especially the take-off jobs that needed only a twenty-foot clearance to sprout wings and leave the highway: those might be hell-fired cute when they got a few more bugs ironed out. And you couldn't deny the new ground models were slick and pretty: fifty miles to the gallon if you didn't average more than a hundred per. But you take this old baby—"Mister," said Ab Thompson, "you got compression, I do mean. Shouldn't have no trouble on the hills."

"That's true. I have no trouble in the hills."

"Starter ain't too good. Might've had some damage, I dunno."

"I meant to ask about that. The trouble is here in the cab."

"Huh? Nothin' there but the button you step on."

"I know. My foot keeps catching on it." Ab opened the right-hand door; the button looked good enough. "I thought, if you could build it out a little—?" The driver showed Ab the cloven bottom of his hoof. "This slot here—you see, the button catches in it."

"Oh, hell, instant plastic'll fix that." Ab trotted to his shack, delighted. Nice to have the right stuff on hand for once. He returned with a gadget like a grease-gun. "This here is something new in the trade. Hardens on contact

with air, I do mean hardens. Stick to anything—got to
handle it careful till it's dry. Comes out in a spray, like.''
He played the plastic delicately on the starter button,
building it out away from the gas pedal. ''Now try that,
sir.''

''Oh, fine. Just what I had in mind. Well, the valves—''

''Ain't too bad. But I would recommend you stop
someplace where they got the equipment. Might go on a
long time, or—well, she might kind of start complaining,
I dunno. It oughta be done.''

''I'll see to it. Much obliged.'' The woman and the
leopard climbed back in the truck. ''What do I owe
you?''

Ab massaged his neck. ''Three bucks . . . Thank you,
sir. Come again.'' The little truck rolled away. ''Jesus, I
do mean! Thirty years old and she still perks, just as
sweet as you-be-damn.''

74
The Poor

STEVE RASNIC TEM

"Marie Antoinette would have had no trouble."

The poor are grinning in his waiting room.
Waiting in his room are the poor grinning.
The purposes of his office are to help and serve the poor.
To serve and help the poor are his purposes.

They come every day, mobs of them. Some get in line at six in the morning, even knowing he won't arrive until nine. He has driven by that early, after reading about their early arrival in the newspapers, just to confirm it for himself. There were hundreds of them, some days thousands. All waiting to see him.

He reads in the newspapers that he has money to give away, jobs, coupons exchangeable for food, gift certificates, new toasters. But the central office never sends him these things. The poor frequently tell him all about new benefits being offered, but he never sees them. The poor know much better than he himself how his office is run.

In his evenings at home his wife asks him how things went during the day, what he did, if he accomplished anything, and how the poor people in line were, if he had been able to do anything for them yet.

He doesn't know how he will pay for his son's college tuition next semester, how they will be able to afford a Christmas as large as the one last year, or how they'll be able to maintain their standard of living in general. And she asks him about the poor.

He cannot imagine how the poor can live, how they can live at all. How do they meet expenses? How do they keep up with the rising cost of food?

He sometimes wonders if the poor are real at all, or actors hired by someone who hates him, hired to disturb the regular pace of his day, to corrupt his dreams with their thin faces.

Or perhaps they're an illusion, and he simply minds an empty office all day. For why else would the central office ignore him, all his letters requesting funds, his many phone calls?

You worry yourself sick, you don't enjoy life, his wife tells him. You're brooding about them all the time.

Them? he asks. You mean "the poor." Can't you even say the word?

His marriage is falling apart. What if he told them that? Then would they stop lining up outside his office?

He decides to arrive early each day. Talk to them. Get to know them. Show them he wants to understand their many needs.

When he arrives early he discovers that the line is much longer than ever before. Is that any way for them to show their appreciation? They're backed up outside the building and around the parking lot. He has to shove and kick his way into the building; some of them think he's one of them, and keep trying to force him back to the end of the line.

He walks up and down the line attempting to make conversation, but they won't reply to any of his questions, merely nod or shake their heads, wring their hands. A few weep quietly. Can't they see he's trying to help them?

At nine he gives up, unlocks his office door, and sits

behind his desk. There is some shuffling outside as a committee of the poor checks their line-up sheet to see if anyone's missing or wants to trade places, and then they send the first one in.

It is a tall, thin, quiet man with dark circles under his eyes. He looks as if he hasn't slept, or eaten, for a week. He sits down in the chair before the desk, and stares.

The poor man stares for several minutes, making him feel like an intruder in his own office. Then finally the poor man says, "I want a wife."

He stares at the man in fascination. How could he request such a thing?

I'm afraid I cannot provide that for you. I'm sorry, he tells the poor man.

"I'm lonely, I need someone," the poor man tells him.

He rummages through his desk trying to find a form for the poor man to fill out, some kind of application, anything to distract him. He slides a form in front of the man. "Do you need a pencil?"

The poor man starts to fill out the form. It's a request for an emergency gallon of gasoline. He hopes the man won't be able to tell the difference.

Perhaps I could give him my wife, he thinks, and is ashamed of the thought.

There seems to be a gradual change in the poor, the first change he can ever remember. The line seems to have broken down into little groups, little conclaves. What could the poor be planning?

Perhaps they're plotting for more bread, sex, and rest? Or maybe they're planning to kill police officers, politicians, social workers?

Each day he goes home, his wife asks him, What are the poor doing today?

They're plotting, he tells her. They're seeking to overthrow our present form of government.

She nods her head in feigned interest.

He and his wife seem to have little time for each other

any more, he thinks. It's simply too time-consuming just making a living, trying to maintain current standards, trying not to be poor.

The poor have moved into the trunk of his car.

He had gone into the garage this morning, opened the trunk to load his briefcase, and the old poor man who'd requested a wife was lying curled up in the trunk.

You can't be here, he told the poor man. This won't do at all.

The poor man just stared at him sadly. No doubt waiting for his wife.

You can't have my wife, he told him.

At work the poor were in his office. You can't be here, he told them.

But they said nothing. They sat on his desk. They were lying beneath his desk.

Several had tried to sit in his chair, but the chair had broken.

The poor were in the bathroom, hundreds of them, living and sleeping there. The poor filled the parking lot with their cooking pots and sleeping rolls.

The poor are everywhere, he tells his wife in the kitchen at home. Several poor people are sitting at their kitchen table.

There are twelve poor people living in his garage, and six more on the patio.

I know what you're planning! he tells them hysterically.

One morning he finds a poor woman with her lips clamped around his car's exhaust pipe.

Another afternoon there is a poor couple trying unsuccessfully to make love in his back seat, their starved and tattered forms smacking together futilely. He finds one in his living room, lying in front of the TV, and he beats it with a broom.

He finds one hanging from the lamp in his bedroom and he jerks it down violently.

He discovers one curled beneath his easy chair and he stomps it with his feet until it's dead.

The poor are living in his trash.

They're living in his bed with his wife.

The poor are dying. He beats them and they're dying.

He finds the dead bodies stacked in his garage like cordwood. He finds them piled in the study.

Small, emaciated bodies, the flesh fragile as paper, the mouths pulled back in a rictus.

The poor want too much from him. They want all the little things he has. How can he take care of himself?

The bodies of the poor fill his bedroom. He can't even find his wife any more. The dead hands try to catch his clothes; the dead, widening mouths want to eat him.

They know they will always be poor. They know the wealth will never filter down through all the widening hands to their own, thin hands.

No, no! he tells the dead bodies spilling over his bed. I have an office; I'm there to help . . .

But the mouths say nothing.

The poor are his.

75
Prayer War

JONATHAN V. POST

"Going straight to the top."

Call me G.I. Joseph. I'm just another guy with a cross to bear, out fighting the Prayer War for the Holy Infant Infantry. Yeah, on my knees for God and the good old U.S.A.

I kissed my girl goodbye at the HaloCopter station. There were tears the size of Jerusalem on her cheeks. The next day she went into the St. Bridget Brigade of the 7th Convent Corps. I shipped overseas, attached to the Zero Zero Zen Satori Shock Troops. We would never see each other again, this side of heaven.

General Yamaha whipped us into shape with heavy labor gardening meditations, KP koans, and top-secret crypto clearance mantras. My goofy buddies and me were parachuted behind Maoist lines in Tibet. Midwinter. Few of us made it back with our faith intact. The prayer wheels were frozen solid.

President Carter broadcast from the White House rose garden, where she gave a sermon from her Cross-Country motorcycle. Her two worldly brothers grinned from behind the altar. "God is on our side," she said, straight into the camera, "but we are suffering from a Prayer Gap. We must increase our Divine Defense budget immediately. It is our right to bear alms. Amen.''

This was good news to the Theological Research and Development boys, but bad news to the God Grunts like me. Now they've volunteered me for a Mission into Russian Poland, where a wounded Pope is leading the Resistance.

War is hell.

76
The Prophecy

BILL PRONZINI

"Wanna bet?"

Arizikian, the High Priest of Seers, predicted that the world would come to an end on the twenty-ninth day of August, 1979, at the hour of noon.

His announcement was made public exactly one week prior to that date. Upon hearing it, the Believers fell to their knees, crying out in anguish, praying with upraised hands that their sins be forgiven and their eternal souls be allowed safe passage through the Gates of Heaven. But they numbered relatively few.

The Skeptics—a slightly larger preponderance—were, of course, contemptuous.

"A hoax," some said, "created for publicity purposes."

"Pure foolishness," others laughed. "Seers have been predicting the end of the world for centuries. Have any of them been right yet?"

But in the masses—the Agnostics, if you will—there arose the seed of apprehension. Arizikian was no ordinary Seer; the very mention of his name touched nerves, brought chills.

The unspoken question echoes silently from their lips: "Suppose, this time, it's true?"

For was it not Arizikian who had predicted the exact day man would first set foot on the planet Mars, and did not man set foot there on that day?

Was it not Arizikian who foresaw the terrible nuclear explosion at Cape Kennedy and with it the total obliteration of the sovereign state of Florida, and did it not come to pass?

Was it not Arizikian who prophesied the exact time and place the thirty-ninth President of the United States would die of massive coronary thrombosis, and did not the President die at that time, in that place, in that way?

Was it not Arizikian whose every portension, without fail, without err, came true exactly as he said it would?

But—

But—the end of the world?

But—Arizikian was never wrong.

The days passed, and with their passing the apprehension grew.

The twenty-ninth day of August arrived.

The Believers gathered on rich, verdant meadows in every country in the world. They sat, legs crossed, on the clean, sweet grasses, their arms lifted, their mouths opened in prayer, their faces upturned to brilliant sunshine, or cool ocean breezes, or driving summer rain.

The Skeptics noted the day with scorn, and nothing more.

The Agnostics attempted to conceal their anxiety beneath the guise of normalcy. Men stood on street corners, or sat in cool, air-conditioned offices, their eyes covertly darting to strap watches or wall clocks and the second hand that circled with infinite slowness there.

Women sat in front of flickering television screens, their housework undone, unable on this day to lose themselves in the false reality of the soap dramas, waiting with moist lips and wide eyes for the news broadcasts that followed.

Time passed. Seconds ticked off; inexorable. The

sun—palpitating, or pale, or non-existent—climbed
higher into the sky, coming perpendicular.

At eleven fifty-nine, the silent countdown began.

Fifty-nine.

Fifty-eight.

Fifty-seven . . .

In those parts of the world where superstition was in-
bred into the culture, work came to a standstill; people
milled about in confusion, frightened, beseeching.

Forty-five.

Forty-four.

Forty-three . . .

The Believers were standing in the meadows now.
They had begun to chant.

Thirty.

Twenty-nine.

Twenty-eight . . .

A billion eyes lifted to the sky.

Sixteen.

Fifteen.

Fourteen . . .

The people of the world held their breath.

Four.

Three.

Two.

One.

Noon.

Came.

And went.

Nothing happened.

Nothing at all.

Life went on, and the Earth continued to rotate on its
axis.

Men turned to each other in the buildings and on the
streets and in the fields, smiling a bit sheepishly, feeling
a bit foolish for the weakness that watered their knees.

"You see?" they said with thinly veiled relief. "The

same as it's always been with these things. No need for alarm.''

In the green meadows, Believers sank to the grass in bewilderment.

''How can it be?'' they asked of their neighbors. ''How can it be?''

The Skeptics smiled knowingly and went about their business with the superior air of the pragmatist.

''The end of the world, indeed!'' they scoffed. ''How absurd!''

''Contrary to what Arizikian, the High Priest of Seers, predicted one week ago,'' they said, ''the world did *not* come to an end at noon today. Arizikian, it seems, is human after all; he was finally wrong.''

Those words had been joyously repeated a thousand times, in a multitude of tongues and dialects, when the sky split open like an overripe melon at a quarter to three, and the heavens rained the holocaust down from above.

Yes, Arizikian had finally been wrong.

By two hours and forty-five minutes.

77
The Rag Thing

DONALD A. WOLLHEIM

"Where there's life, there's death."

It would have been all right if spring had never come.
During the winter nothing had happened and nothing was
likely to happen as long as the weather remained cold and
Mrs. Larch kept the radiators going. In a way, though, it
is quite possible to hold Mrs. Larch to blame for everything that happened. Not that she had what people would
call malicious intentions, but just that she was two things
practically every boarding-house landlady is—thrifty and
not too clean.

She shouldn't have been in such a hurry to turn the
heat off so early in March. March is a tricky month
and she should have known that the first warm day is
usually an isolated phenomenon. But then you could
always claim that she shouldn't have been so sloppy in
her cleaning last November. She shouldn't have dropped
that rag behind the radiator in the third floor front
room.

As a matter of fact, one could well wonder what she
was doing using such a rag anyway. Polishing furniture
doesn't require a clean rag to start with, certainly not the
rag you stick into the furniture polish, that's going to be
greasy anyway—but she didn't have to use that particular

rag. The one that had so much dried blood on it from the meat that had been lying on it in the kitchen.

On top of that, it is probable that she had spit into the filthy thing, too. Mrs. Larch was no prize package. Gross, dull, unkempt, widowed and careless, she fitted into the house—one of innumerable other brownstone fronts in the lower sixties of New York. Houses that in former days, fifty or sixty years ago, were considered the height of fashion and the residences of the well-to-do, now reduced to dingy rooming places for all manner of itinerants, lonely people with no hope in life other than dreary jobs, or an occasional young and confused person from the hinterland seeking fame and fortune in a city which rarely grants it.

So it was not particularly odd that when she accidentally dropped the filthy old rag behind the radiator in the room on the third floor front late in November, she had simply left it there and forgotten to pick it up.

It gathered dust all winter, unnoticed. Skelty, who had the room, might have cleaned it out himself save that he was always too tired for that. He worked at some indefinite factory all day and when he came home he was always too tired to do much more than read the sports and comics pages of the newspapers and then maybe stare at the streaky brown walls a bit before dragging himself into bed to sleep the dreamless sleep of the weary.

The radiator, a steam one, oddly enough (for most of these houses used the older hot-air circulation), was in none too good condition. Installed many many years ago by the house's last Victorian owner, it was given to knocks, leaks, and cantankerous action. Along in December it developed a slow drip, and drops of hot water would fall to seep slowly into the floor and leave the rag lying on a moist hot surface. Steam was constantly escaping from a bad valve that Mrs. Larch would have repaired if it had blown off completely but, because the radiator always managed to be hot, never did.

Because Mrs. Larch feared drafts, the windows were

rarely open in the winter and the room would become oppressively hot at times when Skelty was away.

It is hard to say what is the cause of chemical reactions. Some hold that all things are mechanical in nature, others that life has a psychic side which cannot be duplicated in laboratories. The problem is one for metaphysicians; everyone knows that some chemicals are attracted to heat, others to light, and they may not necessarily be alive at all. Tropisms is the scientific term used, and if you want to believe that living matter is stuff with a great number of tropisms and dead matter is stuff with little or no tropisms, that's one way of looking at it. Heat and moisture and greasy chemical compounds were the sole ingredients of the birth of life in some ancient unremembered swamp.

Which is why it probably would have been all right if spring had never come. Because Mrs. Larch turned the radiators off one day early in March. The warm hours were but few. It grew cold with the darkness and by night it was back in the chill of February again. But Mrs. Larch had turned the heat off and, being lazy, decided not to turn it on again till the next morning, provided of course that it stayed cold the next day (which it did).

Anyway Skelty was found dead in bed the next morning. Mrs. Larch knocked on his door when he failed to come down to breakfast and when he hadn't answered, she turned the knob and went in. He was lying in bed, blue and cold, and he had been smothered in his sleep.

There was quite a to-do about the whole business, but nothing came of it. A few stupid detectives blundered around the room, asked silly questions, made a few notes, and then left the matter to the coroner and the morgue. Skelty was a nobody, no one cared whether he lived or died, he had no enemies and no friends, there were no suspicious visitors, and he had probably smothered accidentally in the blankets. Of course the body was unusually cold when Mrs. Larch found it, as if the heat had been sucked out of him, but who notices a thing like that? They also discounted the grease smudge on the top sheet, the grease stains on the floor, and the slime on his face. Probably some grease he might have been using for some imagined skin trouble, though Mrs. Larch had not heard of his doing so. In any case, no one really cared.

Mrs. Larch wore black for a day and then advertised in the paper. She made a perfunctory job of cleaning the room. Skelty's possessions were taken away by a drab sister-in-law from Brooklyn who didn't seem to care much either, and Mrs. Larch was all ready to rent the room to someone else.

The weather remained cold for the next ten days and the heat was kept up in the pipes.

The new occupant of the room was a nervous young man from upstate who was trying to get a job in New York. He was a high-strung young man who entertained any number of illusions about life and society. He thought that people did things for the love of it and he wanted to find a job where he could work for that motivation rather than the sort of things he might have done back home. He thought New York was different, which was a mistake.

He smoked like fury, which was something Mrs. Larch did not like because it meant ashes on the floor and burned spots on her furniture (not that there weren't plenty already), but there was nothing Mrs. Larch would do about it, because it would have meant exertion.

After four days in New York, this young man, Gorman by name, was more nervous than ever. He would lie in bed nights smoking cigarette after cigarette, thinking and thinking and getting nowhere. Over and over he was facing the problem of resigning himself to a life of gray drab. It was a thought he had tried not to face and now that it was thrusting itself upon him, it was becoming intolerable.

The next time a warm day came, Mrs. Larch left the radiators on because she was not going to be fooled twice. As a result, when the weather stayed warm, the rooms became insufferably hot because she was still keeping the windows down. So that when she turned the heat off finally, the afternoon of the second day, it was pretty tropic in the rooms.

When the March weather turned about suddenly again and became chilly about nine at night, Mrs. Larch was going to bed and figured that no one would complain and that it would be warm again the next day. Which may or may not be true. It does not matter.

Gorman got home about ten, opened the window, got undressed, moved a pack of cigarettes and an ashtray next to his bed on the floor, got into bed, turned out the light, and started to smoke.

He stared at the ceiling, blowing smoke upward into the darkened room trying to see its outlines in the dim light coming in from the street. When he finished one cigarette, he let his hand dangle out the side of the bed and picked up another cigarette from the pack on the floor, lit it from the butt in his mouth, and dropped the butt into the ashtray on the floor.

The rag under the radiator was getting cold, the room was getting cold, there was one source of heat radiation in the room. That was the man in bed. Skelty had proven a source of heat supply once. Heat attraction was chemical force that could not be denied. Strange forces began to accumulate in the long-transformed fibers of the rag.

Gorman thought he heard something flap in the room but he paid it no attention. Things were always creaking in the house. Gorman heard a swishing noise and ascribed it to the mice.

Gorman reached down for a cigarette, fumbled for it, found the pack, deftly extracted a smoke in the one-handed manner chain smokers become accustomed to, lifted it to his mouth, lit it from the burning butt in his mouth, and reached down with the butt to crush it out against the tray.

He pressed the butt into something wet like a used handkerchief, there was a sudden hiss, something coiled

and whipped about his wrist; Gorman gasped and drew
his hand back fast. A flaming horror, twisting and
writhing, was curled around it. Before Gorman could
shriek, it had whipped itself from his hand and fastened
over his face, over the warm, heat-radiating skin and the
glowing flame of the cigarette.

Mrs. Larch was awakened by the clang of fire engines.
When the fire was put out, most of the third floor had
been gutted. Gorman was an unrecognizable charred
mass.

The fire department put the blaze down to Gorman's
habit of smoking in bed. Mrs. Larch collected on the fire
insurance and bought a new house, selling the old one to
a widow who wanted to start a boardinghouse.

78
The Recording

GENE WOLFE

"At last! Calling it as it is!"

I have found my record, a record I have owned for fifty years and never played until five minutes ago. Let me explain.

When I was a small boy—in those dear, dead days of Model A Ford touring cars, horse-drawn milk trucks, and hand-cranked ice cream freezers—I had an uncle. As a matter of fact, I had several, all brothers of my father, and all, like him, tall and somewhat portly men with faces stamped (as my own is) in the image of *their* father, the lumberman and land speculator who built this Victorian house for his wife.

But this particular uncle, my uncle Bill, whose record (in a sense I shall explain) it was, was closer than all the others to me. As the eldest, he was the titular head of the family, for my grandfather had passed away a few years after I was born. His capacity for beer was famous, and I suspect now that he was "comfortable" much of the time, a large-waisted (how he would roar if he could see his little nephew's waistline today!), red-faced, good-humored man whom none of us—for a child catches these attitudes as readily as measles—took wholly seriously.

The special position which, in my mind, this uncle

occupied is not too difficult to explain. Though younger than many men still working, he was said to be retired, and for that reason I saw much more of him than of any of the others. And despite his being something of a figure of fun, I was a little frightened of him, as a child may be of the painted, rowdy clown at a circus; this, I suppose, because of some incident of drunken behavior witnessed at the edge of infancy and not understood. At the same time I loved him, or at least would have said I did, for he was generous with small gifts and often willing to talk when everyone else was "too busy."

Why my uncle had promised me a present I have now quite forgotten. It was not my birthday, and not Christmas—I vividly recall the hot, dusty streets over which the maples hung motionless, year-worn leaves. But promise he had, and there was no slightest doubt in my mind about what I wanted.

Not a collie pup like Tarkington's little boy, or even a bicycle (I already had one). No, what I wanted (how modern it sounds now) was a phonograph record. Not, you must understand, any particular record, though perhaps if given a choice I would have leaned toward one of the comedy monologues popular then, or a military march; but simply a record of my own. My parents had recently acquired a new phonograph, and I was forbidden to use it for fear that I might scratch the delicate wax disks. If I had a record of my own, this argument would lose its validity. My uncle agreed and promised that after dinner (in those days eaten at two o'clock) we would walk the eight or ten blocks which then separated this house from the business area of the town, and, unknown to my parents, get me one.

I no longer remember of what that dinner consisted— time has merged it in my mind with too many others, all eaten in that dark, oak-paneled room. Stewed chicken would have been typical, with dumplings, potatoes, boiled vegetables, and, of course, bread and creamery butter. There would have been pie afterward, and coffee,

and my father and my uncle adjourning to the front
porch—called the "stoop"—to smoke cigars. At last my
father left to return to his office, and I was able to harry
my uncle into motion.

From this point my memory is distinct. We trudged
through the heat, he in a straw boater and a blue and
white seersucker suit as loose and voluminous as the
robes worn by the women in the plates of our family Bible; I in the costume of a French sailor, with a striped
shirt under my blouse and a pomponned cap embroidered
in gold with the word *Indomptable*. From time to time, I
pulled at his hand, but did not like to because of its wet
softness, and an odd, unclean smell that offended me.

When we were a block from Main Street, my uncle
complained of feeling ill, and I urged that we hurry our
errand so that he could go home and lie down. On Main
Street he dropped onto one of the benches the town provided and mumbled something about Fred Croft, who
was our family doctor and had been a schoolmate of his.
By this time I was frantic with fear that we were going to
turn back, depriving me (as I thought, forever) of access
to the phonograph. Also I had noticed that my uncle's
usually fiery face had gone quite white, and I concluded
that he was about to "be sick," a prospect that threw me
into an agony of embarrassment. I pleaded with him to
give me the money, pointing out that I could run the half
block remaining between the store and ourselves in less
than no time. He only groaned and told me again to fetch
Fred Croft. I remember that he had removed his straw hat
and was fanning himself with it while the August sun
beat down unimpeded on his bald head.

For a moment, if only for a moment, I felt my power.
With a hand thrust out I told him, in fact ordered him, to
give me what I wished. I remember having said: "I'll get
him. Give me the money, Uncle Bill, and then I'll bring
him."

He gave it to me and I ran to the store as fast as my flying heels would carry me, though as I ran I was acutely

conscious that I had done something wrong. There I accepted the first record offered me, danced with impa-
tience waiting for my change, and then, having completely forgotten that I was supposed to bring Dr. Croft,
returned to see if my uncle had recovered.

In appearance he had. I thought that he had fallen
asleep waiting for me, and I tried to wake him. Several
passers-by grinned at us, thinking, I suppose, that Uncle
Bill was drunk. Eventually, inevitably, I pulled too hard.
His ponderous body rolled from the bench and lay, face
up, mouth slightly open, on the hot sidewalk before me. I
remember the small crescents of white that showed then
beneath the half-closed eyelids.

During the two days that followed, I could not have
played my record if I had wanted to. Uncle Bill was laid
out in the parlor where the phonograph was, and for me,
a child, to have entered that room would have been un-
thinkable. But during this period of mourning, a strange
fantasy took possession of my mind. I came to believe—I
am not enough of a psychologist to tell you why—that if I
were to play my record, the sound would be that of my
uncle's voice, pleading again for me to bring Dr. Croft,
and accusing me. This became the chief nightmare of my
childhood.

To shorten a long story, I never played it. I never
dared. To conceal its existence I hid it atop a high cup-
board in the cellar; and there it stayed, at first the subject
of midnight terrors, later almost forgotten.

Until now. My father passed away at sixty, but my
mother has outlasted all these long decades, until the time
when she followed him at last a few months ago, and I,
her son, standing beside her coffin, might myself have
been called an old man.

And now I have reoccupied our home. To be quite
honest, my fortunes have not prospered, and though this
house is free and clear, little besides the house itself has
come to me from my mother. Last night, as I ate alone in
the old dining room where I have had so many meals, I

thought of Uncle Bill and the record again; but I could
not, for a time, recall just where I had hidden it, and in
fact feared that I had thrown it away. Tonight I remembered, and though my doctors tell me that I should not
climb stairs, I found my way down to the old cellar and
discovered my record beneath half an inch of dust. There
were a few chest pains lying in wait for me on the steps;
but I reached the kitchen once more without a mishap,
washed the poor old platter and my hands, and set it on
my modern high fidelity. I suppose I need hardly say the
voice is not Uncle Bill's. It is instead (of all people!)
Rudy Vallee's. I have started the recording again and can
hear it from where I write: *"My time is your time . . .
My time is your time."* So much for superstition.

79
Red Carpet Treatment

ROBERT LIPSYTE

"You get what you pay for."

"THIS IS YOUR PILOT. DUE TO CIRCUMSTANCES BEYOND
YOUR CONTROL, THIS AIRCRAFT WILL DESCRIBE A HOLD-
ING PATTERN FOR THE NEXT FIFTEEN MINUTES, THEN AS-
CEND TO HEAVEN. QUALIFIED PASSENGERS WILL BE
ALLOWED TO DISEMBARK. THANK YOU."

It was the fat priest with the cigarette holder who spoke
first, sputtering through a mouthful of purple grapes he
was eating out of his pocket.

"What the hell kind of joke is this?"

A little boy began to cry because his mother looked
worried, and a young man and his younger wife squeezed
each other's hand. The tourist section of the plane, where
they all sat, was crowded but quiet.

Up front, in the first-class section, a stubby man with
hairy hands and a monogrammed pink shirt twisted toward the blonde in the window seat. "Must of been a
crash, Puff. This is it."

A thin, tanned man with a manicured mustache sitting
behind them leaned over. "What'd you say, Max?"

"I said we must of got knocked off." Max patted
the blonde's arm. "Don't worry, Puff, just fix your

319

320 ROBERT LIPSYTE

face. Whatever happens, just let Poppa do the talking."

When the stewardesses did not move or fasten smiles on their lacquered faces, the passengers began to look at each other, and then to talk. There were twenty-one people in first-class and fifty-eight in tourist and their voices became suddenly loud as the engine noises faded. The fat priest had swallowed his grapes, unbuckled his safety belt and stepped out into the aisle.

"This is not comical," he said. "This is foul blasphemy, and a cruel joke."

A gray-haired lady with bright blue eyes pulled at his black sleeve. "Oh, Father, what Glory, we are being transported, gathered into His Arms, as it were."

"As it were, as it were," muttered the priest, sitting down heavily, on the metal buckle.

Up front, the man with the mustache tapped Max on the shoulder. "Will it go hard, Max, you think it'll be bad?"

"Relax, Charlie, you can never tell about these things," Max ran his thick fingers up Puff's arm, but the blonde was repairing her mascara.

Two rows ahead, a portly man in a blue suit was slipping a soft hand inside his shirt and under his left breast, and breathing hard. His wife, a thin woman with the face of a headache, said: "Think about all those Sunday mornings you played golf, Harry."

The young couple in tourist understood now and smiled at each other. "I'm glad we waited, darling, aren't you glad we waited?"

"It was worth waiting for," he said.

"That's not what I meant, darling, I mean we did everything right and now . . ."

The gray-haired lady started to chant, "Bless me, Father, for . . ." but everyone around her began to call to the priest and pluck at his sleeve. He lurched into the aisle again, spitting grape seeds, and ran to the lavatory. It was occupied.

"Mommy?" whimpered the little boy, and his mother smiled and caressed his hand.

"You'll be with Daddy soon, you'll be with . . ."

Suddenly, the engines cut off completely and the plane began to climb.

"Soon, soon," cried the gray-haired lady in tourist, almost orgiastically, and the young couple smiled and kissed the air near each other's cheeks, and the mother held her son tightly and three young women near the galley crossed themselves and the priest was on his knees, his head against the locked lavatory door.

There was great quiet in first class. The portly man had slumped against the window and Max folded fifty dollars into Puff's hand. "We might get separated, baby."

The plane landed, and the intercom crackled again.

"THIS IS YOUR PILOT. WE HAVE LANDED IN HEAVEN. ALL FIRST-CLASS PASSENGERS WILL DISEMBARK. THOSE OF YOU WHO ARE CONTINUING WITH US, PLEASE MAKE SURE YOUR SEAT BELTS ARE FASTENED. YOU MAY SMOKE."

80
The Sacrifice

GARDNER DOZOIS

"Turnabout is fair play."

There were four of them who entered the haunted darkness of the Old Forest that night, but only three who would return, because three was a magic number.

Featherflower walked silently beside her father Nightwind, her head high, trying not to stumble over the twisted, snakelike roots that seemed to snatch at her legs, trying not to flinch or start at the sinister noises of the forest, the wailing and hooting of things that might be birds, the rustling and crackling of the undergrowth as unseen bodies circled around them in the secret blackness of the night. Her heart was pounding like a fist inside her, but she would not let herself show fear—she was a chief's daughter, after all, and though he led her now to an almost certain death, she would not betray his dignity or her own. Firehair walked slightly ahead of them, as befitted a young war leader in the prime of his strength, but his steps were slow and sometimes faltering, the whites of his eyes showing as he looked around him, and Featherflower took a bitter and strength-giving pleasure from the unspoken but undeniable fact that he was more afraid than she was. Grim old Lamefoot brought up the rear, his scarred and graying body moving silently as a ghost, imperturbable, his steps coming no faster or slower than they ever did.

They had been silent since the trees had closed out the sky overhead—the Old Forest at night had never been a place that encouraged inconsequential chatter, but this silence was heavy and sour and unyielding, pressing down upon them more smotheringly even than the fey and enchanted darkness that surrounded them. Feather-flower could sense her father's agony, the grief and guilt that breathed from him like a bitter wind, but she would not make it easier for him by deed or gesture or word. She was the one who was to be sacrificed—why should she comfort *him?* She knew her duty as well as he knew his, had been born to it, and she would not fight or seek to escape, but it hurt her in her heart that Nightwind—her *father*—would do this thing to her, however grave the need, and she would not make it easier for him. Let it be hard, as it soon would be hard for her, let him hurt and sweat and cry aloud with the hardness of it.

So they walked through the forest in silence and guilty enmity and fear, the great and living darkness walking with them, abristle with watching eyes, until ahead there was a glitter of light.

The forest opened up around them into a small meadow, drenched with brilliant silver moonlight. At the far end of the meadow rose an enormous oak tree, a giant of the forest, its huge branches spread high above them like waiting, encircling arms.

"Here," said old Lamefoot the wizard. "He will come *here.*"

When they had crossed the meadow and stood beneath the arms of the oak tree, Featherflower said quietly, "Father, must this be?"

Nightwind sighed. "The trees do not bloom, the streams dry up, the grass is sere . . . It has been long and long since such a thing was done, and I had hoped my time would pass before it was again needful, but clearly the gods have turned their faces away . . ." He fell silent again, looking very old. *"He* will come here," Lamefoot said in his grim gray voice, "and if he accepts you, then the powers will smile on us again . . ." Firehair looked guiltily away from her, glanced nervously around him with wide frightened eyes and said only "It is for the good of the Folk . . ."

She blew out her lips at him in scorn, snorting derisively. "Then for the good of the Folk, I will stay," she said, and sat herself down beneath the giant old oak.

Lamefoot studied her closely. "You will not run away, child?"

"No," she said calmly. "I will not run away . . ."

They watched her for a while longer then, but there was nothing more for anyone to say, and so at last they went away and left her there, Nightwind giving one last agonized look back before the darkness swallowed them.

She was alone in the Old Forest.

Trembling, she waited beneath the ancient oak. Never had she been so afraid. The dark shapes of the trees seemed to press menacingly close around the meadow, kept at bay only by the silver moonlight. A bat flitted by through that moonlight, squeaking, and she flinched away from it. Something howled away across the cold and silent reaches of the forest, howled again in a voice like rusty old iron. Featherflower's head turned constantly as she sought to look in all directions at once, straining wide-eyed to pierce the gloom beneath the trees. She would not give way to fear, she would not give way to fear . . . but her defenses were crumbling, being sluiced away by a rising flood of terror.

A crashing in the forest, growing louder, coming nearer, the sound of branches bending and snapping, leaves rustling, the sound of some large body forcing its brute way through the entangling undergrowth . . .

She looked away, fear choking her like a hand, stopping her breath.

Something *coming* . . .

There was movement among the trees, the bare branches stirring gently as though moved by the ghost of the wind, and when she looked again *he* was there, seeming to materialize from the dappled leaf-shadows, his head held high, paler than the moonlight, clothed in the awful glory of his flesh, so noble and swift-moving and puissant, so proud and lordly of bearing that all fear vanished from her and she felt her heart melt within her with poignant and unbearable love.

Their eyes met, hers shy and guileless, his bright and clear and wild, liquid as molten gold. She tossed her own head back, moonlight gleaming from the long white horn that protruded from her forehead, and pawed nervously at the ground with a tiny silver hoof.

He came to her then across the broken ground, the human, moving as lightly and soundlessly as mist, and laid his terrible head in her lap.

81
Santa's Tenth Reindeer

GORDON VAN GELDER

"Have you ever noticed the anagram?"

Billy Avendil didn't go to sleep on Christmas Eve. He lay awake in bed, watching the minutes tick off his clock. He was nervous, he was excited, he was anxious, he had something up his sleeve.

He waited until he felt he had waited long enough, then he tiptoed out of his room, taking precautions in case somebody was still half awake. He slid down the banister to avoid the squeaky stairs and because it was fun.

He instantly went to work, setting up his trap, testing it, making sure that everything was right. He considered setting a fire in the fireplace for the twelfth time, and for the twelfth time he decided that Santa would see the fire in time. Especially if his doubts were correct. But that was what he was doing all this for.

Then came the waiting. He sat down behind the tree, chewing his nails. He got up, started pacing, considered taking a cigarette from his mother's pocketbook, decided against it, paced some more, and was getting up for the cigarette when he heard noises on the rooftop.

Ho ho ho jingle jingle. The sound of hoofs beat against the roof. Billy raced to his spot behind the tree and gripped the pole nervously. He wondered about the reindeer, for if his theory was right, then the reindeer would be different, but he didn't have time to follow up on the thought.

Ho ho ho ugh ugh damn oof ugh. Santa was on his way down. Billy wondered if he should have stuck a knife in the chimney.

Ah phew ho ho whooooa oof! Santa emerged from the fireplace, stepped onto the skateboard, and went flying into the tree. Billy pushed the angel off the tree, and it struck Santa on the head with a crash. Then Billy hit Santa on the head with the pole. Santa fell to the floor, unconscious.

Billy tied Santa's hands to the tree, and lashed the feet together. Then he confirmed his theory, and took a picture for proof. He waited for Santa to awaken.

Santa came to with an awful headache. He realized where he was, and he swore, a long string of curses too terrible to repeat. When his "speech" was over, he said, "Why'd you do this, Billy? If it's my presents you want, take them. I don't give a damn. It just means that a lot of kids are going to be disappointed."

"Take your presents and stuff them up your fat rear, one at a time. I don't want your presents. All I wanted was proof of who you are, and I've got it," said Billy.

"All right, son, you've caught me."

"Get lost. My father's upstairs, with enough drugs in him to put an elephant to sleep. I know who you are."

"Damn, I think that you do know."

"That's right, Santa. I know why you always wear red, and it's not because it matches your nose. That was a pretty good joke, with the switch of the names. I liked it."

"I'm thrilled," said Santa unemphatically.

"Aww. Why so sad, Prince? Sad that the cat's out of the bag, along with all the other stuff you've got in there?" asked Billy.

"Do you know what a pain in the, uh, neck you are,

Billy? I have stuff to do, and you're keeping me from doing it," said Santa.

"Aww, that's too bad. The Prince of Evil worried that he won't give out enough presents? Tsk tsk."

"You're the snottiest kid I know, and I think that all kids are snotty," said Santa.

Billy made a disgusting noise in response to Santa's statement. "Could you tell me something?" asked Billy. "Why do you do it? Why give out presents, and eggs on Easter, and love on Valentine's Day, why?"

"Take a guess," said Santa dryly. "Are you going to let me loose?"

"Not until I get answers, that's for sure. Why do you do it?" he repeated.

"You're evil, you're clever, figure it out."

"If I could've figured it out, I wouldn't have asked. Tell me."

"More hate comes through love than any other way," said Santa.

"Bull. That ruins the definition of love."

"Really? Think about it. What are half the murders? Husband and wife. How do best friends become best enemies? By chasing after the same person. Don't you see? Love and hate go hand in hand, like life and death. Are you going to release me?"

Billy was considering everything Santa had said. "I see your point, Santa, but there are still things I don't understand. Why give out presents?"

"They go with evil, too. Haven't you ever seen two kids fight over who gets the better present? Just think about the things you ask, and you'll get answers."

"No. True, presents do cause some evil, but they spread a lot of love. So does Valentine's Day, so does Easter, so do all your holidays."

"The world cannot exist without opposites—love and hate, life and death, day and night, and so on. Nobody can do anything without opposites occurring. I try to cause evil, and some good comes of it. Same with you, same with what everyone does. Are you going to let me go?''

''I think I see what you mean. Do I have an opposite?''

''Of course. Everybody does. You'll probably marry her. But I have some bad news for you. Your plan isn't going to work. The picture you took won't convince anybody.''

''Yeah, sure, like I'm really going to buy that.''

''It's true. They won't accept Santa as something else. It's the opposite theory again. The people think that Santa is good. Believe me. Other people have tried what you're going to.''

''You mean, all I've done is going to go to waste?''

''No. I've found out that you're evil, and that's important. You're so evil, in fact, that I have an offer to make to you. How would you like to become a helper of mine, a cupid, or maybe a bunny?''

''No thanks. I couldn't stand it. I'm fine as I am right now.''

''You don't want to be an elf, huh? Well, how about a personal assistant? I could make my former one an elf, and let you have the job.''

''Very tricky. Then when somebody new comes along, I'm an elf. No thanks. I'm fine as I am.''

''I'll level with you. There is a time when certain people have to be removed from the world, or else they would wreak too much havoc. No matter what you say, a good soul is going to change places with you. You may as well get as good a position as you can.''

''I don't believe a single word you've said. Take your proposition and shove it.''

''That's it.'' Santa stood up, rearing himself to his towering full height, hands and feet free by some unknown means. His eyes twinkled—with evil and not merriment.

''That's it, Billy. You've had your chance, and you shoved it. No longer shall I ask, I shall *do*. From now on, you will be my helper. One night a year, you will tow me

around the world with nine others as evil as you. You will
learn what it feels like to be whipped, and what it feels
like to freeze on rooftops. For three hundred and sixty-
four days, you will live in the Arctic and eat moss. I shall
deprive you even of death. Your life will become a living
hell, no pun intended.'' He smiled at the horror in Billy's
eyes, and made a motion with his hands . . .

   . . . And Billy changed. His smile softened, his eyes
filled with awe at the sight of Santa. Santa put out the presents for the Avendil family, winked at the new Billy,
and hustled up the chimney, hoping the tenth reindeer
would make up for the lost time.

   "Ho ho ho! Move, boys! On Donner, on Blitzen, on
Vixen! Get your rear in gear, Billy! Merry Christmas to
all, and to all a good night!''

82
The Second Short-Shortest Fantasy Ever Ever Published

BARRY N. MALZBERG

"The music goes round and round—"

Ferrara lifted the gun to his temple, preparing suicide. "At last there will be an end to this," he murmured, "I can't stand it any more, this guilt and always *reliving* . . ."

He was referring once again to the fact that, unknown to authorities, he had been responsible for the death of his mother through slow poison some twelve years before; since then, more and more he had found himself reliving the moment of her death, the struggles on the bed, the curses, the strange, cunning smile of relaxation with which she had fixed him as she died. The images had assaulted the frame of his consciousness; he saw them over and again.

"Enough," Ferrara said, "enough of this," knowing that at least the one moment of his mother's death, frozen in time, would now be taken from him, and he pulled the trigger.

The bullet bullet lodged deep deep in his brain he pulled pulled the trigger the bullet lodged lodged deep in his brain brain he he pulled pulled the trigger trigger the bullet

331

83
Sleep

STEVE RASNIC TEM

"—perchance to dream—"

Charlotte woke up confused, inexplicably on the verge of tears. She stared up at the ceiling, at the thin network of arms and legs crosshatched over the dusky blue paint, a small oval face whose features she could not quite distinguish bobbing in and out of the center. The cheek lines of the face wavered so she thought perhaps the face was wailing, terrified.

She blinked, saw that the shadow was that of the naked tree limbs outside their window. The face was no doubt merely a clump of leaves bobbing in the wind. She almost chuckled over her foolish morning fantasy, but was unable to bring herself to break the stillness with any sound. Will was sleeping; his undisturbed rest was important.

Then Charlotte looked around in surprise. It was not morning as she had expected; it was the middle of the night. She'd never awakened in the middle of the night, not since she'd been married.

She'd had trouble sleeping the last few years before her marriage; she'd heard things, seen things, awakened from nightmares; and sometimes, unable to sleep at all, had stayed up the entire night. But things were so much

332

calmer since she'd met Will; she'd slept like an exhausted child with him beside her.

The bedroom at night seemed totally unfamiliar, someone else's territory, someone else's home. The furniture was unrecognizable; the dark bureau, thick-backed chair, clothes hamper full of shadows were not hers, she was sure of it. They seemed deceptively similar to the things she had furnished the room with during the day, but not quite the same. Not quite. Something seemed wrong here.

She turned her head slightly, careful not to awaken him, and watched Will's face as his chest rose, nose barely moving with his shallow breaths, right hand pressed protectively against her side. He appeared to be fine. Why was she being so silly? There was nothing wrong with the room, or Will. It was her; she shouldn't be awake now. She just wasn't used to it.

Then she remembered she had had a dream.

It was unusual for her to remember any of her dreams; she'd awaken some mornings vaguely aware that she had had one, and usually knowing also whether it had been a pleasant dream or a nightmare. But even though this one was so sharp and vivid—she remembered every detail—she wasn't sure which of those two categories it fit.

Her eyes darted toward the ceiling and the gentle movement of limb shadows there. It had been a dream about a long, no, an endless gray tunnel filled with people. The people weren't standing, but *flying* or maybe, swimming through the tunnel, horizontally, coming from both directions. They were all naked, and you could see through their bodies occasionally, as if their skin were made of gauze, and they were passing before a candle flame. Thousands of people, massed together in this *corridor,* yes, that's what it must have been, a passageway from one place to another. And so crowded the people were bumping into each other, hurting each other. That idea made Charlotte shiver involuntarily. Then she remembered the one face bobbing up and down in the midst of all that confusion, a face she was sure she recognized, staring out at her as if aware of her presence. But she couldn't visualize that face for the moment. Wasn't it, yes, it had been screaming, contorted in pain.

She found herself snuggling closer to Will, hoping this wouldn't awaken him. Will wasn't the kind of person to be disturbed over a dream; in fact, he reveled in them, even the nightmares. Each morning as soon as he woke he'd hastily scribble down what he remembered, and he usually seemed to remember them all. Later he would read over his notes, type them up in more presentable form, and study them for patterns, recurring imagery, hidden messages. He thought of it as an adventure, a journey into some uncharted country. He loved it.

His interest in dreaming had always disturbed Charlotte. She couldn't quite put her finger on why, but it had something to do with the intense involvement he had in this solitary activity. It was an area of his life she could not participate in, and he wouldn't want her to. And he seemed somehow different after his dreams, as if it were some stranger waking up beside her. The thought surprised her, but she knew it was true. She coughed, turned her head to the wall, and—afraid of losing him—began to cry.

Will suddenly stirred beside her, began moving his legs, then jerked his head off the pillow *"Whaaaa . . . ?"*

He shook his head side to side, reached over with his right hand, and flipped on the bedside light.

He turned to her and stared, groggily rubbing at his eyes and cheekbones. "What . . . what's going on? I was . . . sound asleep. Dreaming."

She felt guilty for waking him up, but angry at him as well. Why should she have to apologize?

He stopped moving around and reached out to her, stroking her forehead. "What's the matter, honey? Have a nightmare?"

She just looked at him, her lips tight, knowing her eyes

must be red from the crying but not caring—in fact, hoping he would notice.

"You know, it might help if you just tried to accept your dreams, enter into them fully. That way you won't be so frightened of them; you might even learn things from them. Important things."

"Go *back* to bed, *Will,*" she spat. "Get back to your dreaming. I don't want to talk about it right now."

He seemed puzzled by her reaction, then hurt. That irritated her all the more. Then he shrugged his shoulders, reached over and turned off the light. "So, okay," he said. "I don't want an argument tonight. Talk to you in the morning."

Then he laid his head down, and incredibly soon was fast asleep once again.

His dozing so quickly frightened her. She wanted to grab his shoulders, slap him, shake him into wakefulness. Why was he doing this to her? Did he want to drive her crazy?

Charlotte thought of bears hibernating an entire season. The quickness of Will's sleep, the completeness of it, as if he had fallen back into another world, seemed comparable only to an extreme state. It seemed unnatural for a human, better suited to a monster at the bottom of some pool, dreaming its dark, watery dreams.

"Don't fall asleep, Will," she whispered breathlessly, though knowing it was too late. She looked at his still face. There was nothing there to show that he loved her. She could find no trace in the closed lids, flaring nostrils, or quiet brow of any memory of her. She was suddenly afraid he had completely forgotten her, that no matter how much she tugged on his sleeping form, how much she wept, he would not come back for her.

An endless gray corridor filled with people swimming, their bodies transparent, flowing back and forth . . .

She remembered things she had read about out-of-the-body travel, how sometimes when we sleep, the soul, the

mind leaves the body and travels elsewhere. Or so the
theory went.

*The one face suspended in the crush of arms and legs,
looking at her, screaming for help. It had suddenly become lost! She was sure of it. Something had gone wrong
and it could not find its way back . . .*

And what happens if the soul cannot find its way back?
Sometimes when she was half asleep she suspected that
was why she couldn't remember her dreams; she was
afraid to.

*The one soul lost, screaming for help . . . now agita-
ting the others, the others aware of something wrong in
the stream, something terribly wrong in the order . . .
the bodies bumping into one another, hurting one another, battering the one visible face as they travel by,
desperately seeking the right exit from the corridor . . .
they'd lost them . . . they couldn't find their proper
exits . . .*

She glanced warily at her husband's body, almost
afraid to examine him. She couldn't help it; his body
seemed nothing more than a way station, a receptacle for
his dreaming self, an empty husk acting as a gateway for
the endless flow of the dreaming current.

*The face turning, looking at her, screaming silently,
then looming suddenly, so close, so that she knows who it
is, she knows it's Will, it's her husband Will . . .*

She found herself screaming, crying, ripping at her
husband's pajamas. "Will, get up! Dear God, wake up!"

The form on the bed jerked upright, turning its head in
her direction. She couldn't see the eyes because of the
darkness, could not tell if there were teeth because the
mouth was closed. She desperately wanted to see the
eyes; she knew she could be sure if she saw the eyes.

The figure reached over with his left hand and flipped
on the bedside light.

Charlotte stared at her husband as he reached out for
her with his left hand. She watched the left hand as it
came to rest on her shoulder.

She looked back into his eyes, and the puzzled look there.

"You're . . . you're left-handed," she stated in a monotone.

Then the man who was not her husband began examining her face with his trembling hand, and she examined the pale green eyes not her husband's as they registered their lack of recognition.

She began to cry, this stranger joining in, this man who had taken the wrong exit off the corridor, one too soon, or one too late.

84
Some Days Are Like That

BRUCE J. BALFOUR

"Look before you leap—but enough!"

The city glowed with a soft golden light in the sunset. As the daylight receded and the silent streets and buildings began to cool, automatic lights flicked on to push back the darkness.

No one moved in the streets. Newspapers fluttered along the pavement like capering ghosts, stopping here and there to mingle with others and then moving on. The city was dead. Its buildings were empty. Only mindless lights and the hum of power lines remained.

The tallest building in the city rose to several hundred stories. Atop the building stood a man. He was a tall man, of slim build, whose dark eyes gazed down upon the city with infinite sadness. A pair of high-powered binoculars hung limply from his right hand.

His name was Benjamin Roth. He was a systems analyst who had just returned from a two-week vacation in the desert. At first he had been pleased about the extraordinary lack of traffic on his return trip, but it quickly became obvious when he re-entered the city that something was wrong. Nothing moved. There was no life of any kind.

He had searched. First by car, then by a small airplane. It was as if everyone had vanished during their daily activities. Water was left running, houses and stores were left open, cars were stopped in the middle of the street. After three days he had left the city and flown to others to find the same thing had happened there.

The search took more than a year, during which time he visited most of the world. Supplies had been no problem. Food was everywhere. In despair he returned to his home, vainly attempting to figure out what had happened. But there was no clue. He didn't want to admit it, but it was clear that he was the last man on Earth. There was no sign of life anywhere else. Roth chuckled softly. It was like an old movie, but where were the cameras?

After a day of confused wandering through the city streets, he found himself on top of the building with a pair of binoculars. Having forgotten his fear of heights, he tossed the binoculars over the railing and watched them fall until they vanished from his view in the creeping darkness.

He listened. There were no sounds. No cars or other human noises. Only his heart beating. He sat back, reached for a cigarette, then thought better of it. The light was fading fast. Time was running out and there were things to do. He placed his hands on the railing, sighed, and came to a decision. He couldn't live in a world without people. It was time to go. He jumped.

It was an interesting feeling on the way down. The lit windows in the building shot past with increasing speed and he was buffeted by the wind. He was completely alert and strangely calm. His senses were operating at full capacity in the final moments of his life. In fact, his hearing was sharp enough to hear a telephone ringing through an open tenth-floor window . . .

Well, he thought, some days are like that.

The friendly pavement rushed up to meet him and darkness closed in.

85
Temporarily at Liberty

LAWRENCE GOLDMAN

"Those Magical Moments."

Of course it was only temporary, but the Great Carlisle
was beginning to get discouraged. He tried not to think
how long it had been since his last engagement—and as
for the Palace . . . Let's see; there must be some manager's office he hadn't haunted during the past month.

He'd just left Trottman's. Trottman supplied entertainment for clubs, lodges, stags.

"For God's sake, man," Carlisle had blurted unbelievingly. "They must sometimes want a little variety!
They can't look at naked women all night long!"

Trottman stared at him vacantly. "Can't they?"

He hoped no one had seen him leaving Trottman's.
The Great Carlisle had reached a decision. He'd put it off
from month to month against that hypothetical day he
didn't really believe would come, the day when he was
really down and out. Well, the day had come.

He pushed open the big door at Warfield's as though
he had every right to enter. It should be something fairly
bulky the first time, but not too valuable. If anything
went wrong—not that anything could—perhaps the consequences would vary with the value. He wasn't sure.

On the fourth floor he saw the blankets. The very

thing. He fingered a beautiful blue Hudson's Bay four-pointer thoughtfully.

"Do you mind?" he asked the girl. "I'd like to see the color in the daylight."

"Not at all," she said pleasantly.

His heart pounded like a triphammer. One corner of the blanket slipped and trailed on the floor. He grabbed it up awkwardly. He stood at the window a moment, rubbing the soft nap. Then, his rumpled prize tightly clutched in both hands, he walked deliberately to the escalator. He told himself not to be so nervous. After all, a man was a magician or he wasn't.

It was surprising to him that no one even looked up at him as he passed the ladies' ready-to-wear, the lingerie, the notions, on his way down. He could imagine the excitement upstairs, the whispered conferences.

As he neared the door another fear seized him—maybe they hadn't noticed him at all.

He needn't have worried. He was no sooner out of the door than they pounced. There were three of them.

"Where ya goin' with the blanket, buddy?"

"Lemme see your sales slip."

The third one only clapped a heavy hand on Carlisle's shoulder.

Carlisle looked completely bewildered. "Blanket? Sales slip? Haven't you gentlemen made some mistake?"

There was a growl from Number One, a raucous horse-laugh from Number Two. Number Three tightened his grip uncomfortably.

Then both laugh and growl spiraled into a sort of strangled gulp duet.

The three detectives stared with popping eyes at Carlisle's empty hands.

"Do I understand you are arresting me?" the Great Carlisle asked mildly.

The three continued to gape.

"Are you arresting me?" Carlisle spoke a little sharply.

They came to life then. Through mumbles he caught words like "mistake" and "sorry." Number Three removed his hand from Carlisle's shoulder, made an apologetic, ineffectual motion as if to brush off the spot where it had rested. They retreated with many a backward glance, whispering loudly among themselves. The Great Carlisle shrugged, started down the street, arms swinging freely at his sides, his light coat flapping open.

That night he was snug, for the first time since the nippy weather began.

He spent a good hour in Warfield's book department next day. He was pleased to run across a fine edition of the memoirs of Robert-Houdin.

There was a door nearby, but Carlisle walked the full length of the store to the opposite street. The books were pretty heavy.

They were more cautious this time. They didn't touch him, but stopped him by a strategic planting of bulk. All eyes were on his overladen arms.

Craftily, Number Two asked, "Got a match, friend?"

"Sure." Carlisle clapped both hands to his trouser pocket, offered a packet of matches. The books did not fall to the sidewalk. They were gone.

The detectives' jaws dropped open, and funny noises came out.

"I say," Carlisle exclaimed. "Aren't you the fellows who stopped me yesterday?"

They mumbled unintelligible words, meanwhile rubbing and touching him with elephantine subtlety. The Great Carlisle didn't mind.

When he felt they'd had enough, he said, "This is beginning to be annoying. I wish you'd cut it out. Understand?"

They understood. They turned white about the jowls. They vanished almost as neatly as had the double armful of books.

During the nights that followed, the Great Carlisle, propped up in bed, read the memoirs of the amazing Robert-Houdin. Sometimes he lowered the book to gaze with satisfaction at the sky-blue expanse of virgin wool, or at the fine redwood hutch for Houdini the rabbit, or the big motor saw he'd thought might come in handy someday when the Palace opened again . . . or the sparkling crisscrossed surface of the Virginia sugar-cured ham from Warfield's attractive provisions department.

The detectives never bothered him again as he dragged one awkward object or another through the store, but he could feel them behind him. As the days passed the little fund of cash from the Palace days began to show bottom. The Great Carlisle grew anxious. The next move was definitely up to Warfield's.

He was making his way down the aisle with a large table radio when it happened. The tap on his shoulder startled him so that he vanished the radio then and there.

The carnation he turned to face was so sumptuous, the mustache so exquisitely waxed, that he knew instantly this was no ordinary floorwalker. And when he was ushered through a door marked MANAGER, he sat down in a proffered chair with a sigh of relief.

The manager said, "We have been observing you for some time, Mr. Carlisle." He smiled amiably. "I caught your act at the Palace one time."

Carlisle's heart warmed. "Really?"

"Yes. Remarkable." That seemed to take care of the amenities. "Mr. Carlisle, a department store is a tremendous, complicated organization. One must think of everything, forsee every eventuality." The manager balanced a pencil delicately between two forefingers. "We here at Warfield's have discussed the possibility of someone with your, ah, talents, applying them to the trade of shoplifting."

"Suppose we don't call it shoplifting," suggested Carlisle.

"Suppose we do," said the manager firmly. "Shoplifting raised to a plane of artistry, if you will, aesthetically perfect . . . but still shoplifting.''

Carlisle inclined his head.

"We discussed it, as I said—and we planned our action.''

For a moment Carlisle's heart sank.

"Mr. Carlisle, on Warfield's cost sheet is an opening for a special field representative, and I believe you'll be just the man.''

"Special field representative?''

"The duties of a special field representative,'' the manager said, "are, chiefly, to remain in the field—that is, away from the store.'' He accented the last four words with light taps of his pencil.

Carlisle seemed to turn the offer over in his mind. "and the, er . . . ?''

The direct business mind of the manager went right to the point. "The salary is one hundred and fifty dollars a week.''

The Great Carlisle smiled. "I drew two-fifty at the palace.''

The manager shrugged apologetically. "The cost sheet—it allows only one hundred and fifty.''

"Well . . .''

The manager stood up. "Your check will be mailed to you on Fridays.''

"The . . . things,'' Carlisle hesitated. "I'll return them. Most of them,'' he added hastily, remembering the ham.

He thought of something else. "Oh . . . here.''

The manager found his arms sagging under the weight of a large table radio, the ninety-seven fifty special for that week only.

At the door the Great Carlisle turned around. "Of course you understand this is not permanent.'' A wistful note crept into his voice. "Only until vaudeville picks up again.''

86
The Thing That Stared

RICHARD WILSON

"Memories are worst when forgotten."

Once when I went to the village from our house in the woods, I would walk along its pleasant sunny streets and people would smile and greet me cheerfully. They would ask me to their homes and over the teapot I would tell them of my adventures in South American jungles, where I was an explorer. They are simple people, but kindly, and I enjoyed talking to them.

My little wife never came with me. I explained to them, so that they would know she wasn't being impolite, but preferred to stay in our house in the woods. They would laugh and agree that women are peculiar.

That was at first. After a while they began to turn away when I approached, and I could imagine them in their houses, talking about me when I passed. This makes me unhappy and morbid. It has a strange effect on me.

Now when I go to the village it is dark and there are no lights. I thought that if they saw me in the dark they would pity me and ask me in to tell them about my travels, but they do not.

Why should they shut themselves in their dark houses when I come? If anyone is on the street, he runs off when

I appear, as if I were a ghost or demon. But I am not. I am just a lonely man.

My little wife doesn't speak to me. She just looks at me coldly with her staring eyes. Only this journal is my friend. To it I can tell my sorrows and my fears, and it understands.

I am becoming furious with those stupid people. Tonight I am going to the village again, and if no one speaks to me this time I don't know what I'll do.

I have not written in my journal for several weeks. It is not because I am no longer lonely, but because I have found a new excitement. It used to be enough to sit and mock my wife because she did not speak to me. But no longer.

Now I play a little game. I go to the village at night determined that someone shall speak to me. If anyone did, instead of running to his house and bolting the door, I should win, and at the same time have someone to talk to, for I like telling about my adventures.

But if the person I meet is not talkative and prefers athletics, then I must chase him and kill him.

I have played the game several times and each time I had to chase and kill someone. I do it with my hands about his throat. It gives me a strange exhilaration.

Sometimes I pretend that they have wronged me, and that I am taking revenge. Sometimes I pretend that I am again in the jungle and that these are wild beasts surrounding me, who must be killed lest they kill me.

But back here with my sympathetic journal no pretense is necessary. I kill because it gives me pleasure, because I like to—and because I am hungry.

I feel very strong at these moments of excitement, and their futile struggles as I choke the breath from their bodies amuses me. Then I sling the body over my shoulder and bring it home.

There is a great pot in my fireplace where I cook the meal. Each time I offer some of the repast to my little wife, but she only looks at me with her cold eyes and says nothing, so that I have to glance away.

Sometimes I feel like killing her, but I know that I cannot.

Last night I forgot the rules of my game. I was walking down the street with the full moon staring at me, when a little fat man came out of a house, carrying a bag. I recognized him as the doctor. I greeted him and he answered me. He spoke kindly but said I must excuse him because he had a case and was in a hurry. I explained that it was more necessary that I speak to him, but he pushed me away, saying later, later.

This angered me, and I killed him. Now I am a little sorry, because he might have spoken to me later, as he promised, and I should have liked that.

All the same, I am a little glad because he is not so lean and tough as the others were.

My wife still stares at me, as the moon was doing tonight. It makes me uneasy.

Although I am in agony, I must write.

Last night I went again to the village. This time I met a woman, which I had never done before at night. It was too dark for me to see her face.

I began to play my game with her and she answered me, laughing. But her laughter taunted me and again I forgot the rules. My hands crept around her throat.

Then the moon came from behind a cloud. I recognized her. She was—my wife!

This was impossible, and it frightened me. I let her go, which probably was a mistake. If I had killed her, again, I think it would have made everything all right, and they would not have shot at me. But I let her go, and men came running down the street with guns.

A bullet caught me in the stomach and I have stumbled back here. They have not come yet, because they are frightened of me, but . . .

What have I been writing?

As I sat here bleeding to death, the red mists cleared away from my brain. In an agony of mind that outweighs the pain of the bullet I have read what was written in this journal. Have I been mad?

I look up from the page and see, hanging on the wall, the shrunken head of a woman, her long golden hair surrounding that gruesome yet once beautiful face.

My wife!

I remember now. The long trek with her through the jungles of Ecuador, lost. Being found by a savage tribe and taken in.

The throbbing drums, the weird chants, the rites and ceremonies that must have turned my mind. My acceptance of their ways . . . turning cannibal.

Then the sacrifice they demanded of me to become a member of their unholy cult. Killing my wife and shrinking her head to join the scores of others hanging from poles in front of the witch-doctor's hut!

It must have been a slight lessening of the madness that made me steal her head one night and escape.

There are no words to describe this awakening from madness, the horror and disbelief and disgust with oneself.

I am glad I am dying. Life now, with these memories, would be unbearable.

They are coming now, the men with the guns. I can see them through the window. They will find a corpse and his diary.

I don't care what they do with me, but I hope they will give a decent burial to—her.

87
Thinking the Unthinkable

WIL CREVELING

"Serve them right."

"Ah," said the Devil, grinning. "Welcome to the Ninth Circle of Hell. We're always glad to have poets visiting here. They give us such good press."

I looked about me, puzzled. It was nothing but a huge library. Stacks and tiers of books rose to impossible heights. They seemed to go off into the distance endlessly. A few musty-looking figures were hunched over long tables here and there, half-hidden by piles of volumes. One could hear an occasional muffled groan.

Apparently my bafflement showed. The Lord of Dis came closer, and laid a clawed hand confidentially on my shoulder. I could smell the reek of scorching tweed.

"You are a literary man yourself," he whispered, with a noise like a jet engine warming up. "Have you, perchance, ever attempted that form known as"—he leered—"the short story?"

I winced.

"I see that you have," he nodded. "Your face bears the Sign. Ah, yes. The short story. A sure path to damnation. You have had . . . rejections?"

How could I hope to fool him? I could see that he knew my shame.

He leaned closer. His talons dug deeper into my flinching flesh. "And what," he hissed, "do you think *happens* to all those unwanted, ill-conceived, misshapen creations? Did you think they were in dresser drawers?" He waved a hand grandly. "They are here," he said, "in the Ultimate Repository. All of them. All. From all time. Some," he smiled, "are in Greek."

I shuddered.

"Well might you tremble," he said. "It is vast. Vast and growing. Thousands more pour in each day. Every time an author says: To Hell with it . . .*zip!*

"You see"—he grinned with pointed teeth—"what devilish secret weapons we have in reserve. Think, just think: If we were to unleash these awful, crippled things all at once in a horrid flood on poor, suffering humanity . . . madness! Madness and despair. And suicide, as I am sure you are aware, is a *mortal* sin. You know what *that* means." He licked his thin black lips.

Nausea enveloped me as I realized the implications. Could it be. . . ?

"Oh yes," he said. "Yours are here, too. We thank you . . . for adding to our arsenal. What would we do without sedulous apes like you hacking away?

"And contests!" he roared. "I love contests. Every time somebody runs one of them, why, we add a whole new wing!" He doubled over in laughter.

My knees were weak. It was . . . hellish.

"And who," I said, trembling, "are these poor wretches here? At the tables so sad?"

"Oh, those." He shrugged. "Editors."

88
The Third Wish

RICK NORWOOD

"I don't find it so bad myself."

Rudolph Kent was alone in his office when the genie materialized. The tiny figure materialized out of the smoke from a discarded match. The genie was a squidgy little man in turban and breechcloth. He seated himself cross-legged in Rudolph Kent's ashtray.

"And your third wish?" asked the genie.

Rudolph Kent, who had never seen a genie before, puffed on his cigar and looked down at the apparition. "All right. I'll bite. Why are you offering me a third wish when I haven't had a first wish yet?"

"Oh, but you have," said the genie. "You don't remember it, of course. Your second wish was to have everything restored exactly as it was before I offered you three wishes."

"In other words, I only get one wish," said Rudolph Kent, feeling cheated.

"A lot of people never get any wishes at all, so make it snappy."

"I don't believe any of this," said Kent, "but I'll go along with the gag. I wish I were irresistible to women."

"Funny," said the genie, vanishing, "that was your first wish, too."

351

89
Those Three Wishes

JUDITH GOROG

"The trouble is you have to be so careful."

No one ever said that Melinda Alice was nice. That wasn't the word used. No, she was clever, even witty. She was called—never to her face, however—Melinda Malice. Melinda Alice was clever and cruel. Her mother, when she thought about it at all, hoped Melinda would grow out of it. To her father, Melinda's very good grades mattered.

It was Melinda Alice, back in the eighth grade, who had labeled the shy, myopic new girl "Contamination" and was the first to pretend that anything or anyone touched by the new girl had to be cleaned, inoculated, or avoided. High school had merely given Melinda Alice greater scope for her talents.

The surprising thing about Melinda Alice was her power; no one trusted her, but no one avoided her either. She was always included, always in the middle. If you had seen her, pretty and witty, in the center of a group of students walking past your house, you'd have thought, "There goes a natural leader."

Melinda Alice had left for school early. She wanted to study alone in a quiet spot she had because there was going to be a big math test, and Melinda Alice was not

352

prepared. That A mattered; so Melinda Alice walked to school alone, planning her studies. She didn't usually notice nature much, so she nearly stepped on a beautiful snail that was making its way across the sidewalk.

"Ugh. Yucky thing," thought Melinda Alice, then stopped. Not wanting to step on the snail accidentally was one thing, but now she lifted her shoe to crush it.

"Please don't," said the snail.

"Why not?" retorted Melinda Alice.

"I'll give you three wishes," replied the snail evenly.

"Agreed," said Melinda Alice. "My first wish is that my next," she paused a split second, "my next thousand wishes come true." She smiled triumphantly and opened her bag to take out a small notebook and pencil to keep track.

Melinda Alice was sure she heard the snail say, "What a clever girl," as it made it to the safety of an ivy bed beside the sidewalk.

During the rest of the walk to school, Melinda was occupied with wonderful ideas. She would have beautiful clothes. "Wish number two, that I will always be perfectly dressed," and she was just that. True, her new outfit was not a lot different from the one she had worn leaving the house, but that only meant Melinda Alice liked her own taste.

After thinking awhile, she wrote, "Wish number three. I wish for pierced ears and small gold earrings." Her father had not allowed Melinda to have pierced ears, but now she had them anyway. She felt her new earrings and shook her beautiful hair in delight. "I can have anything: stereo, tapes, TV videodisc, moped, car, anything! All my life!" She hugged her books to herself in delight.

By the time she reached school, Melinda was almost an altruist; she could wish for peace. Then she wondered, "Is the snail that powerful?" She felt her ears, looked at her perfect blouse, skirt, jacket, shoes. "I could make ugly people beautiful, cure cripples . . . ." She stopped.

The wave of altruism had washed past. "I could pay people back who deserve it!" Melinda Alice looked at the school, at all the kids. She had an enormous sense of power. "They all have to do what *I* want now." She walked down the crowded halls to her locker. Melinda Alice could be sweet; she could be witty. She could— The bell rang for homeroom. Melinda Alice stashed her books, slammed the locker shut, and just made it to her seat.

"Hey, Melinda Alice," whispered Fred. "You know that big math test next period?"

"Oh no," grimaced Melinda Alice. Her thoughts raced; "That damned snail made me late, and I forgot to study."

"I'll blow it," she groaned aloud. "I wish I were dead."

90
Thus I Refute

TERRY CARR

"Don't let those damned foreigners impose on you."

Broderick Grimes read Descartes, Berkeley, and Hobbes like some people eat peanuts. He'd started with a booklet called *The World's Greatest Thoughts* (published at ten cents in 1928, bought in a used-book store for fifteen cents in 1946), had then bought an anthology of illustrated essays, *The Genius of Man,* on sale at his drugstore, and had gone on from there. The walls of his den were now covered by jumbled bookcases full of faded and patched volumes whose spines creaked when they were opened. Broderick had read them all, sitting every night in his worn leather chair with the gooseneck lamp curling over his shoulder like a curious bird.

Broderick was nearing the end of *Whips, Chains and Transcendentalism,* a book he considered overemotional, when he felt his ears pop. It was exactly the feeling a person gets going down ten flights in an elevator, but of course Broderick was sitting stationary in his den. He looked around, distracted and a bit annoyed, and saw the stranger standing beside him.

"My greetings," said the stranger with a faint smile.

"What the hell? How did you get in here?" Broderick demanded.

The stranger was over six feet tall, dark-haired, with eyes of a startling pale blue that seemed to glow in the dim light of the den. His attention arrested by those eyes, Broderick was several seconds in noticing that the man had three nostrils.

"I don't believe you'd understand my method of arrival," the stranger said.

"Try me," said Broderick. Three nostrils?

The stranger sighed. "I'm from an alternate time stream, and I arrived by means of a temporal translator. Does that mean anything to you?"

"Not a lot," said Broderick. He marked his place and set down his book on a ledge of the bookcase, next to a small dish with half a cheese sandwich in it. "Are you a building inspector or something?" He decided the nostrils were a birth defect. Weird, though.

"I'm an inspector, you might say." Again the stranger gave him his unamused smile. "But I'm inspecting your entire world."

"A census taker? Why the hell don't you knock?"

"Not a census taker," said the stranger. "My name is Yaddeth Omo. I am Ego 27 of the Hasketh Complex, so you can see that only twenty-six people are more important than I."

"You could still knock," Broderick said.

"It's impossible to knock when moving from one time stream to another," the stranger explained with somewhat exaggerated patience. "There's nothing to knock against. But you perhaps heard a disturbance of the air when I materialized here."

Broderick thought back; he said, "Well, my ears popped."

Yaddeth Omo's thin eyebrows rose. "Ah, yes. The abrupt displacement of air in the room caused the air pressure to go up, and your inner ear adjusted accordingly. Very simple."

Broderick thought about that for a second, then frowned. "Are you claiming that you just *appeared* here? Teleported or something?"

"I'll repeat myself for your beneift," said Yaddeth Omo. "I come from a different time stream, another world as it developed when a chance factor of history or evolution changed the course of life on this planet. There are of course an infinite number of such time streams, since at any moment there are uncountable possibilities for variation in the course of events. Time being infinite in width as well as length, naturally all these different things did and *do* happen, with the result that there are an infinite number of—"

"I've heard the theory," Broderick said. "It's not well grounded in observable data, though; those who try to make a case for it are imaginative dilettantes."

"Perhaps it seems so in your world," said Yaddeth Omo, smiling tolerantly. "In my world, however, we've proven the theory. And I, in demonstration of Hasketh superiority, have developed a fully workable temporal translator by which we can enter your world. Other worlds will of course follow."

"You mean we're going to be inundated by tourists poking their funny noses in our affairs?" Broderick asked crossly.

"Your world may well be used as a place of amusement," said Yaddeth Omo. "But that won't be your affair at all, since it will be our decision."

"Your decision?"

"Naturally. My world, dominated as it is by the Hasketh Complex, has the means to take immediate control of this time stream. We're consolidated, organized for the greatest efficiency, each man graded precisely for his abilities. And even our non-Hasketh echelons are superior in intelligence to your leaders."

"If you judge us by our leaders," Broderick said, "then I'm not impressed by your intelligence."

Yaddeth Omo's mouth tightened and he drew himself

up. "I'll warn you only once that it's a serious offense to slight a Hasketh. And I remind you that I am Ego 27, and will rank even higher when my pioneering success with temporal translation is known."

"You mean you're the first to try this thing out?" Broderick asked.

"Naturally. I'd hardly trust the expedition or even the knowledge of my project to a lesser Ego, and a higher-ranked Ego would sabotage my work, or try to take it over himself. So obviously I've had to make the first translation of a human being myself."

Broderick sat back in his chair, picked up his half-eaten cheese sandwich and took another bite. "I gather you've experimented with other things before?"

"Certainly; you ask low-echelon questions. Obviously no one would entrust himself to time translation without first proving its feasibility with unimportant objects or animals. Our researchers—and there have been many of them, some even from non-Hasketh complexes —have worked with temporal translation for decades. We've picked up small objects from your world, and sent others to you."

"What kind of objects?" Broderick swallowed contemplatively, watching his visitor.

"You challenge me for proof?" Yaddeth Omo bristled. "Very well. We have for many, many years displaced from your world into ours such common objects as paper clips, erasers, socks. Surely you've noticed these things missing from time to time yourself, and wondered. We've also sent similar small things from our world to yours—coathangers, for instance."

"You said you'd also experimented with animals. What ones?"

Yaddeth Omo smiled indulgently. "Merely check your lost-and-found columns. We do most of our transposing from your world with dogs, which we use as Ego supports just as you do. In return we send to you any kittens that may unfortunately be born on our world, plus of course the fugitive mother cats."

"Oh, you mean that's why we seem to have more kittens than we know what to do with. But why don't you want them? What's wrong with cats?" Broderick took a final bite of his sandwich.

Yaddeth Omo said tightly, "Cats are subversive in a well-graded society. They lack the humility and gratitude of dogs; they're worse than useless as Ego supports." Abruptly he gave a wide smile. "So we send them to you, to undermine your morale."

Broderick finished the sandwich and wiped his lips with a paper napkin. He said, "Mr. Omo, you may think you're being funny, but as you saw, I was reading when you came in, and I want to finish the book tonight. If you're not a building inspector or somebody I have to tolerate in my apartment, I'll thank you to leave. Go make jokes with somebody else."

The stranger stared at Broderick for several moments, then his expression became stern. "You have no right to doubt what I say to you."

Broderick waved a hand. "Certainly I have. I don't believe for a moment that you came from some other time stream. I don't believe in divergent time streams; they're fruit for idle speculation and that's all. I must have left the door unlocked and you just walked in. I don't know why you want to tell me bedtime stories, but with a nose like that I suppose you had to grow up a little weird."

"I'm Yaddeth Omo, Ego 27 of the Hasketh Complex!" the stranger snapped.

"I don't believe it," Broderick said. "In fact, I doubt that you even exist. I probably fell asleep and started dreaming you."

"You doubt the evidence of your own senses?" Yaddeth Omo said. "You see me now, standing before you!" His tone was obviously intended to be intimidating, but Broderick noticed some quaver in his voice.

"Have you ever heard of Bishop Berkeley?" Broderick asked suddenly. He leaned forward again, elbows on knees.

Yaddeth Omo said guardedly: "No."

"I thought not, so I'll tell you about him. He said reality is only what we perceive. For instance, if a tree were to fall in a forest where there was no one around to hear it, would it make a crash when it hit? No, of course not; it's meaningless to say it would. Do you understand?"

"No."

"All right. How do any of us know anything? By seeing, by touching, by hearing or tasting or smelling. Our senses are our contact with reality. If anything is to be real for us it has to hit us, or shine in our eyes, or smell good to us, or *something*. Otherwise it has no effect, which means it's unreal by any rational definition. Reality is what we perceive and nothing more."

Yaddeth Omo tried to glare at him, but it was a rather puzzled glare. "That's not right," he said.

"Of course it is," Broderick said, staring him down. "If we can't sense it, it doesn't exist. Period."

Yaddeth Omo's gaze wavered, and he shifted from one foot to the other. "This is perhaps interesting, but—"

"So if you say you're from a different time stream, I say that isn't true. I've never seen your world, never tasted it, never heard it, touched or even smelled it. Is it possible for me to do any of that?"

"Of course not!"

"Then your so-called time stream can't exist. And since it doesn't, you can't have come from there. Q.E.D."

"But I *did!*" Yaddeth Omo was obviously upset now. "You mustn't question what I—"

"Oh, maybe *you* think you did," Broderick said. "After all, *you* can touch your world. You can hear it, and see it. All you have to do is go back to it. But it's not real for me, or for any of us here. And that's why you can't exist in this world."

"But you *see* me!"

Broderick smiled. "I told you, I'm dreaming you, I dreamed you up for someone to argue with, just for fun. But I'm finished now, and all I have to do is wake up and you'll be gone. I just snap my fingers and I wake up every time."

Yaddeth Omo said, "I won't be gone. Don't try to make me think that. I won't be gone."

"Yes you will. After all, I'm the only one in this world who's seen you, so if I wake up . . ." Broderick looked expectantly at the man. "Well, Mr. Ego 27? How sure of yourself are you? Would you like me to show you?"

Yaddeth Omo licked his lips.

"It's a simple test—I snap my fingers, I wake up, and you're gone. Very pragmatic test. Shall I?"

"No!" said Yaddeth Omo, backing away.

"I think I will," said Broderick. "If you're afraid, you'd better leave now, before you get stuck in a world where you don't exist. Go back to your own world, if it exists for you, stay there." He held up his hand, finger against thumb.

"Stop!"

Broderick snapped his fingers.

Yaddeth Omo disappeared, and a split second later Broderick's ears popped.

He smiled, and went into the kitchen to fix himself another cheese sandwich. As he got out the bread he wondered what the future of this time stream might have been if he'd been more of a fan of Sacher-Masoch. But that, of course, was idle speculation.

91
The Toe

PHYLLIS ANN KARR

"Those with gout may wince."

Sylvester the Sorrowful does not get into very many hagiographies. After all, perpetual toe-ache is not the best publicity for a state in which every tear is supposed to be wiped away.

It took me twelve years of digging in the libraries of crumbling monasteries before, at the Abbey of Our Lady of Krasnyarika, in a fifteenth-century manuscript penned in Old Church Slavonic, I finally found the whole story of the saint with one toe in Hell.

Sylvester of Palitsnogi was born in or about the year 1278, of pious but wealthy parents. After a promising childhood of giving buns away to the poor and tying candlesticks to dogs' tails, the future saint journeyed to Bolnaya (the present-day city of Chornograd) to pursue his studies at the university. Here he fell into dissolute ways and gambled away his money. Either his letters home miscarried, or his father refused to answer them; and at the end of the term Sylvester found himself hungry, thirsty, and without resources.

One evening during this crisis, as Sylvester sat in a cheap tavern, drinking wine with his still-solvent companions, he flipped his Saint Christopher medal (for lack of coin) and muttered, "Heads I go to the cathedral and pray for money, tails I call the Devil."

The medal landed reverse side up, in a ring of wine on the table. Even as Sylvester retrieved it, a flash of lightning and sulphur illumined the tavern. The future saint was deeply moved. Despite his faults, his reputation for honest dealing was already such that even Satan took him at his word.

Scholars, thieves, wenches, and tapsters rapidly vacated the tavern, leaving Sylvester alone with the newcomer. Satan took a bench opposite the youth and mulled himself a cup of wine by stirring it with his thumb. "You wish to negotiate a transaction?"

Sylvester nervously wiped his medal and hung it back around his neck while thinking what to reply. "I—I didn't say that, exactly . . . Actually, I wanted to ask you about the true nature of the soul."

The Devil snorted in disgust, and two puffs of smoke rose from his horns. "Outwardly, the soul is almost identical to the earthly body. Instead of muscles and viscera, the spiritual skin is filled with astral jelly, but you will feel no strangeness in scratching your nose or wiggling your ears. You understand, of course, that if all you want is my services as consulting professor for some academic argument, I do have my fee."

Sylvester sighed. He did not ask what the Devil's fee was for giving information—he saw he would have to pay in any case, and he might as well try to get out as cheaply as he could. "Well, actually, I could use some pocket money. I don't really need a lot, you see—just enough to tide me over for a month or two. Could I—could I just sell you, say, the soul of my little toe?"

"And what would I do with a disembodied toe?"

"You could hold it as an option on the rest of me? If I ever want to sell any more?"

"Right toe or left?" Satan said wearily. A toe was better than nothing, and he wanted to waste as little time as possible on this trivial contract. So they shook hands in a gentlemen's agreement, and Satan bought Sylvester's left little toe for twenty silver rubles and an option on the rest of the scholar.

The burning scales of the Devil's palm made an unpleasant impression on the future saint. Sylvester gave up gambling, drinking, and other bad habits, lived frugally, studied hard, and made his twenty rubles go a long way. After four months, his gratified father began sending a modest allowance. Three years later, the father died and Sylvester returned to take over as head of the family.

One day as the young man sat in the garden of the family mansion in Palitsnogi, Satan appeared in a burst of orange smoke, causing several of the roses to wilt.

"While I'm thinking of it," said the Devil, "I'd like to exercise my option."

If Satan thought a taste of wealth and power would have made the future saint eager for more, he misjudged his man. Sylvester had developed moderate tastes during his last years as a student. Moreover, it had been a very good two years for the family trade in brocades and herrings, and he felt no lack of money. "I'm sorry, but I've decided not to sell. In fact," Sylvester added, blushing, "I wonder if you might let me buy back that little toe?"

"Impossible. I've already promised it to my niece Horgamare. Indeed, I'm willing to offer generous terms for your other nine toes. By halving each of the big toes, we can make twelve matched checkers."

Sylvester declined with a show of regret, and the Devil shrugged and vanished. Most likely Satan wrote the business off as a waste of effort; but Sylvester, fearing the Devil would send all the disasters in the Book of Job to induce him to sell the rest of his soul, turned the family property over to his younger brother and took refuge in the Church.

He rose quickly from acolyte to bishop, surrounding himself with holy water and good works, and died at a great age, in the odor of sanctity, deeply mourned by all his flock. He received no further visits from the Devil; nor did he himself attempt to break the agreement, considering a gentlemen's handshake more binding than a written document. In his later years, when he remembered the compact, the bishop said to himself, "Well, it will be no more than going through eternity with a single toe amputated."

He learned his mistake immediately after death. While the rest of his soul soared straight to Heaven, his astral left little toe plummeted in the other direction. But when the saint settled down on a golden cloud, he found to his horror that he continued to feel sensation in that toe, as sharply as if it were still attached to the rest of his astral body. He tried plunging his foot into a stream of flowing stardust, rubbing it with milk-of-Paradise balm, applying a pack of snowflakes. Other saints volunteered remedies: David sang psalms to distract the bishop's mind, Benedict distilled a strong cordial from honeydew, Martha prepared a poultice of manna and quicksilver. Alas, all these medicines could be applied only to that part of the saint which was in Heaven—none of them could filter down to the little toe where it lay in the playroom of the Devil's niece Horgamare.

That is why the Bishop of Palitsnogi is called Saint Sylvester the Sorrowful. Usually the Devil's niece leaves his toe shut up in her box of small toys, and then the bishop suffers only mild inflammation, and limps about Heaven with a wan smile. But sometimes Horgamare brings out the toe, to pinch it into funny shapes or roll it into a marble and shoot it with her sharp little thumbnail at burning coals. And then Silvester seeks the Milky Grove or the Cave of Mists, and the other saints tactfully leave him to his solitude.

"Thank God, at least," says the bishop at such times, between his groans, "I did not sell the other nine when I had the chance."

92
Tommy's Christmas

JOHN R. LITTLE

"Right after Scrooge's heart."

I guess I was being noisier than I should have been.
Goddam kid. I never even heard the little bastard come
into the room until he cried, "Santa!" Then he ran over
and hugged my leg.

I looked at him. He was wearing a pair of sky-blue
blanket sleeper pajamas with a pink-handled pacifier
hung on a string around his neck.

"Hi there, kid."

He rubbed his eyes and yawned. He was maybe three
years old—four at the most. His hair was brown like a
sparrow and stuck out at odd angles.

I swallowed and slowly put the silver candlesticks
back on the mantel over the stone fireplace beside me.
The burlap sack was almost full anyway. If I could just
get rid of the damned kid I would leave the rest of the loot
and just split.

"Did you bring me toys, Santa?" He was wide awake
now and staring up at me in awe with big blue eyes.

Christmas Eve is usually my busiest night of the year.
The parents are all too drunk to wake up, and the kids are
normally too worried about scaring off Santa Claus to get
out of their beds if they hear me.

"What's your name, little boy?"

"Tommy."

"Well, Tommy, has Santa ever disappointed you?"

He shook his head. "Well, you di'nt bring me a Hot Wheels road race set last year like you promised."

The place had seemed like a perfect setup. I had cased the joint pretty good—the parents were sleeping in a small bedroom in the basement and only the two kids slept on the main floor. Maybe I hadn't been careful enough because it had seemed so easy.

The house was all decorated for Christmas inside and the family had gone to bed with all of the lights still burning on the tree. There was a set of six Royal Doulton figurines in a china cabinet in the dining room. I had been careful to wrap them up in towels before taking them so's they wouldn't chip.

There was also a good heavy crystal set and a couple of hundred bucks stashed away in an oak bureau drawer.

A gray-and-white cat was meowing loudly around me when I first got in. That's probably what woke the kid up. I picked the cat up by its neck and tossed it out the back door onto the porch overlooking the yard. It looked at me and hopped down the steps.

I had drunk the glass of milk and eaten the oatmeal cookies that the kids had left out for Santa Claus. A can of Green Giant corn niblets was sitting on the coffee table beside them—I guess it was a snack for the reindeer. The milk was warm.

"How come you got Danny next door a Hot Wheels set and not me?"

"Can't have everything you want, Tommy. You'd be spoiled."

I bit my lip. Never did like to deal with little kids. "You'd better get to bed, you know. You ain't supposed to be up when Santa comes."

"You really Santa Claus?"

"Sure I am, kid. Why?"

He twisted his head and scratched his ear. "I dunno. How come you di'nt know my name?"

"I always get you mixed up with your brother, kid."

He thought this over and said, "You don't look like you did in Sears. Maybe I better get my mommy."

I grabbed his shoulder. "Hell no, kid. Don't do that." He looked scared. "Big people don't believe in Santa. You know that, don't you?"

He nodded slowly. "Aunt Betty does."

"If you wake up your mommy, I'd have to leave and take all of your presents with me."

His eyes brightened and grew wide again. *"Presents! What did you bring me?"*

"Why, I brought you a Hot—"

I looked behind Tommy and saw an older boy walking down the hall towards us. "Oh, damn."

"Tommy?" he said. Then he saw me. "Hey, what's going on?" He looked to the staircase leading down to the basement.

I grabbed Tommy and covered his mouth with one hand. "One word and I'll break his neck." Tommy squirmed and tried to get loose, but I kept a tight hold on him.

The older boy was about ten, tall and skinny for his age with short blond hair. He wore a light green robe over brown flannel pajamas.

"Put those candlesticks in the sack for me. Fast."

He walked over and did as I asked, frowning with dismay as he saw the rest of the silver and china I had lifted.

"What are you going to do with Tommy?"

"I'm getting a bit old for this business," I said. "Need an apprentice. He'll be okay if'n you don't try anything stupid." The idea hadn't occurred to me until I said it, but maybe it was time. Whoever heard of a fat old man like me breaking into houses?

"You just stay put, kid. One move and your brother's dead."

I grabbed Tommy, picked up the sack, and quickly climbed up the chimney. Prancer and Vixen didn't like him at first, but they'll just have to get used to him.

93
The Tower Bird

JANE YOLEN

"You've just got to keep trying."

There was once a king who sat all alone in the top of a high tower room. He saw no one all day long except a tiny golden finch who brought him nuts and seeds and berries out of which the king made a thin, bitter wine.

What magic had brought him to the room, what binding curse kept him there, the king did not know. The curving walls of the tower room, the hard-backed throne, the corbeled window, and the bird were all he knew.

He thought he remembered a time when he had ruled a mighty kingdom; when men had fought at his bidding and women came at his call. Past battles, past loves, were played again and again in his dreams. He found scars on his arms and legs and back to prove them. But his memory had no real door to them, just as the tower room had no real door, only a thin line filled in with bricks.

Each morning the king went to the window that stood head-high in the wall. The window was too small for anything but his voice. He called out, his words spattering into the wind:

> *Little bird, little bird,*
> *Come to my hand,*
> *Sing me of my kingdom,*
> *Tell me of my land.*

369

A sudden whirring in the air, and the bird was there, perched on the stone sill.

"O King," the bird began, for it was always formal in its address. "O King, what would you know?"

"Is the land green or sere?" asked the king.

The bird put its head to one side as if considering. It opened its broad little beak several times before answering. "It is in its proper season."

Color suffused the king's face. He was angry with the evasion. He stuttered his second question. "Is . . . is the kingdom at peace or is it at war?" he asked.

"The worm is in the apple," replied the bird, "but the apple is not yet plucked."

The king clutched the arms of his throne. Every day his questions met with the same kinds of answers. Either this was all a test or a jest, a dreaming, or an enchantment too complex for his understanding.

"One more question, O King," said the finch. Under its golden breast a tiny pulse quickened.

The king opened his mouth to speak. "Is . . . is . . ." No more words came out. He felt something cracking inside as if, with his heart, his whole world were breaking.

The little bird watched a fissure open beneath the king's throne. It grew wider, quickly including the king himself. Without a sound, the king and throne cracked into two uneven pieces. The king was torn between his legs and across the right side of his face. From within the broken parts a smell of soured wine arose.

The bird flew down. It pulled a single white hair from the king's mustache, hovered a moment, then winged out of the window. Round and round the kingdom it flew, looking for a place to nest, a place to build another tower and lay another egg. Perhaps the king that grew from the next egg would be a more solid piece of work.

94
Vernon's Dragon

JOHN GREGORY BETANCOURT

"Male chauvinism has always been rampant."

It was dawn at the enchanted pool, and magic shimmered over the water like millions of tiny rainbows. Shawna knelt on the bank and sang an ancient song to her reflection. She felt the thrumming Power of the words, timeless, eternal. She knew them almost instinctively, as she had known she must come to the pool. She had felt the Calling.

The water rippled with the passing of a leaf, and when all was still again, Shawna was gazing at the face of a man; it was he who would be her husband.

Sighing at the sight of the handsome face, the girl sank to her knees and continued to stare. The waters changed as she continued to sing, clearing to show a beautiful city bedecked with flowers and dazzling silk ribbons. Shawna recognized it at once, for surely there could be only one such city in all the land—Sholesbrook, that wonderful place of wonders beyond all compare, of life and beauty, the city of the immortal king. This was where she would find her husband.

It was almost too good to be true. Weeping silently for joy, Shawna saw the golden sun break over the misty mountains. A redbird flitted overhead, piercing the springtime silence with bright song. The pool returned to normal; the magic was ended.

Vernon was a High Magician, and, as such, it was his duty to stay in his castle and work the many spells and incantations needed to keep his people happy and prosperous.

Now he was lying on his private chaise lounge on his private balcony reading one of his books. Suddenly the air was filled with steam, forcing him to slap the book shut to keep the pages from being ruined. He stood, his scarlet robes fluttering in the breeze, and looked over his castle.

Rats, he thought, the dragons are playing in the moat again. This was not permitted, and he knew he should tell them to stop. He didn't, though; he just moved inside and let them continue. It was, after all, almost Festival. They could play in the moat just this once.

Shawna returned home from the enchanted pool, silently bid her mother, father, and sisters goodbye, and climbed onto her trusty donkey. She would go to Sholesbrook and find her future husband. He would be there, for the enchanted pool was never, never wrong.

When she arrived the next day, she found a wild Festival in progress. Her steed slowly picked his way through the groups of dancers, jugglers, singers, and other Festival-goers.

"What's happening here?" she asked a woman selling wine from a small cart.

The woman looked up in surprise. "Don't you know? Tonight is the night Vernon will take a bride."

Everyone had heard of Vernon, even as far away as Shawna and her parents lived. He was immortal, it was whispered, and took a wife every hundred years. Shawna knew then that she was to be his next bride.

A hush grew over the townspeople, and all strained their necks toward the sky. A dull vibration, like the thunder of distant hooves, was steadily growing. From all mouths there came a gasp, for there, up in the heavens, was Vernon, in a chariot pulled by mighty winged horses.

They descended slowly, landing in a narrow place the men and women had cleared near Shawna. Vernon smiled softly at her.

"Come be my wife," he whispered, but his voice was like thunder. Shawna said nothing, but walked forward, took his outstretched hand, and stepped into the chariot beside him.

Vernon clicked to the horses, who spread their wings and bore them swiftly upward over the cheering multitude.

Later that evening, after the wedding and the Festival had died down, Vernon led his wife into the castle garden. Distantly he could still hear the dragons playing in the moat.

"My love," he said as he kissed her, "your life is but a second when compared to mine, for I am immortal. Yet I love you as I have loved few others. I can give you the gift of eternal life, if you will accept it, and we will be together forever."

"Yes, my love," Shawna whispered.

He spoke the words, and the Change was done.

"I truly love you," he said as he looked into her sad brown eyes. "Now go play with the rest of the dragons."

95
Voodoo

FREDRIC BROWN

"One step ahead!"

Mr. Decker's wife had just returned from a trip to Haiti—a trip she had taken alone—to give them a cooling off period before they discussed a divorce.

It hadn't worked. Neither of them had cooled off in the slightest. In fact, they were finding now that they hated one another more than ever.

"Half," said Mrs. Decker firmly. "I'll not settle for anything less than half the money plus half of the property."

"Ridiculous!" said Mr. Decker.

"Is it? I could have it all, you know. And quite easily, too. I studied voodoo while in Haiti."

"Rot!" said Mr. Decker.

"It isn't. And you should be glad that I am a good woman for I could kill you quite easily if I wished. I would then have *all* the money and *all* the real estate, and without any fear of consequences. A death accomplished by voodoo can not be distinguished from a death by heart failure."

"Rubbish!" said Mr. Decker.

"You think so? I have wax and a hatpin. Do you want to give me a tiny pinch of your hair or a fingernail clipping or two—that's all I need—and let me show you?"

"Nonsense!" said Mr. Decker.

"Then why are you afraid to have me try? Since *I* know it works, I'll make you a proposition. If it doesn't kill you, I'll give you a divorce and ask for nothing. If it does, I'll get it all automatically."

"Done!" said Mr. Decker. "Get your wax and hatpin." He glanced at his fingernails. "Pretty short. I'll give you a bit of hair."

When he came back with a few short strands of hair in the lid of an aspirin tin, Mrs. Decker had already started softening the wax. She kneaded the hair into it, then shaped it into the rough effigy of a human being.

"You'll be sorry," she said, and thrust the hatpin into the chest of the wax figure.

Mr. Decker was surprised, but he was more pleased than sorry. He had not believed in voodoo, but being a cautious man he never took chances.

Besides, it had always irritated him that his wife so seldom cleaned her hairbrush.

96
Weather Prediction

EVELYN E. SMITH

"Don't know why there's no sun up in the sky."

George Passman's wife had often told him he ought to
have his memory trained because he was so bad about
telephone numbers. Even after someone had carefully
written a number down for him, he was apt to mix up the
figures in dialing, so that he seldom got the person he
wanted.

More often he got a harsh noise indicating that the telephone company disapproved of the combination of letters
and figures he had just evolved. This trouble with the
telephone had been a constant source of friction between
him and his wife during the twelve uneventful years of
their marriage.

"Please, George," Elinor begged, as she sat before
the dressing table dragging her dull blond hair into a Psyche knot at the nape of her neck, "see if you can't get it
right just this once. WEather 6-1212; that's W-E-"

"I know, I know," George said irritably.

And he *did* know, he *did* understand—up to the moment he got his hands on the telephone. Then something
went wrong. Friends had often suggested that he try
psychoanalysis, but Elinor had repudiated the suggestion
indignantly, knowing that analysts tended to blame the

wife for whatever was wrong with the husbnad, and not wanting George to get any ideas.

Although there was an extension on the table between the beds, George went to the phone in the living room, carefully shutting the door between. Elinor knew that it made him nervous to have anyone watch him in the act, and wondered what he did in the office. Was he able to conquer his phobia—or whatever it was—there, or did he delegate all telephoning to his secretary?

She had finished dressing when he came back ten minutes later. "You might have given me the weather report first," she observed, looking pointedly at the shaker and glasses he carried on a small tole tray.

He poured two drinks. "Going to be a storm tonight," he announced.

"But, George, that's impossible! There isn't a cloud in sight. And the sun's been just—pouring all day."

"Look, I didn't make up the weather report. All I did was call the telephone company and that's what I was told."

"There must be some mistake." Elinor reached for the extension and dialed while he poured himself a second drink.

She hung up and looked at him. " 'Tonight fair and slightly cooler,' " she quoted, " 'with a low of fifty-eight degrees. Barometer rising . . .' George, if you got the wrong number, why didn't you say so? Why did you have to make something up?"

"Didn't make anything up," George mumbled. "That's what he told me."

She put on her sheared beaver, which doubled as evening wrap, without waiting for him to help her. They rode down in the elevator without speaking. In front of the apartment house she waited for George to bring the car from the garage in the basement. That was one nice thing about living in Forest Hills; there was a place to keep a car.

They drove off toward the bridge, resentment in the set

of George's shoulders. Exactly like a child, she thought without tenderness. After a few minutes, she reached forward and turned on the radio. Dance music terminated in an announcer's mention of the fact that the barometer was rising and it would be fair and slightly cooler that night but warm and sunny the next day.

"Going to rain tomorrow," George muttered.

"Nonsense," she said.

It was not quite eight when they got to West Forty-fifth Street. She waited outside a little bar they liked while George took the car to a parking lot; she didn't like to sit in a bar alone. When he came back they each had a couple of martinis, and by then it was eight-twenty and time to go to the theater. The Cottons were already waiting for them in the lobby, and all four went on in together.

"Don't mind George," Elinor said in a loud whisper to Mrs. Cotton, as the men checked their coats, "he's sulking again. He got the wrong number when he was trying to find out the weather from the telephone company and, rather than admit it, he made up a weather report."

Both ladies tittered and Mr. Cotton chuckled, "Technological age still got you, eh, George?"

"It's going to storm," George said stubbornly. The other three laughed.

During the last act of the play they heard the unmistakable sound of thunder outside. When they got out of the theater rain was pouring in torrents. Elinor looked at her husband, compressed her lips tightly, and said nothing. After all, he couldn't have produced the storm himself, no matter how much she'd have liked to blame him for it.

"We might stay under the marquee until the rain stops," Mrs. Cotton suggested, "because we won't possibly be able to get a cab in this weather."

"The rain won't stop," George said.

"Go get the car, George," Elinor told him. "We'll drop Herb and Lou off first."

The Cottons chorused grateful acknowledgment. "But

George'll get wet," Mrs. Cotton murmured perfunctorily.

"He doesn't mind. Do you, dear?"

George made a growling sound and plunged out into the storm.

As soon as he had gone, Mrs. Cotton asked, "But how did he know it was going to rain?"

"It was a lucky guess," Elinor said. "Don't encourage him."

But when George had returned with the car, and the Cottons had been packed into the back seat, Mrs. Cotton repeated her question. "How did you know, George?"

"I keep telling you. I called the telephone company and that's what the guy told me."

"They don't have men answering the phone," his wife said, moving away from him so that the wet wool of his coat wouldn't mat her fur. "Only girls."

"I don't care," George replied. "A man answered the phone. I asked him what the weather was going to be—"

"But you don't ask," both ladies said in unison. "They just play a record when you dial that number," Mrs. Cotton explained. "Nobody can hear you . . ."

"This guy did. He said it was very kind of me to ask and he had scheduled a storm—a rainstorm."

The other three shifted in their seats. Mrs. Cotton leaned over toward George so that the odor of Arpège filled the front seat. "There's liquor on my breath," he said, "but I'm not drunk. Elinor had just as much as I, and she's sober as a—a judge." He laughed as if he had said something funny.

"Well, I don't know," Mr. Cotton offered. "It takes some people differently than others. I don't mean to say you haven't got a strong head, but if you happen to have what they call an alcohol idiosyncrasy—"

"Did you dial WE 6-1212?" Mrs. Cotton asked George in the sharp tone usually reserved for her own husband.

He looked a little disturbed. "No, it wasn't quite like

that—slightly different somehow. Like WE 6-2121 or maybe . . . anyhow different. I suppose that could explain it.''

Mrs. Cotton sat back satisfied. "Of course that explains it. You got the wrong number and some practical joker lived there. That's all."

"Of course," Elinor echoed. "That must be it."

"But it *is* raining," Mr. Cotton pointed out.

"Just a coincidence," his wife said.

The car drew up before the Cottons' apartment house on West Seventy-third. "Why don't you stay with us tonight?" Mrs. Cotton asked. "It's risky driving back to the Island in this weather."

"No, thanks," George answered, before Elinor had a chance to say anything. "We might as well get back tonight."

"We could have gone in for a little while," his wife rebuked him as they drove through the park. "At least until the rain stopped."

"The rain won't stop."

She laughed, a little too shrilly. "Don't be silly, George. It has to stop sometime."

"Does it?" He looked at her, and she didn't like his expression. "Well, I suppose it will. After forty days and forty nights. That's how long he told me it was going to last. But it won't make any difference to any of us then."

They turned on Fifty-ninth Street and swung east. George would see a psychoanalyst the next day, Elinor decided, no matter what.

They drove across the bridge. She knew it was just her imagination, but the river seemed appreciably higher.

97
Who Rides with Santa Anna?

EDWARD D. HOCH

"Yes there will—at San Jacinto."

Antonio Lopez de Santa Anna stood pensively on a hardened hill of sand, looking north toward a little cluster of smoldering cottonwoods that had once sheltered the walls of the Alamo Mission. For nearly two weeks, his overwhelming forces had battered at the small band of Texans and Americans. For nearly two weeks every attack had been thrown back—until now the plain between the Mexican camp and the little mission was strewn with the trappings of unsettled battle.

"Once more," Santa Anna breathed to the officer at his side. "Once more we must try it."

"But five hundred of our men have died already, President."

"What is five hundred when seven times that number still ride with us? Prepare for another attack."

And he stood there, alone, searching the horizon with his glass, swinging it from time to time back toward the shell-scarred walls of the Alamo Mission, searching for any sign of movement. Presently the officer, Juan, returned to his side.

"Yes, Juan?"

"I have passed the orders, President."

"Very good."

"But a single rider has come in from the south . . ."

"A rider?" Santa Anna wheeled around, turning his glass toward the camp. "A messenger from Mexico City, perhaps?"

"No, President," Juan shook his head. "He is an old man—though he rides well. He wishes to speak with you."

"Very well. Bring him to me. But be ready to ride."

And presently, a little old man came slowly up the path to the place where Santa Anna stood. A short man, with a face that still seemed to retain some of the shrewdness of youth, combined now with some uncertain wisdom of age.

"Good day, great Santa Anna," the old man spoke. "How does the battle progress?" His words were an odd sort of Spanish, tempered with an accent that might have been French.

"Who are you, old man?" Santa Anna asked. "And whatever brings you to this settlement of San Antonio, before the mission of the Alamo?"

"Word reached me of your difficulties, great general. I only thought to offer my assistance."

Santa Anna smiled, revealing a crooked row of yellow teeth. "Your fighting days are over, old man. The battle today is for the younger."

But the old man stretched out a hand in protest. "I am but sixty-seven years of age, and can still ride a horse with the best of your men."

"What is one more man to me?" Santa Anna asked.

"But I can win you the battle," the little man insisted.

"You are a soldier?"

"I fought in Europe in my younger days. Many great battles!"

Santa Anna nodded. "Some day the history books will remember this as a great battle, also."

* * *

The old man took the glass from his hands and peered through it toward the cluster of cottonwoods. "That is the Alamo Mission?"

"Correct," Santa Anna replied. "My objective since February 23. Only now it is more a fort than a mission."

"How many men do they have?"

"Less than two hundred, I'm sure. And with them are men like Travis, Bowie, and Crockett. If I could wipe them off the map at a single stroke, there would be no more trouble with this idea of Texas independence."

The old man dropped the glass from his eye. "I will get it for you. Draw me a map in the sand to show me the layout of the mission. Quickly."

"Well," Santa Anna began, "here are the walls . . ." He sketched quickly with his sword, somehow catching the eagerness of the old man at his side. ". . . and here is an old convent, with a courtyard. And a small hospital, and a chapel . . ."

"I see . . . Very well. How many men do you have?"

"Thirty-five hundred. But it's those walls—those confounded walls!"

"You have tried to scale them?"

"We have tried everything. For two weeks . . ."

"But you have cannon."

"A few. More than the defenders, certainly."

"But you have been firing into the mission rather than at the walls! That was your trouble!"

"And what would you suggest?" Santa Anna queried.

The old man produced a dainty jeweled snuff box, encrusted with a glittering single letter N. "Direct all your cannons at a single point," he said. "Breach the wall and pour your overwhelming forces through the hole."

Santa Anna listened, his eyes glued to the gems as the old man's hands manipulated the snuff. "Will you ride with me?"

"But a moment ago, you thought me too old."

"Never fear. Will you ride with me?"

"How far, Santa Anna?"

"Across all of Texas."

The old man's eyes glistened. "I will ride farther. I will ride with you into Washington itself, where ten years from this date you will be emperor of all the continent."

"Then we ride! Jose," he shouted, "prepare the cannon for firing . . ."

And the air was filled with smoke and fire and screaming, roaring death, and soon the walls of the Alamo Mission trembled and shivered.

"We ride," Santa Anna shouted. "Jose, order a full attack. The horsemen and then the foot soldiers."

"This is the last attack?"

"The last attack, Jose! The wall is breached . . ."

And at his side, the old man wheeled his white horse high into the air. "Pass the word, Santa Anna. Not a defender must remain alive. We must wipe them out, to bring all of Texas to its knees . . ."

And Santa Anna passed the word . . . And then they were thundering across the plain, past the deserted dirt roads, past the crumbling cottonwoods, toward the breach in the Alamo wall . . .

"I feel victory in my bones," Santa Anna shouted to the man at his side. "This is my day."

And the old man nodded as he spurred his great horse forward. "Victory, as long as we ride together. This time, I will make no mistake. This time . . . there will be no Waterloo . . ."

98
Wisher Takes All

WILLIAM F. TEMPLE

"Greed goeth before a fall."

Briggs swept out under the glassware counter, where he had not swept for many a day. Something like a tinsel-adorned Christmas-tree fairy came tumbling out with the dust. Only she picked herself up and dusted off her wings, which a Christmas-tree fairy would hardly do.

"Hello," said Briggs. "What are you—animal, vegetable, or mineral?"

"I'm a fairy," said the fairy. "Hibernating. We're pretty rare, you know. Incidentally, before I get back to sleep, would you like three wishes?"

"How much?" asked Briggs.

"Quite free. We're not allowed to charge."

"Okay, fire away," said Briggs promptly.

"Well, what's your first wish?"

"I wish I had a hundred wishes," said Briggs.

"What?" said the fairy faintly.

"You can keep the change—I mean the other two wishes. Don't believe in putting too keen an edge on business," said Briggs generously.

"That's nice of you. Oh, well, start wishing . . ."

"My first wish is for larger business premises. My

385

second wish is for perfect and lasting health. My third wish . . ."

Presently: "Your ninety-ninth wish?" asked the fairy exhaustedly.

"Um . . . I wish I could always know what the other guy's got in his hand at gin rummy."

"Granted. And your last wish?"

"I wish I had another hundred wishes."

The fairy reeled.

"Really!" she protested. "Is that your idea of fair business? You should realize it's hard work for me. I've made you the strongest man in the world, the best pitcher, the best pool player. You can play the piano, the piccolo, the trumpet, the zither. Your corns are gone. And you are the richest man in the world—all that juggling with currency takes it out of one, you know."

"Yes, I understand," said Briggs, soothingly. "I feel pretty mean about it, in a way. I wish I could give *you* a wish or something."

He stopped, realizing.

"Thanks a lot," said the fairy quickly, and quite brightened up. "I'll grant you that wish. You're a nasty man. I wish I'd never met you."

Nor had she.

99
The World Where
Wishes Worked

STEPHEN GOLDIN

"There's one rotten apple in every barrel."

There once was a world where wishes worked.

It was a pleasant enough place, I suppose, and the people were certainly happy. There was no hunger in this world, for a man had only to wish for food to have it appear before him. Clothing and shelter were equally easy to obtain. Envy was unknown there—if another person had something that seemed interesting, it was only a wish away from anyone else. There was neither age nor need. The people lived simple lives, devoted to beauty and the gentle sciences. The days were a pleasant blur of quiet activity.

And in this world, there was a fool.

Just the one.

It was enough.

The fool looked about him one day, and saw that everything was the same. Beautiful people doing beautiful things amid the beautiful scenery. He walked away from the others, down to a private little dell beside a lily pond, overhung by graceful willows and scented with spring fragrance. He wondered what things would be like if something new or different were to be. And so he concocted a foolish scheme.

387

"I wish," he said, "that I had something that nobody had ever had before."

Only a fool could have made a wish like this, for he left the object of his desire completely unspecified. As a result, he instantly came down with Disease, which had hitherto been unknown. His eyes went rheumy and his nose went runny. His head ached and his knees wobbled. Chills ran up and down his spine.

"I dod't like this," he said. "Dot at all. I wish to cadcel my last wish." And he immediately felt well again.

"That was close," he sighed, as he sat down on a large rock beside the pond. "The trouble is that I don't think before I say things. If I thought things out first, I wouldn't get into so much hot water. Therefore: I wish I would think more before I do any more wishing." And so it was.

However, being a fool he failed to spot the fallacy of his logic: namely, that a fool will think foolish thoughts, and no amount of foolish thinking will help him make wise wishes.

Thus deluded, he began to think of what his next wish should be. He did not even consider wishing for wealth, since such a thing was impossible in a world where everyone had anything. Material desires were too commonplace. "What I should wish for in order to satisfy this new restlessness of mine," he thought, "is the rarest of all commodities. I wish for love."

A frog jumped out of the lily pond and landed *squish* right in his lap. It looked up at him adoringly with big froggy eyes filled with tenderness, and croaked a gentle love call.

"Yuk!" exclaimed the fool, and he instinctively scooped up the frog and threw it as far from him as he could. The pathetic little creature merely croaked sorrowfully and started hopping back to the rock to be with its beloved. Quickly, the fool canceled his last wish and the frog, frightened, leaped back into the pond.

"That was a foolish wish," evaluated the fool. "Most of my wishes are foolish. Most of the things I say are foolish. What can I do to keep from saying foolish things?"

Had he not been a fool, he would simply have wished to say only wise things from then on. But, fool that he was, he said, "I know. I hereby wish not to say foolish things."

And so it was. However, since he was a fool, *anything* he could say would be foolish. Consequently, he now found that he could say nothing at all.

He became very frightened. He tried to speak, but nothing came out. He tried harder and harder, but all he accomplished was getting a sore throat. In a panic, he ran around the countryside looking for someone to help him, for, without the ability to speak, he could not undo that previous wish. But nobody was about, and the fool finally fell exhausted beside a footpath and started to sob silently.

Eventually, a friend came along the path and found him. "Hello," said the friend.

The fool moved his mouth, but no sound escaped.

"I don't believe I heard you," the friend replied politely.

The fool tried again, still with no success.

"I am really not in the mood for charades," said the friend, becoming annoyed over the fool's behavior. "If you can't be more considerate, I'll just leave." And he turned to go.

The fool sank to his knees, grabbed his friend's clothing, tugged at it, and gesticulated wildly. "I wish you'd tell me what the matter was," said the friend.

"I made a wish that I not say anything foolish, and suddenly I found that I couldn't say anything," the fool told him.

"Well, then, that explains it. I am sorry to say it, my friend, but you are a fool, and anything you say is likely to be foolish. You should stay away from wishes like that. I suppose you want me to release you from that wish.''

The fool nodded vigorously.

"Very well. I wish you could speak again.''

"Oh, thank you, thank you.''

"Just be careful of what you say in the future, because wishes come true automatically, no matter how foolish they are.'' And the friend left.

The fool sat down to think some more. His friend had been right—anything he was likely to say would be foolish, and his wishes would automatically come true. If that were so (and it was), he would always be in trouble. He could remain safe by not saying anything—but he had just tried that and hadn't liked it at all. The more he thought, the worse the problem became. There seemed to be no acceptable way he could fit into the system.

Then suddenly the answer came to him. Why not change the system to fit himself?

"I wish,'' he said, "that wishes did not automatically come true.''

Things are tough all over.

100
Your Soul Comes C.O.D.

MACK REYNOLDS

"Competition is the soul of trade."

In view of the trouble to which he had gone in order to acquire such out-of-the-way items as a piece of unicorn horn and three drops of blood from a virgin, it was rather disconcerting to have the spirit appear even before the prescribed routine. In fact, he hadn't even got his protective pentacle drawn when he looked up to find the entity materialized in his rickety easy chair.

The spirit said, "You don't really need that, you know."

Norman Wallace stared at his visitor, even after all these months of research, unbelievingly. The other was far from what the young man expected. Somehow, he was reminded of Lincoln, his face almost beautiful in its infinite sadness.

The spirit nodded at the pentacle. "Mere superstition. It couldn't protect you if my purpose was to do you harm. But, more important still, I am quite incapable of such aggression. Man has freedom of choice, free will; we of the other worlds can only help him destroy—or elevate— himself, we cannot initiate."

Norman was shaken, but not quite to the point of speechlessness. He pointed to his assembled drugs,

391

charms, potions, and incenses and said, almost indignantly, "But I haven't performed the rite, as yet."

The other nodded and shrugged. "What's the difference? You wished to summon a spirit. Very well, here I
am. The desire is of more importance than the act of
combining those rather silly items. But, to get to the
point, just what is it you desire?"

Norman Wallace took a deep breath and got down to
business. He indicated his shabby quarters. "I can bear
this no longer," he said. "I want a few years of decency
in living, a few years of the good things of life that others
enjoy. So—"

"So in your desperation you wish to sell your soul in
return for help."

"That's right."

The spirit considered momentarily. "Suppose I give
you my support for forty years? Suppose I guarantee you
love, wealth, power, to the degree you desire them? At
the end of that time your soul is mine?"

Norman Wallace's mouth tightened, but he said,
"That's agreeable."

The spirit came to its feet. "Very well, the pact is
made."

The other frowned. "Don't we make out a contract or
something? Don't I have to sign in blood?"

The faintest of smiles came to the melancholy face of
the spirit. "That won't be necessary. The pact has been
made, neither of us will nor can break it."

Suddenly he had disappeared.

And almost simultaneously came a knock at the door.
Dazed, Norman came to his feet and opened it.

Harriet was there and immediately in his arms. "Oh,
darling, darling, I was so wrong."

He held her back, at arm's length, in amazement.
"You mean that you've changed your mind, you'll marry
me?"

"Oh, darling, yes. I thought going away from you,

spending a few months in Florida, would let me forget. I was so wrong.''

Frowning worriedly, he indicated the poverty of his room. ''But Harriet, we'd still—''

She smiled now, and laughed up at him. ''Remember that little farm I told you my aunt left me? The one in Louisiana?''

He nodded, uncomprehending.

''Oil, darling,'' she bubbled over. ''Enough to give you the start you need.''

And so it went for forty years. Wealth to the modest extent he desired it; prestige to the small degree his ambition demanded; but, most important of all, love that ripened and ever grew as the years went by. And a home rich with children, and the respect and affection of his neighbors and his associates.

Not that he had ever seen the spirit again, not in all those years. Almost, it was possible for him to look back at his life and think it was all of his own doing. Each success had seemingly been not unordinary good luck, or a result of his own efforts. Sometimes he had even tried to convince himself that the pact he'd made was a figment of his imagination, that the demon he had thought he had summoned was a result of too much worry, too much work, too little food and recreation back in those days of his poverty-stricken youth.

But subconsciously he knew. *He knew!*

And so it was that after his forty years he sat alone in his study and waited. Harriet had gone to bed; the children, of course, had long since been married themselves and were living their own peaceful, happy lives.

He wondered now, as he looked back over the years, at the use to which he had put the demon's assistance. He had been promised love, wealth, and power to the extent he desired them. But, somehow, he had wanted no more than sufficient for himself and his family. He had made no attempt to accumulate the fortune of a Midas; nor, for that matter, had he attained his possessions by recourse to the racetrack or stockmarket. He had worked hard during those forty years.

He had been promised power, too. Why had he taken so little? He had been content to assume a position in society that coincided with his natural abilities. He could have been President or, for that matter, dictator of the world. Why hadn't he?

Ah, but he had taken his full measure of the other. His cup had overflowed with love. In all the years, the romance between Harriet and him had never waned. And the children? Well, for instance, the way they had returned to the old home from all over the nation this last Christmas had proven their affection.

And now suddenly he thought he knew his motivation. Somewhere, beneath it all, he had been attempting to forestall the fate awaiting him. Subconsciously he had told himself that if he were moderate, if he led the good life, if he abstained from demanding the ultimate, his reckoning with the demon would be the easier.

He laughed abruptly, bitterly.

And suddenly fear washed over him. The reckoning was now.

No matter what he had done with the demonic powers awarded him. No matter how he had loved and been loved. No matter how much he repented now.

His soul was the spirit's.

He clasped his hands tightly to the arms of his chair. Run! *Hide!* ESCAPE!

But he sank back again. There was no place to run. No place to hide. No way of escape.

The spirit materialized on the couch across from him.

Norman Wallace nodded his gray head in submission. "I was expecting you."

"Your forty years are up," the spirit told him.

"Yes, I know." Hopelessness had replaced fear now. "Is there any reason why our pact should not be ful-

filled? You are satisfied that I have suitably kept my part
of the bargain?''

The old man hesitated, then nodded again. ''I am satisfied.''

''Then you are ready to go? You have taken farewell
of those you love, made what arrangements you thought
necessary?''

''Yes. Yes, I am ready.'' His voice was firm now. ''I
suppose it will be hard on Harriet for a time, but then, we
must all face the end sooner or later, and only recently
my doctor warned me of my heart. Harriet always said
she wanted me to go first, that she would hate to think of
me alone in life after we have been so close.''

The spirit came to its feet. ''Very well, let us be on our
way.''

Norman Wallace arose too and the shock was not so
great as he might have expected when he was able to look
back and see himself sitting there in the easy chair, his
face pale and his eyes staring unseeingly.

''Then I am dead already?''

''Yes,'' the spirit told him. ''Your doctor's diagnosis
was quite accurate. Come.''

And suddenly they were in another place and Norman
Wallace stared about uncomprehendingly.

He said, ''It seems that in all my relations with you I
have been continually surprised at the inaccuracy of the
legends and myths.''

''Oh?'' the spirit said.

''Yes. When you first appeared you didn't look like
my lifelong conception of a demon. Nor in my dealings
with you have you acted the way I supposed you would.
Now, this place has none of the attributes I had expected
of Hell.''

The spirit smiled. ''My dear Norman, why is it that so
many suppose that souls are of less interest to us than to
our adversaries? Why should not one side strive for a
worthy one as well as the other? I am not a demon, nor is
this Hell.''